Cathy Glass

SUNDAY TIMES BESTSELLING AUTHOR

The Girl in the Mirror

A NOVEL INSPIRED BY A TRUE STORY

HARPER

This novel is entirely a work of fiction. The names, characters and
incidents portrayed in it are the work of the author's imagination.
Any resemblance to actual persons, living or dead, events or
localities is entirely coincidental.

HARPER

An imprint of HarperCollins*Publishers*
77–85 Fulham Palace Road,
Hammersmith, London W6 8JB

www.harpercollins.co.uk

First published in Great Britain by HarperCollins*Publishers* 2010
This paperback edition 2010

4

© Cathy Glass 2010

Cathy Glass asserts the moral right to
be identified as the author of this work

A catalogue record for this book is
available from the British Library

ISBN 978-0-00-729927-0

Printed and bound in Great Britain by
Clays Ltd, St Ives plc

Mixed Sources
Product group from well-managed
forests and other controlled sources
www.fsc.org Cert no. SW-COC-001806
© 1996 Forest Stewardship Council

FSC is a non-profit international organisation established to promote the
responsible management of the world's forests. Products carrying the FSC
label are independently certified to assure consumers that they come
from forests that are managed to meet the social, economic and
ecological needs of present and future generations.

Find out more about HarperCollins and the environment at
www.harpercollins.co.uk/green

Most families have secrets – skeletons in the closet that are never spoken of. Sometimes the secret is so painful, and buried so deep, that it becomes 'forgotten' by the family.

This is the story of Mandy, who wasn't aware she held the key to her family's dreadful secret until a crisis unlocked it.

AUTHOR'S NOTE: Attitudes to the administering of pain relief are slowly changing.

The Girl in the Mirror

Prologue

')'m sorry,' Mandy said, stopping Adam's hand from going any further. 'I'm sorry. I can't. Not now.'

'It's OK,' he said a little too quickly, moving away. 'I could do with an early night.'

She watched him cross her bedsitting room to the chair where he'd left his jacket. Throwing his jacket over his shoulder he continued to walk away from her — to the door. Stop him, now, Mandy told herself. Stop him before it's too late. 'Adam?' she said.

He turned. 'Yes?'

She hesitated, and then shrugged. 'Nothing. I'll see you tomorrow?'

He gave a non-committal half-nod. 'I'll phone.'

She watched helplessly as he let himself out. Idiot! she cursed herself. Go after him and try to explain. You've done this once too often. It'll serve you right if he makes it the last time and you lose him for good. But even if she went after him what could she say? She didn't understand why she behaved as she did, so how could she possibly explain it to him?

Tears stung the back of her eyes. She stood up, moved away from the bed and slowly crossed to the easel propped against the far wall. She stared at the canvas on it. It was entirely blank: an added testament to her failure. Failure as an artist; failure as a lover; failure as a daughter; failure even as a person. Her life was one long failure. She picked up the paintbrush and, deep in thought, stood for a moment holding it at either end, absently flexing the wood. It bent, and then snapped in two. The sound of splintering, cracking wood was satisfying in its finality. It was broken and could never be repaired.

One

Mandy woke with a start. The room was not as it should be; she could sense it. Something had woken her – something close and imminent. Something wrong? She raised her head and looked around. The room was empty, as it should be. Adam had gone and although he had a key he would never use it without asking her first.

Yet something had disturbed her. It was too early for her to wake naturally. The room wasn't properly light yet, and even the weakest of suns came through the thin and faded curtains. And the street noise filtering through the ill-fitting Victorian sash windows of her bedsitting room suggested very early morning. Mandy turned on to her side and reached over the edge of the bed for her phone. Bringing it to her eyes she peered at the time: 6.29 a.m.

What sounded like hailstones landed against the window and she guessed it was the hail that had woken her. Another wet day, she thought, and to make it worse she'd argued with Adam. She closed her eyes again and hoped the day would go away. No rain followed the hail. She heard a car door slam and the engine start, and a lone police siren in the distance. Then another blast of hail.

A pattern of sound began to emerge as Mandy lay enfolded in her duvet, eyes closed, trying to keep the day at bay. A blast of hail, sand-like against the window, then silence, then another blast of hail. It gradually occurred to her in the half-light of her thoughts and consciousness that the pattern of noise was too regular, too neatly spaced to be hail. She decided it was more likely to be Nick from the attic flat, having locked himself out. As he'd done once before he was now throwing gravel against her window to wake her to let him in, rather than pressing the main doorbell and incurring the wrath of the whole house – six residents in self-contained bedsits, or studio flats as the landlord liked to call them.

Why Nick didn't secrete a spare front-door key in the garden, as she had done, Mandy didn't know, but would shortly ask. She knew he had a spare key for the door to his room hidden not very imaginatively under the mat outside his door, but that key was obviously useless if he couldn't get in the outer door first. It crossed her mind to leave him there a while longer to teach him a lesson. But Nick had been helpful in the past – changing a light-bulb for her which had rusted into its socket, and disposing of a large spider lodged in a crevice of the window and out of her reach. Living this semi-communal existence had one advantage, she thought: they helped each other; that, and it went with the bohemian lifestyle she'd chosen to try and make it as an artist.

With a sigh Mandy left the warmth of her duvet and felt the cold air bite as she crossed the room to the bay window. One of the disadvantages of this lifestyle, she quickly acknowledged, was that feeding the electricity meter for heating had to be discretionary – almost a luxury. Easing back one of the curtains she looked down on to the front path to check it was Nick and not their local down-and-out hoping for a hot drink and a bed, as had happened once before. From her first-floor room she had a clear view over the front garden and path. The only place she couldn't see was the porch – where Nick must now be, for the path and garden were empty.

She continued to look down, waiting for Nick to reappear. A moment later a man stepped from the porch and stooped to pick up more gravel. It wasn't Nick but her father!

'What!' Mandy exclaimed out loud, and tapped on the window to catch his attention. Whatever was he doing here?

Arrested half into the act of picking up another handful of gravel, her father looked up and, seeing her, straightened. He mouthed something she didn't understand, then he pointed to the front door and she nodded.

Dropping the curtain, she crossed the room and pulled her kimono dressing gown from the top of the dressing screen. What the hell? she thought again as she tied the kimono over her pyjama shorts and T-shirt. Her parents hadn't been anywhere near her bedsit (or her bohemian lifestyle, come to that) since she'd taken a year off from teaching art to follow her dream of becoming an artist and paint full time. Now, here was her father, throwing gravel at her window to wake her at 6.30 a.m.! Shrugging off the last of her sleep she realized with a stab of panic something had to be wrong, badly wrong. And given it was her father who was here and not her mother, something must have happened to her mother!

Mandy's heart raced as she ran down the threadbare carpet of the wide Victorian staircase. Arriving in the hall she turned the doorknob and heaved open the massive oak front door. 'Mum?' she gasped, searching his face. His expression seemed to confirm her worst fears.

'No, your mother's fine,' he said sombrely. 'I'm afraid it's your grandpa, Amanda. He's taken a turn for the worse.'

'Oh ...'

'He has left hospital and has gone to your aunt's. I am going there now.'

'Oh, oh, I see,' she said, relief that her mother was safe and well quickly turning to anxiety that dear Grandpa was very ill.

'I thought, as you're not working, you'd like to come with me,' her father continued. 'Your mother prefers not to go while Grandpa's staying at your aunt's.'

This came as no surprise to Mandy for, while her mother got on well with her in-laws, ten years previously there'd been what her father had called 'a situation', which had resulted in her parents severing all contact with Aunt Evelyn, Mandy's father's sister, and Evelyn's family. Now, ten years on, and with no contact in the interim, her father was going to his estranged sister's house! Mandy knew he would never have gone had his father not been ill and staying there; and her mother was still refusing to go.

'Yes, I'll come,' Mandy said quickly. 'I'd like to. I didn't realize Grandpa was so ill.'

'Neither did I. Your aunt phoned late last night.'

As he came in and Mandy closed the door behind him, she tried to picture the stilted conversation that must have taken place between her father and his sister – their first conversation in ten years. She wondered if her mother had spoken to her sister-in-law and decided probably not.

'Is Grandpa very ill?' she asked once they were in her room.

'Your aunt said so,' her father said stiffly.

'So why is he at Evelyn's and not in hospital?'

'He *was* in hospital but your aunt had him discharged. She said she could look after him better at her home than the hospital could. Your gran agreed. She's staying at your aunt's too.'

'I see, and what have the doctors said?' Mandy felt fear creeping up her spine.

'I'm not sure; we'll find out more today.' He thrust his hands into his trouser pockets and shrugged. 'I don't know, perhaps your mother was right and Evelyn is being hysterical, but I have to go and see him just in case ...'

Mandy decided to make do with a quick wash rather than her normal shower so she turned on the hot tap, which produced its usual meagre trickle of lukewarm water. 'Sit down, Dad,' she said. 'You haven't seen my bedsit before. What do you think?'

In the mirror above the basin she saw him cast a gaze over the 1950s furniture, which had clearly given good service. He gave a reserved nod. 'Is all this yours?'

'No, it came with the room. Apart from that Turkish rug. And I bought a new mattress for the bed.' She squeezed out the flannel and ran it over her face and neck. 'Would you like coffee?'

'No, thank you. I had one before I left.'

Taking the towel from the rail, she patted her face and neck dry and then crossed to the chest of drawers where she took out clean underwear, trainer socks and T-shirt. Collecting her jeans from where she'd dropped them on the floor the night before, she disappeared behind the Japanese-style dressing screen. In one respect it was just as well Adam had gone off in a huff the night before, Mandy thought. It would have been embarrassing if her father had come in to find him in her bed. But she was sorry she'd behaved as she had and if Adam didn't phone as he said he would she'd phone him – and apologize.

'Is Mum OK?' she asked from behind the screen.

'Yes, though she's worried about your grandpa, obviously. She sends her love.'

'And how are Evelyn and John?'

There was a pause. 'Your aunt didn't say much really.'

'I guess it was a difficult call for her to make.'

Through the gap between the panels of the hinged dressing

screen, Mandy could see her father. He was sitting in the faded leather captain's chair, hunched slightly forward, with a hand resting on each knee and frowning.

'By the way Evelyn spoke,' he said indignantly, 'you'd have thought I hadn't seen my father in years. I told her I'd have visited him in hospital again if he'd stayed.' Mandy heard the defensiveness and knew the peace between her father and his sister was very fragile indeed and only in place to allow them to visit Grandpa.

Dressed in jeans and T-shirt, she stepped from behind the dressing screen and crossed the room. She threw her kimono and pyjamas on to the bed and went to the fridge. 'I'm nearly ready, I just need a drink. Are you sure you don't want something?'

'No thanks.' He shook his head.

The few glasses she possessed were in the 'kitchen' sink, and to save time, and also because she could in her own place, she drank the juice straight from the carton. 'Ready,' she said, returning the juice to the fridge. She wiped her mouth on a tissue and threw it in the bin.

Her father stood and followed her to the door. 'Have you painted many pictures?' he asked, nodding at the empty easel.

Mandy saw the broken paintbrush and wondered if he'd seen it too. 'Yes,' she lied. She took her bag from the hook behind the door and threw it over her shoulder. 'Yes, it was the right decision to give up work. I have all the time in the world to paint.' Which was true, but what she couldn't tell him or Adam – indeed could barely admit to herself – was that in the seven months since she'd given up work she'd painted absolutely nothing, and her failure in this had affected all other aspects of her life. So much so that she'd lost confidence in her ability to do anything worthwhile, ever again.

Two

Checking her mobile, Mandy got into her father's car. There was no message from Adam but he would only just be up. She fastened her seatbelt as her father got in. On a weekday Adam left his house at 7.30 a.m. to catch a train into the City. Her heart stung at the thought of how she'd rejected him and she now longed for the feel of his arms around her. Bringing up a blank text she wrote: *Im rly rly sorry. Plz 4giv me. Luv M*, and pressed *Send*. She sat with the phone in her lap; her father started the engine and they pulled away. A minute later her phone bleeped a reply: *U r 4given. C u l8r? A x*. Thank God, she thought. She texted back: *Yes plz. Luv M*. Returning the phone to her bag, she relaxed back and looked at the road ahead.

It felt strange sitting beside her father in the front of the car as he drove. Despite the worry of Grandpa being ill, it felt special – an occasion – an outing. Mandy couldn't remember the last time she'd sat in the front of a car next to her father. When she'd travelled in the car as a child her place had always been in the back, and later it had been her mother who'd taken her to and collected her from university. When she'd started work she'd bought a car of her own which she'd sold to help finance her year out. No, this was definitely a first, she thought. I don't think I've ever sat in the front next to Father.

'The hospital was pretty grim,' her father said, breaking into her thoughts. 'Apparently it's a brand-new building, but staffed by agency nurses. Your aunt said there was no continuity of care and your grandfather was left unattended. She suggested they paid for him to go into a private hospital but your grandfather wouldn't hear of it.'

Mandy smiled. 'That's my grandpa!' Like her father, he was a man of strong working-class principles and would have viewed going private as elitist or unfair. She noticed her father referred to his sister as 'your aunt' rather than using her first name, which seemed to underline the distance which still separated them.

'I expect he wanted to be out of hospital,' Mandy added. 'It's nice to be with your family if you're ill.'

'Perhaps,' he said. 'As long as he's getting the medical care he needs.'

She nodded.

'It's good weather for the journey,' he said a moment later, changing the subject. 'Not a bad morning for March.'

March, she thought. She was over halfway through her year out – five months before the money ran out and she would have to return to the classroom.

'Does Sarah still live at home?' Mandy asked presently as the dual carriageway widened into motorway.

'I don't know, your aunt didn't say.'

'It would be nice to see her again after all these years. I wonder what she's doing now.'

Mandy saw his hands tighten around the steering wheel and his face set. She hadn't intended it as a criticism, just an expression of her wish to see Sarah again, but clearly he had taken it as one. When her father had fallen out with his sister ten years ago and all communication between the two families had ceased, Mandy had been stopped from seeing her cousin Sarah, which had been very sad. They were both only children and had been close, often staying at each other's houses until 'the situation' had put a stop to it.

'It was unavoidable,' he said defensively. 'It was impossible for you to visit after ... You wouldn't know, you don't remember. You were only a child, Amanda. It should never have happened and I blame myself. I vowed we'd never set foot in that house again. If it wasn't for Grandpa being taken there, I wouldn't, and I've told Evelyn that.'

Mandy felt the air charged with the passion of his disclosure. It was the most he'd ever said about 'the situation', ever. Indeed, it had never been mentioned by anyone in the last ten years, not in her presence at least. Now, not only had he spoken of it, but he appeared to be blaming himself, which was news to her. And his outburst – so out of character – and the palpable emotion it contained made Mandy feel uncomfortable, for reasons she couldn't say.

She looked out of her side window and concentrated on the passing scenery. It was a full ten minutes before he spoke again and then this voice was safe and even once more.

'There's snow forecast for next week,' he said.

'So much for global warming!'

A few minutes later he switched on Radio 3, which allowed Mandy to take her iPod from her bag and plug in her headphones. It was a compilation – garage, hip-hop, Mozart and Abba; Mandy rested her head back and allowed her gaze to settle through the windscreen. The two-hour journey slowly passed and her thoughts wandered to the trips she'd made to and from her aunt's as a child. The adults had taken turns to collect and return Sarah and her from their weekend stays. Mandy remembered how they'd sat in the back of the car and giggled, the fun of the week-end continuing during the journey. Then the visits had abruptly stopped and she'd never seen Sarah again. Stopped completely without explanation, and she'd never been able to ask her father why.

They turned off the A11 and Mandy switched off her iPod and removed her earpieces.

'Not far now,' her father said.

She heard the tension in his voice and saw his forehead crease. She wasn't sure how much of his anxiety was due to Grandpa's illness, and how much by the prospect of seeing his sister again, but Mandy was sure that if she hadn't agreed to accompany him, or her mother hadn't changed her mind and come, he would have found visiting alone very difficult indeed. His dependence on her gave him an almost childlike vulnerability, and her heart went out to him.

'Don't worry,' she said lightly. 'I'm sure Evelyn will be on her best behaviour.'

He smiled and seemed to take comfort in their small conspiracy. 'We won't stay too long,' he reassured her.

They slowed to 30 m.p.h. as they entered the village with its post-office-cum-general-store. Mandy remembered the shop vividly from all the times she'd stayed at her aunt's. Auntie Evelyn, Sarah and she had often walked to the store, with Sarah's Labrador Misty. When Sarah and she had been considered old enough, the two of them had gone there alone to spend their pocket money on sweets, ice-cream, or a memento from the display stand of neatly arranged china gifts. It had been an adventure, a chance to take responsibility, which had been possible in the safe rural community where her aunt lived, but not in Greater London when Sarah had stayed with her.

Mandy recognized the store at once − it was virtually unchanged − as she had remembered the approach to the village, and indeed most of the journey. But as they left the village and her father turned from the main road on to the B road for what he said was the last part of the journey, she suddenly found her mind had gone completely blank. She didn't recall any of it.

She didn't think it was that the developers had been busy in the last ten years and had changed the contours of the landscape; it was still largely agricultural land, with farmers' houses and outbuildings dotted in between, presumably as it had been for generations. But as Mandy searched through the windscreen, then her side window, and round her father to his side window, none of what she now saw looked the least bit familiar. She could have been making the journey for the first time for the lack of recognition, which was both strange and unsettling. Swivelling round in her seat, she turned to look out of the rear window, hoping a different perspective might jog her memory.

'Lost something?' her father asked.

'No. Have Evelyn and John moved since I visited as a child?' Which seemed the most likely explanation, and her father had forgotten to mention it.

'No,' he said, glancing at her. 'Why do you ask?'

Mandy straightened in her seat and returned her gaze to the front, looking through the window for a landmark – something familiar. 'I don't recognize any of this,' she said. 'Have we come a different way?'

He shook his head. 'There is only one way to your aunt's. We turn right in about a hundred yards and their house is on the left.'

Mandy looked at the trees growing from the grassy banks that flanked the narrow road and then through a gap in the trees, which offered another view of the countryside. She looked through the windscreen, then to her left and right, but still found nothing that she even vaguely remembered – absolutely nothing.

She heard her father change down a gear, and the car slowed; then they turned right and continued along a single-track lane. Suddenly the tyres were crunching over the gravel and they pulled on to a driveway leading to a house.

'Remember it now?' she heard him say. He stopped the car and cut the engine.

Mandy stared at the house and experienced an unsettling stab of familiarity. 'A little,' she said, and tried to calm her racing heart.

Three

It was like *déjà vu* – that flash of familiarity, sensed rather than consciously thought. A dizziness; a feeling of not being there. It was as though she'd been given a glimpse of another life. It had been fleeting, and without detail, but as Mandy looked at her aunt's house, panic rose. She'd been here lots of times as a child but couldn't remember any detail. It was like looking at a holiday photo in someone else's album of a place she too had once visited.

She read the old wooden signboard – Breakspeare Manor – and then looked at the house again. It was a large sprawling manor house with two small stone turrets and lattice period windows. The front of the house was covered with the bare winding stems of wistaria. Instinctively Mandy knew that in a couple of weeks the entire front of the house would be festooned with its lilac blooms, like the venue for a wedding reception at a far-off and exotic location. She knew it without remembering – a gut feeling – and also that the house was 150 years old.

'Ready?' her father asked after a moment, gathering himself.

She nodded and, taking a deep breath, picked up her bag from beside her feet and got out. The air smelt fresh and clean after London but it had a cooler, sharper edge. Drawing her cardigan closer, she waited for her father to get out. He reached inside the car for his jacket, straightened and, pointing the remote at the car, pressed to lock it. Mandy looked around. There were no other cars on the sweeping carriage driveway, and the double garage – a separate building to the left of the house – had its doors closed. None of the rooms at the front of the house had their windows open and the whole house looked shut up and empty.

'There must be someone in,' her father said, echoing her thoughts. 'Grandpa's here and we're expected.'

She walked beside her father as they crossed the drive to the stone arched porch. Mounted on the wall to the right of the porch was a black-on-white sign announcing 'Tradesmen', with an arrow pointing to the side of the house. Mandy didn't remember the sign but knew her aunt had insisted the butcher, housekeeper, gardener, newspaper boy, plumber and electrician used the side entrance, while friends and those arriving in big cars used the front door. She also remembered this had seemed strange to her as a child. At her house everyone used the front door, including those delivering goods and reading the gas and electric meters; the side gate was only used to take out the garbage.

'Shall we let ourselves in the tradesmen's entrance?' her father asked, taking a step out of the porch and looking up at the front. 'I don't want to press the bell and disturb Grandpa if he's sleeping.'

'The gate is kept locked and the bell is even louder than this one. So they can hear it from the kitchen and laundry room.' Her father looked at her, mildly surprised she'd remembered this detail. She shrugged and hid her discomfort.

Mandy didn't know how she knew about the bell; her reaction had been instinctive, as though she'd absorbed the information from being part of her aunt's family during all the times she'd stayed as a child. And while she still couldn't remember visiting the house as such, nor had the least idea what the rooms would look like once they were inside, she found she knew that break-fast and lunch were taken in the morning room and supper in the dining room, and that Wednesday was the housekeeper's day off. Perhaps she'd remembered this because it was all so very different from her own family's modest home and routine, she thought.

Her father pressed the bell and almost immediately the door opened. For a moment Mandy thought the dark-haired woman standing before them was her aunt, until she saw the apron.

'Good morning. Please come in,' the housekeeper said, clearly expecting them. 'Mrs Osborne is busy with her father.' She smiled warmly and stood aside to let them in.

Although Mandy couldn't have described the housekeeper from when she'd visited as a child, she felt sure this wasn't the same woman, but they clearly used the same polish. The faint but distinctive smell of beeswax drifted into the hall from the dining room, and Mandy instinctively knew that the dining table needed a lot of polishing.

'Please come through to the sitting room,' the housekeeper said, leading the way along the wooden panelled hall, which seemed vaguely familiar.

Mandy felt the same vague familiarity as she entered the sitting room, while not actually recalling ever being in the room. She looked at the off-white sofa and matching armchairs, the light beige carpet, curtains and soft furnishings, and wondered if she and Sarah hadn't been allowed in this room as children, which could explain her lack of recall.

'Sit down and make yourselves comfortable,' the housekeeper said, waving towards the armchairs and sofa. 'I'm Mrs Saunders. Mrs Osborne will be with you shortly. Can I get you coffee?'

'Yes please,' Mandy said, and her father nodded.

'That's not the same housekeeper who was here when I used to stay, is it?' Mandy asked her father as soon as the door closed behind her.

'No. That was Mrs Pryce. She left —' He stopped as though he had been about to say something but had thought better of it. 'This one is new.'

They sat for a while, both gazing out of the French windows and on to the upper terraces. Although it was only March the gardener had clearly been busy. Brightly coloured spring blooms dotted the terracotta pots on the patio and the neatly tended flower beds beyond. Instinctively Mandy knew that further down the gardens, out of sight on the lower lawns, there used to be swings, which Sarah and she had played on as children.

The room was quiet, save for the ticking of the brass pendulum clock mounted in the alcove by the fireplace. Indeed, the whole house seemed quiet; unnaturally so, Mandy thought. It was a sharp contrast to her studio flat where the comings and goings of the other occupants meant there was always noise of some sort.

'I don't know why we have to wait here,' her father grumbled after a moment. 'I've come to see my father, not drink coffee.'

'The housekeeper said Evelyn was busy with Grandpa,' Mandy soothed. 'I'm sure she won't be long.'

He harrumphed. Mandy could feel his tension and knew that unless he changed his attitude he was going to start off on the wrong foot when he met his sister again after all these years.

'Has this room changed much?' she asked shortly, still unable to place it and trying to cut the silence with conversation.

'I don't know,' he said quickly. He looked away, deflecting further questions.

They sat in silence again, gazing out of the window, until a knock sounded on the door and the housekeeper returned carrying a large silver tray with coffee, and biscuits arranged on a white porcelain plate.

'Help yourselves,' she said, placing the tray on the coffee table between them.

'Thank you,' Mandy said, grateful for the biscuits, having not had breakfast. Her father nodded.

'You're welcome. Mrs Osborne is on her way.' She smiled and left the room, closing the door behind her.

Mandy put sugar in one cup and passed it to her father and then picked up the other cup and took a sip. It felt very odd sitting here drinking coffee with the sense that it was all familiar while not actually recalling it – like watching someone's home movie. You saw the intimacy of their lives but weren't part of it. The sitting-room door opened again and Evelyn came in. Mandy knew immediately it was her aunt: a smaller, female, and slightly younger version of her father. Her father stood as she entered and put down his cup. There was a moment's hesitation before Evelyn came over and they air-kissed. 'Hello, Ray,' she said, and then, turning to Mandy: 'Good to see you again, love, though it's a pity it's in such sad circumstances.'

Mandy felt another stab of familiarity as she stood to kiss her aunt. Evelyn had always called her Mandy, as her friends and work colleagues did, while her parents still used her full name: Amanda.

'How's Dad?' her father asked.

Evelyn took a step back and Mandy saw the anxiety in her face. 'Very poorly. Sit down while I explain what has happened. You need to know before you see him.'

Mandy thought he was going to protest at being kept longer from his father, but he clearly thought better of it. He returned to the armchair while Evelyn sat on the sofa beside her. Drawing her hand anxiously across her forehead, she looked from Mandy to her brother, her face sad and serious.

'Dad is very old,' she began slowly, 'and his heart is weak. He was lucky to recover from the stroke last year, but it has taken its toll. His body is slowly closing down. As you know he was admitted to hospital two weeks ago with a chest infection. They put him on intravenous antibiotics. Although the chest infection cleared, his general condition deteriorated.' She paused and Mandy thought she was choosing her words very carefully, as though trying to let them down slowly.

'Dad had never been in hospital before,' she continued, 'apart from when he had pneumonia as a child. He was very upset by the whole experience. He felt no one cared and he insisted he wanted to go home. Clearly it was out of the question for him to go to his house – Mum couldn't have coped, so I made the offer for them both to come here, which they accepted. Ray,' Evelyn said, looking directly at him and her eyes misting, 'Dad won't be returning to hospital, nor to his home. He has come here so he can have peace and quiet among his loved ones at the end.'

'But I don't understand,' her father said abruptly. 'You said Dad responded to the antibiotics, so why shouldn't he make a full recovery?'

Evelyn paused and glanced at Mandy, almost for support. 'His body is slowly shutting down. He's tired, Ray. He's had a long life and a good one, and now it's coming to its natural end. I don't know how else to put it, Ray, but Dad is dying.'

There was silence. Mandy looked from Evelyn to her father, who was clearly as shocked as she was. He had gone very pale and was absently wringing his hands in his lap. Presumably Evelyn had had time to come to terms with the seriousness of Grandpa's condition while they had not. 'Has the doctor said this?' he asked at length.

'Not in so many words,' Evelyn said gently, 'but it will be obvious when you see him.'

18

'I'd like to see him now, please,' he said, standing. 'And I think we should leave the prognosis to the doctor.'

Mandy felt embarrassed by her father's curtness and hoped Evelyn appreciated it was a result of the shock of hearing how poorly his father was, and didn't take it personally.

'I'll take you to him now,' Evelyn said evenly, also standing. 'We've converted the study into a sick room. Mum sits with him for most of the day.' She hesitated and looked again to Mandy for support. 'Be prepared to see a big change in him. He's lost a lot of weight.'

'Why? Isn't he eating?' her father asked as they crossed the sitting room. Mandy knew he hadn't really grasped the implications of what Evelyn had told them.

'He takes a little water sometimes,' Evelyn said. 'But even that is getting less. He's sleeping more and more. My hope is that in the end he'll just fall into a deep sleep from which he won't wake.'

Four

M andy felt her pulse quicken as she followed her aunt and father along the hallway at the rear of the house. When her father had said Grandpa had taken a turn for the worse she hadn't for a moment thought he could be dying, only that he was ill. She was struggling to take in what Evelyn had told them; she could see her father was too. They walked in silence down the wood-panelled hall, which, like the reception hall and the other rooms they passed, seemed vaguely familiar. Evelyn stopped outside a closed door on their right and, giving a brief knock, eased it open. 'All right, Mum?' she said, poking her head round. 'Ray and Mandy are here.'

They followed her in. Gran was sitting beside a single bed, a little away from the wall, where Grandpa lay on his back asleep. 'Don't get up,' her father said as Gran began struggling on to her walking frame to greet them. He went over and, kissing her cheek, helped her back down. Mandy saw his face crumple as he looked at the bed.

'He's asleep,' Gran said protectively, her voice small and uneven. 'He's very poorly. I'm so pleased you've both come.'

Her father nodded but couldn't say anything.

Mandy kissed Gran, hugging her thin shoulders, and then looked at Grandpa. She could have wept. It was only three weeks since she'd last seen him and although he was in his eighties he'd been fit and well. He'd taken her on a tour of his garden and had

20

proudly shown her the spring bulbs and the forsythia which was about to flower. Now he lay on his back propped on a mountain of pillows, his previous ruddy complexion waxen and his cheeks hollow. His jaw had relaxed in sleep and his mouth hung open as his head lolled to one side. His right arm, thin and wasted, jutted from the sheet and Gran held his hand. It was pitiful how quickly someone of his age could deteriorate, Mandy thought. She looked at her father and saw her own pain reflected.

'The nurse has just left,' Gran said, her voice slight. 'He'll sleep for a while now. It tires him out being messed around with.'

'The nurse was washing him, Mum,' Evelyn qualified. 'Not messing him around.'

'It's all the same to him,' Gran returned smartly, ever protective of her husband of fifty-nine years.

They fell silent and all that could be heard for some moments was Grandpa's heavy and laboured breathing. Mandy looked at her father, who was standing beside Gran, one hand resting reassuringly on her shoulder. She saw his creased brow and the pain in his eyes, and knew he was as shocked as she was by Grandpa's physical decline. And perhaps, Mandy thought, he saw his own end reflected in his father, for they had been very much alike in stature and temperament, until now. Mandy looked at the outline of Grandpa's wasted body beneath the sheets and could see none of her father's strong and muscular frame, nor his pride and dignity. As she watched saliva ran from the corner of Grandpa's mouth and dribbled on to the pillow. Evelyn took a tissue from the box on the desk and wiped the corner of his mouth. 'There, there, that's better,' she soothed, as though tending a baby. Mandy cringed inwardly.

She looked at her father. 'Why don't you sit down, Dad?' she asked softly.

He nodded. Evelyn took the chair from the desk and set it next to Gran beside the bed. 'I'll leave you to chat with Mum,' she said, 'while I go to the kitchen to see Mrs Saunders about lunch. I take it you will be staying for lunch?'

The mention of lunch in the sick room where Grandpa lay so ill seemed grotesquely out of place, but again Mandy supposed Evelyn had had time to adjust in the five days since she'd brought Grandpa home from hospital, and of course they had to eat.

Mandy looked at her father, who gave a vague shrug.

'Yes, please,' she said.

Evelyn nodded and, straightening the sheets on the bed, went out of the study, closing the door behind her.

Mandy hovered for a moment at the end of the bed, unsure of what to do or say, and then sat in one of the two brown leather armchairs at the other end of the room. It was a large study, big enough to retain the armchairs, desk, coffee table, filing cabinet, and a free-standing bookshelf even with the addition of the two single beds. Grandpa was in the bed in front of her while Gran's nightdress lay neatly folded on the pillow of the other bed, which was against the opposite wall. Her grandparents had lived in a bungalow for as long as she could remember and Mandy knew that although Gran could still manage stairs with her arthritis it was a struggle. Mandy had no idea what the study had looked like before the furniture had been arranged to accommodate the beds, nor did she have any recollection of ever having been in it. But that was hardly surprising, she told herself, for Sarah and she wouldn't have been encouraged to play in the study, and in all likelihood had probably been banned from it.

Mandy looked at her father and Gran sitting beside the bed watching Grandpa. All that could be heard was the sound of

Grandpa's laboured breathing, the breaths deeper than normal breaths, with more time in between; exaggerated, she thought, as though each breath was a statement of living that shouldn't be ignored or taken for granted.

'How's Jean?' Gran asked her father quietly after a moment. 'She didn't come with you?'

'No. She sends her love, and apologies. She'll visit next time.'

'Don't worry, Ray,' Gran said. 'I understand. I'm glad you felt you could come. When Evelyn first suggested Dad and I came here to stay I was worried you wouldn't visit. Evelyn said she would phone you and make it all right. It would have been dreadful if you hadn't visited and been able to say goodbye to your father –' She stopped as her voice broke.

Her father took her hand between his and patted it reassuringly. 'It's OK between Evelyn and me now, Mum. Honestly.'

Mandy looked at them. What Gran had just said – her worry that the past would stop her father from visiting – was the most she'd ever said in front of her about 'the situation'. First her father had referred to it earlier, and now Gran. She wondered when someone was eventually going to tell her what had happened all those years before. At twenty-three she was able to deal with a skeleton or two in the family closet. She was beginning to resent her exclusion. She doubted that whatever had happened could be that horrendous, not in their family. They were squeaky clean. And Mandy now wondered, as she had before, if it had anything to do with her mother and Uncle John – Sarah's father. As children Sarah and she had giggled that they seemed to like each very much and always kissed each other hello and goodbye on the mouth rather than the cheek.

Her thoughts were broken by a change in Grandpa's breathing. His breaths had suddenly become shorter, and then the next didn't come. She sat upright, senses alert. There was a short rasp followed by a dry cough. 'He's waking,' Gran said.

Mandy rose and crossed to the bed where she stood next to her father. They looked at Grandpa and his eyes slowly opened. Turning his head towards them, he smiled. His eyes were moist from sleep and his skin was so pale and thin it was almost translucent. Mandy could see the effort it took for him to speak. 'Hello,' he said, his voice catching. 'Good to see you. Can you get me some water, please?'

'Of course, Dad,' her father said, patting his shoulder.

'It's on the desk,' Gran said to Mandy.

Mandy crossed to the desk where a silver tray with a water jug was at one end, away from the laptop, printer and phone. On the tray, beside the covered jug, were a glass and a plastic feeding beaker.

'Use the beaker, love,' Gran said. 'He can't manage a glass any more. It spills down his front.'

Mandy glanced over and saw the shock on her father's face – that Grandpa could no longer drink from a glass but was reliant on what looked like an adult version of a toddler's training cup. She took the lid off the beaker and poured the water, then snapped the lid on and carried it to the bed.

'Evelyn usually gives it to him,' Gran said anxiously. 'I can't lift his head.'

Mandy glanced at her father, wondering if he wanted to help Grandpa with the drink, but he shifted uncomfortably, unsure of what was required.

'Grandpa, shall I hold the beaker?' Mandy asked, leaning forward so she was in his line of vision.

He gave a small nod. Her father eased back his chair so she could get closer to the bed. Leaning over, she wriggled her left hand under the top pillow and slowly eased Grandpa forward and upright. His dry, lined lips closed around the funnel of the feeding beaker. Mandy gradually tilted it as he sucked and then swallowed. He took three sips and collapsed back, exhausted. Mandy lowered the pillow and moved to one side.

It took a moment for him to gather his strength again to speak. 'I'm pleased you came,' he said slowly, forming each word separately and with effort. 'I'm not very good at present. Have you spoken to Evelyn and John?'

'Yes, Dad,' her father said. 'I've seen Evelyn and everything is fine.'

Grandpa smiled, reassured, and allowed his eyes to slowly close. Mandy watched as his hand came from under the sheet, searching for his son's hand. Her father took it in his and his mouth quivered as he fought back emotion. Men in her family rarely showed their feelings; it wasn't considered the 'manly' thing to do. It was more than Mandy could bear to watch her father and Grandpa exposed and their emotion raw. Thank goodness we came, she thought. Thank goodness Dad was able to surrender his pride and take the opportunity to see his father at his sister's house.

'Is Jean with you?' Grandpa asked as Gran had done, his eyes still closed.

'No, Dad. She sends her love. She'll come next time.'

'If there is a next time. I'm very tired, Ray, and the pain is getting worse.' It was said without self-pity, but Mandy saw her father flinch.

'Are you in pain now?' he asked, sitting forward and still holding his father's hand.

Grandpa shook his head.

'The nurse gave him something,' Gran said. 'But it wears off too quickly.'

'You shouldn't have to suffer in this day and age,' her father said. 'I'll speak to Evelyn and we'll have a word with the doctor.'

Grandpa nodded, but his eyes stayed closed. Then his breathing slowed and deepened as he drifted once more into sleep. Her father eased the bedclothes up round his neck with a tenderness Mandy found exceptionally touching. He stood. 'I'm going to the bathroom,' he said and Mandy knew it was to hide his emotion.

'Will you tell Evelyn that Dad has taken some water?' Gran called after him. 'She'll be pleased. It's a good sign, isn't it?'

He nodded without saying anything, unable to give Gran the false hope she desperately sought. Glancing pointedly at Mandy, he left the room. Mandy moved into the chair her father had vacated, next to Gran and beside the bed. She looked at Grandpa, his chest rising and falling beneath the sheet as his laboured breathing once more filled the air. Until now he'd always appeared much younger than his eighty-five years, but now his illness had aged him enormously. Mandy found it almost impossible to equate the upright, agile person that had been her grandpa a few weeks ago with the shell of a man before her now, who hadn't even the strength to raise his head for a drink.

'It is a good sign, isn't it?' Gran said again. 'Water is good for you. You can do without food, but not water.'

Mandy gave the same non-committal nod her father had done, feeling the same reluctance to fuel what was obviously an unrealistic hope. She wondered if the seriousness of Grandpa's condition had been explained to Gran. Had the doctors, Evelyn or John said that her husband wouldn't be getting better; if so, had she accepted it?

'So tell me about your painting,' Gran suddenly said, her voice lightening as she changed the subject. 'Have you finished that masterpiece yet? I want to be the first to see it.'

Mandy gave a small, dismissive laugh. 'No, not yet, but I promise you'll be the first to see it, if and when it happens.'

'You mean when, not if,' Gran said.

Somehow, in the strange intimacy of the sick room, with Grandpa's laboured breathing as a backdrop, Mandy now found herself able to share her thoughts and frustrations with Gran in a way she couldn't with her parents or even Adam. 'You see, Gran,' she began, 'I think I've got the equivalent of writer's block. It's nearly eight months since I stopped work to paint and I haven't painted anything. I might just as well give up the idea and return to work. When I had little time and I was under pressure, the ideas seemed to pour out. I painted at weekends and some evenings after work. Now I have all the time in the world I can't do anything. I've lost confidence. I haven't a single thought in my head.'

'Like me then.' Gran smiled, lightly touching her arm. 'But, Mandy, the main thing is you tried, love. That's so important. Even if nothing comes of it you had a go. And you know Grandpa's favourite saying?'

Mandy frowned questioningly. 'I don't. He's got lots of sayings. Which one?'

Gran paused, looked at Grandpa as though bringing him into the conversation, and then quoted: '"It is better to have tried and failed, than never to have tried at all."' She looked again at Mandy, and there were tears forming in her eyes. 'Don't give up on your dreams, love. Stay with them or you'll regret it for the rest of your life. I'm sure you're talented, and I know when you find the right subject you'll be able to paint. Then it will be from your heart and the painting will be perfect.'

Five

As her father returned from the cloakroom Mandy said she would go.

'It's down the hall to the right,' he said, pointing to the front of the house. 'And your aunt said lunch is about to be served in the dining room. Apparently they always have lunch at this time,' he added, 'while Dad sleeps.'

'OK, I'll join you there,' she said and left the study.

Mandy knew exactly where the cloakroom was without her father giving directions. It was reassuring that she remembered, but hardly surprising, given the number of times she must have used the downstairs toilet when she'd stayed as a child. Down to the end of the hall, turn right, and she knew the door marked 'Cloakroom' would be set in a recess on her left. It was a large room, she remembered, far larger that their toilet downstairs at home. In addition to the loo and washbasin, there had been a dressing table and matching chair, and another recess like a walk-in wardrobe where the coats and outdoor shoes were stored.

Eyes down, deep in thought, and concentrating on the pattern of the inlaid wooden floor, Mandy turned the corner. She stopped with a small cry of alarm. 'I'm sorry,' she exclaimed, flustered. 'Sorry, I didn't see you.' She took a step back and looked at the man she'd just walked into. He was smiling at her, finding it amusing.

'Hello, Mandy,' he said, in a voice that she'd not heard for a long time. 'Good to see you again. How are you?'

She looked at him, heard his voice and then her silence, and knew he had heard her silence too – the hesitation before she recognized him. 'Uncle John. I'm sorry. I didn't know you were in the house. Evelyn didn't say.'

He laughed indulgently. 'Didn't she? I was having a lie-down upstairs. I was up all night with Grandpa. How are you?'

'I'm fine,' she said, embarrassed she'd not immediately remembered him. He'd been like a second father to her when she'd stayed as a child but he'd changed dramatically since she'd last seen him and was nothing like the man in the one photo she had of him – playing with her and Sarah on the swings. He was obviously ten years older, but he'd put on weight and his face seemed wider, more jowly. What was left of his previous black hair was now grey. Only his voice had remained more or less the same.

'You're looking good, Mandy,' he said, flashing the smile she remembered from her childhood. 'I'd have recognized you anywhere.'

'Thanks,' she said, still embarrassed. 'And you.'

He laughed. 'I don't think so but it's nice of you to say so.' His eyes held her until, uncomfortable, she looked away. 'Anyway, it's good to see you again,' he said. 'I understand lunch is ready.'

'Yes, I'll be there shortly.' She stepped past him and into the cloakroom.

Closing the door behind her, Mandy slid the bolt. She leant with her back against the door, her heart pounding and thoughts racing. It had been a shock bumping into Uncle John like that – not only the suddenness of coming round the corner and walking straight into him, but actually seeing him again. Why hadn't Evelyn said he was in the house – warned her? Perhaps it had slipped her mind, but then again there was no reason for Evelyn to warn her – she didn't know there was anything to warn her about. Only Sarah had known, and she wouldn't have told her mother. It was their secret, just theirs; they had sworn on their lives. For in the instant Mandy had recognized John she'd also remembered the crush she'd had on him. Going on thirteen and at the onset of puberty, she'd confided her crush in Sarah, who then admitted to having a crush on her uncle – Mandy's father. They'd been convinced they were the only ones to have these feelings for older men and that if anyone had discovered they found their uncles attractive they would have been locked up and ostracized for good.

Mandy leant with her back against the cloakroom door. She didn't know whether to laugh or cry. John, middle-aged, overweight and balding, once the object of her desire! How could she? How could she and Sarah? It seemed ludicrous now. But there was something else – something she couldn't quite put her finger on, that was making her legs tremble and heart pound. Something that lurked in the shadows of her mind, another, separate reason for her panic. Something that challenged her explanation that it was the shock of bumping into John and remembering her crush that had made her so uncomfortable and embarrassed. Half remembered and then forgotten, a feeling rather than a thought, similar to when she'd first seen the house: as though she had something to be frightened of but couldn't remember what.

Heaving herself away from the door Mandy crossed to the washbasin and turned on the tap. She splashed cold water over her burning cheeks and then patted her face dry on the hand-towel. The cloakroom looked different from how she'd remembered it – possibly the colour scheme had changed, for the dressing table and chair seemed the same, as did the door to the walk-in wardrobe. Perhaps it was the passage of time and the fact she was now taller that made the room look different? With a small sigh, she reined in her thoughts, used the toilet and then rinsed her hands. She checked her face in the mirror and left the cloakroom.

In the hall the chink of cutlery and china could be heard coming from the dining room at the end of the hall, but there was no conversation.

'It's a buffet, help yourself,' Evelyn said cheerily as Mandy entered the dining room. Evelyn was seated at the far side of the long oak dining table which was covered with platters and serving bowls of food. 'Mrs Saunders will get you something to drink.'

'Just water, please,' Mandy said to the housekeeper, who was waiting by the sideboard, and sat in the chair left vacant next to her father.

She was on the opposite side of the table to Evelyn and Gran, with John to her right at the head of the table. She kept her gaze away from John. So too did her father, she thought. He was concentrating on the table just in front of his plate, looking most uncomfortable. It seemed ridiculously formal for lunch, and the atmosphere was strained with them all together. Mandy looked at the array of cold meats, new potatoes, quiches and salads, and regretted agreeing to lunch; a sandwich on their laps would have been far more appropriate.

'Quite a spread, isn't it?' Gran said dryly, glancing at her from across the table. 'I told Evelyn not to go to so much trouble.'

'We have to eat, Mum,' Evelyn chided. 'And it's no trouble. Help yourself, Mandy.'

Mandy smiled and accepted the platter of quiche Evelyn passed to her. Using one of the silver servers she carefully cut a slice and placed it in the centre of her large gleaming white plate, hoping it would fill up space. Mrs Saunders brought her a glass of water and then moved a salad bowl to within reach. 'Thank you,' Mandy said, and without much enthusiasm took a helping of green salad. She rarely ate much so early in the day; it was only 12.15, and despite not having had breakfast she wasn't hungry. The formality of the setting – upright on their high-back dining chairs and Mrs Saunders hovering ready to assist – certainly didn't help. Indeed it seemed somewhat bizarre, almost grotesque, she thought, that as Grandpa lay desperately ill and barely able to sip water two rooms away they were in here facing a feast. Mandy took a couple of mouthfuls of quiche, drank some water, and then began toying with the salad.

'Leave it if you don't want it,' John suddenly said, making her start. 'You don't *have* to eat it here.'

She looked up and felt her cheeks burn, then glanced at Evelyn. 'Sorry, I'm really not very hungry.'

'Don't worry,' Evelyn said with a tight smile. 'I'll have Mrs Saunders pack you sandwiches for your return journey.'

But John's words had taken Mandy back to her childhood, and one of the first times she'd stayed with Sarah. She remembered she'd sat self-consciously at this very table and toyed with some food she hadn't liked, overwhelmed by the formality of their dining. 'Leave it, Mandy,' John had said. 'You don't *have* to eat it here.' And she remembered the absolute relief she'd felt, for at home her mother had always insisted on a clean plate.

'Sorry,' she said again to Evelyn, setting her knife and fork on her plate. Then she sat with her hands in her lap as they continued eating, not liking to make her excuses but wondering when she could reasonably leave.

Evelyn seemed happy to be at the table, making conversation, perhaps as a diversion from the sick room, Mandy thought, although her talk was mainly about Grandpa: the appalling state of the hospital she'd rescued him from; the doctor who'd been in charge of his case and whom they'd only seen once; and nursing him at home. 'John and I have been operating a rota,' Evelyn said, glancing at her husband. 'John sat with Dad last night so it'll be my turn tonight. Unfortunately I still have to wake John as I can't lift Dad by myself.'

'Why do you have to lift Dad?' her father asked naively, speaking for the first time.

'To get him on to the commode,' Evelyn said.

"Oh.'

'Although Dad's lost a lot of weight, he's still very heavy. I have to be careful of my back.'

Mandy saw her father shift uncomfortably, but he couldn't have known what Evelyn had meant.

'It works all right,' John said amicably. 'I nap when I can during the day. I would rather Evelyn left all the nights to me, so she gets some sleep.'

'Your business is managing without you?' her father asked, changing the conversation.

'Yes, I have a good team. I've briefed them on the situation here, and they phone if there's a problem. I work on my laptop – emails, etc., while Dad sleeps.'

Her father nodded, and Mandy felt a stab of guilt. While John had rearranged his work, house and routine so that he and Evelyn could nurse Grandpa, she and her father had done nothing other than visit, and her mother was conspicuous by her absence. In their defence, Mandy thought, her parents hadn't appreciated the seriousness of Grandpa's condition or the practical implications of nursing him.

'Dad and I could look after Grandpa this afternoon,' Mandy offered, 'while you and Evelyn go out or get some rest.'

'Yes,' her father readily agreed. 'We can hold the fort.'

'Thanks,' John said. 'We might take you up on that if you don't have to rush off.'

'No, not at all,' her father said convivially. 'I'll call Jean and tell her to expect me later.'

Mandy looked at Evelyn and hesitated. 'Is Sarah around?'

'She visited yesterday, with her partner – they live in the town. Sarah finds it too upsetting seeing Grandpa like this. She can't really offer much help. She's worried she'll remember Grandpa as he is now, rather than as he was when he was well. I'm sure she'll visit again later in the week.'

Mandy nodded. 'I understand.' For she was already finding that the image of Grandpa today as he was now, sick and emaciated, was starting to impose itself upon the memory from when she'd last seen him, fit and healthy.

'I've finished,' Gran said, dabbing her lips with the linen napkin. 'I'll go to Will. He shouldn't be left alone for too long.' She turned in her seat, ready to stand, and was drawing her walking frame towards her when a crash came from the study followed by a piercing scream of pain. 'I knew it!' she said, panic-stricken. 'I just knew he wanted something.'

Six

*I*mmediately they were all on their feet, rushing out of the dining room. John went first; Mandy followed with her father while Evelyn held back to help Gran. Arriving in the study they found Grandpa on the floor beside the bed, having fallen trying to get out. He was on his side with one leg splayed behind the other. His eyes were half open and he was struggling to sit up, confused. John and her father went to him as Mandy hovered anxiously behind them. 'Does anything hurt, Dad?' John asked.

Grandpa shook his head and tried to sit up again.

'Let's get you back to bed,' John said. He turned to her father. 'I don't think anything is broken.'

Mandy stood by the bed as her father and uncle, one either side of Grandpa, eased him into a sitting position. He let out a small moan and tried to say something.

'Sorry, Dad?' John said, lowering his ear. 'You've fallen. Ray's here. We'll get you back into bed.'

Grandpa shook his head and whispered something.

'OK, Dad. Hold on a minute.' Then to Mandy: 'Can you take the top off the commode?'

Mandy looked round for the commode.

'It's that chair,' Evelyn said, pointing, having just come in with Gran. 'The top comes off.'

Mandy went to the chair and began grappling with the vinyl-covered seat, not knowing if it lifted or rose on a hinge.

'Give it a good pull,' John said, an edge of impatience creeping into his voice. 'The whole seat lifts off.' To Grandpa he added: 'Hold on, Dad, nearly there.'

She yanked the seat and it came off in her hand, revealing a white plastic toilet seat with a bowl suspended below.

'Bring it closer, will you?' John demanded.

She dragged the commode to just in front of Grandpa. He was still in a sitting position on the floor, supported either side by John and her father.

'On the count of three,' John said to her father. 'We need to lift him and then swing him sideways and down, on to the seat.'

Mandy saw anxiety flash across her father's face. John knew what he was doing but neither her father nor she did.

'One … two … three,' John said, and they began to lift.

Mandy watched with dismay as they lifted Grandpa on to his feet and then manoeuvred him round and down on to the commode like a large rag doll. The second before his bottom touched the seat, John pulled down his pyjama trousers. Mandy looked away. It was pathetic and demeaning: her tall, strong, proud Grandpa who, until a couple of weeks ago, had kept fit by swimming every week, now slumped on the commode, with his eyes half open and pyjama trousers round his knees. He looked like a giant toddler on a potty.

There was quiet as her father and John waited either side of Grandpa. She waited with Evelyn and Gran at the foot of the bed, all of them averting their eyes. Then the silence was broken by the trickle of water as Grandpa began to relieve himself. Her father fled the room. Gran turned her walking frame and followed him out, while Evelyn, focusing on the practical, went to Grandpa's empty bed and began stripping the sheets. 'He needs clean ones,' she said matter-of-factly.

'And pyjama trousers,' John added. 'But his top is dry.'

Mandy watched in awe as John steadied Grandpa with one hand and, kneeling down, began trying to ease off the wet pyjama trousers with the other. Realizing she could finally do something to help, she went to where her father had stood, just behind Grandpa, and placed her hands on his shoulders to support him.

'Thanks, Mandy,' John said. With both hands free he was able to slide off the wet trousers, which he passed to Evelyn. Grandpa relaxed back on the commode.

'I'll check your dad is all right when I've put this in the wash,' Evelyn said to Mandy. 'It's a lot for him to cope with – seeing his father like this.'

'It's a lot for you to cope with too,' Mandy said.

Evelyn met her gaze and in that look Mandy saw not a grown woman in control, but a small girl who was struggling to cope as best she could with her dying father, and wasn't really coping at all.

'Yes,' Evelyn said quietly. 'It is.' Her face crumpled, and as she hurried from the room Mandy saw she was silently weeping.

Mandy stayed by Grandpa, a reassuring hand resting on each of his shoulders, and waited. By standing behind him, at least she was preserving some of his modesty she thought, but it was a pathetically small amount given what he'd lost. John finished straightening the mattress protector on the bed ready for the clean sheet and then came over and lowered his mouth to Grandpa's ear. 'Dad, have you finished?' he asked gently.

Grandpa moaned.

'Dad, have you finished on the commode?' he tried again patiently.

'Yes,' her grandpa said.

'OK, hang on there. Evelyn is fetching some clean pyjamas, then we'll get you back into bed.'

When Evelyn returned with the clean sheets and pyjama trousers she and John fell into what Mandy guessed was a well-practised routine. Evelyn passed the trousers to John and he began easing Grandpa's feet into them while she made up the bed. Mandy remained where she was. She could feel the warmth of his body through the material of his pyjama jacket; could smell the soap that had been used to wash him – different from the one he usually used. He was so quiet and still as they worked she couldn't tell if he was awake or dozing. She kept her gaze directed into the centre of the room and tried to picture Grandpa as he used to be.

'OK, Dad,' John said. 'On the count of three we'll get you to stand. Can you help, Mandy?'

Moving her hands from Grandpa's shoulders, she placed them under his left arm and helped raise him off the commode and into a standing position. As they did, Evelyn quickly pulled up his pyjamas and the three of them then eased Grandpa into bed and on to the pillows. How John and Evelyn had coped alone for nearly a week Mandy had no idea.

'All right, Dad?' Evelyn asked as Grandpa lay back on the pillow. She tenderly stroked his forehead.

He groaned slightly and then gave a small nod.

'Good man,' John said. 'I bet you're exhausted after that. Try and get some sleep.'

Mandy was touched by the dignity John and Evelyn gave Grandpa as well as their ability to actually nurse him. Neither of them had had any nursing experience as far as she knew, but both seemed to know how to manoeuvre him in a way that caused minimum discomfort. Their efficiency seemed to highlight her father's inefficiency and his inability to cope. Since arriving he'd hardly been in the same room as his father, and although she appreciated why, it didn't help. 'I'll go and find Dad,' she said.

Evelyn nodded. 'He's in the morning room with Gran.'

Outside the study, Mandy turned left, instinctively aware she would find the morning room at the end of the hall. It was strange: she seemed to know the layout of the downstairs of the house without any conscious recollection of being in the rooms. Mrs Saunders came towards her, on her way to the kitchen, carrying a tray of plates from lunch. 'Miss,' she said, acknowledging her and smiling as they passed. Mandy thought how odd it must be, having someone other than family in the house, but then again Mrs Saunders appeared so well integrated she was like a family member.

The door to the morning room was slightly ajar. As Mandy approached she could hear her father and Gran talking quietly, in the middle of a conversation.

'I'm not saying anything to her,' her father said. 'Not now.'

Mandy heard Gran tut, then: 'It's your decision, obviously, Ray, but now seems a very good time to me.' And although the 'her' could have applied to her aunt or even her mother Jean, Mandy had the distinct impression they were talking about her, an impression confirmed when they both fell silent and looked at her as she entered.

'Dad,' Mandy said, hovering just inside the door. 'Grandpa will be asleep again soon; I really think you should see him.'

'Yes,' Gran agreed, pulling the walking frame towards her, ready to stand. 'I like to be with him as much as I can, while I have the chance. John put a bed in the study for me, but I can't sleep, he's so restless at night. I think they're moving me upstairs. I hope Will understands.'

'I'm sure he does,' Mandy's father reassured her, falling into step at her side.

* * *

It was nearly 2 p.m. as they settled themselves in the study-cum-sick room, Mandy in one of the pair of leather armchairs at the end of the room and her father and Gran by Grandpa's bed. John and Evelyn had taken up the offer of a break and were in the sitting room trying to have a nap. It seemed most of the day was spent sitting and watching Grandpa sleep; Gran said she sat with him all day and Evelyn and John joined her as and when they could. But although Grandpa's eyes were closed and he appeared to be asleep, he was very restless, and became more so as the afternoon wore on. He called out and sometimes groaned as though in pain, which was not only disturbing for him but upsetting to witness.

Mandy saw her father grow more and more anxious as he watched his mother trying without success to soothe his father. 'It's the medication wearing off,' Gran said at last. 'It seems to be lasting less and less time, and the nurse isn't due until three.'

'Can't Dad have more tablets before the nurse comes?' her father asked.

'He can't swallow tablets any more,' Gran said, 'even when they're crushed. We've tried the liquid the doctor prescribed but that didn't do any good. The nurse gives him injections now, every four hours. It's morphine, I think. That helps for a while, but he needs more. John said he'd speak to the nurse this afternoon.'

The next hour was the worst Mandy had ever experienced in her entire life, she thought, as the morphine gradually wore off and Grandpa became in increasing pain. To begin with they left Evelyn and John having a rest, but as Grandpa's discomfort grew and their efforts to soothe him became less and less effective, her father fetched them from the sitting room. 'I'll call the nurse,' John said when he saw Grandpa, and went to the phone on the desk.

Mandy stood anxiously with her father and Evelyn by the bed and tried to soothe Grandpa. But he tossed and turned, and cried out, shouting words that made no sense at all. Evelyn spoke to him in a calming voice, stroked his forehead and tried to reassure him, but her efforts were pathetic and futile in the face of his pain. Then he began clawing at his arms as though his skin was on fire. Mandy's father tried to stop him by holding his hands, which made him even more agitated, and he swore.

'He doesn't know what he's saying,' Gran excused. 'He's delirious, he doesn't mean it.'

'The nurse won't be long,' John said, hovering by the phone.

But 3 p.m. came and went and the nurse failed to arrive.

'It's not like him,' Evelyn said. 'Normally he's very punctual.'

'Should be, the amount they're paying.'

At 3.15 there was still no sign of the nurse and Grandpa had broken out in a cold sweat from the agony. John said he would phone the nurse again and find out what the hell was going on. He left the study to make the call and when he returned he said the nurse had been called to an emergency and would come as soon as he could.

'That's unacceptable!' her father said, turning on John. 'Let me speak to him! No one should have to suffer like this!'

'If you think it will help, go ahead!' John retorted, almost shouting. 'I don't like to see Dad suffer any more than you do. He's been like a father to me and now I can't help him! We've had almost a week of this – a week of watching him suffer. And I'm not sure I can take much more.' John's face crumpled and he turned away.

'Oh, Will,' Gran said, trying to catch hold of Grandpa's hand. She began to cry.

41

'This isn't helping,' Evelyn said. 'Ray, why don't you take Mum into the sitting room until the nurse has been and Dad is more comfortable?'

Her father hesitated. Mandy saw his resentment at being told what to do by his sister. 'I think it's a good idea,' Mandy said, touching his arm. 'Gran shouldn't see Grandpa like this.' Although it was more about removing her father from the room than Gran, who seemed to be coping far better.

Her father glanced at her and then without speaking helped Gran to her feet. The two of them left the room. Mandy went over and, kneeling by the bed, began gently stroking Grandpa's forehead and talking to him quietly. 'It's Mandy,' she said. 'The nurse won't be long. Dad and Gran are in the sitting room. Try to relax, take deep breaths, it'll help soothe away the pain.'

John and Evelyn hovered close by. 'Thanks, Mandy,' John said, sounding relieved to have some of the responsibility taken from him.

'I'm sure he knows it's you,' Evelyn said. 'He's growing calmer.'

Mandy felt her eyes mist as she continued to stroke Grandpa's brow and whisper words of comfort. She thought he was responding; his legs were still and he was no longer trying to claw at his arms. His eyes had closed and his face seemed more relaxed; perhaps he did know it was her and had taken comfort in her presence. Feeling she might be able to help, and aware this could be her last opportunity to spend time with him, she decided to offer to stay and help, for however long she was needed.

Seven

'I'm sure,' she said. 'I want to. And it's not as if I've got a proper job and need to take time off work. I'd like to help, really.'

'It's much appreciated,' John said. 'Thanks, Mandy.'

'Yes, thanks,' Evelyn echoed.

'I don't know,' her father said again, as he had when Mandy had first told him of her intention to stay.

'Why ever not?' Gran asked, turning from the bed to look at him. 'It's nice that Mandy wants to, and Evelyn and John could do with the help. It will be fine, Ray. I promise. Don't worry.'

They were all in the study grouped once more around Grandpa's bed. He was asleep and pain-free. The nurse had arrived, full of apologies, shortly after 4 p.m., and had given Grandpa the morphine injection which would allow some relief for a few hours at least. It was now 6 p.m. and, having had an early dinner (Evelyn had insisted he ate before setting off), Mandy's father was now preparing to leave. But his reluctance to leave Mandy, combined with Gran's reassuring him: 'It will be fine, Ray, I promise,' and their exchange of meaningful glances, seemed to Mandy there was something she wasn't being told.

'All right.' Her father shrugged, still reluctant. 'But I don't know what her mother will say.'

'Nothing,' Gran said. 'And I think Jean should come and visit, tomorrow, when you bring Mandy's things.'

'I'm sure she will,' her father said defensively. 'Jean didn't realize how ill Dad was or she would have come today.'

'All right,' Gran agreed, and returned her attention to Grandpa.
She was sitting in her usual chair by the head of his bed. There was
more room in the study now. Before dinner her father had helped
John manoeuvre the other single bed upstairs back to the guest
room it had come from, so Gran could have a better night's sleep.

Her father looked at his watch and slowly stood. 'I'd best be
off,' he said awkwardly.

'We'll leave you to say goodbye to Dad then,' Evelyn said. She
and John slipped from the study.

He stood uncomfortably by the bed and Mandy saw how difficult he was finding it to leave. Normally father and son shook
hands on meeting and parting, but clearly that was impossible
now. Grandpa was so heavily sedated it was doubtful he could
even hear, let alone raise his arm.

Her father took a step closer. 'Goodbye, Dad. I'm going now. I'll
see you again tomorrow. I'll bring Jean with me.' He paused and
looked embarrassed, unsure of what to say or do next. Grandpa
gave no acknowledgement, no sign he knew his son was there.
'Mandy is staying to help look after you,' he added. 'Goodbye,
Dad.' He leant over the bed and kissed his father's forehead.
Grandpa's breathing faltered and then resumed. It was impossible
to know if he was aware of his son or not.

Her father turned to Gran and kissed her cheek, easily, as he
always did. 'Goodbye, Mum. Don't get up. Take care. Look after
each other and I'll see you tomorrow.'

'Drive carefully, Ray,' she said, taking hold of his hand. 'And
give my love to Jean.'

'I will.' He kissed her again and then crossed to Mandy who
was waiting by the study door ready to see him out. With a final

glance at his father, he nodded to his mother and quickly left the study.

Mandy walked with him along the hall towards the front of the house.

'Are you sure you'll be all right, Amanda?' he said again as they arrived in the reception hall. 'You know you can change your mind. You don't have to stay. I can take you home now.'

She looked at him carefully. 'Dad, why shouldn't I be all right? I'm with family. I'm staying to help look after my grandpa.'

He looked away and left the question unanswered. 'Well, if you're sure.'

'Dad, please don't worry.' She touched his arm. 'I'll be fine, and Evelyn and John desperately need some help. They're exhausted. If you could get my clothes from the flat that would be great. You've got my list and key?'

He nodded. 'We'll stop by on the way tomorrow. You mother will have a better idea of where to find things. I must go to the office in the morning so we should be here late afternoon.'

'OK.' She kissed his cheek. 'Text me to say you got home safely.'

He gave a small laugh. 'I'll try.' She had recently taught him to text but his fingers seemed too big for the tiny buttons and he rarely did so, saying it was easier to phone.

'I'm going now,' he called to John and Evelyn, and they appeared from the sitting room.

'Safe journey,' John said.

Her father shook John's hand and then kissed his sister's cheek – his previous awkwardness slightly eased by the time spent with her. Saying goodbye, John and Evelyn made their way back down the hall, leaving Mandy to see her father off. He opened the front door and Mandy folded her arms against the cool evening air. She watched him cross the drive towards the car. The sky was only just beginning to darken as the days were lengthening towards spring. He pointed the remote at the car; the locks flew up and the interior light went on. He paused before getting in and looked back to give a little wave. 'Take care, love,' he called. 'See you tomorrow.'

'Yes.' She smiled and waved too.

She watched him climb into the car and the door close. The interior light faded and went out. The engine started and the tyres crunched over the gravel as the car slowly moved forward, round the curve of the carriage drive and towards her. As the car drew level her father ducked his head and peered through the side window to give another little wave. She waved back. He continued past and her gaze fell on the rear of the car as it slowly pulled away. Then in the half-light of dusk something strange happened which froze her to the spot. As she watched the receding car, the shadowy outline of a girl appeared in the rear window. The child turned to look at her and their eyes met. She was about twelve and her long fair hair was tied in a ponytail. Tears stained her cheeks and her face was creased in sorrow. Mandy knew instinctively the girl was frightened and needed help but she also knew there was nothing she could do to save her. She stared after the car with an overwhelming sense of despair as it continued down the drive, and away from her. The image of the girl faded and then vanished.

Eight

Mandy stayed where she was, staring at the now empty drive. The air was still and the door to the house stood open behind her. Her heart was racing and her mouth was dry. It must have been a trick of the eye, she said, trying to calm herself, an illusion in the twilight. Of course there wasn't a girl in the back of your father's car. Don't be ridiculous. You're worried about Grandpa, and tired – it was nothing more than your imagination.

So, as a child accepts its mother's reassurance that there is nothing lurking under the bed while not wholly convinced, Mandy turned from the drive and went into the welcoming warmth and light of her aunt's house.

'How would you feel about staying up with me tonight?' John asked as she entered the study. He was in one of the pair of leather armchairs with his laptop open on his knees; Gran was in her usual chair by the bed. 'Evelyn could do with a night's sleep,' he added.

'Yes,' Mandy said, and sat in the chair next to Gran at the side of the bed.

'Only if you want to,' John said. 'You don't have to. There's a bed ready upstairs otherwise.'

'No, it's fine, really,' she reassured him, and looked at Grandpa. Now the medicine had taken effect and he was sleeping comfortably, she could enjoy her time with him; they all could. One of his hands jutted from beneath the bedclothes and Gran was stroking it tenderly. 'Was your dad all right?' she asked after a moment.

Mandy nodded. 'He's going to text when he gets home. Oh,' she said, suddenly realizing, 'I've forgotten to tell Adam where I am.'

'Best phone him now,' Gran smiled. She'd met Adam many times and liked him.

Mandy stood, retrieved her handbag from where she'd dumped it in the corner of the study and took out her mobile. There were five texts: two from Adam as well as a missed call from him. 'I won't be long,' she said, and left the study.

Going a little way along the hall, she pressed Adam's number and he answered immediately. 'Are you OK, Mandy?' he asked, concerned. 'Wherever have you been?'

'Sorry. I've had my phone on silent all day. I'm at my aunt's in Cambridgeshire. Grandpa's very ill.' She then explained what had happened since her father had come to her flat early that morning. Adam sympathized; his pique of the night before had gone.

'If there is anything I can do, promise me you'll phone,' he said kindly. 'I know what you're going through.' His own grandfather had died the year before.

'Thanks,' she said, touched by his sensitivity and reminded of what she stood to lose. 'And sorry again about last night.'

'No problem. Take care.'

When they'd finished the call she texted him: *Luv u*, which she knew she needed to start showing more as well as saying.

Returning to the study, Mandy sat next to Gran and replied to the other texts, from friends. She sent the same message to all three: *Stayin at my aunts. grandpa ill. will fone on return.* Leaving her mobile on silent, she dropped it into her bag and took out her iPod. Gran was dozing now and John was still working on his laptop. She plugged in her earpieces and gazed at Grandpa. He was still relatively peaceful. Occasionally his arm jerked, or a muscle twitched in his face, giving the impression he was frowning, but there was no sign of the shocking pain that had engulfed him during the afternoon. Perhaps the nurse had changed the medication, or given him a stronger dose of morphine? She hoped so, for as her father had said no one should have to suffer in this day and age. Her iPod was playing a Michael Jackson ballad, 'Will You Be There', and in the now calm atmosphere of the study with Grandpa sleeping peacefully, there was something almost perfect, almost ethereal in the love she felt for him, and she was so very pleased she'd stayed to help.

At 8.15 p.m. Gran was still dozing when Evelyn poked her head round the study door. 'Mandy, I usually make Gran an Ovaltine drink at this time, before I help her get ready for bed. Would you like an Ovaltine?'

'No thanks. Is it all right if I make myself a tea later?'

'Of course. I'll show you where everything is in the kitchen, just as soon as I've seen to Gran.'

Evelyn left the study and as the door closed Gran opened her eyes. 'She thinks Ovaltine helps me sleep at night,' she whispered conspiratorially, 'but I haven't noticed any difference.'

'You'll be better tonight, upstairs,' John said from the end of the study. Gran started, having forgotten he was there.

'It's very kind of Evelyn, though,' Gran added quickly, looking guilty. Mandy smiled.

Evelyn reappeared ten minutes later with the hot drink. Gran sat by the bed with the cup cradled in the palms of her hands and slowly sipped it. At nine o'clock Evelyn returned, took away the cup and saucer, and then reappeared almost immediately.

'Bedtime now,' Gran said stoically to Mandy. 'It takes me a while to get ready and I need some help.'

Mandy stood aside as Evelyn helped Gran to her feet and on to the walking frame.

'If only I had your youth,' Gran said to Mandy. 'Goodnight, love. See you in the morning. And thanks for staying.'

Mandy gave her a hug and kissed her cheek. 'Night, Gran.' She watched as Gran slowly crossed the study with Evelyn following, ready to assist if necessary.

John closed his laptop and set it on the coffee table. 'I'll give them a hand getting upstairs. Are you all right here alone, Mandy? I won't be long.'

'Yes, of course.'

The three of them left the study in a small slow procession as Mandy sat again by the bed and looked at Grandpa. On his back, with his jaw gaping in sleep, the only sound was that of his laboured breathing. Longevity didn't really have much to recommend it, she thought, if it reduced you to this. Yet she had to admit that her grandparents had gained something special from growing old together; they had a lifetime of shared experiences and mutual support to look back on and draw strength from. Growing old with a loved one, Mandy thought, was far better than growing old alone – old age didn't seem quite so threatening if you had someone to share it with.

Twenty minutes later John returned to the study and said Gran was in bed. 'Evelyn's in the kitchen, so if you'd like to go through she'll show you where everything is now.' He said it with a cocked eyebrow in a slightly disparaging tone as though he thought Evelyn was fussing unnecessarily, but should be indulged. It was a collusion Mandy had noticed him attempt with her before and, as before, she ignored it.

'Thanks,' she said lightly, and left the study.

The kitchen was huge, nearly as big as her entire bedsitting room, and was clearly brand new. 'We've had it refurbished,' Evelyn said proudly, standing in front of the disarming array of oak cupboards and granite work surfaces, which shone in the concealed lighting and seemed to go on for ever.

'It's lovely,' Mandy said admiringly.

Evelyn smiled, pleased, and began opening and closing the cupboard doors, showing her where things were kept. 'Tea, coffee, drinking chocolate and sugar, etc.,' she said, 'are here. Mugs, glasses, cups, here. The fridge and freezer are in here, and the dishwasher is here.' Everything was behind an oak door – even the oven. 'Help yourself to whatever you want,' she said. 'If you fancy a sandwich, the bread is here, or cake and biscuits here.'

'Thank you,' Mandy said again.

'And upstairs,' Evelyn continued, 'I've sorted out some overnight things to see you through until your dad returns tomorrow with your own. I've put them in one of the guest rooms, which will be your room. If you come up now, I'll show you, then I'll go to bed. Are you sure you're all right to stay up tonight?'

'Positive. I don't need much sleep.'

Evelyn smiled. 'No, I didn't at your age either.' She led the way out of the kitchen up the stairs.

Mandy found she remembered going up the stairs from when she'd stayed as a child. It was a huge winding staircase with a small landing halfway up, and so unlike her staircase at her parents'. There was a window on the landing with a windowsill that had always contained a vase of fresh flowers. The vase was still there but without the flowers. Mandy remembered the polished brass handrail which she and Sarah had been told off for using as a slide. At the top of the stairs she followed Evelyn into a bedroom at the rear of the house, overlooking the gardens. Neatly folded on the bed was a set of towels, face flannel, soap, tooth-brush, toothpaste, nightdress and two pairs of new pants.

'Thank you very much,' Mandy said, impressed that Evelyn had produced this at such short notice.

'Thank *you*, for staying. It's much appreciated. I'll sleep better knowing John has your help. But for goodness' sake wake me if I'm needed.'

'I will,' Mandy said, and then hesitated. She glanced around at the magnolia-emulsioned walls and flowered duvet. 'Evelyn, is this the room I used to sleep in when I stayed as a child?'

Evelyn looked at her, clearly shocked. 'No. You had the Pink Room, at the front of the house. Don't you remember?'

'No, not really.'

'But, Mandy, you stayed with us regularly. How can you not remember? You were always here – weekends and school holidays. You and Sarah were inseparable between the ages of four and twelve. You'd turned thirteen the last time you came.' She stopped as though suddenly realizing something and looked at her oddly.

Mandy gave a small shrug. 'I know,' she said carefully. 'But my memory is very bitty. I have vague recollections of being in the house but no detail. I guess ten years is a long time.'

Evelyn held her gaze and Mandy could see that not only did her aunt not know what to say, but that she wasn't sure whether to believe her.

'I suppose it is,' Evelyn conceded after a moment. 'Anyway the guest bathroom is next door.' With a brief air-kiss she said good-night and quickly left.

Mandy crossed to the curtains and, parting them, looked out. This room was at the rear of the house; Evelyn had said the Pink

Room was at the front. Although it was pitch dark outside she could see the upper terraces subtly lit by small round sunken lights. This view was unfamiliar whereas the view from the Pink Room would presumably be familiar from when she'd stayed as a child. The Pink Room, Evelyn had said, expecting her to remember it, and the name almost rang a bell. Almost. Somewhere in the crevices of her mind Mandy thought she had stayed in that room. Possibly. But at thirteen of course she should have remembered, and in detail. No wonder Evelyn had looked at her oddly. But apart from a vague feeling that she'd heard the name before, she could recall nothing else about it. And in the backwater of her mind an unsettling premonition told her it was better it stayed that way.

Nine

Mandy washed her face and brushed her teeth in the guest bathroom, and then went downstairs. Most of the main lights in the house were off now, and she guessed that while she'd been in the bathroom Evelyn or John had locked up for an early night. A single wall-light lit the landing at the top of the stairs, and a lamp on an onyx table lit the front hall. A light glowed in the porch and through the leaded light window of the front door Mandy could see the silhouette of a tree stirring eerily in the wind outside. Towards the back of the house, the rear hall was lit by a nightlight, and the doors to the morning room and dining room were closed. The kitchen door had been left open but the light was off, Mrs Saunders presumably having gone home. Mandy had never liked the dark, particularly in a strange house; as a child she'd imagined all sorts of ghoulies and ghosties lurking in the shadows. She'd slept with a lamp on in her room at university, and even for the first three months of living in her flat, despite the room never being dark because of the street lamp right outside her window.

The door to the study was closed. Giving a small knock, she turned the handle and gently eased open the door. Here, too, the main light was off, and she was surprised to find a red glow illuminating most of the room. It came from a lava lamp on a table in one corner. Mandy went in and silently closed the door behind her. Grandpa was asleep on his back, mouth open and breathing heavily. John was dozing in one of the armchairs. She quietly crossed the room, sat in the other armchair and looked across the room at the lamp. She hadn't noticed the lava lamp during the day, presumably because it hadn't been switched on. Its red glow now gave the room a strange, almost surreal hue. As she looked, a red bubble of oil in the lamp slowly elongated upwards and a smaller bubble appeared to the right. She was surprised her aunt and uncle had such a modern and popular (to the point of tacky) artefact amidst their antiques and hand-crafted reproduction furniture. It seemed incongruous.

Reaching down beside the chair into her bag, Mandy quietly slid out her mobile and checked for messages. There were three texts: one from a friend replying to her earlier text, one from her father staying he'd arrived home safely and would 'c' her tomorrow, and the third from Adam: *'Luv n miss u 2. hugs n kisses. adam'*. Mandy smiled to herself as she returned the phone to her bag. She'd been forgiven. Resting her head back she gazed at the lava lamp. The larger of the red bubbles of oil was still contorting upwards, becoming thinner and longer, while the smaller one was growing rounder and fatter. The trouble with lava lamps, she thought, was that your eyes were drawn to them, and you had to watch, whether you wanted to or not. Like a television left on with the sound off, it was difficult to look away or concentrate on anything else.

It was only 9.50 p.m. but with the early start and the emotional rollercoaster she'd been on all day it seemed much later and she felt pretty exhausted. Grandpa's heavy and laboured breathing continued in the background; she saw his legs occasionally twitch beneath the sheets. She wondered if the medication was wearing off already. The nurse had come again at 8 p.m. and given him another injection, which also contained a sleeping draught and was supposed to see him through the night.

Tired, reasonably comfortable in the upholstered chair, and mesmerized by the swirling glow of the lamp and Grandpa's almost hypnotic breathing, Mandy's eyes slowly began to close. His breathing seemed louder now her eyes were shut, and with nothing else to concentrate on she found herself silently counting the seconds in the rhythm of his breathing. In – one, two, three, four, and then a pause of five seconds before he breathed out for three seconds. It was far, far slower than her own breathing – she'd taken nearly three breaths to his one. She assumed it was his medication slowing his body rhythm at the same time as it suppressed the pain. Counting the seconds of his breathing was as soporific as counting sheep and, combined with the warmth of the room, soon made her doze.

She was a child again, in this house, and looking out of a window at the front, looking down on the driveway below. She was in the Pink Room, so named because it was decorated pink. Mandy could see herself standing at the window and looking down on to the drive. It was late at night and very dark outside. A car was pulling away, leaving the house, its headlights illuminating the gravel ahead. It was her father's car and there was someone in the back. As she watched, the girl with the ponytail turned to look at her, just as she had earlier that evening when she'd waved goodbye to her father. Tears streamed down the girl's cheeks and Mandy could feel her terror and distress. 'Help! Someone help me. Daddy, no!'

'Help, Mandy, quick.' Mandy's eyes shot open. 'Wake up. I need your help!' John's voice.

The dark of the night outside had gone, and so too had the red glow of the lamp, replaced by the main light of the study. Mandy was immediately on her feet, going to the bed; her heart raced from the shock of suddenly waking. 'He needs the toilet,' John said, struggling to get Grandpa out of bed and over to the commode. Grandpa groaned but his eyes stayed closed; he was a dead weight and powerless to help.

Mandy pulled the commode to the bed and then yanked off the lid, but it was too late. As John lifted Grandpa on to the commode, he groaned again, and they heard the rush of water as a wet patch appeared on his pyjama bottoms. 'I'm sorry,' he mumbled in a small voice, and Mandy could have wept.

'It's not your fault, Dad,' John reassured him. 'I should have woken sooner.'

So should I, Mandy thought, if I'm going to be of any help.

Grandpa's eyes stayed closed as John steadied him, a hand on each shoulder. Mandy knelt at his feet and carefully slid off the wet pyjama trousers, one leg at a time. 'Thanks, love,' he said, his eyes still closed.

'I'll get you clean ones,' she said quietly, humbled by his humility.

He gave a little groan of acknowledgement but didn't open his eyes.

'You'll find the clean stuff either in the dryer or the airing cupboard – in the laundry room, behind the kitchen,' John said.

Mandy rolled up the wet pyjamas and left the study. She knew she'd let Grandpa down by not hearing his calls for help. The rear hall was lit only by the nightlight and now seemed even darker after the main light of the study. She passed the kitchen, which was still in darkness, and then stopped outside the next door which John had said would be the laundry room. Turning the knob, she felt inside for the light switch and clicked it on before entering. The room was bare and cold compared to the rest of the house, and smelt of pine disinfectant.

She saw the washing machine straight in front of her and next to that the dryer. Crossing the red slate-tiled floor, Mandy pushed the wet pyjama trousers into the washing machine ready for the next wash the following day, then opened the dryer door. There was a single sheet from Grandpa's bed and two pairs of his pyjama bottoms, still warm from drying – Evelyn must have put them in before going to bed. She gave them a shake and loosely folded them over her arm. She guessed this room was mainly the domain of the housekeeper, Mrs Saunders; her apron hung on the back of the door and the shoes she wore in the house were paired just inside the door. Switching off the light, Mandy came out and returned to the study. If she'd ever been in the laundry room as a child she certainly didn't remember it.

Grandpa was as she'd left him: on the commode, eyes closed, with John standing behind, holding him. 'Well done, you found them,' John said, glancing at the clean laundry draped over her arm. Grandpa didn't stir and could have been asleep.

Leaving the sheet and spare pair of pyjama trousers on the foot of the bed in case they were needed later, Mandy knelt and concentrated on easing Grandpa's red and swollen feet into the pyjamas, first one leg then the other. His legs were like dead weights, and there were notches of blue veins clustered on both ankles where the blood had flowed down from sitting. She drew the trousers up to his knees; his pyjama jacket hung over his lap.

'Ready,' she said to John, and straightened.

'On the count of three, Dad,' John said. 'One. Two. Three.' As John lifted, Mandy quickly pulled up the pyjama trousers as she'd seen John previously do, which gave Grandpa as much privacy as possible. 'Now into bed,' John said.

Taking most of the weight, John swung Grandpa towards the bed and Mandy guided in his legs. Grandpa moaned but his eyes stayed closed. She pulled up the sheet and tucked it around his neck, as John straightened the pillows. The commode was empty and Mandy moved it to one side, but left the lid off ready for next time. They waited by the bed for Grandpa's breathing to slowly regulate, signalling he was asleep.

'Shall I make us a cup of tea?' Mandy asked, now wide awake.

'Please. Mine's skimmed milk with no sugar. And thanks for your help, Mandy. It's so much easier with two. We make a good team – you and me.' His gaze lingered appreciatively.

Mandy looked away. *A good team.* She would have given her right arm to have heard him say that when she'd had her schoolgirl crush. Perhaps it was the embarrassing reminder of that time, or the intimacy of the sick room, but she suddenly felt uncomfortable. 'I'll make that tea then,' she said with a small nod, and left the study.

As she moved around the unfamiliar kitchen, trying to remember where Evelyn had said things were, her thoughts went to her parents. She was pleased her father hadn't stayed; he would never have coped with seeing Grandpa so vulnerable and compromised, not even able to make it to the commode without wetting himself. Now she was worried her mother wouldn't be able to cope either when she visited tomorrow. For although her parents hadn't spoken to John and Evelyn in ten years, they'd always been in close contact with Gran and Grandpa. Indeed her mother saw more of her in-laws than she did her own parents, who lived a long way away. Her mother would be devastated when she saw how ill Grandpa really was and Mandy hoped her father would warn her, although in truth, she thought, nothing could prepare you for the reality of his decline.

She made tea and placed the two mugs on a tray, together with a plate of digestive biscuits, and returned to the study. Grandpa was asleep and John was in his usual armchair with his laptop open before him. He had switched off the main light and the red glow of the lava lamp once more fell across the room, supplemented by the brightness coming from the computer screen. Mandy placed the tray on the coffee table between them, closed the study door and sat in the other armchair, next to John.

'Thanks, Mandy,' he said without looking up. 'You don't mind if I catch up on a few things?'

'No, of course not.'

Taking one of the mugs and a couple of biscuits, she sipped the tea and dunked the biscuits as John tapped on the keypad, occasionally extending his arm to reach for his mug. She resisted the temptation to look at the screen, although her eyes were drawn to it. The lava lamp didn't give off enough light to read a book by and she wanted to stay awake to help if Grandpa woke. Finishing her tea, she checked her phone again. The time showed 11.43. There were no new messages; most of her friends and certainly her father would be in bed now. Returning the mobile to her bag she took out her iPod. Suddenly Grandpa's legs jerked and he cried out in pain. It was a cry like no other and seemed to rip straight from his body into hers. She was immediately on her feet; so too was John.

'It's all right.' With a hand on each shoulder he began gently massaging, trying to ease away the pain.

Grandpa's eyes were screwed tightly shut and, despite John's comforting hands, his face contorted in pain. Then his clenched fists began pummelling the bed either side of him and his legs drummed beneath the sheet. 'Make it stop. I'm begging you. Please, John!' he pleaded. 'I can't take any more.'

His agony was even worse than it had been that afternoon. Tears sprang to Mandy's eyes. She felt utterly helpless in the face of his pain. She saw the anguish in John's face too as he continued rubbing Grandpa's shoulders, trying to give some relief.

'Is there nothing we can do?' she asked in desperation.

'If it doesn't pass soon I'll call the nurse to give him another shot.'

'Shouldn't we call him now?'

'If he gives him a shot now he'll have to delay the next one. It's morphine. Too much could kill him.'

Mandy stared in horror as Grandpa's body arched in pain and John tried impotently to soothe him. It seemed there was nothing they could do to help him and it made her afraid. Guiltily, she thought an overdose of morphine was preferable to this suffering; she would have given it to him herself if it had been possible. Grandpa cried out again. John continued massaging and talking to him in a low, reassuring voice: 'The pain will pass, Dad. I promise. It will go just as it did last night. Mandy is here with you. Ray has been, and Jean will come tomorrow. We all love you, Dad.'

Tears stung her eyes. Clearly a deep bond had developed between the two men in their nights together, when John had had to deal with Grandpa's suffering alone and as best he could. Putting aside her own fear she moved closer and, taking one of Grandpa's hands between hers, began rubbing it. Suddenly his back arched again and, just as Mandy was sure he couldn't take any more, the pain seemed to peak and subside. His body went limp, collapsing flat on the bed. He was so still and quiet that for a moment she thought he was dead.

'Thank God,' John said quietly, taking his hands from Grandpa's shoulders. 'He should sleep now.' Only then did she hear Grandpa take one long deep breath and saw his chest rise and fall.

Mandy remained where she was at the side of the bed, frozen in the horror of what she'd seen. Her heart raced and she felt icy cold. Never before had she witnessed someone in such torment.

61

Grandpa shouldn't have to suffer; he was a good, kind man, proud and caring, who'd always done the best for his family. He shouldn't have to end his life begging for release; he should leave it as he lived it – with dignity and self-respect.

She felt the tears escape and run down her cheeks. She turned away from the bed so John couldn't see. Her gaze fell on the lamp as a red bubble of oil stretched to its limit and the top broke away. She heard John's voice behind her, tender and close. 'Are you all right, Mandy?'

Then she felt his hands lightly on her shoulders. Then he was turning her around to face him. Without meeting his eyes and grateful for his support she rested her head against his chest and cried openly. His arms closed around her, safe and secure; he held her tight and comforted her just as he had when she'd been a child.

Ten

It was as though John had to reaffirm his loyalty to Evelyn, Mandy thought later, when he told her yet again how very supportive Evelyn had been. Supportive when the recession had bitten and his business had suffered, and when he'd made an error of judgement in his private life some years before — although exactly what he didn't state. Evelyn had always been there for him, John said, his rock, and now he was pleased to have the chance to help her by shouldering some of the responsibility for looking after Grandpa.

It was just before dawn. Through the parting in the curtains of the study Mandy could see the distant edge of skyline beginning to lighten. John and she had been talking and dozing intermittently all night in the peculiar intimacy of the sick room with its red bubbles of moving light. Grandpa had woken every couple of hours in discomfort and in need of reassurance, but the pain hadn't been as bad as that first time, when Mandy had cried and John had comforted her. When she'd stopped crying and had thanked John, he'd seemed embarrassed and had apologized. Since then he'd been extolling Evelyn's virtues at every opportunity as though he felt guilty. Why he should feel guilty for comforting her, Mandy didn't know.

At 6.30 a.m. she thought she'd take a shower while all was quiet. John was again dozing in the chair and Grandpa, more peaceful than he'd been all night, seemed in a deep sleep. Mandy stole quietly from the study and upstairs to the bedroom Evelyn had previously shown her. Taking the fresh underwear her aunt had placed on the bed, she went into the guest bathroom and locked the door. Selecting body-wash and shampoo from the array of small bottles on the glass shelf, she showered and washed her hair. Half an hour later, dressed and feeling more refreshed, she returned to the study. As she entered she was surprised to see Evelyn sitting where John had been, also dressed, lipstick on and apparently ready to face the new day.

'Morning.' Evelyn smiled brightly.

'Morning,' Mandy said, going over and kissing her aunt's cheek.

The curtains were now fully open and the early-morning sun filtered through the lattice window of the study. The room seemed more optimistic now the natural light had replaced the red glow of the lamp.

'Shall I fetch you a hairdryer?' Evelyn asked.

'No, thanks. I let it dry naturally. Where's John?'

'Taking a nap upstairs. He might have to go to the office later. I understand you had a pretty rough night.'

Mandy nodded. 'But John is so good with Grandpa.'

'Yes, I don't know what I'd do without him.' Evelyn stood up. 'I usually make coffee now, before Mrs Saunders arrives at eight to make breakfast. Would you like one?'

'Love one. Thanks.'

A routine then fell into place which Mandy guessed had developed during the past week since Grandpa had come to stay, and would probably continue for as long as it was needed. Evelyn returned to the study a quarter of an hour later with Mandy's coffee but didn't stay. 'I drink mine on the hoof,' she said, 'while

I see to a few things in the kitchen.' At just gone 8 a.m. Mrs Saunders knocked on the door and came in carrying a fresh jug of water. She said good morning, swapped the fresh jug of water for the one on the tray and, collecting Mandy's empty coffee cup, asked if she needed anything, which she didn't. At 8.45 Gran came slowly into the study on her walking frame, having being helped downstairs by Evelyn, who then disappeared. Mandy kissed Gran good morning and they sat by the bed until 9 a.m. when Mrs Saunders reappeared and announced that breakfast was ready.

'We have breakfast in the morning room while Evelyn sits with Will,' Gran explained to Mandy. On cue Evelyn came in and said she would sit with Grandpa while they ate breakfast. Gran flashed Mandy a knowing smile.

Mandy helped Gran to her feet and walked by her side along the rear hall to the morning room. As she entered the room she felt she was on a film set for *Brideshead Revisited* or a similar period piece. Mrs Saunders was standing by the oak sideboard where five silver tureens had been arranged with matching silver serving spoons. The circular oak table was now formally laid for two, with silver cutlery, Aynsley rose-patterned china cups and saucers, and a ringed linen napkin beside each place setting. 'If you'd like to help yourself ...' Mrs Saunders said to Mandy, removing the lids from the tureens. 'There's scrambled eggs, bacon, sausage, mushrooms, grilled tomatoes, and toast in the rack.'

Mandy wondered if they always breakfasted like this, and what Grandpa, with his simple tastes and dislike of pretension, would have made of it. Not a lot, she thought. But she was hungry.

'Thank you,' she said, accepting the breakfast plate Mrs Saunders handed to her. She then went along the sideboard and took a spoonful from each of the tureens while the housekeeper served

Gran. Coming to the end she took a glass of orange juice from the tray and then sat at the table opposite Gran. But unlike the day before, when she'd found the formal meals served in the dining room quite bizarre and somewhat distasteful given what was happening to Grandpa, she now found the ritual almost reassuring. Despite the turmoil and anxiety of the family crisis, here was something that could be relied upon: dependable, consistent, and a complete distraction. It was presumably why Evelyn continued with the routine of formal meals.

Shortly before 9:30 the doorbell rang. 'That'll be the nurse,' Gran said. 'Evelyn or John will see to him.'

'I think John's asleep,' Mandy said.

'Then Evelyn will see to him. Evelyn likes me to stay here until the nurse has finished. I usually do as I'm told.'

Mandy returned Gran's smile and they continued eating. They heard Mrs Saunders answer the front door and then Evelyn's voice greet the nurse in the hall. When they'd finished eating Mrs Saunders cleared away the plates and they remained at the table until Evelyn had seen the nurse out and came into the morning room and said Grandpa had had his wash and injection.

Evelyn helped Gran onto her walking frame and Mandy followed them to the study. As she entered she saw the commode had gone and a capped polythene bottle was now beside the bed. Gran noticed it too.

'He won't use that,' Gran said indignantly.

'We'll give it a try, Mum. It should stop the accidents and make it easier for Dad.'

'And his pain relief?' Gran asked. 'You were going to see if it could be increased.'

'It's all taken care of. Don't you worry, Mum.' Mandy thought Evelyn sounded patronizing but Gran either didn't hear it or chose to ignore it. She nodded and returned to her chair by the bed.

'Why don't you have a lie-down?' Evelyn suggested to Mandy. 'Grandpa should sleep for most of the morning now, and I'll be popping in and out.'

'If I'm not needed I might go for a short walk,' Mandy said. 'Get a breath of fresh air.'

'Of course, love. Do whatever you please.' Evelyn smiled. 'We're all very grateful you stayed.'

'I'm pleased I stayed, really I am,' Mandy said. 'I think I might walk into the village. Do you want anything from the shop if I get that far?'

Mandy saw the smile on Evelyn's face vanish. There was a short pause before she replied, tightly: 'No, no thank you. I don't use that store any more.' Throwing Gran a pointed glance she said something about having to see Mrs Saunders and left the room.

Mandy looked at Gran for explanation but Gran had returned her attention to Grandpa. 'See you later then,' Mandy said. 'Do *you* want anything from the store?'

'No thanks, love, but you can give my regards to Mrs Pryce. She works there.'

'Will do.' Picking up her bag from beside the chair Mandy threw it over her shoulder and, kissing Gran and Grandpa good-bye, left the study.

Pryce? Mrs Pryce? The name sounded familiar, Mandy thought as she went to the cloakroom before setting off. Why it should sound familiar she didn't know, nor why Evelyn had behaved oddly when she'd mentioned the village store. But one thing she did know was that there were no toilets on the walk into the village, and if you got caught short you had to go behind a hedge. She remembered that Sarah and she had had to take turns to squat out of sight of the road, while the other looked out for passing cars or, worse, someone walking their dog along the path.

Tucking her mobile into her jacket pocket – Adam had texted earlier saying he would phone mid-morning – and with her bag slung over her shoulder, Mandy let herself out of the front door. It was a lovely fresh spring morning, like yesterday – which had been Tuesday, she had to remind herself. Too much food, too little sleep and being closeted in the hot study were making her brain sluggish, but her body restless. A brisk walk was exactly what she needed, she thought, to 'blow away the cobwebs' as Gran would say.

Mandy followed the path around the edge of the drive and turned right on to the narrow tarmac footpath which ran beside the single-track lane. It was the road her father had driven along yesterday, the only road leading to and from the house and which led to the main road and then into the village. Mandy walked quickly, invigorated from being outside in the fresh air, and also from the luxury of being alone. She wasn't used to having company and making conversation for large parts of the day. Since she'd given up work she'd had solitude each day during the working week to concentrate on her painting. She'd only seen Adam in the evenings. In this at least I've been disciplined, she thought cynically, although she had to admit her time alone had produced very little: a few half-baked ideas, the odd sketch, but no painting. If I could just finish one painting, she thought, I'm sure it would restore my confidence and make a difference – to everything.

She passed the driveway which led to her aunt's closest neighbour, although the bungalow, standing in its own substantial grounds, was so far away from Evelyn's house it hardly constituted a 'neighbour'. Indeed, all the properties she passed had their own land and were very secluded; 'exclusive' was the word an estate agent would have used, she thought. And although the houses were slightly familiar from when she'd passed them in the car the day before, she had no other memory of the road despite Sarah and her often walking into the village.

Mandy felt her phone vibrate in her pocket and quickly took it out.

'Miss you,' Adam said, as soon as she answered. 'When are you coming home?'

'Miss you too,' she said, appreciating the sound of his voice. 'Adam, I've said I'd stay and help. My aunt and uncle are exhausted.' And grateful for the chance to off-load she told him of the dreadful pain Grandpa had been in between the shots of morphine, and the night she'd spent in the study-cum-sick room. She felt herself choking up as she described how John and she had tried to soothe away the pain. 'He's very poorly,' she finished, not wanting to cry on the phone. She was about to tell him of the strange thoughts and flashbacks she'd been having since arriving at her aunt's, but she realized how ridiculous it would sound and instead told him of the breakfast laid on the sideboard in silver tureens. Her phone began to bleep, signalling the battery was about to run out. 'Sod it!' she said, annoyed. 'I'll have to phone you back later from the house.' Quickly winding up and swapping 'Miss you's, she said goodbye. Before the battery went completely she texted her father, asking him to bring her phone charger, which she'd left plugged in beside her bed. Unaware she wouldn't be returning home that evening, she hadn't brought it with her. She now wondered how many other things she'd forgotten to ask her father to collect from her bedsit and which she would find she needed. Epilator, she thought. Never mind, I'll buy a razor from the village shop.

The narrow tarmac path Mandy now trod looked like many other country paths and was no more familiar. But the brilliant green of the early spring shoots, the brown earth, blue sky and picture-postcard rural tranquillity suddenly caught her artistic eye. She knew she should try and remember it, as she used to, to paint later. Whenever she'd been out, if she came across a scene that appealed she used to be able to capture it in her mind's eye – freeze-frame it – and then transfer it to canvas when she got home. But in the last seven months, since she'd been unable to paint, the magic of the scene always faded and lost its intensity, so that all she managed were some drawings in her sketch pad. Perhaps this will be different, she thought. Try to be positive. She looked around at the beauty of the countryside and willed herself to remember what she saw.

A house appeared through the trees to her left and then the path broke for a concealed and overgrown driveway. Mandy was about to cross the drive and then jumped back as a car suddenly appeared. As it drew level the driver nodded and she felt a sudden surge of familiarity. Hadn't a car pulled out of one of these driveways when Sarah and she had been about to cross on one of their walks into the village? She thought it had. A Land-Rover with two large cream dogs in the back? She was sure now, for she remembered they'd been so busy chatting they hadn't seen the Land-Rover until the last second, and had had to jump back on to the path to avoid being knocked down. Perhaps it was the shock of it nearly happening again that had triggered this memory, like the shock of suddenly bumping into John when she'd first arrived had reminded her of her schoolgirl crush. She wondered if the man in the muddy Land-Rover who'd told them off for not looking where they were going still lived in the house along here. But which one? She had no idea. She also wondered why her recollections were so piecemeal and random, and why she had no control over them. It was not only strange but disturbing. Better not to dwell on it. She concentrated on the path ahead and checked the driveways for cars.

Coming to a halt at the end of the lane Mandy waited to cross the road. Whereas she'd only seen a couple of cars on the lane, now the cars sped by at regular intervals in intermittent rushes of air that fanned her face and blew back her hair. She spotted a gap in the traffic and crossed the road, then began towards the village. She passed a speed camera box and further up a banner announcing 'Bypass Now'. To her right stood the early-nineteenth-century stone church with half a dozen headstones in a small, neatly tended graveyard at the front. A massive oak tree rose on the other side of the church, its branches overhanging the pavement. Beside the church was a duck pond and next to that the village pub with its original signboard of a painting of a red lion suspended from the post outside. The road gently curved away and then rose up and out of the village, finally meeting the blue horizon in the distance. Mandy focused on the village scene ahead, so unlike London, but which did seem vaguely familiar. She made her way along the narrow pavement, keeping close to the cottage walls and well away from the traffic that flashed by.

Close up, the village shop was even more familiar than it had been when they'd driven past the day before. Mandy was sure the door was the same shade of green as when she'd visited as a child. With a pang of nostalgia, she saw the window displays were as cluttered, enticing and unsophisticated as ever. It was one of those small village shops where a sample of virtually everything they sold appeared in the bay windows: greeting cards, cooking utensils, a pan, nails and a hammer, pencils, tea, sugar, paper, a rug; and the small china ornaments which Mandy knew had appealed so much to her and Sarah as children, and which they'd saved up their pocket money to buy.

The bell clanged as she opened the door and entered the store. She glanced around. It was as familiar inside as it had been out, and she was sure the layout had barely altered in ten years. But then if you carried this much stock, she thought, there wasn't much you could alter – all the floor space was taken up by tiered shelving. A woman was being served by a young assistant at the post office counter and an elderly man was examining greeting cards. Over to her right two middle-aged women chatted in front of a glass display counter, and behind the counter a similar-aged woman in a nylon overall stood patiently waiting to serve them. She looked at Mandy with a brief smile. Mandy met her gaze and returned her smile. Then she stared and felt her heart miss a beat. She was sure that the woman was Mrs Pryce, the woman Gran had asked to be remembered to. But what Mandy hadn't realized when Gran had mentioned her was that Mrs Pryce had been the housekeeper at her aunt's during all the years Mandy had visited as a child. Mrs Pryce had looked away; she hadn't recognized her.

Eleven

It was a shock suddenly seeing her like that – a flash from the past. And why hadn't Evelyn or Gran said something? *You'll remember Mrs Pryce. She used to be the housekeeper here when you stayed.* True, Gran had asked to be remembered to Mrs Pryce, but why not tell her who she was? Mandy didn't understand, and understood even less Evelyn's pointed remark about not using the store any more; unless of course Mrs Pryce had been dismissed from her service? That could possibly explain it.

Mandy made her way between the narrow aisles of display stands, careful not to nudge anything that could send an item toppling. The shop door clanged open and shut again and a small child came in with his mother who cautioned him not to touch anything. Mandy looked over as Mrs Pryce said good morning to the woman and asked if her child was better. It was definitely the old housekeeper. She was sure. She'd known her so well from all the times she'd stayed as a child. Mrs Pryce had been in her aunt's service for years, as much a part of the household as Mrs Saunders was now, probably more, for she'd lived in and taken on the role of nanny when Sarah had been little. And while Mrs Pryce certainly didn't seem like someone who'd be given the sack, Mandy couldn't think of another explanation for Evelyn's cool rejection.

Reining in her thoughts, Mandy scanned the tiers of shelves and found the disposable razors she was looking for, then picked up a copy of the *Daily Mail* from the bottom shelf. John had *The Times* and *Telegraph* delivered but Mandy wanted something lighter to read. Going into the next aisle she found the stationery section; on one shelf lay three small sketch pads next to a jar of HB pencils and other writing implements. She took one of the sketch pads and a pencil, and then selected an eraser and a small plastic pencil sharpener. Perhaps if she managed to sketch some of the local country scenes she'd be able to paint them when she returned home.

Picking up a small bar of milk chocolate Mandy crossed to the till. Mrs Pryce was behind the counter, having just served the man with the greeting card. As she approached she felt her stomach flutter nervously. Mrs Pryce looked at her with a polite smile but there was nothing in her manner to suggest she recognized her. Mandy placed the items she was buying on the glass-topped counter and summoned the courage to say something. She felt strangely nervous.

'Are you Mrs Pryce?' she asked, almost blurted, as the woman took the first item to ring into the till.

She paused, surprised, and then looked puzzled. 'Yes. Sorry, do I know you?'

'You used to,' Mandy said. 'My gran is Mrs Edwards. She sends her regards. I'm Mandy.'

Amazement and delight spread across Mrs Pryce's face, and Mandy relaxed. 'Good heavens! Little Amanda. After all these years! I'm sorry, love, I didn't recognize you.'

'It's not surprising really, I was only thirteen when you last saw me, but I recognized you the moment I walked in. You haven't changed at all.'

To a woman in her early sixties this was clearly a compliment, and Mrs Pryce smiled appreciatively. 'How are you, dear?' she asked warmly. 'And how are Mr and Mrs Edwards? I heard they were staying at your aunt's because of Mr Edwards being ill. But I didn't know you were there too.'

'Grandpa is very poorly,' Mandy confirmed. 'I came with Dad yesterday, just for a visit, but I'm staying on to help.'

'That's nice of you, but then you were always a thoughtful child. You look very well. How are you and your family?' There seemed to be no reluctance on her part to ask after her family, Mandy thought, which made Evelyn's attitude towards her even more puzzling.

'Mum and Dad are well, although they're obviously very concerned about Grandpa. They're visiting again later today. I'm sure they'll be delighted when I tell them I've seen you.' Mandy paused, unsure of how to continue now the initial surprise of their meeting was over. 'I seem to remember you looked after Sarah and me when I stayed. I hope we didn't cause you too much trouble.'

Mrs Pryce smiled indulgently. 'Only children having fun. I loved it when you came; there was always so much excitement. Do you still see Sarah?'

'No, not since my visits stopped.'

Mrs Pryce's previous open and obvious delight at seeing her again after so long was now replaced by something closed and more serious. She lowered her gaze and, drawing the items across the counter, began entering them into the till.

'Evelyn said Sarah will visit later in the week,' Mandy added, and Mrs Pryce nodded non-committally.

Mandy didn't know what to say now. She would have liked to have talked about the past and heard what Mrs Pryce had to say about the times she'd looked after Mandy at her aunt's, but she felt the way in was barred. Unhooking her bag from her shoulder, she took out her purse as Mrs Pryce, eyes down, rang up the last item. 'That's £4.78 please, dear. Would you like a carrier?'

'Please,' Mandy said, and took out a £10 note as Mrs Pryce placed the items in a bag. 'You don't see Evelyn and John now?' Mandy tried. 'You were with them a long time.'

'Yes, I was. Fourteen years. I see Mr and Mrs Osborne driving through the village sometimes, but not to talk to, not since I left – ten years ago.' She passed the carrier to Mandy and then counted the change into her palm. Mandy felt a formality had crept into Mrs Pryce's manner, which she was sure had never been there when she'd known her as a child, and indeed didn't sit happily with her now. 'Well, it's been nice meeting you again,' Mrs Pryce said, almost stiffly. 'Please remember me to your gran. I'm so sorry Mr Edwards is poorly. And remember me to your parents too.'

'I will.' Mandy hovered. 'I might pop in again if I need something.'

Mrs Pryce gave a small nod. 'Yes, dear.' She turned to the next customer.

The door clanged shut behind Mandy as she set off along the narrow pavement in the direction of her aunt's. Apparently the only persons Mrs Pryce didn't want to be remembered to were Evelyn and John, she thought. And they hadn't spoken in ten years despite living in the same small village! Clearly the rift between them ran very deep.

Mandy took the chocolate bar from the carrier bag and, peeling back the foil, bit off a chunk. She savoured the creamy sweet texture as it melted on her tongue. Seeing Mrs Pryce again seemed to release a few more memories, and her thoughts returned to her childhood and the times Sarah and she had been left under the watchful eye of the housekeeper while Evelyn was out or busy. Dear, kind Mrs Pryce with her neatly rollered greying hair, so conservative in dress and habit, how they'd teased her and played her up. Mandy cringed as she remembered the time Sarah and she had put damp soil from the garden in the toes of her shoes. Mrs Pryce, like Mrs Saunders, always changed into 'house shoes' when she arrived and she'd been too embarrassed to say anything as she'd pushed her feet into her shoes and felt the wet earth. Or the time they'd put salt in the jug of water on the table at dinner and John had taken a large gulp and spat it out, then blamed Mrs Pryce for not being more vigilant instead of Sarah and her − the real culprits. Mandy remembered too the fantasies Sarah and she had made up about Mrs Pryce: caught in a state of undress with the gardener in the potting shed, or ravishing the butcher as he delivered the meat via the tradesmen's entrance. Or compromised in the laundry room with Fred Hutch, who used to be the handyman. *Very handy*, Sarah and she had giggled. But now, as then, Mandy had to admit that the chances of Mrs Pryce doing anything improper were minuscule, if not non-existent, which made the cloud hanging over her leaving all the more peculiar.

Mandy crossed the road and paused by the churchyard for a better view of the church. When Gran and she were alone, she decided, she would ask her about Mrs Pryce's departure, which might possibly also give her some clue as to why her own visits had stopped. Mrs Pryce had said she'd left Evelyn's service ten years ago, which was the same time she'd been stopped from visiting Sarah. Mandy wondered if the two events could be connected in some way, though she'd no idea how. Try as she might she couldn't remember anything that might have led to 'the situation', as her father called it, and Mrs Pryce didn't seem the type to be responsible for any bad feeling. Finishing the chocolate bar, she screwed up the wrapper and dropped it into the bin by the entrance to the churchyard, then gazed up at the church spire set against the azure sky. She narrowed her eyes, straining to capture the sharpness and detail in her mind's eye with the hope of trying to sketch it later.

Mandy knew the moment Mrs Saunders answered the door something was different. Something wrong? 'Let me take your coat, miss,' she flustered. 'Go straight through to the study, please.'

She quickly passed her jacket to the housekeeper as Evelyn called from the study: 'Mandy, is that you? Come in quickly.'

She heard the urgency in her aunt's voice and, fearing the worst, rushed down the hall and into the study. To her amazement and absolute delight Grandpa wasn't in pain, his condition having worsened as she feared, but was propped up in bed on a mountain of pillows, wide awake and smiling at her.

'Grandpa!' she cried, dropping her handbag and carrier bag by the door. 'You're awake!' She nearly ran to the bed, and kissed his forehead. 'Grandpa,' she said again delightedly, pressing her cheek against his. 'It's so good to see you.'

'Hello, love. How are you?' His voice was slow and rasping. It was obviously a lot of effort to speak, but he was awake and talking!

'I'm fine, Grandpa,' she said, perching on the bed. 'I'm so pleased you're awake. I've been for a little walk to the village. How are you?'

'Could be better,' he slowly rasped, and managed a small chuckle. Someone had given him his glasses and they hid his sunken eyes, which made him look more like he used to before his illness.

'He's so much better,' Gran said. She was sitting in her usual chair by the bed, with Grandpa's hand in hers. 'He woke and asked for something to drink earlier.'

'That's fantastic,' Mandy said. She glanced at Evelyn, who was standing just behind her.

'He came round about fifteen minutes ago,' Evelyn said. 'I was hoping you'd be back in time to see him. But I've warned Gran not to expect miracles. He's still very poorly.'

All right, Mandy thought, we know he's very ill but we can at least enjoy this moment. She placed her hand on his arm and gently stroked the dry and paper-thin skin. 'So, Grandpa,' she joked, 'what have you been up to in my absence?'

'Not much,' he rasped, and then gave a small congested laugh. 'Won't be running the marathon this year, love.' He laughed again. 'How about you? Painted that masterpiece yet?'

'Not yet, but when I do you'll be the first to see it.'

He smiled and his red and watery eyes focused on her. 'Paint a picture of me, will you, Mandy?' he said, suddenly serious. 'And give it to your gran. Something to remember me by when I'm gone. But not like this. Paint one of me young and handsome – when she fancied me.' He stopped, exhausted.

Mandy felt her eyes well, and swallowed hard. She also felt a sudden wave of panic at what she was being asked. 'I haven't painted a portrait since I was at Uni,' she said. 'But I'll try. I promise I'll try, for you.'

'Thank you,' he said quietly. 'You used to paint lovely portraits. I remember the one you did of your mum.' A smile crossed his lips and his eyes slowly closed.

'Mum and Dad are coming later today,' Mandy said quickly, willing him to stay awake. 'I hope you'll be able to see them.'

There was a long pause, and then he took a deep breath, summoning the strength to answer. His eyes briefly flickered open. 'I hope so too, love,' he said. His voice drifted off and his eyes closed.

'Grandpa?' Mandy said, rubbing his arm. 'Grandpa, stay awake. I love you so much. Please stay and talk to us.'

But his eyes remained closed and his breathing deepened as he once more lapsed into unconsciousness. His head slowly lolled to one side. 'Grandpa?' she tried again, but there was nothing; he could no longer hear them.

Evelyn came forward and removed his glasses, folding them into the case. 'It was nice he was awake long enough to see you,' she said. 'He asked for you as soon as he came round.'

They were supposed to be words of comfort, but they made the pain worse. She stood up and fled the room. Hurrying down the hall she went into the cloakroom and locked the door so she could cry in private. Dear Grandpa; she loved him so very much. She really couldn't bear the thought of losing him. He and Gran had been such a large part of her life, for as long as she could remember. She'd always had a special bond with her grandpa; they were similar in many ways and shared the same view on life and sense of humour. Her parents had often said she took after her grandpa, and the thought of never seeing him again was more than she could bear. Of not being able to speak with him on the phone again, or pop in on the off chance and see his face light up at her surprise visit, or share a joke or discuss politics, which he loved. It surely couldn't all end here. And although her rational mind told her he was very old and everyone had to die some time, her heart wasn't ready to let go. 'Damn and blast!' she said angrily. 'It's not fair.'

Taking a tissue from the floral box on the dressing table, she blew her nose, then looked at her face in the mirror. Her eyes were bloodshot, her skin was red and her brow was knitted with pain. But as she looked in the mirror it wasn't her reflection she saw but that of a young girl with fair hair, her expression frightened and her cheeks wet from crying. Mandy stared at the image, horrified yet mesmerized, willing the girl to go away but at the same time needing her to stay. She held her gaze, looked deep into her eyes and saw her pain and sorrow. It was the same girl she'd seen in her father's car and in the dreams she'd had in the study. Not taking her eyes from the mirror she reached out and touched the glass. The girl vanished.

Burying her head in her hands she cried openly – for Grandpa, and for whatever had happened in the house.

Twelve

Fifteen minutes later Mandy pulled herself together. Drying her eyes, she checked her face in the mirror and returned to the study, hoping no one would notice she'd been crying. There was only Gran in the study and she was dozing in the chair beside the bed and Grandpa, while restless, was asleep. Mandy took the sketch pad and pencil from the carrier bag, sat in the armchair, and with determined effort began drawing the outline of the church, more for distraction than from any real desire to draw. Concentrating on the delicate lines of the steeple began to direct and channel her thoughts. The girl in the mirror and all her unhappiness faded.

Gran woke and Mandy told her she'd seen Mrs Pryce who sent her best wishes. 'Thank you,' Gran said, nodding thoughtfully. Mandy was about to ask her why Mrs Pryce had left and if it had anything to do with her own visits stopping but Evelyn popped in to check on Grandpa. In fact Evelyn was in and out of the study all morning so there was no chance to talk to Gran. Evelyn seemed nervous and Mandy guessed it was because her parents were expected later that afternoon, when she would be meeting her sister-in-law for the first time in ten years.

They had lunch in the morning room while the nurse visited and then returned to the study. Gran dozed, Mandy continued with the sketch, and then a little after 3 p.m. Mandy heard the door chime. She wasn't expecting her parents until later and remained in the study, but suddenly Evelyn was showing them in. 'Mum, Dad!' she cried, standing to kiss them.

'How are you, love?' her mother asked, concerned.

'Not bad. I'm glad you came.'

'How are you, Mum?' her mother asked, turning to Gran.

'Mustn't grumble. I'm pleased you felt you could come here, Jean. It means a lot to Will and me.'

Her mother smiled, then looked properly at Grandpa for the first time. Mandy saw the shock on her mother's face and she joined her at the bed. Evelyn hovered for a moment and then left, closing the study door behind her.

'The housekeeper is taking your case up to your room,' her father said, still not looking at Grandpa. 'I remembered your phone charger, and your mother packed some clothes.'

'Thanks. Was everything all right at the flat? I feel like I've been away for weeks, not two days.'

'It looked fine. There were a couple of letters for you and those are in your case too. Let me return your keys before I forget.' Delving into his trouser pocket he handed the keys to her. 'How's Grandpa been?' he said, finally looking at the bed.

'Up and down. Last night was bad, but he was awake earlier and recognized me. I told him you were coming this afternoon.'

He nodded, obviously pleased, and they both looked at the bed. In sleep Grandpa's head lolled to one side and his mouth hung open, causing his hollow cheeks to look even more pronounced.

'He's lost so much weight,' her mother said quietly, clearly still shocked by his deterioration. 'Three weeks ago he was digging the garden, getting it ready for spring. Now ...' She stopped as her voice faded. Gran touched her arm reassuringly. 'Can we wake him?' her mother asked after a moment. 'I'd like to talk to him.'

'It's not that kind of sleep,' Gran said. 'It's more unconscious-ness – due to the morphine and also because he's just drifting off.' Mandy heard the phrase 'drifting off' and knew what Gran was really trying to say, and the word they were all carefully avoid-ing. 'He had his last injection at midday,' Gran continued, patting Grandpa's arm. 'They're every four hours. He was in so much pain, John spoke to the nurse and had the dose increased. John has been very good; I don't know what we'd have done without him.' Mandy saw her mother tense at the praise for John. 'Have you seen John?' Gran asked.

'Evelyn said he was at work,' her father replied, while her mother said nothing.

'Hopefully he'll be back before you leave,' Gran said. 'It would be nice for you all to be friends again. It would make Grandpa happy.'

'I thought I did all right yesterday, considering,' her father said, childlike in his defence.

Gran gave a small reserved nod.

'Considering what?' Mandy asked, and heard the silence.

'Oh, nothing,' her father said after a moment, and changed the subject.

They stayed in the study for the next three hours but Grandpa didn't wake. He slept fitfully, occasionally calling out in his sleep but didn't regain consciousness. Mandy was relieved at one level, for had he woken in pain it would have been dreadful for her parents to have witnessed, but if he'd woken pain-free, as he had done that morning, it would have been wonderful – a memory they could have taken with them. As it was they sat by his bed, just spending time with him and chatting to Gran. 'I think he's had too much morphine,' her father said.

'Better a little too much than not enough,' Gran said.

John didn't return during the afternoon so there was no opportunity for Gran's hope of John and Jean meeting and all 'being friends again'. Her parents stayed until 6 p.m. and then politely, refusing Evelyn's offer to stay to dinner, her father said, 'We need to be getting on the road,' and her mother agreed.

They said goodbye to Grandpa then they all went to the front door, where they hugged and kissed. 'Drive safely,' Gran said.

'Take care,' Evelyn added with warmth.

'I'll come again at the weekend,' her father said. 'Thanks again, Mandy, for all you're doing.'

'I'll phone if there's any change,' Mandy reassured him.

After they'd gone, Evelyn disappeared upstairs while Mandy returned to the study with Gran. She helped settle Gran in her usual chair beside the bed and then checked her phone which was charging on the socket by the desk. Five minutes later John appeared, still in his suit, apparently having just returned from the office.

'Sorry I missed your parents,' he said to Mandy. 'How's Grandpa?'

'He slept all afternoon,' Mandy said. 'Mum and Dad said they were sorry to have missed you too.'

Gran threw Mandy a small appreciative smile, then said to John: 'Ray thinks Dad might be having too much morphine. Apart from quarter of an hour this morning he hasn't been awake at all today.'

'I doubt it,' John said tersely, 'but I'll speak to the nurse this evening. Now I need to shower and change before dinner.' Mandy wondered if he'd taken her father's comments personally – everyone in the house was so sensitive. It crossed her mind to say something and try to explain but decided it was better just left.

* * *

The routine of her first evening in the house was now largely repeated for the second. They ate at 7 p.m. and then Gran and she returned to the study until Evelyn came in with Gran's Ovaltine at 8.30. At nine o'clock Evelyn helped Gran to bed, then John reappeared in the study. 'Mandy, do you feel up to doing the night shift again?' he asked. 'Evelyn could do with the rest.'

Mandy had assumed she would be doing the 'night shift' again, and although tired hoped that as Grandpa was more peaceful she'd be able to sleep in the armchair, or failing that take a nap the following day. 'Of course,' she agreed.

Evelyn went to bed once she'd seen Gran up and then shortly before 10 p.m. the nurse arrived on a new schedule to give Grandpa his injection. Mandy thought she would take the opportunity while the nurse was there to go upstairs and sort through the suitcase her parents had brought. Mrs Saunders had taken it to the bedroom she was using. Opening the case she found her mother had done a good job in choosing which clothes to pack: three pairs of jeans, an assortment of tops, underwear, slippers, her kimono dressing gown and clean pyjamas. She opened the two letters her father had mentioned: a bank statement and a circular from her local art centre detailing forthcoming events. Returning the letters to the case she went into the guest bathroom where she washed and brushed her teeth ready for her night in the chair; she'd shower again in the morning. When she came out she found the main lights were off and the landing and stairs were again lit by nightlights, John presumably having locked up after the nurse had left. She made her way down the staircase, past the lamp on the onyx table in the hall and to the study where the lava lamp was once again the only light. John was in his usual armchair and concentrating on his laptop. Grandpa was on his back, asleep, breathing very slowly and heavily.

'The nurse said the dose is right,' John confirmed without looking up. 'I don't think your father or Gran has accepted the inevitable yet.'

'No,' Mandy agreed, and wasn't sure she had fully accepted the inevitable either.

She sat in the other chair and unplugging her phone from the charger — the battery was full — she checked for messages. There were four texts; two from Adam asking if she was all right, and she suddenly realized with everything going on she'd forgotten to return his call from the morning when the battery had gone flat. It was a bit late to phone him now. He'd be on his way to bed with work the following morning. She quickly texted: *Sorry. im ok. mum n dad visited. ill call tmrrw. luv&miss u xxx.*

'Boyfriend?' John asked, glancing up with a smile that invited intimacy.

'Yes,' she said non-committally.

'Serious?'

'Possibly.' She wasn't going to be drawn into discussing her relationship with Adam.

'Sarah's living with her partner, Simon,' John offered. 'He's got a good job in finance. Hopefully you'll meet him when they visit.'

'That would be nice.' Mandy smiled, and concentrated on her phone.

John returned to his laptop; Mandy answered the texts and then closed her phone and dropped it into her bag. She rested her head on the chair-back and allowed her eyes to close. The warmth of the room soon combined with the soothing red glow of the lava lamp and she began to doze. Grandpa's slow and heavy breathing continued in the background with the tap tap tap of John's laptop close by. Some time later she awoke with a start and was already out of her chair and going towards the bed before she heard John's voice: 'Don't worry, Mandy, I've seen to him. Sorry, I didn't mean to wake you.' Mandy looked over. John had just opened the study door and was about to go out. In his hand was the plastic bottle, now containing a small amount of dark orange urine. 'Sorry,' he said again. 'He needed a wee. I'm just going to empty this.'

She nodded and John left.

With her heart racing from suddenly waking Mandy remained where she was in the middle of the room and looked at Grandpa. He was on his back, his breathing still light from having recently woken. She felt a pang of regret that John hadn't needed her help and woken her, for it was a missed opportunity to tell Grandpa her parents had visited. Any opportunity to talk to him was precious and it was impossible to know when the chance would come again – or, indeed, if it would.

Stiff from sleeping in the chair, she flexed her arms and rolled her head from side to side; her neck clicked. She'd no idea of the time or how long she'd been asleep. John's laptop was open on the coffee table with the screensaver coloured boxes flying across the screen. Instinctively, without thinking, as she would have done at home to check the time if her laptop was on, she reached down and drew the cursor towards the time icon in the lower right-hand corner of the screen. As her fingers touched the mouse the screensaver vanished and in its place was a photograph of a child, aged about three or four and completely naked. The photo automatically enlarged to fill the screen. It was her.

Mandy stared at it and felt a cold tingle run up her spine. Without even their pants on, she and Sarah were playing in the garden of this house on what was clearly a hot summer's day. The two of them had obviously stripped off to run under the sprinkler – it could be seen watering the lawn in the background. Sarah and she were apparently unaware the photograph was being taken. Sarah was in the background, on the far side of the sprinkler, while she, the subject, was in the foreground. On the left of the screen were three 'thumbnail' pictures of photographs John had already viewed in the same folder. She looked closer. Obviously taken at the same time, she and Sarah were naked in all of them. The top one showed Sarah and her holding hands and running though the spray; the next showed them trying to catch the spray. The third showed them throwing a brightly coloured ball through the jet of water with John laughing in the background. In all of them Sarah and she were playing unselfconsciously and oblivious to their nakedness as young children are. The counter on the toolbar showed the open photo was the fourth out of a set of sixty.

A sharp intake of breath came from the bed behind her and Grandpa stirred in his sleep. Mandy took a step back, away from the laptop, and stared at her image. Family photographs? She supposed they must be, but couldn't remember them being taken or ever having been shown them. Who else had been present? John was in the background. Who had taken the photograph? Evelyn? Her father? And while there was nothing wrong in John reminiscing over a family album, Mandy felt deeply uncomfortable that he had been doing so – viewing her naked – in a semi-darkened room, while she slept in the chair beside him. It didn't feel right and something told her it wasn't right, not at all.

Thirteen

Mandy continued to stare at the screen, willing the coloured flying boxes of the screensaver to reappear. It was embarrassing enough to have stumbled on the photographs, it would be even worse if John returned and found her looking at them. The setting on the timer for the screensaver could be anything from one minute to sixty; she'd set the one on her laptop to five minutes, but obviously had no idea what John had set his to. A couple of minutes had already passed. How much longer before the screensaver timed in and the photo disappeared? And how long before John finished rinsing the bottle in the cloakroom and returned?

Another minute passed. Mandy stared at the screen as her heart thumped loudly and the image persisted. Then she heard a movement in the hall outside and quickly snapped shut the lid on the laptop. She sat back in the armchair; having to admit to shutting his laptop was preferable to him coming in and seeing, and then her having to explain. Grandpa stirred in his sleep and a second later the door opened and John came in. He had the clean urine bottle tucked under his arm and a mug in each hand.

'Thought you might like a tea,' he said, pushing the door to with his foot. His eyes immediately went to the laptop.

'Sorry, I brushed against it, and the lid shut. I hope I haven't lost your work.' The lie sounded pathetic even to her.

He placed the two mugs on the coffee table beside the laptop, and then returned the urine bottle to beside the bed. 'No harm done,' he said lightly. 'Closing the lid doesn't lose the information.' Which Mandy knew. She also knew that when John lifted the lid again, the last open document, i.e. the photograph, not the screensaver, would reappear. Why she didn't simply admit to what she'd done she wasn't sure, for she hadn't been prying; she had stumbled on the photographs by accident. It was more to do with the embarrassment of him seeing her naked, albeit as a child, together with the persisting feeling that it wasn't proper for a man to be storing pictures on his laptop of his niece without her clothes on.

'Thanks,' she said, picking up her mug of tea. She took a sip and looked across the room at the slow-moving red bubbles of the lava lamp. Out of the corner of her eye she could see John sipping his tea, elbows resting on the arms of the chair, and making no attempt to open his laptop. Grandpa's deep and laboured breathing once more filled the air, signalling he had again lapsed into heavy unconscious sleep. Mandy continued drinking her tea until the silence became uncomfortable and she had to break it. 'I walked into the village while you were at work,' she said with forced casualness.

John nodded and took another gulp of tea. 'Yes, Evelyn said.'

'I needed a few things, and some exercise.' She paused. 'We used to go to that store a lot when I stayed here. It was strange going back. It's hardly changed at all.'

'No. We order our groceries online now and have them delivered. Did you see Mrs Pryce?'

Mandy was surprised by his directness; perhaps it was only Evelyn who'd had the argument with the former housekeeper.

'Yes. I recognized her straight away but she didn't recognize me. Not surprising really, after all this time. Why's she working there? She always seemed so happy here.'

John rubbed his thumb around the rim of the mug, and then flashed her a sideways glance: 'Didn't she tell you, Mandy?'

'No.'

He gave a small, dismissive shrug. 'I guess she just wanted a change. She'd been with us a very long time.' And Mandy knew for certain he was lying. Something in his tone and the casualness of his reply, together with Mrs Pryce's reaction, told her this was not the reason, but she also knew he wouldn't tell her what the real reason was.

Without saying anything further he finished his tea, set his mug on the coffee table, and then picked up his laptop and left the study. When he returned five minutes later and lifted the lid to resume work, her photograph had gone and a half-composed email filled the screen. That he had left the room to close the file added to her feeling of disquiet – as though he had something to hide. But to bring up the subject now would turn it into an issue, she thought, and it wasn't the time or place. Later, if her feelings of unease persisted, she would work out what to say and ask him about the photograph.

Her gaze once more drifted to the red bubbles of moving light on the far side of the room as Grandpa's drawn-out breaths filled the air. It was now nearly 2.30 a.m. and she felt the long hours before dawn stretch ahead. She thought of Adam and bitterly regretted the way they'd parted on their last night together. While he'd forgiven her, now they were apart she felt her rejection of him even more and could have kicked herself for being so cold. How she now longed for the warmth and security of his arms around her; his straightforward and uncomplicated manner. He

92

was a good, kind person who said what he thought and kept his word. There was no side to him, no hidden agenda. Not many would have put up with her blowing hot and cold – wanting to make love one moment but not the next. Were all women like this? She wondered. She'd no idea; it wasn't something she'd ever felt comfortable discussing with her friends.

As happened before when there was no conversation in the study Mandy found herself absently counting off the seconds of Grandpa's laboured breathing. The breaths – too long apart, which began and ended with small rasps – seemed to be taking more and more effort. She doubted she would ever forget the sound of his breathing and the long silences between. She was sure the gaps were growing longer; unnaturally long, she thought, as though each breath could be his last. Was that what happened in the end? Was that how life ended? One long breath and then nothing – the moment of death? Was that it, or did the person say something or cry out? Mandy had never been with anyone who had died, but had heard stories about the dying waking at the end and experiencing a moment of lucidity just before they passed away. Her mother had told her of a very old aunt who, unconscious for a week, had suddenly sat up in bed at the moment of death and, reaching out her hand, had said: 'I'm ready now. I'm coming with you,' as though someone had been sent to meet her. Mandy's mother had found comfort in this – proof there was an afterlife, but Mandy wasn't sure. For someone with no religious faith, it would be a terrific leap to view death as anything other than the depressing finality she now accepted it to be.

Grandpa's breathing faltered for a second before he cried out – an agonized howl that struck terror into her soul. She was already out of the chair and by the bed when the second cry came.

John was at the bed-head. Taking hold of Grandpa's shoulders he began massaging them as he had the night before. 'We're here, Dad,' he reassured him. 'The pain will pass.'

Mandy took one of Grandpa's hands in hers and stroked the back. It felt cold and clammy, and too smooth, almost like gloss paper. When the next anguished cry came, his face contorted and his hand clutched hers so tightly his nails dug into her flesh. 'Grandpa, it's Mandy,' she said urgently, but he was oblivious. His back arched and he shrieked again. She looked at John and saw her own fear reflected.

'It's all right, Dad. We're here,' John tried to soothe him.

Mandy knew the pain was worse than it had been the night before, and she was sure it hadn't peaked yet. The medication had worn off and Grandpa was being forced into consciousness by the agony. It was horrifying, humiliating, and out of control. His back arched and his eyes screwed shut as his face contorted, but his words were clear and unmistakable: 'No more. I want to die. Help me to die, please, John!'

'I'll call the nurse,' John said. 'He'll give you an injection to stop the pain.'

'No. I want an end. Once and for all.' Then his whole body suddenly jolted as though an electric current had passed through, and he began to retch.

Mandy grabbed the plastic bucket from beside the chair as John turned him on to his side. She held the bucket beneath his chin as his body stiffened and he retched, over and over again. First saliva trickled from his open mouth and then a thick brown liquid shot into the bucket. It smelt foul and Mandy felt her own stomach contract.

'Christ!' John said. 'What's that? He hasn't eaten for a week.' Mandy glanced in the bucket and then looked away. It was disgusting.

John kept his hands on Grandpa's shoulder, steadying him on his side as he retched again. Mouth open, his whole body caught in the act of vomiting, like a dog. The smell coming from the bucket and also from his mouth was putrid, more like excrement than vomit. His retching peaked, and more of the disgusting brown liquid shot into the bucket. Then he let out a loud groan and his body went limp. Mandy swallowed the bile rising in her throat.

John gently laid him flat on his back. 'Can you get him some water, Mandy,' he said quietly, clearly shocked.

Placing the bucket to one side, she fetched the beaker of water from the tray on the desk, and also a tissue. She wiped away the brown saliva from Grandpa's lips. John slid his hands under Grandpa's shoulders and eased him off the pillows as she tipped the beaker to his lips. Veins stood out on his neck where he had been retching, and thread veins had broken across his nose and cheeks, making his skin look purple. His dry, lined lips closed around the beaker, but his eyes stayed shut. He took a sip and with great effort swallowed. Then his head dropped back, exhausted.

'Would you like another sip?' Mandy asked softly.

There was a faint: 'No.'

She stayed by the bed. Although Grandpa's eyes were closed and his body was still, from the lightness of his breathing she knew he was still conscious. John was very pale – until now he'd been in control, able to ease Grandpa through the pain, but this last attack had left him powerless to help, and he was visibly shaken. Now the pain had peaked Mandy hoped Grandpa would drift into unconsciousness as he had done the night before. They watched and waited. He stirred and tried to say something, although his eyes remained closed. 'Sorry, Dad?' John asked gently, lowering his head closer to Grandpa's mouth.

'John?' he groaned.

'Yes, I'm here. So is Mandy.'

'Mum and Dad visited today,' Mandy said quickly. 'They send their love.'

Grandpa nodded. 'John?' he said again, struggling to tilt his head in the direction of John's voice.

'Yes, Dad?'

'I need you to promise me …' he began, his voice slow and rasping, each word punctuated by a breath. 'I want you to promise me … if it gets any worse … you'll end it … for me. I can't do it … or I would.' His eyes briefly opened and he squinted in John's direction, trying to focus, before they closed again. Mandy saw John's look of horror. It had been said rationally with a detachment and seriousness that was almost cold.

'I'll phone the nurse to make you more comfortable,' John said, moving away from the bed.

'No,' Grandpa cried. John stopped and looked at him, surprised by the strength in his voice. 'Please, John, I need you to promise,' he rasped, struggling for breath and trying to open his eyes. 'This might be my last chance to ask. For the love of God, and the sake of my wife and family, please end it for me.' He desperately tried to raise his head but failed and collapsed back on to the pillow with a groan.

Mandy saw John flinch. How could he give such an undertaking? Yet after the agony he had just witnessed … 'I understand,' John breathed after a moment. Then, more strongly: 'I promise I won't let you suffer.'

A small smile seemed to flicker across Grandpa's lips and then his face relaxed and his breathing slowly deepened as he once more lapsed into unconsciousness. Leaving the end of the bed John picked up the bucket. 'I'll get rid of this,' he said, and left the room.

Mandy turned from the bed as a bubble of oil in the lamp elongated and stretched to the limit. As she looked, the top broke away and, forming a bubble of its own, floated free. Behind her Grandpa's breathing reluctantly continued.

Fourteen

After that night Mandy felt there was an unspoken pact between John and her that whatever happened with Grandpa in the study stayed there and would never be spoken of – now or in the future. When Evelyn came into the study at 6.30 a.m. the following morning, washed and dressed, and asked what sort of night Grandpa had had, John said, 'Restless,' and Mandy agreed. When Gran arrived downstairs at 8.45, helped by Evelyn, John had gone for a lie-down, so Mandy repeated the half-truth. 'Not too good,' she said, 'although he did wake briefly. I was able to tell him Mum and Dad had visited.' Which pleased Gran and made her a little bit happier.

After breakfast with its silver tureens arranged along the sideboard in the morning room, Mandy showered and changed. She was on her way to the study when Evelyn intercepted her. 'Mandy, I was wondering if you could do me a favour?'

'Yes?'

'Gran could do with some more clothes from home. Could you run her over to the bungalow to get what she needs? You could take my car.'

'Yes, of course,' Mandy said, feeling that far from it being a favour for Evelyn she would be grateful for a change of scenery and also to spend some time alone with Gran.

She went with Evelyn into the study where Evelyn told Gran of the proposed outing. Gran glanced anxiously at Grandpa.

'Don't worry,' Evelyn reassured her. 'He'll be fine. You won't be long.'

While Evelyn fetched Gran's shoes and coat Mandy checked her phone. She answered the two texts – one from a friend and one from Adam – and then pressed to return her father's missed call.

'Just wondered if there was any change?' he said. He was at his office desk.

'No, not really. He had a restless night, but he is comfortable now.' There was no point in worrying her father further by telling the truth. 'Gran's here. I'm taking her to get some things from home. Would you like to speak to her?'

'Yes, please. We'll be over again on Sunday.'

Mandy passed her mobile to Gran. 'Hello, Ray,' she said, and then, unused to mobiles, took the phone from her ear to speak into the microphone. 'Pardon?' she said, having missed Ray's reply.

Mandy smiled and repositioned the phone to Gran's ear and they spoke for a few minutes.

'Incredible,' she said when she'd finished and returned the phone to Mandy. 'What will they think of next!'

'We could buy you a mobile,' Mandy said. 'I'd teach you how to use it. It isn't difficult.'

'We'll see. Will's got one, he knows what to do.' She smiled wistfully.

Fifteen minutes later Gran was sitting beside her in Evelyn's Fiat, an automatic that was very easy to drive. They were five minutes into the twenty-minute journey and Mandy thought Gran was appreciating the outing as much as she was. She was very alert, looking out of her side window and making comments on the passing scenery. Mandy recognized that while Gran would never have complained about all the time she spent with Grandpa, first going to the hospital and then in the study-cum-sick room, clearly her life had narrowed too.

A couple of minutes later Mandy decided it was a good opportunity to ask about Mrs Pryce. 'I recognized Mrs Pryce straight away yesterday. But she didn't recognize me.'

'Well, it's been a long time since she last saw you,' Gran said, still looking out of her window. 'You've changed a lot.'

'Ten years,' Mandy agreed. 'Do you still see her?'

'Occasionally. I used to see her at the Women's Institute, but I haven't been this year.'

Mandy smiled to herself: she could picture Mrs Pryce and Gran swapping recipes and flower arranging or whatever they did at their WI meetings. 'The village shop hasn't changed either,' Mandy said, glancing at her. 'Why doesn't Evelyn use it now?'

'Not sure,' Gran said with a small shrug. 'She used to walk the dog into the village and pop in the store. Perhaps Evelyn's feeling her age, like me. She doesn't walk into the village. They order a lot of their stuff on the computer now.'

Mandy didn't think Evelyn would be pleased if she knew someone thought she might be 'feeling her age', for she'd said more than once that the fifties were the new thirties and age was only 'a state of mind'. Neither did Mandy think the walk was the reason Evelyn no longer patronized the store, not from the abruptness of Evelyn's 'I don't use that store' and the way Mrs Pryce had gone quiet on being reminded of the time she'd left Evelyn's service. 'Why did Mrs Pryce leave?' Mandy asked after a moment. 'Do you know?'

There was a short pause, perhaps a small hesitation, before Gran replied. 'Not sure, love, although I could guess.' Mandy waited for her to continue, but she didn't.

100

'Why do you think she left?' Mandy persisted, concentrating on the road ahead.

'Because it would have been very difficult for her to have stayed,' Gran said matter-of-factly. 'What reason have John and Evelyn given for Mrs Pryce leaving?'

This was like playing conundrums, Mandy thought, all of them referring to each other for explanation. 'John said she just wanted a change.'

'Well then,' Gran said.

Well then, nothing, Mandy thought. Either she was becoming paranoid and seeing conspiracy everywhere or Gran was being deliberately obtuse and not telling her something. If she dropped the subject now it would be more difficult to pick up again later and she might not get another opportunity. Gran usually appreciated directness so Mandy decided to take the bull by the horns. 'Mrs Pryce left at the same time I stopped coming to visit Sarah,' she said. 'Was that coincidence or were the two connected?'

'Probably connected,' Gran said, now looking straight ahead.

'How?'

There was another short pause before Gran replied, a little tersely: 'You will need to ask your father that.'

'Dad?' Mandy glanced at her, puzzled. 'I don't understand. Why should he know about Mrs Pryce leaving?'

Gran met her gaze, her expression serious yet doubting. Mandy returned her attention to the road and heard Gran say quite sternly: 'Do you really not remember, Mandy? Or is it that you don't want to?'

Mandy felt her heart start to race as a now familiar sense of unease began to descend. 'Remember what?' she said. 'Mrs Pryce leaving?'

'No. The day *you* left Evelyn's for the last time. The reason your visits stopped and the two families never spoke again.'

Mandy's fingers tightened around the wheel as she searched the crevices of her mind for some long-forgotten clue, some hint of what she was being challenged to remember. 'No. Until I came here three days ago, I wasn't even aware there was anything to remember.'

Gran said nothing. There was silence. When Mandy spoke again her voice sounded strained and uneven. 'Gran, Mum and Dad have never spoken of the day I left. But since I've come back I've been having strange thoughts and dreams, and seeing things. I don't know how they link, but I'm usually thirteen years old. What happened, Gran? Did I do something dreadful? Is that why I wasn't allowed to visit Sarah any more? For it seemed quite possible she had done something terrible that had stopped her visits and no one dared speak of.

She glanced at Gran and, just for a second, Mandy thought she was going to tell her something, but then her face stilled again. 'It wasn't exactly your fault,' she said slowly, 'although you were involved. I can't tell you, Mandy. I'm not allowed to. You'll need to speak to your father. He was the one who stopped your visits and forbade us to talk about it. He thought it was for your own good, but I was never sure.' She turned her head and looked out of the side window again, signalling the matter was closed.

Mandy stared at the road ahead while her thoughts somersaulted. So there *was* something, something very bad by the sound of it, and she *had* been involved. She searched her mind again for anything that would allow her into the past, but there was nothing beyond the unsettling flashbacks – if that's what they were – which had plagued her since entering the house. She glanced at Gran, who was still resolutely looking out of the window, and knew it would be unfair to press her further.

Five minutes later she pulled on to the drive of Gran's bungalow and cut the engine.

Fifteen

Inside, the bungalow was exactly as Mandy had last seen it when she'd visited before Grandpa had been taken into hospital, but without her grandparents it had lost its welcoming warmth. Uninhabited for nearly three weeks, it already had that shut-up smell.

'I'll get what I need from the bedroom,' Gran said. 'I won't be long.'

'Do you want some help?' Mandy asked as Gran made her way down the hall towards the main bedroom at the rear.

'No, sit yourself down in the lounge. I can manage.' Mandy thought she probably preferred to do it alone, appreciating the small independence after being waited on at Evelyn's.

Going into the lounge, Mandy sat in the armchair she usually sat in when she visited and gazed around the room. The dated furniture, heavy velvet curtains and knick-knacks arranged along the mantelpiece, which had helped create that feeling of cosiness and security, now seemed faded and worn. A folded newspaper lay on Grandpa's chair as though he had just put it down for a minute and would shortly return and continue reading. Then as she directed her gaze over to the coffee table she saw his flat cap: the tweed cap he always wore and had done for as long as she could remember – in winter to keep him warm and in summer to protect the top of his head from the sun. He never went anywhere without his cap and not having it with him now seemed to underline just how ill he was. On impulse she reached over and picked it up; she would take it with her. Even though he didn't need it and it was unlikely he would ever wear it again he should still have it with him.

A few minutes passed and then Gran called from the bedroom: 'Mandy, can you give me a hand, love?'

She stood and went into the bedroom. Gran was by the bed with one hand on her walking frame, struggling to get some clothes into a zip holdall with the other.

'Here, let me,' Mandy said, going over.

Laying the cap on the bed she began packing the clothes Gran had laid out: two dresses, some of her underwear and a fresh nightdress; Grandpa's pyjamas, his socks, underwear, a pair of trousers and a shirt, although it was doubtful he'd ever need them. Lastly, Mandy laid the cap carefully on top of the other clothes in the case. 'Is that everything?' she asked.

Gran nodded. 'Let's go,' she said quietly.

Mandy saw her face and knew how difficult it was for her being here without Grandpa. Closing the case, Mandy took it off the bed and with the case in one hand she linked Gran's arm with the other and they crossed to the door. In the hall Gran gave a quick glance around and then led the way out, in no hurry to stay. She locked the front door and then asked Mandy to check it. 'Will usually does it,' she said.

'It's fine,' Mandy said, pushing her shoulder against it.

She helped Gran into the car, and then stowed the walking frame and case in the boot. Climbing in, she paused before starting the engine. She looked at Gran, who was staring through the windscreen deep in thought. 'All right?' she asked gently, touching her arm.

Gran nodded.

'We can come again another day if you need anything else.'

'Thanks, love. But I can't imagine Will's going to be needing much more.' She smiled sadly.

'Is there anywhere else you need to go?'

'No thanks, love. Best be getting back.' She threw Mandy the same sad smile, and then folded her hands in her lap, resigned and accepting.

Mandy started the engine and reversed off the drive. They were quiet, then Gran began to nod off. Mandy thought of the conversation they'd had on the way to the bungalow and immediately felt her pulse quicken. What was it Gran seemed to think she should be able to remember? What was it about Evelyn's house and the people in it that had stopped her visits? Clearly Gran thought she should know and had even suggested she was deliberately not remembering: *Do you really not remember, Mandy? Or is it that you don't want to?* In the past she'd counted on Gran for her honest opinion. Why wasn't she being honest now?

Mandy came to with a jolt, braking as the red lights of the car in front suddenly loomed. Gran woke too. 'Sorry,' Mandy said, 'he stopped a bit quickly.'

She kept her concentration fully on the road for the rest of the journey.

When they arrived Evelyn greeted them in the hall and said lunch was ready.

'Lunch!' Gran exclaimed. 'We've only just had breakfast.' But she dutifully followed Evelyn into the morning room where the table was laid with quiche and salad.

Mandy ate very little, partly because she too felt she'd only just had breakfast, but mainly because she was still unsettled by the conversation she'd had with Gran. A conspiracy seemed to be building around her, a conspiracy of silence which stretched back ten years. As soon as was reasonable she asked to be excused and said if she wasn't needed she would go to her room for half an hour. 'Good idea,' Evelyn said. 'Get some rest while you can.'

But it wasn't rest she needed; she needed to be alone to try to make sense of the tangle of thoughts that was writhing in her head. Going into the bedroom she kicked off her shoes and flopped on the bed. It was only 1.30 p.m. but she felt utterly exhausted – and not only from lack of sleep. She was emotionally drained.

Resting her head on the headboard Mandy lay back and stared at the ceiling, willing herself to think back and remember. She tried to visualize herself in the house and garden as she might have been on one of her many visits. In the sitting room, morning room, the conservatory-cum-playroom – what was she doing? She knew from John's photographs that she'd played in the garden under the sprinkler, but could she remember actually being there and doing it? She wasn't sure. But she was sure she'd been in the cloakroom in tears, and also that she'd been driven away from the house in the back of her father's car, distraught. If and how the two incidents were connected, she didn't know. And these were isolated and limited recollections – snapshots from the album of her past which should have been overflowing with memories from all the times she'd stayed with Sarah. The rest was blank.

'Why did Father stop all contact and then forbid everyone to talk about it?' she said out loud as though that might prompt an answer. It must have been something dreadful. Gran's comment – *It wasn't exactly your fault, although you were involved* – suggested she was an accomplice, and therefore partly to blame. Was Sarah the other perpetrator in the unspeakable, unknown crime? It was possible. If so, what could they have done that had led to her being banished from the house? Stolen from the village store? Set fire to something? Drunk wine from the cellar? Or had their pre-pubescent crushes on their respective uncles been discovered? Mandy shuddered at the possibility, yet surely none of these was severe enough for her father to stop all contact between the two families for ever?

'Shit!' she said, clenching her fists. 'Someone needs to tell me what I've done!' It crossed her mind to go downstairs now and demand an explanation. But how could she make a scene and risk upsetting everyone with Grandpa so ill? She remained propped on the bed, frustrated and angry at her inability to remember. Then, just for a second, through the fog of time, she thought she heard her father shouting at Evelyn, as she and Sarah cried openly. Then it vanished.

A tear escaped and ran down her cheek, and another and another. She wept for Grandpa, his pain and suffering, and the loss of their once open and honest relationship. It was inconceivable everyone knew apart from her, especially her beloved grandparents, with whom she thought she'd shared almost everything. Now they too were part of the conspiracy of silence, which her dear grandpa would take to his grave.

Sixteen

Half an hour later Mandy dried her eyes, heaved herself from the bed and pushed her feet into her slippers. If she was staying to help she needed to get a grip and be of some use, otherwise she might as well go home. Putting on a face to mask feelings seemed to run in the family and she was sure she could do it just as well as anyone else. There would be time later to consider the past; now she needed to simply get on with it and help. Smoothing her hair flat, she checked her face in the dressing-table mirror and then returned downstairs.

Evelyn was coming out of the study with the urine bottle. 'I'm just going to empty this,' she said. Mandy nodded. 'Sarah phoned while you were asleep. She and her partner, Simon, are visiting tomorrow.'

'That will be nice,' Mandy said, 'I'll look forward to it,' and returned to the study. It was nearly 2 p.m.

Gran was in her usual chair beside the bed. Someone had unpacked Grandpa's flat cap and it now lay on the coffee table next to his glasses as though at any moment he might step from the bed and put them on. She sat in one of the armchairs and gazed across the room towards the bed and the chair where Gran sat holding Grandpa's hand. All that could be heard for some time was Grandpa's breath, then Gran began to doze. Mandy checked her phone and then listened to her iPod. Ten minutes later Evelyn returned with the empty urine bottle and tucked it beside the bed. Gran stirred and Evelyn said she was 'seeing to the arrangements for our guests': Sarah and Simon on Friday, and Mandy's parents on Sunday.

As the afternoon passed Mandy felt a rising sense of occasion. Evelyn looked in regularly to check they were all right and give updates on what she was doing to prepare for the guests: she was having Mrs Saunders give the house an extra clean and polish; she was trying to decide on the menus – did her parents like rainbow trout? She'd have to go into the town rather than order online, and so on and so on. Mandy took her earphones out each time Evelyn came into the study and Gran woke and smiled and nodded politely. 'She's a great one for entertaining,' Gran commented dryly after one visit.

Presently Evelyn reappeared looking concerned. 'Are you certain your parents like rainbow trout?'

'I'm certain they do,' Mandy said. 'But please don't go to any trouble.'

'No trouble. We'll have the trout with new potatoes and French runner beans on Sunday when your parents come, and the lamb tomorrow when Simon and Sarah visit.'

'I'm sure that'll be lovely,' Mandy assured her.

Without doubt all Evelyn's preparations were a distraction from what was really going on, Mandy thought, and she hoped her parents could be persuaded to stay for lunch or dinner, or whichever meal the trout was for, otherwise Evelyn would be sorely disappointed, and the tenuous relationship her aunt had with her parents would be strained even further.

After Evelyn's last visit worrying about the trout Gran gave up trying to doze and stayed awake. Mandy put aside her iPod and took out her sketch pad. She drew a large picture of a trout with its mouth turned down in a sulk. She headed the sketch *Trout with a Pout* and showed it to Gran, who laughed out loud. No matter how upset you were you couldn't be sad all the time, Mandy thought, it simply wasn't possible.

Grandpa's pain always seemed more manageable during the day, but then during the day the nurse came every four hours to give him a morphine injection, compared to the one at 10 p.m., which, with the sleeping draught, was supposed to see him through the night. When the nurse made his 6 p.m. visit they remained in the study and the nurse said Mr Edwards's pulse was noticeably weaker in his neck. Gran and John nodded stoically as though they knew what this meant and had been half expecting it, but Mandy didn't know and thought it sounded bad.

'My parents aren't coming again until Sunday,' she said anxiously to the nurse. 'Should I tell them to come sooner?'

The nurse looked up from Grandpa and smiled kindly. 'I don't think there's any immediate concern. I'm sure Sunday will be fine. Your grandpa could stay the same for many days, but not weeks. I'll check again when I settle him for the night.'

When the nurse returned at 10 p.m., after Gran and Evelyn had gone to bed, he took Grandpa's pulse and said he was 'holding his own' and his pulse hadn't weakened further, which seemed good news. After this 10 p.m. injection Grandpa slept reasonably peacefully until just after 2 a.m., when he awoke with a start and cried out. Mandy was already awake, with her iPod on low, and went straight to the bed, followed by John. John took his shoulders and she took Grandpa's hands and together they tried to soothe him. But it had no effect and he grew delirious. 'Get it off me!' he cried, trying to knock something off his chest. Then, squinting towards the curtains: 'Close the windows! They're getting in!'

'The windows are closed,' John reassured him. 'Nothing can get in.'

Mandy tried to hold Grandpa's hands to stop him from hitting his chest while John soothed his forehead, but he kept pulling away. And while Mandy wouldn't have admitted it she was slightly spooked by Grandpa's insistence that 'they' were getting in, for the threat seemed real. She glanced around the room at the shadows in the corners and then put the main light on. 'He hasn't got a temperature,' John said, feeling his forehead. 'It's probably all the morphine making him see things.'

With the main light on Grandpa gradually began to calm down as though the light had banished the demons. The hallucinations stopped and he lay back on the pillows, exhausted, and slowly drifted into unconsciousness. They'd just returned to their chairs when he called out again; they were immediately by his bed. The pain was as bad as the previous night now and although John massaged his shoulders and Mandy stroked his head, all the time talking and trying to calm him, it had no effect. Then his eyes suddenly shot open and he stared up at John. 'End it now,' he gasped between breaths. 'You promised. I've had enough.'

Mandy looked at John, who'd visibly paled. He took his hands from Grandpa's shoulders and crossed to the phone on the desk. 'Sorry, Dad, I can't. I'll call the nurse.' Grandpa groaned.

As they waited for the nurse they soothed and comforted Grandpa as best they could. The agony drove him in and out of consciousness. In his waking moments he shouted out and stared around, not knowing where he was, then his eyes rolled upwards and he was unconscious again. The minutes ticked by and John kept glancing at his watch. 'Where the hell is he?' he demanded, channelling his worry into anger.

At last the pain seemed to peak and was subsiding when he began to retch. Mandy grabbed the bucket and he vomited the thick brown foul-smelling liquid. The doorbell rang. 'Thank God,' John said.

Mandy stayed where she was and wiped his mouth on a tissue while John answered the door. 'The nurse is here,' she soothed, but there was no reply.

Coming into the study, the nurse took charge. Mandy stood away from the bed as he turned Grandpa on to his side and gave him the morphine injection in his thigh. He opened a sterilized packet containing moistened cotton buds and carefully wiped the inside of Grandpa's mouth. The smell rose from the bucket. 'It's faecal vomiting,' the nurse said. 'When the lower bowel becomes obstructed it contracts and forces the waste up through the intestines where it is ejected as vomit.'

Mandy thought she was going to puke.

John grimaced. 'Can you think of anything more degrading than being forced to vomit up your own excrement!' he said bitterly.

'It won't happen again,' the nurse promised. 'I'll make sure he has an anti-nausea drug in with the morphine. You're doing a good job,' he added, touching John's arm reassuringly. 'Mr Edwards is a lucky man to be able to die at home surrounded by his family.'

Mandy flinched at the word 'die', which they'd all been carefully avoiding.

'Is he?' John said tightly. 'I wouldn't want an end like this.'

Mandy silently agreed.

Seventeen

The following morning, as usually happened, everything returned to 'normal', and John and Mandy continued their collusion by withholding the details of the night and passing it off as 'restless'. Once breakfast was over and 12 noon began to approach – the time Sarah and Simon were expected – excitement over the 'sense of occasion' fuelled by Evelyn continued to rise. Mandy wondered if Sarah and Simon were always treated to such a 'red carpet' welcome, as if they were visiting dignitaries rather than daughter and boyfriend. It was nothing like Mandy's visits to her parents when she simply dropped in or, if Adam was going too, phoned to say they were on their way. But then Mandy supposed her family (including her grandparents) would be deemed working class while her aunt's family was clearly something more.

By 11.45 a.m. she was feeling quite nervous, partly because of Evelyn's continual fussing and tidying, and also, if she was honest, at the prospect of meeting Sarah again after all this time. What memories would Sarah have of their time together? Would they even recognize each other?

Midday came and went. Gran and she were in the study sitting beside the bed while Grandpa slept. Evelyn and John were upstairs 'getting ready', and Mrs Saunders was busy in the kitchen.

'Sarah's always late,' Gran said. 'She takes after her mother. Evelyn always used to be late until she married John.'

Mandy gave a small nod. 'It doesn't matter. It's not as though we're going anywhere.'

'No, love, that's for sure,' Gran said. 'The only person going anywhere is Grandpa, and he's in no hurry either. Are you, Will?'

Mandy smiled. Gran's humour was like Grandpa's, dry; it had seen them through many of life's downers. The fact that Gran was able to make a joke suggested a semblance of normality – an acceptance of what was happening. Mandy supposed this was a result of gradually coming to terms with Grandpa's condition. Nursing a loved one at home gave you time to adjust, she thought, compared to visiting in the emotional sterility of a hospital ward, where dying was safely removed but left you ill prepared for the end when it came. Whether her parents had made the same adjustment she doubted – it was hands-on nursing that prepared you.

'She'll regret not spending more time with him,' Gran said, breaking into Mandy's thoughts. 'This will only be Sarah's second visit and she only lives fifteen minutes away.'

Mandy could appreciate Gran's concern but she could also understand Sarah's reluctance to visit and see Grandpa so poorly. 'Evelyn said Sarah's finding it very difficult.'

'And you're not?' Gran said, turning to look at her.

Mandy shrugged. 'Perhaps I'm made of stronger stuff. It doesn't mean Sarah cares less.'

'I know that, love. Sarah's been good to us in her own way.'

At 12.20 they heard the door chime; Mandy felt a surge of relief and apprehension. Two minutes later the study door opened and Evelyn came in, followed by Sarah and then Simon, both tall and very smartly dressed. Would she have recognized Sarah? Only from her photograph in Evelyn's sitting room. Mandy stood to greet them.

'Hi! It's my little cousin,' Sarah cried, taking Mandy's hands between hers and air-kissing her cheeks. 'Great to see you again! Fantastic,' she enthused. 'This is my partner, Simon.'

Simon air-kissed Mandy. 'Lovely to meet you,' he said.

'And you.'

'Sarah's told me so much about you. All the time you spent together as children, and the mischief the pair of you got up to. Sounds great fun.'

Mandy glanced at Evelyn, smiled at Simon, and hid her shock. She'd assumed, wrongly, that because she hadn't been allowed to speak of Sarah or her family to her parents during the past ten years the same had been true for Sarah speaking of her. Now she found not only was her name known to Simon, but that Sarah had been reliving fond childhood memories, apparently with her mother's approval. Adam knew nothing of Sarah, beyond that she was a cousin whom Mandy hadn't seen since a family argument a long while ago.

'How's Grandpa?' Sarah asked, going over and kissing Gran's cheek. 'He looks so pale and thin, doesn't he, Si? Not at all like he should.'

Simon nodded and hovered at the end of the bed. Mandy moved to one side so Sarah could get closer to the bed.

'He's holding his own,' Gran said.

'Is he going to wake up?' Sarah asked. 'We'd like to say hi.'

'He's heavily sedated,' Evelyn said. 'It's for the best.'

'Oh dear, what a shame. We're disappointed, aren't we, Si?'

Mandy looked at Sarah and tried to visualize her as a child, but it was difficult. Like so many things connected with the house and the time she'd spent here she had the vague feeling of familiarity without the clarity of proper recall. Had Sarah always been this flamboyant and extrovert? Mandy thought she might have been. And she was sure Sarah had always been the taller. Now, at about five feet nine inches, Sarah was still five inches taller than Mandy – the reason she referred to her as 'little cousin'. Simon was tall too, and they made a handsome couple: confident, sleek and slender. Sarah's fair hair shone in a fashionable bob, and her light make-up accentuated her high, aristocratic cheekbones and clear blue eyes. Her smooth pencil skirt and short-sleeved cashmere jumper were clearly not chain-shop; suddenly Mandy felt under-dressed in her jeans and T-shirt. Simon's grey flannel trousers and matching V-neck jumper complemented Sarah perfectly. Evelyn was right to be proud of Sarah, Mandy thought; there was a sense of occasion in being with her.

'Is there anything we can do, Mummy?' Sarah asked, looking at Evelyn.

'Not really, pet. Dinner will be at one thirty. Mrs Saunders is making Simon's favourite.'

'Not the rack of lamb?' he asked, his eyes widening.

Evelyn beamed and nodded, flattered by his enthusiasm.

'Mum, you'll spoil him,' Sarah cried, squeezing Simon's arm. 'You know I can't cook, although I am going to join an evening class next term.'

'Not a moment too soon,' Simon joked. Sarah poked him playfully in the ribs.

Mandy wondered how long Simon and Sarah had known each other and decided it couldn't have been long. They were very attentive, constantly touching and exchanging glances, as you do with a new partner, treating each other with exaggerated care. They hadn't yet developed the more comfortable, take-each-other-slightly-for-granted behaviour that came from knowing someone a long time. She thought Adam and she had reached that comfort zone, except of course when she threw a wobbler and couldn't bear him to touch her and rejected him. Then he recoiled for his own protection and put distance between them and she panicked at the thought of losing him.

'I'll be in the dining room if I'm wanted,' Evelyn said.

'We'll come with you,' Sarah said quickly. 'We need to speak to Dad.' Then, flashing Mandy a smile: 'Will you call me if Gramps wakes?'

'Of course.' Mandy returned her smile.

Sarah and Evelyn left the study with Simon right behind them.

'What does Simon do?' Mandy asked, returning to sit beside Gran.

'A broker in the City, I think. He's always talking about stocks and shares.'

'And Sarah?'

Gran smiled to herself. 'Not a lot. John set her up with a beauty salon, but it's never made any money. I overheard him saying he can't prop it up for ever. I expect that's why she needs to talk to him – it's usually about money.' Gran paused. 'I wouldn't let anyone else say this about Sarah but I can as her gran. John and Evelyn have spoilt her and it's given her airs and graces. She'll be twenty-five next birthday. She should be standing on her own two feet instead of relying on them. She needs to get a proper job and do an honest day's work.'

Mandy didn't comment, it wasn't her place; and she was aware that she wasn't exactly doing 'a proper job' either at present. Yet Gran had given her nothing but encouragement in her venture to paint full time, and Mandy wondered if it was Sarah's 'airs and graces' that needled Gran, for she could see, even in their brief meeting, that Sarah's flamboyant, dizzy nature had the potential to irritate.

* * *

Grandpa slept on, unaware there were visitors in the house. Sarah didn't appear in the study again until 1.15 when she came in with Simon and announced lunch was nearly ready: 'Mummy says if you need to use the cloakroom could you do so now.'

Gran said she did want to and Mandy helped her on to her walking frame. Sarah said she would go with Gran so Mandy would have a chance to get to know Si. Mandy wasn't sure she needed to know him, and Simon looked unconvinced too. They watched Sarah and Gran leave the study, glanced at each other awkwardly, and then looked at Grandpa who was on his back, mouth open and breathing heavily.

'You're doing a good job,' Simon said. 'I'm afraid Sarah can't help much. It makes her too upset seeing him like this. She's very sensitive.'

Mandy nodded.

'I hear you're an artist?'

Mandy looked at him, surprised. How did he know? Presumably Evelyn had said something. 'Not really,' she said, embarrassed. 'I'm just treating myself to a year off. A bit of self-indulgence really.'

'I used to be pretty good at art at school, but I don't have the time now. May I have a look at your drawings?'

It seemed churlish to refuse, so reluctantly Mandy crossed to the armchair and picked up the carrier bag from beside the chair. Taking out the sketch pad she passed it to him. 'There isn't anything exciting,' she apologized. 'Just a few views I've seen since I've been staying here. I thought I might try and paint them when I go home.' She waited self-consciously as Simon flipped through the pages, examining the half-dozen drawings. He laughed at the picture of the trout.

'They're good,' he said. 'I like your style – very realistic.'

'Thank you.' She returned the pad to the carrier bag and tucked it out of sight beside the chair.

A moment later the study door shot open and Sarah appeared. 'Lunch is ready!' she cried. Grandpa stirred but didn't wake. 'Mandy, Mummy said to tell you Gramps will be OK alone while we eat, but to leave the study door open so we can hear him.'

Sarah linked Simon's arm and Mandy followed them into the hall. 'Si used to paint,' Sarah said over her shoulder at Mandy, 'but he doesn't have the time now he goes into the City.'

'No,' Mandy agreed. 'It's very difficult to get out the brushes after a day at work.'

'I want him to paint me,' Sarah said, turning to Simon as they walked. 'I could pose draped over a couch, like one of those Ruben-esque women.'

'Mnnn, sounds good to me,' Simon said seductively and kissed the end of her nose.

They filed into the dining room and settled around the table. Mrs Saunders set the dishes and platters down the centre of the table with a serving spoon in each as John opened a bottle of wine. They helped themselves and began eating. Mandy found she didn't have much to say during the meal, which was just as well as there wasn't a great deal of opportunity. Sarah was clearly the star attraction and occupied centre stage, which she did naturally and successfully, Mandy thought. She talked continuously – to the neglect of her lunch – of her beauty salon and the media clients who patronized it; Simon's success in the City; their apartment; entertaining; and their most recent holiday in Gran Canaria. Sarah's monologue was only interrupted by the occasional and very small portion of food, which she delicately forked into her mouth where it seemed to dissolve rather than be chewed; and confirmation from Simon that what she was saying was true –

'Isn't that right, Si?' she said, to which he invariably replied, 'Absolutely.' And Mandy thought, a little unkindly, that appreciation from Sarah's audience ran on a decreasing scale – from Evelyn and Simon who laughed and agreed unreservedly with everything Sarah said; to John who nodded occasionally; to Mandy who smiled faintly but appropriately; and Gran who, on the same side of the table to Sarah, said nothing, clearly used to Sarah's chatter and refusing to indulge her.

The door chime rang at 2 p.m. and Evelyn left the table to let the nurse in. Gran had finished her main course and told John she didn't want pudding but would go and sit with Will instead. Sarah paused briefly from talking to help Gran on to her walking frame. Sitting down again she resumed the story she'd been telling. Mandy would have liked to have excused herself from the table too, but Sarah was seated directly opposite her and was addressing much of her monologue to her. She was reaching the climax of what had been a long story about a mouse which had got into her salon one night and scared her senseless in the morning. Her voice rose, her eyes flashed and she waved her arms as she described the search of the premises that had resulted in the mouse escaping out of the back door. Mandy smiled and nodded.

The meal drew to a close with fruit salad and ice cream shortly after 2.30. Once finished they stood and began moving away from the table and out of the dining room. Sarah said she was going to the 'little girls' room', and after she'd gone Mandy suddenly found herself alone with Simon in the front hall. 'Sorry,' he whispered. 'Sarah always talks too much when she's nervous.'

Mandy glanced at him and smiled, unsure of what he meant.

'She can talk for England when she's worried, but she's got a heart of gold. She was worried about meeting you again.'

'Was she?' Mandy asked, surprised, for Sarah hadn't given the impression of being nervous. Far from it.

He shrugged. 'She thought it might be embarrassing meeting again, given what happened. But you're fine about it all now, aren't you?'

Mandy turned to look at him squarely. They had come to a halt at the end of the hall. Evelyn and John were still in the dining room, talking to Mrs Saunders – congratulating her on the meal. 'Fine about what?' Mandy said.

'You know, what happened when you were kids.'

She stared at him, completely taken aback. She didn't know 'what happened'! She hadn't got a clue, but clearly Simon knew. 'Why exactly was Sarah worried?' Mandy asked carefully, watching his expression.

'Oh, well, she thought you might want to keep talking about it, you know, like some people do. There's a guy I work with who was on the tube when the bombs went off – he had a few cuts but nothing serious. He keeps talking about it – reliving it, over and over again. Post-traumatic shock, I suppose. But you're not like that. I can tell. You've moved on from the past. I expect your painting helped – it's a type of therapy, isn't it?'

Mandy continued to stare at him, dumbfounded. What the hell was he talking about? Post-traumatic shock? Therapy from her painting and moving on from the past? Sarah must have told him something about their shared past, but what? Simon was watching her, waiting for an answer – confirmation that she was all right now. She felt her cheeks flush and her legs go weak. She continued to look at him, searching for a clue and unable to give him the reassurance he sought.

'I'm sorry,' he muttered after a moment, realizing he'd made a mistake. He took a step back. 'I'm sorry, I shouldn't have said anything. Sarah was right.'

Mandy heard his pity and collusion with Sarah about her unknown past. 'What exactly did Sarah tell you?'

'Nothing,' he said curtly. 'I shouldn't have said anything. Forget I ever mentioned it, please. I'm sorry.'

'I'm going to see Grandpa,' she stammered and backed away. She needed to get away from Simon.

She nearly ran to the end of the hall and then left, into the study. Gran looked up from where she was sitting beside the bed. 'What's the matter, Mandy?'

'Nothing. I'm going out.' Grabbing her bag from beside the chair and before Gran could say anything further, she fled the study.

Out into the hall again and past Simon who had now been joined by Sarah. She felt their eyes on her as she passed, heading for the front door. She kept her head down and said nothing, and hoped they wouldn't say anything either. Her heart was racing, she felt hot and a strange buzzing noise filled her ears. Suddenly she heard a child cry and felt her cheeks damp with tears. Then she saw her father appear beside her, his face red with anger, his hand on her arm, holding it tightly – too tightly, hurrying her towards the door. He paused before opening it and they turned. She could see Evelyn at the far end of the hall, white from shock and crying. On her left was Sarah as a young teenager with her head buried in Mrs Pryce's shoulder; both were sobbing openly. Mandy saw her father's face, felt his anger and was very afraid.

Eighteen

Outside, instead of being bundled into the back of her father's car and being driven away in tears, as she thought she'd be, Mandy found herself running down the driveway and then turning right into the lane. She continued running along the path at the edge of the lane in the direction of the village; her only thought to get away. Get away from the house and everyone in it, for good. The air was chilly without a coat but Mandy didn't feel the cold. She was hot – boiling hot, but not from running; it was fear that was making her sweat. Sarah knew, Simon knew, and they had even discussed it! But what? What had happened that everyone knew about, apart from her? What had made Mrs Pryce, Evelyn and Sarah stand in the hall and cry, and her father so angry that she'd been afraid of him? What had she done to upset them all – that had caused her father to drag her from the house, never to return? Suddenly she realized that whatever it was must be so awful that her father had decided it was better she didn't know. That the wall of silence was there to protect her – from herself.

Out of breath, with fear gripping her, she was forced to slow to a walk. Her throat was dry and sore and her heart beat wildly. Dear God, whatever was it? Something so horrendous that not even her dear gran could bring herself to tell her. *You'll need to speak to your father. He was the one who stopped your visits and forbade us to talk about it.*

The lane ran out and she crossed the main road and walked to the bus stop. Ten minutes later she was on a bus taking her to the station. From there she would catch a train into London and a tube home. Home: her bedsitting room that held no secrets and was safe and secure; where she could close the door and be alone. Where she was Mandy who had taken a year off work to paint and no one knew the dreadful secret of her past. Her heart stung at the thought of Gran and Grandpa whom she'd abandoned without even saying goodbye. She might never see her dear grandpa again. But the thought of the shame she'd brought upon them and the secret of her dirty past that they'd been forced to carry tore through her like a knife. She couldn't stay in that house, not with everyone knowing.

At 3.20 Mandy boarded the train for Paddington and her phone began to ring. She took it from her bag; it was Evelyn's landline number. Leaving the call to go through to her voicemail she switched the phone to silent and returned it to her bag. She chose a window seat in an empty part of the carriage. Resting her head back, she stared out at the platform. Her head was throbbing and her neck ached. She screwed her eyes shut at the thought of Simon telling Sarah what he'd said. She could hear Sarah's response: *It's not your fault, Si. She's obviously not over it yet.* Over what? Mandy wanted to shout. Her phone vibrated in her bag and she ignored it. Two young children scrambled on to the seat opposite but were thankfully called to another seat by their mother. Mandy stared unseeing through the glass window. A moment later the doors closed and with a small shudder the train pulled away.

It was dusk by the time she turned the corner into her street, the last of the daylight being replaced by the street lamps flickering on. She was exhausted and longed only to climb into her bed and curl beneath the duvet. Her phone had been buzzing with missed calls throughout the journey and she'd ignored it. At some point she'd have to phone Evelyn and tell her she was OK, but not now. Not yet. She couldn't face it.

Taking her keys from her bag, Mandy went down the short path between the untrimmed hedges and unlocked the front door. The slightly musty smell of the old under-heated house hit her, familiar and reassuring. She flicked on the hall light and climbed the stairs, praying she wouldn't bump into another tenant and have to talk to them. Rounding the landing she saw a faint light coming from under her door. She must have forgotten to turn off the light when she'd left with her father in the early hours. It was a wonder it hadn't drained the meter by now. Turning the key in her lock, she opened the door and started. 'What are you doing here?'

'I could ask you the same thing!' Adam stood up and came across the room. 'Where the hell have you been, Mandy? Your father phoned me, worried sick! He hasn't dared tell your mother you're missing. What the hell did you think you were doing, running out of your aunt's like that?'

She pushed the door closed behind her and met him face to face. He was angry but so was she. The last person she needed to find here was Adam looking for an explanation. 'I don't remember asking you to come here!' she said. 'Did I ask for your help?'

'No, but you obviously need it. What's going on, Mandy? What's the matter?'

She glared at him and he stared back. Then she saw the concern and anxiety in his eyes and her anger melted. Her face crumpled and the tears she'd held back all the journey flowed.

'Oh, Mandy, love,' he said, folding her in his arms. 'Whatever is it? What's happened?'

She shook her head and buried her face in his shoulder. 'I don't know,' she sobbed. 'I wish I did.'

He held her close, then after a moment steered her towards the bed that they used as a sofa. He sat her down and sat beside her. She felt his arm around her shoulders and she rested her head against his. When he spoke again he was gentle as he usually was. 'Evelyn phoned your dad and said you'd run off. She said you were very upset and you weren't answering your phone. Your dad left a message on your voicemail and then phoned me. He's very worried. We need to tell him you've been found safe. Shall I send him a text?' Mandy nodded.

Moving slightly away, Adam took his phone from his pocket and texted her father that she was safely home. Returning the phone to his pocket, he put his arm around her again. 'Mandy, can you tell me now what's the matter?'

She shook her head. 'No, I can't, I'm sorry.'

She felt him stiffen slightly at the rebuff. 'Why not? Evelyn told your father that it might have had something to do with a remark Simon made. I understand Simon is her daughter's boyfriend?' Adam paused, waiting for a response. 'What did he say, Mandy? Did he do something to you?'

'No, nothing like that. I can't explain. I don't know.'

In her bedsit, seated next to Adam, Evelyn's house and its hauntings seemed so far away it was almost unreal. To try and explain to Adam what she had seen and felt was impossible. She didn't know where to begin. 'I had some strange dreams, and they unsettled me,' she tried, and knew it sounded pathetic.

He looked at her, puzzled. 'Mandy, you don't run off without a word to anyone and come all the way home because of a dream.'

'No,' she agreed, 'but I don't know anymore.'

127

They sat side by side for some moments in silence. Mandy knew she should say something but also knew she couldn't. For while the hallucinations she'd been having at her aunt's now seemed fanciful, she was still acutely aware that something had made her father stop her visits to John and Evelyn's and then forbidden everyone to talk of it. It was all so confusing she was beginning to think she didn't know what was real and what was imagined any more.

After a while Adam lowered his arm. 'Do you want me to stay, Mandy?' he asked gently.

'It's difficult for me right now. Perhaps not.'

He nodded and stood up. He looked down at where she sat on the bed, his face serious. 'Mandy, I'm not going to pressure you. I never have. But whatever you've fled from won't be solved by running away. I'm going home now. Phone if you need me. Take care.' He kissed the top of her head, turned and, without looking back, crossed the room and let himself out.

Mandy stayed where she was, perched on the bed, and stared into the room. The fridge hummed and a few moments later she heard the front door slam in the hall below as Adam let himself out. The heavy oak door with its leaded light window was not dissimilar to the one at Evelyn's house, the door her father, his anger brimming over, had dragged her towards on that last night. Why had he been so angry? What had she done? Why were Sarah, Evelyn and Mrs Pryce crying, and where was Uncle John? If she closed her eyes she could see that hall; she could feel her father's fingers gripping her arm, see his face tight with anger. Before he'd opened the door he'd turned and raised his fist.

Mandy's eyes shot open. Yes, he'd shaken his fist in anger but it wasn't at her. It was Evelyn he was angry with. It was Evelyn he'd shouted at. Mandy screwed her eyes shut and concentrated.

128

She pictured the scene that night as she'd seen it on fleeing Evelyn's. There he was pulling her towards the door; she could see the leaded light window. Just before he'd opened the door he'd turned and raised his fist and shouted. And now she remembered the words he shouted. 'If you ever come near my family again, I'll have the lot of you arrested!' Yes it was Evelyn he'd been so angry with, not her. But why? Try as she might she couldn't remember any more.

Nineteen

The following afternoon, Mandy got off the bus in the village. She'd chosen the stop closest to the village store rather than the one near the lane that led to her aunt's house. It had started to rain, and while she now had a jacket — brought from home — she hadn't thought to bring her umbrella. She quickened her pace, her heart racing at the prospect of what she was about to hear. It had occurred to her during the night, in the normality of her bedsit, that as Mrs Pryce had been in the hall that last night then it was likely she knew what had happened and, not bound by the family's vow of secrecy, could tell her.

Mandy crossed the road to the shop. The door clanged open and an elderly couple came out. They smiled at her and put up their hoods before hurrying off. Mandy went in and the door clanged shut behind her. The shop was busier today, Saturday, than it had been on her last visit. She looked over to the till on the right where she'd last seen Mrs Pryce, but a girl in her twenties with long blonde hair was serving a customer. Mandy went further in and peered down the aisles, but there was no sign of Mrs Pryce. She went round the corner and looked into the recess that housed the post office counter; a woman, a similar age to Mrs Pryce, was serving behind the security grille. Mandy waited until the customer had finished and, having checked that no other customers were waiting, went up to the counter. The woman smiled and looked at her questioningly. 'I was wondering if you could help me?' Mandy said. 'I'm looking for Mrs Pryce. Is she here? I'm an old friend.'

'I know who you are,' the woman said kindly. 'Mary mentioned you'd come in last week. It's Amanda, isn't it?'

Mandy gave a small nod; clearly nothing went unnoticed in the village.

'I'm afraid Mary's not in today,' she said. 'She only works part-time. Can I give her a message? I should be seeing her at church tomorrow.'

Mandy hid her disappointment. 'No, no message, thank you.' She began to move away.

'I'll tell her you came in,' the woman called after her. 'She'll be working again on Tuesday.'

'Thank you,' Mandy said, and left the store. Tuesday. It seemed a lifetime away.

Outside large drops of rain splattered on the pavement and the sky had darkened. Mandy crossed the road and walked quickly along the path away from the village and towards the lane that led to her aunt's. She was bitterly disappointed. She'd had her hopes set on asking Mrs Pryce; now she'd have to wait until Tuesday, assuming she was still at Evelyn's. Thunder rumbled in the distance and Mandy knew she shouldn't go down the lane with its overhanging trees if there was any chance of lightning. When she'd stayed as a child her aunt had often warned Sarah and her, once they were old enough to come into the village alone, to wait until a storm passed and not to shelter under the trees. She could hear Evelyn saying it: *Wait under the bus shelter in the village if there's a storm. Don't shelter under the trees.* Mandy remembered her warning and also the game of dare Sarah and she had played when they'd gone into the village one summer's afternoon and a storm had broken. Sarah had wanted to wait under the bus shelter as her mother had told her, but Mandy had goaded her cousin until she'd agreed to go down the lane. It had been fun and dangerously exciting – hearing the thunder and then seeing how many trees they could run under before the lightning struck. Mandy remembered their squeals of laughter; how they'd arrived home soaking wet; and the huge telling-off they'd been given, which had been directed at Sarah. 'You're old enough to know better,' Evelyn had said. 'You should have waited.' Mandy remembered Sarah had accepted the telling-off without passing on the blame and afterwards Mandy had thanked her. 'That's what friends are for,' Sarah had said.

How I can remember this, she thought, frustrated, but not the important things? I can remember a silly game of dare but not why my father shouted at his sister and I was never allowed in the house again. It was as if a curtain had been drawn over this part of her mind, a curtain which occasionally parted to let her peep in, but not for long enough to make any sense of what she saw.

The rain was falling heavily through the canopy of bare branches overhead and Mandy began to jog along the lane. She was nervous at the thought of seeing everyone again. She'd phoned Evelyn after Adam had gone the night before and had apologized for disappearing, saying she'd just needed a break. Although Evelyn had been understanding and hadn't pressed her, her running off after Simon's remark must have sparked speculation. Doubtless she had been talked about and discussed, but now she needed to go back. Adam had been right: running away wouldn't solve anything, and she'd also realized she couldn't desert her grandparents.

Five minutes later, wet and out of breath, she jogged down the drive, past the wooden sign saying 'Breakspeare Manor', and to Evelyn's front door. She pressed the bell, heard it chime, and then a moment later Evelyn opened the door. 'Good to have you back, Mandy!' she exclaimed, relieved and pleased to see her. She gave her a quick hug. 'You're soaking. I'll get you a towel.'

'Thanks. How's Grandpa?'

'About the same.'

Mandy stayed on the doormat just inside the hall and took off her sopping wet jacket and shoes, which had leaves and dirt stuck to the soles. The house was quiet and only Evelyn's car had been parked on the drive. Evelyn reappeared and passed her the towel.

'Is John here?'

'No. He's gone to visit his mother. He goes every Saturday. She's in a nursing home now.'

Mandy nodded and rubbed her hair on the towel. So John was out, and Gran would be in the study. While she had the opportunity, and before her courage failed her, she should ask Evelyn what she knew. She concentrated on rubbing her hair and carefully avoided Evelyn's gaze. 'Last night I was thinking about when I last stayed here,' she began, her voice unnaturally light. 'Can you tell me why you and Dad fell out? What happened to stop me coming here?'

She heard her aunt's silence. Then she met her gaze and saw her look of shock and disbelief – the same disbelief she'd seen on Gran's face when she'd asked her.

'You really don't know, Mandy?' Evelyn asked, amazed.

Mandy stopped rubbing her hair. 'No, I really don't. But you do, and I'd like you to tell me. I used to see Sarah regularly and then suddenly I wasn't allowed to come here any more. Something happened, something very upsetting, and I'd like you to tell me what.'

Evelyn's look of disbelief slowly vanished, replaced by confusion, then her face set. Mandy could guess what was coming next.

'No, I can't be the one to tell you,' she said firmly. 'You'll have to ask your father; it was his decision to stop you coming here. If he hasn't told you he's got some explaining to do. I always thought burying it would make it worse, and now it has.' Evelyn stopped. 'You'd better change before you catch cold.' She turned and went down the hall.

Mandy stared after her as the door to her past once more slammed shut in her face. She seethed inwardly with anger and frustration. It crossed her mind to run after Evelyn and demand the truth – make a scene if necessary, until she told. But scenes weren't a part of their family – one thing Evelyn and her father still had in common was their self-control and dislike of raw emotion!

Her phone began ringing in her bag. 'Yes?' she said. It was Adam. They hadn't spoken since he'd left her bedsit the evening before.

His voice was subdued. 'How are you?'

'OK.' She crossed the hall and started to climb the stairs as she spoke.

'Are you at your aunt's now?'

'I've just arrived. How did you know I was coming here?'

'Your dad phoned me this morning.'

'I see.' She pushed open the door to the bedroom and, dumping her bag on the floor, began pulling off her wet jeans.

'You're sure you're OK?' he asked.

'Yes.'

'Mandy, your parents have asked me if I want to come with them when they visit tomorrow. I said I would like to but I wanted to make sure it was all right with you first?'

She hesitated. 'Yes, why not? Gran will be pleased to see you.'

'And you?'

She sat on the bed in her T-shirt and pants and pulled off her damp socks. 'Yes.'

'Sure?'

'Yes, come. I'd like to see you.'

'Good. Is there anything you need?'

'No, I don't think so.'

'I'll see you tomorrow then.'

'Yes.'

Saying goodbye, she closed her phone and returned it to her bag. She knew she should have tried to sound more enthusiastic, but in some ways seeing Adam right now just felt like an added pressure – more emotion and unresolved issues to deal with. Recently – even before Grandpa's illness – whenever they'd seen each other he'd gone away hurt and she'd ended up feeling a shit. But she wanted to see him, she always looked forward to seeing him; it just seemed to go pear-shaped. She would make a big effort tomorrow.

Having changed into dry jeans and socks, she tucked her phone into her pocket and went downstairs. She needed a drink of water before she went into the study. Evelyn was in the kitchen making sandwiches for supper. She didn't look up as Mandy entered.

'Adam is coming with Mum and Dad tomorrow,' Mandy said. 'I hope that's OK?'

Evelyn nodded and continued slicing tomatoes.

'Don't worry about lunch for him, though; he never eats until the evening.'

'Of course he must eat,' Evelyn said bluntly. 'There'll be plenty.'

Mandy felt the atmosphere charged and heavy. 'Can I get myself a drink of water?'

'Of course.'

She took a glass from the cupboard and went to the tap. Evelyn concentrated on the sandwiches.

'Do you want some help?' Mandy asked, trying to break the tension.

'No, I've nearly finished. We'll have these for supper. I've given Mrs Saunders the day off as she's coming in tomorrow.'

Mandy nodded and started towards the door.

'Mandy?'

She stopped, turned and met her aunt's gaze.

'What I said earlier. You do understand why your father has to be the one to tell you? It was his decision to handle it in the way he did. I can't risk upsetting him again, and having another ten years without speaking.'

Mandy gave a small shrug. 'I guess. As much as I understand anything at present.'

'So you'll talk to him?'

'Yes, but not tomorrow. Later, when this is all over.'

Evelyn gave a faint smile and appeared relieved. 'Thanks, Mandy. And thanks for coming back to help. We're very grateful. John says he doesn't know what he'd have done without you, and he feels it has helped smooth things between you.'

'What was there to smooth between John and me?' Mandy asked, surprised.

Evelyn looked away. 'Oh, you know ... it wasn't easy for any of us. But your father must be the one to tell you.'

There was clearly no point in pressing Evelyn and making her feel uncomfortable. Mandy continued into the study where Gran was sitting beside the bed, holding Grandpa's hand, exactly as she'd left them the previous afternoon. She glanced up and smiled. 'I knew you wouldn't desert us, Mandy.'

'No. I wouldn't do that.'

Twenty

andy thought she was dreaming – a proper dream, a pleasant dream, not the disturbing flashbacks that had plagued her since arriving at her aunt's. It was very realistic. She could hear Adam's voice close by, smell his favourite shower gel, and feel the warmth of his breath on her cheek as he kissed her. It was a lovely vision of how things had been between them once, and how she hoped they could be again. Then she opened her eyes and saw she wasn't dreaming. Adam was perched on the edge of her bed. 'What are you doing here?' she said, sitting up.

He laughed. 'It's Sunday. I said I'd come with your parents. Remember? We've just arrived; they're downstairs. Your uncle showed me up, then left me to wake the sleeping princess. How are you?'

She rubbed her hand across her forehead, disorientated from sleep. 'I came up for a lie-down and must have dropped off. What time is it?'

'One thirty.'

'I've been asleep for two hours!' She struggled further up and looked at him. 'Thanks for coming, Adam.'

He smiled and kissed her cheek, then put his arms around her and began slowly rubbing her back. It felt good. Her head relaxed against his chest as his chest and his arms encircled her: safe, strong and protective. This was what his touch should feel like, not the threat it sometimes seemed and from which she recoiled.

She felt his lips on her neck, heard his small sigh of pleasure. 'Do you think we'd be missed downstairs?' he breathed into her hair.

She laughed. 'Unfortunately, yes.'

'Pity. Your aunt said lunch was nearly ready.' With a final kiss he moved slightly away. 'I was going to take you out for a pub lunch, but Evelyn said she'd laid a place for me.'

'That sounds like Evelyn.' Mandy smiled, kissed the end of his nose and gave him another hug. Swinging her legs over the bed, she sat on the edge and looked at him seriously. 'I'm sorry I've been such a pig. I don't know what gets into me sometimes. I love you, yet sometimes I behave as if I hate you. Staying in this house hasn't helped. I mean I want to be with Grandpa but there's a lot of stuff going on here.'

'What sort of stuff?' Adam asked, puzzled.

She shrugged. 'All I know is that Dad and Evelyn had a huge argument when I was a child and somehow I was involved. I was taken from this house in the middle of the night. Then they didn't speak for ten years.' She stopped and hesitated. 'Dad hasn't said anything to you, has he?' As they'd spoken on the phone recently she wondered if he had.

'No. Yesterday he said you'd run out. When he phoned today he seemed to think it was because you were upset about Grandpa – that you needed a break. I know how you feel, Mandy. I was close to my granddad too.'

She nodded and looked at him, saw his empathy and concern, and was truly grateful. 'Grandpa's so poorly. Have you seen him yet?'

'No, I came straight up here to see you.'

'We had the nurse out twice last night, which was why I was so tired.' What else could she tell him? Now he was here normality had returned with him – sensible, level-headed Adam. She was here to help nurse Grandpa, and the strange visions from her past seemed distant and ludicrous again. 'I guess we should go down if lunch is ready,' she said, standing.

'Yes, I don't want to get in your aunt's bad books when we've only just met.'

She crossed to the dressing table and, picking up her hairbrush, ran it through her hair, then smoothed her jumper. 'Ready,' she said, crossing to the door.

Adam came up behind her and, nibbling her neck, gave her bottom a playful tap. 'Perhaps we could go for a walk later? Somewhere secluded,' he said.

'Yes, I'd like that.'

Downstairs there was a distinct smell of fish and Adam pulled a face. He was about to comment, but Mandy pointed to the kitchen door, which was slightly open, and Evelyn and Mrs Saunders could be heard putting the finishing touches to lunch. They continued through to the study, where Mandy kissed her parents and Adam kissed Gran. 'How are you, love?' her mother asked, concerned. 'I understand you had a rough night?'

Mandy glanced at Grandpa, whose legs were tapping restlessly beneath the sheets. 'We had to call the nurse out. He gave Grandpa an extra shot of morphine.'

Her father nodded. 'Evelyn explained.'

Her father looked tired and strained, Mandy thought. She knew how difficult it was for him to see his father like this. He was keeping a tight grip on his emotions but Mandy could see his vulnerability, which was so often masked by his reserve. Their roles seemed to have reversed since Grandpa became ill, and she was the one more in control, and she wanted desperately to protect him. 'Grandpa is always kept comfortable,' she said. 'He's never in pain. We make sure of it.' There was nothing to be gained by telling him other than what he desperately needed to hear.

The smell of fish crept into the study and Gran sniffed pointedly.

'It's rainbow trout,' Mandy said to her parents. 'I told Evelyn you liked it. I hope you do.'

'I hope so too,' Gran said dryly.

'She shouldn't have gone to all that trouble,' her mother said.

'My sentiment exactly,' Adam added.

'Now, now,' Mandy cautioned lightly, feeling the need to defend Evelyn in her absence. 'You can leave it, if you don't like it. Evelyn won't be offended.' It was too easy, Mandy thought, to come into the house and make fun of Evelyn and her meals if you didn't know it was their planning and preparation that probably kept her sane, and the routine of mealtimes that held their day together when everything else was falling apart.

Half an hour later they were all seated at the dining-room table tucking into the fish, apart from Adam, who apologized to Evelyn and said he rarely ate at midday, which was more or less true. Mandy found it strange having Adam suddenly seated at her aunt's table as one of the family – strange, but comfortable, natural. John talked easily to Adam, asking him about his work and the car he was rebuilding in the garage at his parents'. Mandy also noticed the conversation between John and Evelyn and her parents was more relaxed than it had been the last time her parents had visited. Gran noticed it too.

'Aren't they doing well?' she said quietly to Mandy across the table. 'Just shows they can behave when they want to.'

Mandy smiled in collusion. Gran sometimes referred to, and treated, her son and daughter like children, more so than she ever did her. But given they'd quarrelled and not spoken for ten years, it was hardly surprising: they'd behaved like children. Mandy wondered at the pain the family rift must have caused Gran, although she'd never mentioned it during the previous ten years. How ironic that it had taken something as sad as Grandpa's illness to heal the rift and have the whole family once more seated around the table and making conversation.

As the meal ended the nurse arrived and Evelyn suggested they take their coffee through to the lounge until the nurse had finished. Adam caught Mandy's eye. 'Shall we go for a walk?' he suggested.

'Sure,' Mandy said, and made a move towards the door.

'Don't go far,' Evelyn warned. 'Rain is forecast. You don't want another soaking, like yesterday. Why don't you go for a stroll in the grounds?'

'Suits me,' Adam said. 'There's a lot to see.'

Mandy agreed. She hadn't been in the grounds since arriving and she didn't really mind where they went. Adam waited in the hall while she changed into her outdoor shoes and then she led the way out through the side door. The air, like yesterday, was very fresh, and she shivered. 'Shall I get your coat?' Adam asked.

'No, you can keep me warm,' she giggled and, lifting his arm, draped it around her shoulders, then snuggled into his side.

They followed the path that led from the side door. It took them round the edge of the grounds to the rear of the pagoda where they couldn't be seen from the house. Adam paused and drawing her to him, kissed her passionately on the lips. She felt the tingle of desire and returned his kiss before they walked on.

'I'm so glad you came,' she said, wrapping her arms around his waist. 'I've missed you.'

'I've missed you too,' he said, and paused again for another lingering kiss.

The path they followed passed the sheds and greenhouses, away from the house and towards the lower gardens. They came to some steps and paused, looking out to the boundary fence in the distance. 'Is all this your uncle's?' Adam asked, impressed.

'Yes,' she said, following his gaze. 'But they have a full-time gardener. He has the weekend off.'

'Your uncle must have done very well. He told me he built up his business from scratch?'

'So I believe.' Mandy paused. 'But money isn't everything. I mean happiness is more important and money doesn't guarantee happiness, does it?'

'Agreed,' Adam said mischievously, 'but you can have both. I mean I'd be very happy with you if I won the lottery.'

She laughed and, tapping his arm, kissed his cheek. She felt light-hearted now and alive. This was how she wanted to be with Adam: receptive, tactile, and fun to be with, not moody and irritable. They continued down the steps and then followed the path as it curved to the right. As the lower lawns appeared Mandy let out a small squeal of delight. 'The swings! And slide! I don't believe it. They're still here. Sarah and I used to play here for hours. There was a wooden see-saw as well, but I guess that's rotted away.'

Grabbing his hand in excitement, Mandy ran with him to the slide, like a child in a park. The slide was very tall and old, and made of wrought iron. Metal steps led up to a wooden platform with short handrails where you waited for your turn. Mandy dropped her head back and looked up at the platform; saw it framed against the clouds beyond, exactly as she had done as a child.

'I haven't seen one like this for ages,' Adam said. 'Health and Safety would have a fit.'

'Do you think it's still safe to use?' Mandy asked.

'Stay there and I'll find out.'

Before she could stop him he was running up the steps two at a time, his shoes clattering on the metal. Arriving at the top, he tested the wooden platform with one foot and then stood on it and looked out. 'It's fine,' he called. 'You can see for miles up here!'

'Be careful!' she warned. She hated heights and could remember feeling dizzy up there, although she'd never had the nerve to stand and look out as Adam was doing now. She'd always made the transition from the top step to sitting on the slide by kneeling on the platform, and without looking down.

She watched as Adam turned to survey the view behind him; his body towered precariously above the short safety rail. She felt dizzy just watching him and looked away. Eventually he sat on the platform ready to slide down and she went to the end of the slide to watch his descent. Years of disuse had dulled the once shining metal and Adam came down slowly, squeaking and jerking, unlike when Sarah and she had whizzed down, she thought, so fast it had made their eyes water. He ground to a halt a yard from the end and jumped off. 'It needs polishing,' he said. 'Have you got a tissue?'

'No, I left my bag in the house.'

'Never mind, it will polish up. Race you!' he shouted.

Running round the slide he beat her to the steps. He was on the fourth rung as Mandy arrived, laughing. He raced up the steps two at a time as she followed more slowly. The metal handrails felt cold and rough and Mandy remembered her aunt saying one winter they shouldn't really wear gloves as it could make their hands lose their grip.

At the top Adam stood on the platform and beat his chest, then let out a Tarzan-like cry before disappearing down the slide.

Mandy laughed. Arriving at the top step she experienced the light-headedness she had done as a child while her heart raced with fear and excitement. *Don't look down,* she heard John say as he used to. *Hold on and look straight ahead.*

Keeping low, and gripping the handrail, she knelt on the wooden platform. Then, gingerly manoeuvring her legs into a sitting position, she pushed off.

Keep your hands in your lap, she heard John call, *or you'll get friction burn.* She shook her head and tried to clear her thoughts. She didn't want John here now – she was with Adam and trying to enjoy the day.

She waved at Adam waiting at the bottom and slowly descended. There was no chance of friction burn now – the unpolished surface acted as a brake and her descent was very slow. When she came to a halt she jumped off. 'I'm having another go!' she shouted.

'Me first!' he yelled and tore round to the foot of the steps, arriving just ahead of her. Laughing, she followed him up, faster this time, her confidence growing. With another Tarzan-like cry Adam beat his chest, then disappeared over the top and down the slide. She went after him. Jumping off the end, she chased him round and up the steps again, their feet clattering in pairs. Over and over again. Each time they came down the slide it was a little faster as their jeans polished the metal surface. She was out of breath, but enjoying herself so much; the house and Grandpa were out of sight and temporarily out of mind. They were like children, completely absorbed and playing unselfconsciously, just as … just as she had on the last weekend she'd stayed here.

Abruptly, without warning, she was jolted back into the past. *Mandy's turn,* she heard John call. It was a hot sunny afternoon, a Saturday, and she'd just climbed to the top of the slide. Evelyn and John had visitors. They'd all come down to the play area after lunch. The visitors had two small children who were too young to go on the slide or swings. She could see them playing with a large brightly coloured beach ball, which was nearly as big as they were. Sarah and she were taking turns racing down the slide. She was sitting at the top on the platform waiting for Sarah to finish and climb off the end. She could feel her hands clenched tightly around the rails either side; could see her legs straight in front, ready for the off. Her stomach was tight and her heart was racing from the rush of anticipation and fear she always felt as she waited for her go, so high up. It was a lovely day, the air was still and the sun beat on her face and head. She watched Sarah come to a halt and then jump off the end. Smoothing her dress down and taking a gulp of air she pushed off, remembering to put her hands in her lap as John instructed.

Down, down, she went, fast, faster, gathering speed, her dress billowing up in the rush of air and causing the bare skin on her thighs to squeak uncomfortably on the hot metal. A man appeared at the foot of the slide – not John, he was standing over to the left, but the male visitor whom she called Uncle. He was squatting on his haunches with his arms outstretched, waiting to catch her as he had done once before that afternoon. He was grinning over his thick moustache. She could see the whites of his teeth. She didn't want to be caught by him. She was thirteen and too old to be caught and tickled, but there was nothing she could do. She sailed down the last part of the slide, straight into his waiting arms. He lifted her high into the air, way above his shoulders, so she thought he and John could probably see up her dress. He set her down and she felt his moustache scratch her cheek as he gave her a little kiss. At the same time his fingers tickled under her arms. She turned to run after Sarah and felt his hand playfully slap her bottom.

'Don't do that!' she snapped, rounding on him. 'I don't like it!'

'Sorry,' Adam said, surprised, raising his hands in surrender. 'You should have said.'

'Oh.' She stared at him, confused. They were standing at the foot of the slide. She'd just come down and Adam must have slapped her bottom as she'd turned to run to the steps for their next go.

'Sorry,' he said again.

'It's OK,' she said quietly and moved away. 'We'd better get back. I don't like leaving Grandpa for too long.'

'No, all right.' He fell into step beside her, and then, slipping his arm around her waist, tried to kiss her, but she pulled away.

'We can be seen from the house,' she said.

Adam nodded. They walked side by side and in silence with his arm loosely around her waist. She knew she was being a cold, heartless bitch but the man with the moustache had unsettled her. She didn't want Adam to kiss her now, and the feel of his arm around her waist no longer offered the comfort and support it had on the walk down to the swings. She could still feel that man's hands around her waist as he'd lifted her high in the air and John had looked on, laughing. She thought John should have seen her distress and stopped the man. Sarah was a similar age; John should have known the embarrassment this type of attention caused. But he hadn't, indeed he'd laughed, colluding with the man and fuelling her embarrassment and discomfort. She remembered his laugh; it was almost as if he'd enjoyed it.

As they walked Mandy responded to Adam's comments about the grounds and the house with a nod or grunt. By the time they arrived at the side door to the house she'd fallen completely silent. Adam reached out and took her hand to stop her opening the door. 'Mandy, what have I done now?' he said with a sigh.

'Nothing.' She looked at him and shook her head. 'It's just a difficult time for me. I'm sorry.'

'All right, if you're sure. I think I understand.'

She was sure he didn't, couldn't possibly understand.

Twenty-One

Mandy knew there was no way Adam could have understood, even if she'd been able to tell him. Sympathize, yes, offer words of reassurance, but not understand. He couldn't have understood because she didn't understand herself. Why being held by that man had unsettled her and why John's laughter, his collusion, had upset her even more, she didn't know. It was all too much. She had enough to cope with with Grandpa being so poorly; the rest, including Adam, would have to wait.

It was nearly 11 p.m. and Mandy was gazing at the lava lamp, absently following a small red bubble which had recently broken away and was now floating aimlessly. A feeling of normality had returned to the house, and particularly to the study, now the weekend was over and their 'guests' had gone. Her parents were returning the following weekend, with Adam, unless she phoned to say they should come sooner. Evelyn had said that Sarah and Simon wouldn't be returning until the following Saturday either as Simon worked 'long hours in the City'.

They were like soldiers regrouping after an assault, Mandy thought, and she had to admit to a small sense of relief. An unspoken bond, a comradeship, had developed between the four of them from being with and nursing Grandpa, which made it difficult to include 'outsiders'. She was sure Evelyn and John felt it too: a slight resentment at having their territory infiltrated, even by close relatives and loved ones. But at least she'd seen Adam, and her parents had returned home reassured, having spent time with Grandpa who, while not waking, hadn't been uncomfortable between injections.

Mandy suddenly realized the tapping on the laptop beside her had stopped. She turned to look at John. His head rested on the chair-back, his eyes were closed and his lips slightly parted. With his muscles relaxed in sleep, there was little of the suave, successful businessman, who prided himself on keeping fit. More a heavy-jowled, slightly flabby, middle-aged man with deep expression lines across his forehead and either side of his mouth. Mandy wondered why she had chosen him to have a crush on, but then Sarah had chosen her father, which seemed even more incomprehensible. How could your own father have sex appeal! She thought back to John as he had been ten years before and guessed he would have been deemed handsome. He'd also listened and talked to her in an adult way when her parents had still treated her very much as a child, often dismissing her views as inconsequential. 'You'll learn,' had been her father's favourite expression when she'd dared to disagree with his opinion, meaning that when she grew up she'd realize he had been right. Whereas John had listened attentively to her views, taken them seriously, discussed issues with her, and had even sometimes agreed.

She looked at John's laptop. The coloured screensaver boxes flew steadily across the screen. She resisted the temptation to reach over and touch the mouse to see what he'd been viewing. He could wake at any time and she'd almost been caught once. Grandpa whimpered and then tried to sit up. Mandy was immediately on her feet and across the room.

'Grandpa, it's Mandy,' she whispered, leaning over the bed. 'Are you in pain? Do you want anything?' He whimpered again and then said something she didn't understand. 'Say it again,' she said gently, lowering her ear closer to his mouth.

'Water, Mandy,' he croaked.

'I'll get it.'

By the light of the red lava lamp she silently crossed the study and fetched the beaker of water they kept ready on the tray; returning, she knelt beside the bed. Sliding her arm under the pillow she eased Grandpa forward, at the same time tilting the beaker to his mouth. He'd lost so much weight he was light as a feather. He took a sip and licked his lips. 'Do you want some more?' she asked softly.

'No, thanks, love.'

She lowered the pillow and set the beaker on the floor. His eyes were still closed but his hand came out from under the covers, searching for hers. She took it. 'Hi, Grandpa. How are you?' she whispered.

He gave a small nod. 'Good. No pain,' he rasped. Then, very slowly and pronouncing each word separately: 'What time is it?'

'It must be nearly midnight now. It's Sunday. Mum and Dad came to see you today.'

'Ray?' he asked, his eyes opening.

'They're gone now. But Mum and Dad were with you all afternoon.' She rubbed his hand. 'They sat beside your bed and talked to you. You didn't say much.'

He nodded and gave a small laugh. 'And Lizzie?'

'Gran's in bed, asleep. Upstairs,' she added, in case he thought she was still in the single bed in the study. 'She's fine. Will you try and wake and speak to her tomorrow?'

'I'll try, but I'm very tired. I'm sure she understands.'

'I'm sure too.' Mandy smiled, and swallowed the lump rising in her throat. He spoke slowly and with great effort, but he hadn't been this awake for days and he wasn't in pain. She felt touched and privileged to be with him, but sorry Gran and her parents weren't here to be part of it. 'Gran sits here,' she said, tapping the chair beside the bed. 'All day. From nine o'clock in the morning until nine o'clock at night.'

'A twelve-hour shift then,' he said with a small smile.

'A labour of love,' she replied quickly, enjoying the repartee they usually shared.

'She's a good woman, my Lizzie. I'm a lucky man to have her.' He smiled again, and turned his head towards her, his glazed and red-rimmed eyes trying to focus.

'Shall I get your glasses?' Mandy asked.

He shook his head. 'I'll be asleep again soon.' Then he seemed to sense someone else was in the room. 'John?' he asked, trying to raise his head.

Mandy pointed. 'He's asleep in the chair over there.'

He nodded, and relaxed his head on to the pillow again. 'Evelyn?'

'She's asleep upstairs.'

'So there's just you awake, keeping me company?'

'That's right.' She smiled. 'I feel very honoured.'

His eyes, struggling to stay open, now closed. 'You're a good girl, Mandy,' he said faintly. 'It can't be easy seeing me like this. I am grateful.'

'There's no need to be grateful,' she said, now fighting back the tears. 'I like being with you, Grandpa. I'm pleased to help. I love you.'

But there was no reply. His eyes stayed closed and his head slowly fell to one side as he lapsed once more into unconsciousness. 'Grandpa?' she tried, but silence followed.

She remained where she was, kneeling beside the bed and holding his hand. It was a bitter-sweet moment – just the two of them locked together in the warm red glow of the lamp. His breathing slowly deepened and the gaps between each breath grew longer as he descended down through the layers of unconsciousness until his hand became limp in hers.

A few minutes later she heard John stir. Then he woke and stood up. 'Everything all right?' he asked, coming over and seeing the beaker beside the bed.

'Fine. Grandpa was awake.' She returned his hand to beneath the sheet. 'He spoke for a few minutes.'

John looked shocked. 'Are you sure he was conscious? With all that morphine? He hasn't been properly awake for ages.'

Mandy felt a niggle of irritation. 'Absolutely. He spoke very clearly and wanted a drink. He asked where everyone was and I told him. He was pleased Mum and Dad had visited.'

'So why didn't you wake me?' John asked, piqued. 'Didn't it cross your mind that I might want to see him while he was awake!'

'Sorry!' she said indignantly. 'Next time I'll run round and wake the whole house, shall I?'

'Don't be ridiculous,' John snapped, 'but it wouldn't have hurt you to have woken me. I'm in the same room, for Christ's sake!'

'All right! Point made!' she said, her voice rising. Standing, she brushed past him and stormed out of the study, and went down the hall to the cloakroom where she shut the door. He was the one who was being ridiculous. Pathetic! Behaving like a spoilt child who had missed out on a treat. Yet she had to admit there was some truth in what he'd said. If the situation had been reversed she would have wanted to have been woken – a reward for all the hours of nursing Grandpa when he'd been unresponsive. But it highlighted just how narrow and intense their lives had become that John and she had clashed over this.

Ten minutes later she returned to the study and without speaking sat in her armchair. John was intent on his laptop and didn't immediately look up. She went to plug in her iPod but before she did he said: 'I should apologize, Mandy.'

She looked at him. 'Don't worry. I've taken on board what you said.'

'Friends?'

She nodded.

Half an hour later Grandpa woke again and asked for the toilet. 'I'll see to it,' John said. 'You put the kettle on and make us some tea.' Since Grandpa had been using the urine bottle John had been the one to 'see to it', so preserving some of Grandpa's dignity and saving her embarrassment.

When she returned with the two mugs Grandpa was asleep once more. John left the study to empty the bottle. Grandpa woke again at 2 a.m. and was still pain-free and alert. They helped him further up the pillows and he asked for his glasses. Mandy passed them to him and showed him his cap.

He smiled. 'Just in case I pop out?'

'Well, you never know,' she joked.

She sat on the chair Gran usually occupied and John perched on the bed. It took time and concentration for Grandpa to form his words, as though it used all his energy, but he kept asking questions as if trying to regain his grip on the world: 'What's the date?' 'What time is it?' 'What was the weather like yesterday?' 'What's forecast for tomorrow?' 'Is someone collecting my mail?' 'Am I having my Warfarin?'

'Yes, Dad, don't worry,' John said, and Mandy nodded in agreement, but felt a stab of guilt at the last question. They had stopped giving him the Warfarin, which he'd been taking for years for his heart condition, when he'd no longer been able to swallow tablets. The doctor had confirmed there was no need to continue it. But Mandy now wondered if stopping the Warfarin was shortening his life, for with Grandpa awake and pain-free twice in two hours there almost seemed a glimmer of hope.

'Are my slippers here?' he asked Mandy with a knowing smile. 'I might need them tomorrow.'

'Yes, they're here, tucked under the bed.'

'Good. Can't be without my slippers or cap.' The slippers Mandy had given him for Christmas as she gave him slippers every Christmas although she'd tried to persuade him to have something different.

Presently she felt his hand go limp in hers. 'Tell Lizzie I love her,' he said before falling asleep.

He woke again just before dawn, but only briefly. 'You still here, love?' he said to Mandy with a smile, and then fell into a deep sleep. He was still asleep when the nurse came at 9 a.m. John told the nurse he'd been awake and asked about the Warfarin. 'If Mr Edwards wants his pills and can swallow them, he can have them,' the nurse said. 'They won't do him any harm.'

'Will they do him any good?' John asked.

The nurse hesitated. 'At this late stage, it's doubtful,' then added quickly: 'But it's good he didn't need the morphine in the night. He doesn't need another shot now either.'

John waited until they were outside the study and away from Gran before he asked the nurse directly what he thought of Grandpa's progress – for progress was how they'd come to view it. Evelyn was with them in the hall and Mandy watched the nurse as he struggled to find the right words to let them down gently: 'Mr Edwards's pulse is very weak. It's almost gone from his neck.

Reducing the morphine will allow him to be more awake, but call me straight away when he needs another shot.'

Mandy saw her own disappointment reflected on the faces of Evelyn and John as they nodded and knew they had to accept this.

'Doctors aren't always right,' Gran said when Mandy returned to the study, sensing the conversation that had taken place.

'No,' Mandy agreed, and sat in the chair beside her. But seeing Grandpa once more deeply unconscious, his emaciated head lolling to one side and the sickly grey tone to his skin, she understood why the nurse had been cautious and said what he had. It seemed almost impossible Grandpa had been awake and fully conscious or ever could be again. He was a shell of a man.

Yet an hour later he woke and, reaching for Gran's hand, said, 'How's my Lizzie doing?'

'Good!' she said, surprised. Then he asked for a glass of champagne. 'Champagne!' Gran exclaimed. 'You don't want champagne, Will. You need milk to build up your strength.'

Mandy called Evelyn and John and they grouped around the bed. 'If he wants champagne then he will have it,' John said. 'Any particular vintage, Dad?'

Grandpa gave a small chuckle and shook his head. 'Nothing too expensive. Don't want it going to waste.'

'No chance of that, Dad,' Evelyn said gaily, and giggled. There was a buzz in the room, a furtive excitement as though they were planning a forbidden party.

John left the study and Mandy thought it was typical of this house that John could produce a bottle of champagne just like that. She never had a bottle of champagne on hand (let alone a choice of vintage) and she doubted her parents stockpiled it either. John returned with the bottle and five champagne glasses on a silver tray and, with a certain ceremony, set it on the coffee table. The anticipation built as they watched him slowly peel the foil from the top of the bottle of champagne and then release the cork. It shot out with a loud pop that made them jump. Evelyn laughed and held out a glass to catch the foaming liquid.

'Shall I put yours in the beaker, Dad?' John asked.

Grandpa pulled a face. 'Champagne in a plastic beaker?' he exclaimed in mock disdain.

'Whatever was I thinking of?' John laughed. 'Thank goodness one of us hasn't lost his sense of decorum.'

He finished filling the glasses, passed them around and then took one to the bed. He tilted it as Grandpa sipped.

'Hmm, it's a good one,' Grandpa said between swallows.

Evelyn smiled. 'Only the best for you.'

There was something so pathetically touching in seeing Grandpa enjoying this little pleasure Mandy thought she was going to cry. Her heart went out to him almost as much as when he was in pain. But no sooner had he finished the champagne than he started to retch. John put down his glass and grabbed the bucket.

'There!' Gran said as Grandpa brought up the clear, still frothing liquid. 'I knew he should have had milk. It was too strong for his stomach.'

'I can usually hold my drink better than that,' Grandpa quipped. He lay his head back on the pillow and began to doze.

Yet despite not being able to keep down the champagne his progress, if that was what it was, continued throughout the morning and into the afternoon. Grandpa woke every hour or so for about five minutes, spoke to whoever was in the room, and wasn't in any pain. The nurse looked in every four hours, took his pulse and temperature and listened to his heart, but went away again without giving him an injection. Each time Grandpa woke he asked: 'What time is it?' a little anxiously as though he had a flight to catch or an important meeting to attend. Having been told the time, he asked the day, and then wanted confirmation: 'Is it twelve twenty-five on Monday then?' It was as though he wanted to keep a grip on his place in the world.

By three o'clock Mandy was wondering if she should telephone her parents and tell them of Grandpa's progress. She would have phoned them if his condition had deteriorated so shouldn't she give them the chance to see him while he was awake and doing well? She wasn't sure, and asked Gran what she thought.

'Ray will be at work,' Gran said.

'He has his mobile with him. I can phone him at work in an emergency.'

'It's a two-hour journey,' Gran said. 'Will could be asleep again by then. Why not see how he does tonight and phone your dad tomorrow?' Which seemed reasonable and Mandy agreed to.

At 5 p.m. Grandpa asked for something to eat, and their hopes soared further. 'But he hasn't eaten for over a week,' Evelyn said, trying to curb her enthusiasm. 'What would you like, Dad?'

'Something light,' Gran said.

'Bread and jam?' Evelyn suggested.

'Scrambled eggs?' John asked. 'It's what I have when I've got a funny tummy.'

'Scrambled eggs,' Grandpa agreed.

Ten minutes later they grouped around the bed again as Evelyn tucked a napkin under Grandpa's chin and spoon-fed him scrambled eggs from a china bowl. Five minutes later John was holding the bucket as Grandpa vomited it up. 'Will!' Gran said in dismay. 'What are we going to do with you?'

Grandpa shook his head. He seemed not to care. It was as

though his body didn't know what it was supposed to be doing: taking in food for energy and life, or shutting down ready for death. An hour later he asked for some bread and butter, but no sooner had he finished that than it reappeared, to Gran's dismay.

'We can't not give him food, if he asks,' Evelyn said anxiously. 'That would be cruel.'

When the nurse came at 6 p.m. Grandpa was in a light sleep and John told him about the food and vomiting. 'Because Mr Edwards isn't sedated his body is craving food,' the nurse explained. 'Shall I give him something to help him sleep?'

'But he isn't in pain,' Evelyn said. 'Does he need it?'

'Morphine acts as a sedative as well as relieving pain. It's up to you.'

Grandpa stirred and opened his eyes. 'Hello, Mr Edwards,' the nurse said gently. 'I hear you've been awake today. How are you feeling?' He took Grandpa's hand tenderly between his.

'Very tired,' he said, trying to focus.

'Would you like a shot to help you sleep?' the nurse asked, patting his hand.

To their surprise Grandpa answered, 'Yes.'

The nurse looked to them for confirmation. Evelyn reluctantly nodded and John said, 'If that is what he wants.'

Gran smiled sadly. 'Goodnight, Will. Hopefully we'll see you again tomorrow.' She leant forward and kissed him on the lips.

'Goodnight, my Lizzie. I love you.' He held her gaze, looked deeply into her eyes, and the years fell away. Mandy could see he was a young man again courting his Lizzie, his one and only love. Then he extended his arm ready for the injection that would send him to sleep. 'Night, my love,' he murmured as his eyes closed and his hand fell limp in hers.

Twenty-Two

When Mandy awoke just after 6 a.m. she felt pretty good, and rested. Grandpa had only woken twice in the night and had resettled easily, which had allowed her two three-hour sleeps in the armchair – more than she had at home if she'd been out late. She'd grown used to sleeping in the armchair, and because of her routine of showering and changing first thing had come to feel she was 'getting up' in the morning, only it was from a chair not a bed. However, she was aware that John, bigger built and older, was finding it more difficult sleeping in a chair. He rarely managed more than fifteen minutes at a time and always went upstairs for a lie-down in the morning once Evelyn was up.

John was asleep now but restless – more so than Grandpa, who lay on his back very still, breathing gently. Mandy wondered what Grandpa thought about when he was awake and if he'd contemplated or even prepared himself for death. She wondered if that was why he'd accepted the morphine the night before – that having mentally readied himself, and begun the journey, he simply wanted to get on with it. In which case, she supposed, there was something to be said for growing old and dying slowly – it gave you time to adjust; unlike suddenly being snatched from the world in a car accident or being struck down by cancer while young.

Standing, Mandy crept from the study and went upstairs to shower and change into fresh clothes. Having not left the house the day before because Grandpa had been so awake, and following Sunday, when she'd only walked in the garden with Simon, she felt she needed some fresh air and exercise, and also to get away from the house for a while. It was Tuesday and Mrs Pryce would be in the shop so she decided to walk into the village. She ate breakfast as usual with Gran, and once Gran was settled in the study with Evelyn and John had gone for a lie-down Mandy said: 'I was thinking of walking into the village. Do you want anything from the shop?'

She appreciated there was an element of playing devil's advocate in mentioning the store to Evelyn. 'No, thank you,' Evelyn said tartly.

'Can you see if they still do those sherbet lemons?' Gran said. 'I really fancy some of those.'

'Of course.'

'If you fetch my purse I'll give you the money.'

'No you won't,' Mandy refused. 'My treat. Anything else you fancy?'

'No. Thanks, love.'

Five minutes later Mandy slipped on her jacket, left the house and began a leisurely stroll along the lane and towards the village. It was very different from the way she'd left the house last time on Friday, when she'd fled after Simon's comments and had run most of the way into the village and the bus stop. Now she strolled and had time to take in and savour the country views. At nearly 10.40 a.m. the morning was already warm, 'unseasonably warm for the beginning of April', the weather report on her iPod radio had said. Mandy realized with a jolt that March had gone and a week had passed since her arrival at Evelyn's, although in some ways it seemed much longer. As she walked she took her mobile from her bag and texted Adam, asking him to check her flat and bring any mail with him when he came the following weekend. Assuming I'm still here, she thought, and Grandpa is still with us. And the fact that she could now acknowledge Grandpa might not be with them at the weekend showed she was adjusting to and gradually accepting the inevitable. She was better prepared now than she had been a week ago, she thought, and better prepared than she'd been when Lucy — a good friend at university — had suddenly developed a brain tumour in their second year and died three months later. It had been terrifying, the swiftness, and in someone her own age. She still thought of Lucy, who had been a kind and loyal friend. Her death should never have happened, Mandy thought, it was so unfair. And the shock of losing her so suddenly had stayed with Mandy, and would do for a very long time, possibly for ever.

She crossed the main road and continued past the church to the village shop. The bell clanged as she opened the green door, and then again as she closed it. She spotted Mrs Pryce straight away, over to her right, serving at the till. Mrs Pryce looked up to see who had come in and smiled when she saw it was Mandy, her previous coolness apparently forgotten. Mandy returned her smile and made her way round the lines of free-standing display units to the shelf containing sweets. She found a bag of sherbet lemons and chose a chocolate bar for herself. The post office counter in the recess was empty, as indeed was most of the shop. Apart from the woman paying at the till there was only one other customer, flicking through a swatch of curtain fabrics that could be ordered through the shop. Mandy waited until Mrs Pryce had finished serving before going over.

'How are you?' Mrs Pryce asked warmly. 'How's Mr Edwards? I've been thinking of you all.'

'Grandpa's not too bad,' Mandy said. 'Yesterday was very good. He was awake for most of the day, but the nights tend to be worse.'

Mrs Pryce nodded sympathetically. 'And your gran? How's she faring? Poor dear. They've spent a lifetime together; however will she manage without him?' She seemed more at ease and willing to talk than last time, and was making no attempt to ring up the items yet.

'Gran's doing all right, considering,' Mandy said. 'She doesn't say much. She just sits by his bed all day holding his hand. She's asked for these sherbet lemons.'

'Bless her. She always used to buy a packet of these when she could come into the shop. How's her arthritis?'

'Not too bad,' Mandy said. 'She uses a walking frame now.'

'She did the last time I saw her – must be over a year ago.' Finally drawing the items across the counter, she began entering them into the till; £1.65 showed. Mandy passed her two one-pound coins and waited for her change. The only other customer was still at the far end of the shop, now searching through the magazines.

'Thank you,' Mandy said as Mrs Pryce handed her the change. She dropped the coins in her purse and zipped it up, silently steeling herself for what she had to say. 'I hope you don't mind,' she began tentatively, 'but I was wondering if I could ask you something?' She felt her pulse begin to race.

'Yes?' Mrs Pryce asked amicably. 'I'll help you if I can,' supposing, Mandy thought, that she was going to enquire about an item in the store.

'I was wondering …' Mandy said, 'why you left my aunt's house to work in the shop? As I remember you used to say how happy you were – that you wouldn't want to work anywhere else. I'm puzzled as to what made you leave.'

Mrs Pryce's initial expression of affable curiosity vanished and her face grew serious. 'I was asked to leave,' she said stiffly. 'By your uncle.'

'Oh, I'm sorry. I didn't realize,' Mandy said, although it had crossed her mind this might have happened.

'No, well, you were out of the area by then, but most people round here knew. It made things very difficult for me.'

'Yes, I can see that. I'm sorry,' Mandy said again. 'I'd no idea.' She looked at Mrs Pryce, aware she didn't have the right to ask the obvious next question, but knew she had to ask it anyway. The other customer was still occupied at the far end of the shop. They couldn't be overheard.

'I hope I'm not being insensitive,' Mandy began, 'but can I ask why my uncle asked you to leave?'

'You don't know?' Mrs Pryce asked aghast, meeting her gaze. 'No.'

'And you can't guess? You must, surely?'

'No.' Mandy shook her head and felt her pulse beat even faster. Mrs Pryce's expression said she was finding it almost impossible to believe what she'd just heard. Just as Evelyn and Gran had when Mandy had said she couldn't remember. 'I know there was a family argument all those years ago.' She had to say something. 'But I've no idea what. My memory of that time is very fuzzy. I think something bad might have happened, but I really don't know what. Try as I might I can't remember, although I'm sure you were there.' She stopped. Mrs Pryce was staring at her, incredulous.

'I don't know what to say,' she said at last. 'What have your parents told you?'

'Nothing. It's never been mentioned. My parents stopped seeing my aunt and uncle ten years ago, and probably wouldn't have seen them again had it not been for Grandpa going there from hospital. I didn't even know anything had happened until I arrived at my aunt's and realized I could remember some things, but not others. Then I started having strange thoughts, dreams, images – like images from the past.'

Mrs Pryce was still watching her curiously. 'And your aunt and uncle haven't said anything to you?'

'No.'

Glancing away, she pursed her lips. 'So they did hush it up,' she said quietly. 'I thought they might when they fired me and warned me never to speak of it. But your gran?' she asked, surprised. 'You were always close to your gran. She must have explained?'

Mandy shook her head. 'We are still close, but Gran said as it was my father's decision not to speak of it I must ask him, which I will when the time is right. But not now.'

A flash of pity ran across Mrs Pryce's face and then she looked away, collecting her thoughts. When her gaze returned Mandy had a good idea what she was going to say: 'Look, love, I'm sorry you're having to deal with all this as well as your dear grandpa being ill, but it isn't my place to tell you what happened in your family. I expect your father did what he thought was best. Your gran is right – you need to ask him, then your mother can support you.'

'Support me?'

But Mrs Pryce was shaking her head. 'No, I'm sorry, love, you must ask your parents. It was a difficult time for me as well. I don't want to go back over it all now.' She began busying herself with something on the counter and Mandy knew the conversation was at an end and the subject closed, for good.

'I'm sorry,' Mandy said again, moving away. 'I didn't mean to upset you. Thank you for talking to me. Goodbye.'

'Goodbye, and take care,' she said without looking up. Mandy left the shop.

The word 'support' latched itself on to Mandy's mind and wouldn't let go. Support meaning she needed help – as in therapy? Did Mrs Pryce think she wasn't coping and needed therapy – or would do in the future? Those with problems had support; victims of abuse or disasters had support. Was she a victim in need of counselling and support? If so, why? Until she'd come to her aunt's house she'd always considered herself well balanced and, until now, no one had suggested any differently. Her mobile went off, and pulling it from her bag she saw it was Adam's number.

'Yes?' she said tersely, shaken from her thoughts. 'Aren't you at work?'

'I'm on my way to a meeting. I thought I'd grab the chance and give you a ring. Is it a bad time?'

'No, I'm not in the house. I've gone for a walk.' She hesitated, then came to a halt in the centre of the path. She concentrated on the overhanging branch of a tree that was straight ahead. 'Adam, can you think of any reason why I might need support? You know – emotional support, to overcome something?'

'No, why?'

'Someone here thinks I might.'

She heard him give a small laugh. 'They obviously don't know you now.'

'Now? What do you mean *now*? Did I need support in the past?'

'No, I didn't mean … It was nothing, really.'

'I would still like to know. Have I ever needed support?' She heard his pause. He was probably wishing he hadn't phoned. 'Adam?' she persisted.

'All right. When we were first at Uni the word was you didn't date, which was why it took me so long to ask you out. There was a feeling among those who knew you that perhaps you'd had a bad experience with a bloke and didn't want guys near you.'

'What! Just because I wasn't leaping in and out of bed with everyone!'

'I guess. As I said, it was nothing, and once I got to know you I realized you were fine, until ...'

'Until what?'

'Well, recently, you've obviously been under a lot of pressure.' He paused again. 'Look, Mandy, I wouldn't let the comment bother you. You're fine. I've got to go into the meeting soon. How's Grandpa?'

She was silent for a moment, then dragged her thoughts back. 'He was asleep when I left him this morning.'

'And he's comfortable?'

'Yes. I know this sounds insensitive, but in some ways I'll be pleased when this is all over. Grandpa is very old and ill, and I think I've accepted he's not going to get better. Do you realize I've been here a week?'

'Yes, and I miss you.'

She felt a frisson of warmth. 'I miss you too.'

'Good, because I've been thinking. When you get back we should talk about putting our relationship on a firmer footing. Move in together. I think a lot of our problems are because we simply don't get to spend enough time with each other. I know you haven't been keen in the past – wanting to do your painting, but you will be able to continue that. And with my money going into the house it would be easier for you.'

After the way she'd treated him and he still wanted to be with her! She didn't deserve him, she really didn't. But she wasn't sure.

They'd had their problems – what would it be like if they were together all the time and neither of them had a bolt hole? 'Yes, we should talk about it,' she said at length.

'Good. And if you feel getting married would help, we could talk about that too.'

She gave a small laugh. 'OK, we've plenty to talk about!'

She said goodbye and, dropping her phone into her bag, continued down the lane towards her aunt's house. Dear Adam, he was trying so hard to make her happy by doing and saying the right thing. And in some ways it did make sense to move in together, although marriage was a different matter. Had he envisaged moving in with her or was he proposing they rent somewhere new together? He hadn't said. Her thoughts briefly returned to his comment about her not dating at Uni, and she dismissed it. During those first terms at Uni, when many students suddenly discovered the freedom of living away from home, if you weren't having continuous sex you were considered frigid. But as Adam said, once he'd got to know her he knew she didn't have a problem. No, she didn't need support.

Following the footpath Mandy turned the corner and the drive came into view. Immediately she saw the nurse's car; either he was an hour early, which hadn't happened before, or he had been called. She began to run down the drive. Dear God, she had wished it was all over! But she hadn't meant now!

She pressed the bell and Mrs Saunders appeared straight away. Mandy knew immediately from her expression something was badly wrong. 'They're all in the study,' she said quickly, taking Mandy's jacket. 'The nurse is with Mr Edwards now.'

Mandy felt fear curl around her as she hurried down the hall and into the study. The nurse was rolling down Grandpa's pyjamas sleeve, having just given him an injection. Gran was sitting beside the bed, with John and Evelyn standing either side of her. They all looked up as she entered and her fear deepened she saw the look on their faces. 'He woke but was in the most dreadful pain,' Evelyn said, her face crumbling. John put his arm round her and comforted her.

Mandy stood at the end of the bed and looked at Grandpa. Although his eyes were closed and his features were relaxing as the injection took effect, something in his face told her he'd taken a turn for the worse from which he was unlikely to recover. His skin, stretched thinly across his cheekbones, was so grey it seemed impossible that blood was still running through. And there was a stillness about him which tore at Mandy's heart, as though life had become one stage removed. 'Shall I phone my parents and tell them to come?' she asked.

Evelyn and John looked at the nurse.

'I think that would be nice,' he said.

Mandy stepped outside the study. With her fingers shaking and her heart drumming loudly she took her mobile from her bag and pressed her father's number.

'Mandy,' he said, anxiety already in his voice. 'What is it?'

'You need to come now, Dad. Grandpa probably won't make it until Sunday.' She heard her voice break.

'I'm on my way.'

Twenty-Three

wo hours later Mandy fell into her mother's arms, and the
tears she'd been keeping a tight lid on flowed freely. 'I should
have phoned you yesterday, when he was awake,' she sobbed. 'He's
so poorly now. I'm sorry.'

They were in the hall; her father was still in his office suit,
having stopped by home only to collect her mother.

'Don't upset yourself,' her father said awkwardly as her mother
stroked her hair. 'We said our goodbyes on Sunday. Grandpa
understands.'

Evelyn appeared in the hall and, with her guard lowered from
emotion, came over and kissed and hugged her brother and sister-
in-law unreservedly. 'Thanks for coming,' she said. 'It was the right
thing to do. The nurse has been and Dad is more comfortable now.'

They followed Evelyn into the study where John and Gran were
sitting by the bed. John shook her father's hand warmly and then
kissed her mother's cheek. He fetched more chairs from the
dining room, which he arranged around the bed. They sat in a
large semi-circle, mainly in silence, and looked at Grandpa as the
minutes ticked by.

It was as though they were waiting for something, Mandy
thought, although what, exactly, no one could have said. Often
the only sound in the room was Grandpa's breathing, his breaths
so far apart now it seemed impossible he would ever take the next.
His legs and arms occasionally twitched beneath the sheet, and

from time to time he moaned in his sleep, but his eyes didn't open and he didn't appear to be in pain. A strange, almost sweet smell began to drift from the bed, which hung in the air and would not disappear despite Evelyn opening the window. It was unlike anything Mandy had ever smelt before and she wondered if this was what was meant by the 'smell of death'. Did the body give off its own strange perfume as it gradually closed down? An essence distilled from the life it was losing? She knew she couldn't ask, but she could tell the others smelt it too.

They sat grouped around the bed, only leaving to go to the toilet as the day slowly passed. The nurse came again at two o'clock clearly expecting this visit to be his last. But as the hours passed Grandpa's condition began to stabilize. When the nurse came again at four o'clock he said his pulse rate was the same as it had been yesterday. 'That's good,' her father said, and Gran nodded. Mandy wasn't sure.

Shortly after 5 p.m. Evelyn said she would ask Mrs Saunders to make sandwiches and a pot of tea, and they could have it in the study. Mandy's parents nodded gratefully and thanked her, and Mandy was pleased they were staying. But she saw the strain on their faces and knew they were emotionally exhausted and couldn't take much more of just sitting beside the bed, watching and waiting. She had begun to regret phoning them and telling them to come, for what purpose had it served? Grandpa didn't know they were here – the only positive was that it was nice for Gran to have both her children beside her.

After they'd eaten Evelyn suggested she ask Mrs Saunders to make up a bed so they could stay the night. Mandy was relieved her father refused: 'We'll wait until the nurse comes again, and then make tracks,' he said. Mandy knew he couldn't cope with another day of just sitting hour after hour by his father's bed.

Grandpa couldn't have coped with it either if he'd been in the same situation; they were both men who needed to be doing something.

'I'll phone if there's any change,' Mandy reassured her father, although she knew she wouldn't be calling him to bring him to his bedside for more of this.

The nurse returned shortly before 8 p.m. and they all left the study while he washed and changed Grandpa and gave him an injection. When he'd finished he called them in and said he'd put Mr Edwards in incontinence pants as he was wet. Mandy felt their collective guilt at not having noticed Grandpa had wet himself. He'd given no indication he needed the toilet, so no one had thought to check beneath the sheets.

A few minutes later Mandy hovered by the study door as Evelyn and John showed the nurse out, and her parents said what they assumed would be their last goodbye to Grandpa. Her mother stroked his forehead lovingly and told him he was very brave and what a smashing father-in-law he'd been. 'You've been the best,' she said. 'I couldn't have wished for anyone kinder and more supportive.' Her father stood to one side and repeatedly cleared his throat in an effort to choke back his tears. Their pain was pitiful to watch and Mandy wished they would just go.

'Try not to upset yourself, Jean,' Gran said. 'Will's had a good life. He wouldn't want a lot of fuss.' Which made her mother cry all the more and she moved away from the bed.

'Dad,' her father said, finally going forward. He lowered his mouth closer to Grandpa's ear. 'I want you know there's nothing for you to worry about. Evelyn and I have patched up our differences and we're friends again.'

Although Grandpa gave no sign he had heard, Mandy saw the look on Gran's face and could have wept. 'Thanks, Ray,' she said, touching his arm. 'That means a lot. I'm sure Will knows.'

Her father straightened, kissed Gran's cheek and then said goodbye quickly before emotion got the better of him and he broke down completely. Gran stayed in the study while Mandy went with her parents to see them out. She stood in the porch in front of Evelyn and John and watched her parents cross the drive and get in the car. The night air was cold; she shivered and crossed her arms protectively across her chest. The interior light of the car came on, and then slowly dimmed and went out. The wipers flicked across the windscreen, clearing the thin layer of dew, and the engine burst into life. Mandy watched the car slowly come towards them and sweep round the carriage driveway. As it drew level her parents gave a small wave and managed to raise a smile. Mandy smiled and waved, just as she had countless times as a child when they'd dropped her off to stay the weekend, or for a few days during a school holiday. But whereas then she'd brimmed with excitement at the prospect of staying with Sarah, now she felt a deep sense of foreboding which could only partly be explained by Grandpa's condition.

They returned inside and to the study. Evelyn made Gran Ovaltine and then asked Mandy if she would like to sleep upstairs: 'Your dad said you were looking tired. You haven't had a proper night's sleep since you arrived.'

'I'm fine,' Mandy reassured. 'I *do* sleep in the chair, and it's more important you have a reasonable night, with everything you have to do.' But if she was honest she didn't want to sleep upstairs. Something told her it was safer downstairs in the study with Grandpa and the warm red bubbles of moving light.

'All right, if you're sure,' Evelyn said, and then added as she did every night: 'Wake me if I'm needed.'

* * *

172

However, unlike the previous nights Mandy now found she couldn't sleep; in fact she couldn't even close her eyes. There was something different about tonight, something that had begun that morning and, although Grandpa had stabilized, now continued. There was an almost tangible air of expectation, as though the waiting of the afternoon and evening was about to reach fruition. Although how, she couldn't have said. A sign maybe? Chariots of winged angels appearing from the heavens? She didn't think so. But something had shifted and she was sure John felt it too. He was very restless and couldn't settle to his work. Every so often he stood and, placing his laptop on the coffee table, wandered over to the bed and checked on Grandpa, then returned, without speaking, to his chair.

Mandy rested her head on the chair-back and watched the red swirls of moving light coming from the lamp as she absently counted off the seconds between Grandpa's breaths. The gaps had widened considerably over the last week and his breaths had also grown shallower, almost as if he was taking them with token effort, just to keep his family happy. Reaching down beside the chair she took her phone from her bag and checked the time. It wasn't midnight yet, but it seemed an eternity since the daylight had gone and her parents had left. Another red bubble of oil broke off in the lamp and drifted away. The breathing continued in the background, then stopped. Grandpa suddenly sat bolt upright and cried out in pain.

They were both out of their chairs and by the bed. 'It's all right, Dad,' John reassured, placing his hands on his shoulders. 'We're here.'

Grandpa's eyes were screwed shut and beads of sweat stood on his forehead. 'Help me,' he cried, doubling over. 'Don't let me suffer.'

'I'll call the nurse,' John said.

'No! No more. Make it end, please. You said you would help me. You promised!'

John flinched. He hesitated, then said, 'Come and stand here, Mandy, while I call the nurse.'

'No!' Grandpa cried, but John ignored him.

Mandy went round to where John had been at the bed-head and began gently massaging Grandpa's shoulders, trying to ease away the pain. John picked up the phone on the desk and keyed in the numbers he knew by heart. 'Damn! His phone's off. It's gone through to his voicemail.' He severed the line and tried again. Grandpa called out.

'It's all right,' Mandy soothed, supporting and massaging his shoulders. 'John is phoning the nurse.' She could feel his shoulder blades poking through the material of his pyjamas; there was nothing of him – surely not enough to maintain life.

'It's John Osborne,' John said, leaving a message on the nurse's voicemail. 'Please come as soon as you can. Dad is in a lot of pain.' He waited to see if the nurse would pick up; when he didn't he replaced the receiver. Grandpa gave another cry and doubled forward again.

'The nurse is on his way,' John lied. Mandy met his gaze and saw his fear and helplessness.

She stood aside to let him take over and John began massaging Grandpa's shoulders. Going round to the side of the bed, Mandy took one of Grandpa's hands in hers and began rubbing the cold, damp skin. But unlike before, when he'd responded by curling his fingers around hers, they remained rigid with pain. John continued massaging but it didn't help; Grandpa was past being soothed. She looked at his grey face, contorted with agony, and the emaciated neck jutting birdlike from his pyjama collar, and prayed the pain would stop. *Stop it, please, for good, and give him the peace he deserves.* 'Is there nothing we can do?' she asked help-lessly, looking at John.

Grandpa cried out again. 'Help me!' he begged.

John was silent for a moment, then his hands became still and he stopped massaging. His voice was low and tight when he spoke. 'Dad, do you want me to help you end it?'

'Yes,' Grandpa rasped. He clutched his stomach as the waves of pain lashed over him.

In the red glow of the lamp Mandy felt her heart cramp with fear. She looked at John as he slowly took his hands from Grandpa's shoulders and moved away from the bed. He crossed to the desk where the water and beaker were on the tray and took off the lid. She knew he had made a decision but she was too scared to ask what he was going to do. Suddenly they both froze as the door chime sounded in the hall. He looked at her and their eyes locked, complicit in guilt. Neither of them dared move. Then John took his hand from the beaker and headed towards the study door. 'It must be the nurse,' he said. 'It can't be anyone else.'

Mandy allowed herself to breathe again.

Twenty-Four

John had left the study door open and, through it, Mandy could hear him go down the hall and open the front door. She heard him greet the nurse, and then Evelyn, who must have been woken by the door chime, said something, although Mandy couldn't hear what. Mandy sat on the edge of the bed, stroking Grandpa's hand, talking, trying to reassure him. The nurse appeared in the study first, followed by John and then Evelyn, who switched on the main light. Mandy blinked against the sudden brightness after the red glow. She stood and moved away from the bed to allow the nurse access. He took Grandpa's pulse and listened to his chest. Grandpa tried to cooperate by breathing in and out when told. But when the nurse asked if he could lie down Grandpa shook his head and remained bent forward. 'We need to make you more comfortable,' the nurse said, and looked to John for assistance. John went to the bed and, taking a shoulder each, they slowly eased Grandpa down. But as his head touched the pillow and his back straightened, losing the last of the C curve, he cried out in torment.

'Oh Dad,' Evelyn said, her hand shooting to her mouth. Mandy put her arm around her.

'Soon have you asleep,' the nurse said gently. He took two sterilized packages from his bag and, tearing them open, assembled the injection.

'Can't you increase the dose?' John asked in desperation.

'Unfortunately not. I can't even give him all this.' He held up the phial and tapped it. 'On top of what he's already had it could kill him.'

Mandy met John's gaze and knew what he was thinking.

They watched as the nurse shot some of the morphine into a tissue before lowering the waistband on Grandpa's pyjamas and injecting him in the only flesh he had left: at the top of his thigh. Mandy wondered if Grandpa was aware that some of the morphine had been withheld, which to a man who was begging for permanent release from pain would seem like an added torture. The morphine took immediate effect and Grandpa's face relaxed and he drifted into sleep. The nurse disposed of the used syringe and morphine-soaked tissue in a small plastic box, which he returned to his bag. He then took out another sealed package, which Mandy saw held a clean pair of incontinence pants. As she had done previously she left the study while the nurse changed him.

She went into the kitchen, where she filled the kettle and set it to boil. What exactly had John been about to do to end Grandpa's suffering when he'd removed the lid on the beaker? What would she have been an accomplice to had not the nurse arrived in time? In some ways it was a great pity Grandpa had been so opposed to staying in hospital where pain relief was presumably always on hand, and effective.

A few minutes later she heard John and Evelyn see the nurse out. Then they came into the kitchen and Mandy passed them a mug of tea each. They leant against the kitchen cabinets and sipped their drinks, none of them in any hurry to leave and return to the study. Grandpa would be deeply unconscious straight after the morphine so wouldn't need anything for a while, and there was a cosiness and a sense of normality in standing in the kitchen having a hot drink.

'Gran didn't wake then?' Mandy asked after a moment.

'She wouldn't have heard the bell,' Evelyn said, 'not without her hearing aid, poor dear.'

With her hair uncombed and no make-up, Evelyn looked much older than she did during the day. The strain of nursing Grandpa and all the accompanying worry and upset showed in the lines of her face. Mandy felt sorry for her: she seemed so fragile. She was pleased her father and Evelyn had made up their argument and were now comfortable in each other's company. It was just a pity it had taken ten years, she thought, and Grandpa's illness to do it. When Evelyn spoke again there was a finality in her voice that hadn't been there before, as though she'd been considering something and had come to a conclusion. 'God only knows why the nurse didn't give Dad the full injection. In some countries they help people at the end.'

'But not here,' John said. 'If the nurse had given Dad the extra morphine, aware it could kill him, he could have been prosecuted.'

'And who's going to tell? Us?' she challenged. 'Hardly. It would have been a relief for Dad. He can't take any more and he doesn't deserve this. He should be allowed a dignified and pain-free end.'

John glanced at Mandy. There was a small silence when Evelyn's words hung in the air – as though she had just given them permission to do whatever might be necessary. 'I know,' John said quietly after a moment. 'I completely agree. But we can't ask the nurse.'

Evelyn nodded and looked away.

In that moment there was a tacit agreement, Mandy thought, that Grandpa wouldn't be allowed to suffer any longer. But only they could be the ones to put a stop to it. It would be up to them.

After a few moments Evelyn crossed the kitchen and placed her empty mug in the dishwasher. 'Mandy, are you all right to continue or do you want to go to bed?'

'I'm all right,' Mandy confirmed. John nodded.

An hour later John had closed his laptop and was trying to doze, while Mandy, her head resting on the chair-back, was again following the red bubbles of moving light. Although it was only an hour since the injection, Grandpa was already very restless; his limbs jumped beneath the sheets and he groaned in his sleep. Suddenly he was bolt upright again and crying out in torment. They both leapt out of their chairs. Mandy went to the bed as John grabbed the phone to call the nurse. 'Perhaps he'll change his mind about the injection now,' he said bitterly. Mandy saw his anger and frustration and was a little afraid.

The nurse answered and said he would come straight away. 'Twenty minutes,' John said to Mandy as he put down the receiver and joined her at the bed.

Grandpa moaned in agony and, leaning forward, clutched his stomach. 'The nurse is coming,' Mandy reassured him.

'Hold on there, Dad,' John added, a tight edge to his voice.

John moved to the bed-head and tried massaging Grandpa's neck and shoulders, while Mandy sat on the bed and held his hand as they had before. But Grandpa's pain was so far past being soothed that their pathetic attempts seemed risible. Bent double, with his arms closed across his stomach, it was as though he was trying to contain the pain, stop it at its source. He cried out, dry-retched, called on God to help him, and then somehow found the strength to raise his voice at them: 'You promised! You said you'd help me!'

'I know, Dad,' John cried, then: 'For fuck's sake, where the hell's the nurse? It's been twenty minutes.' Storming from the bed he crossed to the desk to phone the nurse again. 'It's on fucking voicemail!' he shouted and kicked the desk chair, sending it crashing to the floor. Grandpa started and then whimpered, upset and frightened.

'That's not going to help!' Mandy snapped.

'And what do you know?' John yelled, rounding on her.

'John?' Grandpa asked weakly and tried to turn his head in the direction of the noise.

'It's all right,' Mandy soothed. 'The nurse won't be long.'

She looked at John standing by the desk with the phone still in his hand. In the red glow of the lamp she could see his face set hard with fury and his eyes wide and staring. She saw his anger and knew at that moment he was out of control. Reason and rational thought had left him; he was capable of anything, and she needed to protect Grandpa.

A few seconds later the doorbell rang. 'Thank God,' she breathed.

John stormed out of the study, flicking on the main light as he went.

'John?' Grandpa asked again. He sounded frightened.

'Don't worry,' she said soothingly. 'John is upset.'

'Because of me?' Grandpa asked, his head still bent forward on his chest.

'No, not because of you, love,' Mandy said. And as she spoke the words she had the strangest feeling she'd heard them before. She could hear them being spoken, but when and by whom? *John is upset ... because of me? ... No, not because of you, love ...* She couldn't place them although she knew they were real. Like the other words and pictures that had come to haunt her they'd landed in her head without warning.

John reappeared with the nurse. Evelyn hadn't come downstairs this time; whether the bell had woken her or not, Mandy didn't know. The nurse took the sterilized packages from his bag and shot some of the morphine into a tissue before injecting him. Mandy thought it was just as well Evelyn wasn't here to see it. 'If you can't give Dad all of it,' John said tightly, his anger just under control. 'Can't you give him something stronger?'

'I'm sorry, Mr Osborne, there really isn't anything stronger. But I'll come as often as required to top up the pain relief. I can be here in under half an hour if necessary.' Mandy saw the look on John's face and knew exactly what he was thinking: half an hour was an eternity when Grandpa was in acute pain.

'I suggested a live-in nurse,' John said quietly. 'But Evelyn won't hear of it. She promised her father she'd look after him.'

The nurse nodded and Mandy looked away as he checked Grandpa's incontinence pad, which he said was dry. He said he'd visit again at 6 a.m. unless he heard from them sooner. The anger had completely left John now Grandpa was out of pain; he thanked the nurse for coming and then showed him out. Mandy switched off the main light and returned to the armchair. She took her mobile from her bag and checked the time. It was 2.23 a.m.

She was half expecting an apology from John, but when he returned to the study he went to the bed, checked on Grandpa, and then sat in the other armchair without speaking or even acknowledging her. Opening his laptop, he began scrolling and typing, so Mandy plugged in her iPod and closed her eyes.

When she woke it wasn't from Grandpa's cries – she still had her earpieces in – but from a hand on her arm, holding too tight and tugging. She opened her eyes, at the same time taking out her earpieces. John was trying to pull her out of the chair. Although startled and disorientated, she was awake enough to realize Grandpa was sitting up in bed in pain. 'What? What time is it?' she mumbled.

'Three fifteen. I want you to leave the room,' John said, and propelled her towards the door.

She resisted. 'Why? Have you called the nurse?'

'No, there's no point. It's only an hour since the last injection. He can't do anything.'

She jerked her arm free and stared into John's face. His pupils were dilated and she could hear his breath coming fast and shallow. Grandpa cried out again and dry-retched. 'I'll call the nurse,' Mandy said.

'No, you won't,' John hissed. 'He can't help any more. There is nothing he can do.' He was standing in front of her, blocking her way to the bed and phone, his face too close to hers. 'Look at him, Mandy!' he demanded. 'Do you want him to go on suffering? Look at him. It's pathetic!'

Mandy looked towards the bed as Grandpa screamed again. He was doubled up, his scrawny neck bent forward and barely able to support the weight of his head. Tears welled in her eyes. 'Do as I say, Mandy,' John said. 'Go into the kitchen and stay there until I tell you.'

She held his gaze and panic gripped her. 'What are you going to do?'

'Don't ask, Mandy, just do as I say. Go into the kitchen and stay there. If Evelyn comes down, keep her there too.' The study door suddenly opened in front of her and she felt his hand in the small of her back. With one small push she was in the hall and the door closed firmly behind her.

Twenty-Five

*D*on't ask. Just do as I say. Keep quiet and you won't be hurt. Her legs trembled and she leant against the work surface in the kitchen for support. *Don't scream or I'll have to kill you.* She could feel her chest tighten as the words spun in her head. She couldn't breathe. Someone was lying on top of her, crushing the air out of her lungs. *Don't ask. Just do as I say.*

Then her two worlds collided and she remembered

It was John, John's voice, then as now. *Don't ask. Just do as I say. Keep quiet and you won't be hurt.* Close, too close – his face pushing into hers, and the pressure of his chest forcing the air out of her lungs. She was on her back, arms pinned to her sides, and John was on top of her. She could smell his sweat mingled with the soap he used, the heat of his body, the stubble on his chin as he tried to kiss her. She was lying helpless in the dark, too frightened to cry out, having woken in the night to find him on top of her, forcing her legs apart, trying to drive himself inside her. She knew now what had happened. Since arriving she'd known something was wrong, something was trying to free itself from her subconscious, something that had to be remembered. And John's words now, nearly identical to those spoken ten years ago, had brought her two worlds together and made her remember. The monster had tried to rape her! And now he was alone with Grandpa!

Her chest heaved, bile rose in her throat, and her head felt as if it was about to explode. She wanted to run, run from the house

183

and never stop, but she knew she had to stay to protect Grandpa. Pushing herself away from the work surface she hurtled across the kitchen and into the hall. Without hesitating and ignoring John's warning to stay out, she flung open the study door. 'Don't touch him!' she cried. 'Keep away from him. I know now! You monster!'

John looked up, startled. He was leaning over the bed with a pillow in his hand. 'Get away from him!' she cried, raising her fist and rushing towards him. John straightened and took a step back. Grandpa's eyes were closed and he lay very still. She couldn't see or hear him breathing. 'What have you done?' she shouted. 'What have you done to him?'

'Nothing,' John said, shocked and confused. 'I couldn't.' The pillow slipped from his hand and fell to the floor. She heard Grandpa take a breath.

'Bastard!' she hissed, turning to John. 'I hate you! All this time and you never said a thing. You sat in here night after night, knowing what you did and pretending nothing had happened. I thought I was going mad – seeing and hearing things. But I wasn't, I was remembering! Something so dreadful my mind had blocked it out, until now. You evil bastard! I was just thirteen and you tried to rape me!' Opening her fist, she slapped his face hard. His hand went instinctively to his cheek as he stared at her. She went to slap him again but he grabbed her wrist and pushed her arm out to one side. 'Mandy?'

'Let go, you monster!' she shouted, and kicked his leg.

He flinched. 'Mandy,' he gasped. 'It wasn't like that. You've got it wrong. I loved you and I –'

'Bastard!' she cried again before he could finish. Wrenching her hand free, she fled the room.

She ran along the hall, tears streaming down her cheeks, praying he wouldn't come after her. Where to go to be safe? She was in a monster's house. She ran into the cloakroom, pulled on the light, slammed the door and turned the key. 'Bastard!' she wept. 'Fucking bastard!' She leant heavily against the door. How dare he say he loved me? How could he? He was my uncle and I trusted him. I looked upon him as a second father. All those nights in the study, caring for Grandpa together, with him knowing and me beside him. How could he! How dare he! She thought of the naked photographs of her on his laptop and her stomach lurched. Words and phrases came flooding back, their meaning obvious now, but buried so successfully she hadn't understood at the time. Mrs Pryce had known. She'd been there when her father had rushed her from the house. Mandy could see her standing in the hall, comforting Sarah, as her father raised his hand in fury at his sister: *If you ever come near my family again, I'll have the lot of you arrested!*

Mrs Pryce knew, her father (and presumably her mother) knew; John, Evelyn, Sarah, even Gran and Grandpa knew – and all of them had colluded in a conspiracy of silence that had lasted ten years. The only person who hadn't known was she: the victim. She felt utterly betrayed – betrayed by her family, the very people whom she should have been closest to; whom she should have been able to rely on for their openness and honesty. And John! Bastard! Did he really think she wouldn't remember eventually, and that when she did it wouldn't matter! Through her tears she now thought how she'd been driven away in the back of her father's car on that last night. Now it all made sense. A sickening, depraved sense.

Heaving herself away from the door, she pulled a tissue from the box and blew her nose, then looked at herself in the mirror. Her eyes were red, her skin was blotchy and pain was etched across her face. But as she gazed it wasn't a woman of twenty-three she saw, but that girl of thirteen. With her hair tied in a ponytail and her cheeks wet from crying, Mandy saw her distress and felt her guilt now as then, for surely her childish crush had encouraged John, and she was partly to blame. But it had only ever been a fantasy, nothing more. He wasn't even supposed to know, let alone do anything.

Taking another tissue from the box, she blew her nose and flushed it down the toilet. There was no way she could face John now, and maybe never would again. Perhaps she should phone her father and ask him to collect her, but she couldn't face seeing him now either. Her head was spinning and she needed time to think – decide what to do for the best. Perhaps she could phone Adam and ask him to collect her, but she doubted she had the words to explain right now. The comment Adam had made on Sunday flew at her like an arrow from a bow: ... *at Uni the word was you didn't date, which was why it took me so long to ask you out. There was a feeling ... you'd had a bad experience with a bloke and didn't want guys near you.*

She went cold and her legs shook. Clearly Adam, and others, had seen something in her that she had not; something she'd been totally unaware of – something unclean. Sullied.

Leaving the cloakroom, she crossed the hall. With her hand gripping the banister she started up the stairs, listening and looking for any sign of John. She would go to her room and try to think what to do. Grandpa was here, she didn't want to leave him, she really didn't, but how could she stay? She supposed John had now phoned the nurse who would be on his way with another injection, which would last another hour.

It was quiet upstairs; Evelyn must have slept through her shouting, and Gran never heard anything without her hearing aid. At the top of the stairs she turned right and went along the landing, but instead of going into the bedroom she was using at the back of the house, she stopped outside the door on her right. This led to the Pink Room, which Evelyn had said she'd used when she stayed as a child, and which presumably she'd been in on her last night – when John had come in.

With her mouth dry and heart pounding, she placed her hand on the doorknob and, slowly turning it, pushed open the door. It was dark inside, but not as dark as it had been on that last night when the curtains had been closed. Now, with no one using the room, the curtains had been left open. Through the window came a faint glow from the lamp on the driveway. Enough to see the wardrobe and chest of drawers to her left, the bookshelves beneath the windows in front and the bed on the wall to the right. All as it had been ten years before.

Taking a step in, she closed the door quietly behind her and, instinctively knowing where the switch was, clicked it on. Colour flooded the room. It was pink, all pink – the reason for its name. The walls and ceiling were emulsioned light pink, and the carpet and curtains were a darker shade of rose. Mandy remembered that as a child pink had been her favourite colour and her aunt had had the room decorated especially for her. It was her room when she stayed. Sarah had liked blue, and the room next door – the Blue Room – had been hers. Sometimes they'd slept together; then they stayed up half the night giggling or telling horror stories and scaring themselves silly. But if they'd had little sleep one night Evelyn always insisted they slept in their own rooms the following night, otherwise they were like 'bad-mood bears', Mandy remembered her saying. She also remembered that when Evelyn and John were in bed Sarah had stolen into her room with midnight feasts. They were good times and even now she remembered how happy she'd been until …

Standing by the door she confronted the room. The furniture had not changed, and it stood in the same place as it had on that last night. The bed wasn't made up, but a pink candlewick bedspread was draped over it. The top of the chest of drawers, where Mandy had kept a few soft toys, was empty. The bookshelf beneath the window was also empty, apart from three small china ornaments arranged on the middle shelf. From the distance of the door, Mandy stared at these, and then shuddered with a stab of recognition, powerful and bitter-sweet.

Moving silently and slowly over the carpet, she crossed the room for a closer look. The ornaments were of dogs, a poodle, collie and King Charles spaniel, each sitting in its own little wicker basket with a small tartan rug. She'd known the names of the breeds of dogs even as a young child. She'd loved dogs and had wanted one of her own. Mandy remembered how Sarah and she had saved up their pocket money and had bought the china ornaments from the village shop. Sarah had collected horses and she had collected dogs. These three were part of a larger collection. The other eleven were on the bureau at her flat, and until now Mandy hadn't been aware any were missing. Now, she realized that in the chaos and outrage of that last night she'd forgotten to pack these three – her most recent purchases. Here they'd sat, unremembered, her mind having blocked out their existence as successfully as it had blocked out everything else connected with the house. Until now.

Straightening, she turned and looked at the bed. The memories and fear came flooding back. Terrified at being suddenly woken in the night, she'd tried to push John off but he was too heavy, and the weight of his body had kept her pinned to the bed.

'Don't scream or I'll have to kill you,' he hissed close to her ear. 'This is our secret, Mandy. Cry out and I'll kill you.' Yet despite her fear she found the courage to cry: 'Sarah! Help! Help me, please!' She felt the sting of John's hand as he slapped her across the face. Sarah appeared in the doorway and screamed. Then Evelyn appeared beside her and screamed too. John fled. But Sarah and Evelyn's shrieks were so terrible that they made her more afraid than ever. She clutched the sheet to her chest, rigid with terror, and wept helplessly. Then Mrs Pryce, who, unlike Mrs Saunders, lived in, arrived, and for a moment the three of them were silhouetted at the bedroom door. She could see the horror on their faces as they stared at her, and she lay paralysed with fear, clutching the sheet to her chin and sobbing uncontrollably.

Mrs Pryce took control and told Evelyn to see to Sarah and phone Mandy's parents. She switched on the main light and came over and sat on the bed. 'It's all right now,' she said in a gentle but firm tone, stroking Mandy's forehead. 'You're safe with me. Nothing can harm you now. There's no need to be frightened any more.' Eventually the words of comfort and her cool, soothing touch reached her and slowly, very slowly, Mandy was persuaded to release the sheet. Mrs Pryce took her in her arms and held her close, cradling her like a baby. Mandy remembered the soft, reassuring warmth of her body after the cold, harsh rigidness of John's. She buried her head in the fabric of her dressing gown and clung to her for all she was worth. Gradually her tears began to subside but she kept tight hold of Mrs Pryce. When she finally dared to raise her head Evelyn and Sarah had gone from the door. Mrs Pryce sat on the bed beside her and comforted her until her father arrived.

She heard the wheels of his car crunch on to the driveway below. 'That'll be your father,' Mrs Pryce had said gently.

The front door slammed below and they heard his voice shouting angrily in the hall. And his anger, after Mrs Pryce's calm reassurances, made Mandy afraid again; that and the look on his face when he finally came into the bedroom.

'Get your things,' he said brusquely.

Mandy clung to Mrs Pryce, not wanting to leave the safety of her arms. 'It's all right, love,' she reassured. 'You're going home. You'll be safe there.'

Mrs Pryce told her father to wait outside while Mandy got dressed, then she helped her into her clothes and packed her belongings. Mandy remembered holding tightly on to Mrs Pryce's arm as she carried her case to where her father waited on the landing. Passing him the case, the three of them went down the stairs in silence, her father first and she still clutching Mrs Pryce's arm.

Evelyn and Sarah were in the hall in their dressing gowns, crying. John was nowhere to be seen. Her father took her arm and began hurrying her towards the front door. Fast, too fast, almost dragging her away from Mrs Pryce, Sarah and Evelyn. She threw off her father's arm and ran into the cloakroom where she bolted the door and sobbed. She clutched the hand basin for support and stared at her distraught reflection in the mirror, tears streaming down her face, as her father hammered on the door. 'Open the door, Amanda,' he demanded. 'Now! We have to leave.' Too afraid to disobey him and aware they had to go, she unlocked the door and allowed him to lead her down the hall and to the front door. As he opened the door he paused and, turning, raised his clenched fist in anger at Evelyn: 'If you ever come near my family again, I'll have the lot of you arrested!' And his shouting, their crying, and the knowledge that she was to blame were more than Mandy could bear. By the time they'd arrived home, two hours later, she was already blocking it out.

Twenty-Six

Mandy stared at the bed from the safe distance of the room. She felt hot and cold at the same time; her cheeks were damp and her legs trembled. She could feel the weight of John's body on hers, the bristly hair around his mouth, and him hard against her legs. All the years the memory had been shut away seemed to have preserved it, and now she could see it, feel her pain crystal clear as though it had been frozen in ice. John on top of her, so heavy he was forcing the air out of her as his body chafed roughly against hers and he tried to force himself into her. But what had happened after she'd left her aunt's house that night and had arrived home with her father, she'd no idea. Had her parents questioned her? Had she seen a doctor or the police? She didn't know. Perhaps those incidents had been traumas in themselves and would need more time to remember. But what she now realized was how she'd subsequently dealt with boys and dating – she hadn't. Adam had been right – she'd shunned all intimacy. And had it not been for his gentle and unthreatening nature, when he'd taken time to get to know her and win her trust, she doubted she'd ever have had a boyfriend or been in love.

She remained standing in the middle of the room, staring at the bed, when suddenly she froze. From the corner of her eye she could see the doorknob moving. She turned to look, fear rooting her to the spot. The doorknob turned and the door slowly opened.

John appeared. She gasped, her hand shooting to her mouth. She stared in horror and disbelief as he took a step into the room; coming to finish what he'd begun ten years before? She watched petrified as he closed the door behind him, then she finally found her voice.

'Get out!' she cried. 'Get out, you bastard!'

'Mandy, let me explain.' He started across the room towards her.

'No, don't touch me!' She backed away.

'Mandy, I need to explain.'

'No, keep away. Don't touch me.' She retreated as far as she could until the wall rose up behind her. She could see the whites of his eyes, hear his breath coming fast and shallow. He was right in front of her now, his face red. Instinctively she put up her arms to cover her chest and protect herself. 'No, I won't let you. Not again! Go away!'

'Mandy, please,' he said, taking the final step that allowed him to touch her. She felt his hand on her arm like a branding iron.

'No!' With all her might she pushed him away. 'Get out! Now!' she screamed at the top of the voice. 'Get out! You bastard!'

He hesitated. She took a step forward and pushed him again, then went to claw his cheek. He pulled back, finally turning from her and heading towards the door. 'Bastard!' she cried after him. 'I hate you!'

She remained where she was, her fists raised and clenched and her heart racing as she watched him cross the room. He went out without looking back and closed the door behind him. Her knees trembled, her legs buckled and she sank slowly to the floor. Kneeling, she held her head in her hands and began to weep as she'd never cried before. The sobs racked her chest and her tears flowed as though they would never stop. Finally she was crying for what had happened on that dreadful night ten years ago and which, now remembered, could never be forgotten. She would carry the scar for ever. She cried for the pain and fear she now remembered, and for what the sordid secret that was her past had done to her as a person. She wept for her parents and grandparents who'd conspired to keep that dirty secret from her, especially Grandpa who would die believing he was still the keeper of her tainted history. Was that why he couldn't let go and die in peace? she wondered. Because he still carried the burden of not telling? She had no doubt he, like her parents and Gran, loved her, and if she believed that, then she had to believe they'd acted in her best interests – to protect her. But how Grandpa and Gran had found it within themselves to forgive John and carry on seeing him, she'd no idea. Was it because if they hadn't forgiven him they would have lost their daughter and granddaughter? Clearly Evelyn and Sarah had forgiven him.

Mandy started as a knock sounded on the door. Not John again, dear God no! Through the blur of tears she stared terrified at the door as a trapped animal fixes on the hunter advancing towards it. The door didn't open. Pushing down on her hands, she stood and ran to the door, then leant on it with all her might to stop it from opening. She could feel her heart thudding in her chest as she pushed against the wood, listening and waiting; dreading hearing the sound of his voice again. Another knock came but the doorknob didn't turn. 'What do you want?' she cried, her voice sounding far off and unreal.

'Mandy, it's Evelyn. May I come in?'

Evelyn? What did she want? To champion John's cause and ask her to forgive him? No, she didn't want to see her aunt; she didn't want to see anyone. She wanted to grab her belongings and go.

Through the window the sky was beginning to lighten towards dawn, and the lone walk along the isolated country lane held fewer demons than staying in the house.

'Mandy?' Evelyn knocked again. 'May I come in? I need to talk to you. Please.'

'No. Why?'

'I must, Mandy, I have to. I need to tell you something. Please.'

She heard the desperation in Evelyn's voice. 'Is John with you?'

'No, he's not.' Her voice caught. 'It's just me. Please Mandy.'

Slowly, very slowly, in case it was a trick and John was outside ready to burst in, Mandy took her weight off the door. She looked through the small gap where the door met the frame but all she could see was the landing light. With her hand on the door ready to close it in a second, she turned the knob and slowly opened it. Evelyn came into view in her dressing gown and slippers. There was no one else beside her. Opening the door wider, Mandy wiped her hand over her eyes and looked at Evelyn. She had been crying too; her eyes were red. It reminded Mandy of that night ten years ago when she'd last seen her in the hall.

She looked at Mandy, her face tense. Mandy stood aside to allow her in and closed the door behind her. Evelyn took a couple of steps into the room and turned to face her. 'Mandy,' she began uncertainly, 'I heard shouting. John came to me. He's very upset …'

'Upset!' Mandy cried, unable to believe what she was hearing. 'He's upset! What about me?'

'Mandy, listen please,' Evelyn said, her brow creasing. 'It's not as you think. Let me speak. Sometimes memories get distorted and –'

'Oh no you don't!' Mandy cried again. 'That won't work. Your memory might be distorted but mine certainly isn't. Not now!

You've kept this from me and covered up for him all these years, but now I remember perfectly!'

'Mandy,' Evelyn said, raising her voice slightly, 'will you please just give me a chance and hear what I have to say? Come and sit down and listen to me. I need to sit while I talk.'

Mandy watched Evelyn cross to the bed. She sat on the edge and lowered her gaze. She was pale and looked absolutely wretched; she was no threat. Putting her own feelings to one side, Mandy went over and sat on the bed beside her.

'Thank you,' Evelyn said.

There was silence as Evelyn appeared to be collecting her thoughts; they both concentrated on the floor. Mandy heard her aunt take a breath, then she looked up and straight ahead. 'Mandy, as you know, your father and I hadn't spoken for ten years, until I phoned to tell him we'd brought Grandpa here. I thought you'd want to visit your Grandpa – you've always been so close, probably closer than Sarah is in some respects. I won't pretend I wasn't worried about meeting you again, given what happened. I thought you might still blame us. I found it strange that none of your family had ever spoken of that night but I was totally shocked when I realized you had no memory of what happened here ' She paused and Mandy waited, with no idea where this was leading. 'Clearly you now have some recollection of what you think happened, and you're right to believe you were attacked – in this bedroom. But it was not as you think.'

Mandy looked up sharply and was about to speak, furious that Evelyn was still trying to cover up for John. 'No, let me finish, please, Mandy,' she said firmly. 'This should have been dealt with at the time, not left to fester for all these years. What I am about to tell you is the truth. I hope you will remember how it really was, and see that what I'm saying is right.'

Mandy continued to look at Evelyn and wondered if she was going to apportion blame, as she herself had been doing: yes, John did come into your bed but you had been flirting with him and leading him on.

'Do you remember that weekend?' Evelyn asked after a moment. 'That Saturday when it happened? I mean during the day, not the night?'

Mandy thought. 'I think so. Some of it's coming back.'

'It was a hot June day,' Evelyn said. 'And we'd had a barbeque, which you and Sarah had helped cook. We'd eaten sitting on the patio, then we'd gone down to the lower lawns where the swings and slide were – still are.' Mandy nodded. 'It was such a lovely day – hot with a warm gentle breeze, and we were all enjoying ourselves, so much that we stayed there all afternoon and well into the evening, only popping up to the house to use the toilet. Mrs Pryce made us sandwiches and jelly and we had a picnic tea on the lawn just before the sun set. Do you remember that day, Mandy?'

Mandy thought. 'Yes. You had guests staying that weekend. A couple with two children, and the children were too young to play on the slide.'

'So you can remember that?'

She nodded. 'I can now.' She realized it was the day she'd remembered when Adam and she had played on the slide.

Evelyn was watching her carefully now. 'The couple who stayed with us that weekend with their two young children are called Jimmy and Natalie. Jimmy was John's brother. I say *was* because John disowned him that night and has never spoken to him since.' She paused. 'Mandy, it wasn't John who came into your room that night and attacked you; it was his brother, Jimmy.'

'No! Absolutely not!' Mandy cried. 'I know what you're up to. You think you can blame it on John's brother because they've fallen out! Or perhaps that's what John made you believe – that it was his brother and not him. Well, if you want to live a lie that's your problem. But don't bring me into it. John attacked me and I caught him looking at photos of me naked as a child!' Shaking with anger she jumped up from the bed and ran to the door.

'Mandy!' Evelyn called after her. 'No, Mandy, please listen.'

'No! I've lived a lie for ten years. I won't have you take the truth away from me now. You'll be telling me next it was my fault – that I led John on!' Flinging open the door she ran across the landing and to the bedroom she was using. Slamming the door behind her she pressed her hands to her ears and screamed. She didn't care who heard. She screamed for what John had done to her and the secret Evelyn was still trying to maintain. But most of all she screamed for what she had just acknowledged – that she was responsible.

Twenty-Seven

Lowering her hands, she began darting around the room. Some of her clothes lay scattered on the floor and others were strewn across the bed. In blind panic she ran around the bedroom, grabbing her belongings and throwing them in her suitcase. She had to get away as quickly as possible. Away from this house and the truth she now knew: that her schoolgirl crush had led John on to the point where he'd believed it was all right to go into her bedroom; that it wasn't rape, but what she'd wanted.

With tears streaming down her face she kicked off her slippers and threw them in the case. She grabbed her hairbrush and cosmetic purse and dumped them in too. A knock sounded on the door. 'Go away,' she cried. 'Leave me alone. I'll be gone soon.'

'Mandy.' It was Evelyn. 'Please, can I come in?'

'No!'

Dragging the zip round to close the case, she heaved it to the floor. The door opened and Evelyn came in. 'Get out!' Mandy shrieked.

Evelyn didn't get out but continued across the room towards her. She had something in her hand. 'Mandy, listen, please. Give me one chance to explain, then if you still want to go I'll call a taxi.' She took another step and stopped.

Mandy looked at her and was about to say no again, grab her case and escape past her, never to return. But something in her look – in her pained and haunted air; something in the pathetic way she now offered up what she held made Mandy hesitate. 'Mandy, please look at this,' she said.

Mandy heard her desperation and took the photograph. She recognized it immediately. It was a snapshot from that Saturday afternoon, when they'd had visitors – the visitors Evelyn now said were John's brother Jimmy with his wife and children.

'I took that photograph,' Evelyn said, 'which is why I'm not in it. John usually took all the photos so he wasn't in many of them. I said it would be nice to have one of him with his brother and his family.' She gave a tight smile. 'Little did I know it would be the last photograph of us all together. Little did I know what Jimmy had in mind as I took it.' Her lip trembled.

Mandy looked at Evelyn and then again at the photograph. John was posing with Jimmy on one side of him and Jimmy's wife on the other. Mandy was next to Jimmy, and Jimmy's two small children stood either side of Sarah at the front. Everyone was smiling, the sky was blue, and the swings and slide could be seen in the background.

'Mandy, look closely at John and Jimmy,' Evelyn said. Mandy looked, and fear crept up her spine. 'John and Jimmy were only fourteen months apart in age,' Evelyn continued, 'and were often mistaken for twins. They were the same height, had the same brown hair and very similar features. Except Jimmy always had a moustache and John never had one, ever. Mandy, I know you remember the attack but in the dark and the terror of being woken you were mistaken about your attacker. Think back. You cried out for help and Sarah heard and came in. She saw Jimmy on top of you and screamed. Do you remember? Then I came and Jimmy fled past me. It was Jimmy who attacked you, not John, I promise you, love. We both saw him.'

Mandy continued to stare at the photograph. John and Jimmy: the same height and build, with features so similar they could easily pass as twins. Only Jimmy had a thick moustache and John didn't. The moustache Mandy remembered scratching her cheek as he caught her off the slide, and then tearing at her mouth as he tried to kiss her that night, when she'd woken petrified to find him on top of her in the dark. She remembered Jimmy and how uncomfortable she'd felt around him even before that night. Her mouth went dry and her legs trembled as she recognized the truth in Evelyn's words.

'Do you remember now, Mandy?' Evelyn was saying. 'Do you remember?'

Mandy slowly nodded. She had gone cold and felt so weak. She sat on the bed. Evelyn sat next to her.

'Your dad blamed us for not protecting you,' Evelyn said, 'and he was right to do so. But we were punished – we crucified ourselves with guilt. John disowned Jimmy that night and we've had no contact with him or his family since. But, Mandy, while your father was right to blame us – we should have seen the warning signs and protected you – he was wrong to simply cut us off and not talk about it. You can't bury something like that. It's not healthy.'

'I know,' Mandy said quietly. 'I know.'

They were silent for some moments. Evelyn placed her hand lightly on Mandy's arm and they both gazed at the photograph she still held. A small weight began to lift from Mandy's shoulders – the truth was out and she wasn't in any way to blame. She'd never encouraged Jimmy, consciously or otherwise, by having a crush on him; far from it, she'd always shied away from him and had kept her distance. She could now remember other times when he'd kissed her cheek, his moustache scratching, or tickled her for too long, or patted her bottom, or winked suggestively when no one was looking: the warning signs Evelyn had referred to. She also remembered how she'd recoiled from his advances. No, she wasn't to blame for the attack, and her relief was enormous.

'What happened to Jimmy?' she asked at length, handing back the photograph. 'Was he prosecuted?'

Evelyn shook her head and slid the photograph into her dressing-gown pocket. 'Your father didn't want the police involved. He thought being interviewed and having to give evidence would cause you even more upset. He wanted you to forget it and move on with your life – he thought that was best. Mandy, I would be lying if I said we weren't relieved. It wouldn't have done us any good if we'd had to go to court and it was splashed over the local newspapers, nor John's business. And I was relieved that Sarah wouldn't have to give evidence, which would have been very upsetting for her.'

'So that was it? Matter finished?' Mandy asked, upset that it had all been brushed away so easily.

Evelyn nodded. 'Although you did see a doctor the following day.'

'And?'

'I don't know the details but I understand it had stopped short of rape. Which confirmed to your father that he needn't go to the police.'

Mandy gave a small cynical laugh.

'I'm sorry, love,' Evelyn said, taking Mandy's hand between hers. 'I really am. I'm sorry we didn't protect you, sorry we lost you, and sorry you had to find out like this.'

Mandy looked at her aunt – so genuine and sincere in her apology, her heart went out to her. 'It wasn't your fault,' she said quietly. 'And I suppose Dad only did what he thought was best.' She let out a small sigh. 'The power of the mind. We didn't speak of it, it wasn't dealt with, so as far as I was concerned it didn't happen. I wonder if I would have ever remembered if I hadn't come back to this house?'

'I think you would have remembered eventually,' Evelyn said. 'Something would have triggered a memory – a chance remark or a smell, then you would have asked a question.' She paused. 'When this is all over and you are home, I think it might be a good idea if you saw a counsellor.'

'Why? Do you think I'm mad?' Mandy asked with a small tight laugh.

'No, far from it. I think you've coped incredibly well. But it's often easier to talk to someone outside the family. Sarah saw a counsellor for a year after it had happened.'

'Did she?' Mandy asked, surprised.

Evelyn hesitated. 'Yes. She was very distressed – by what she'd witnessed and also because she'd lost your friendship. You were so very close, like sisters.'

'I know.' But the irony didn't escape her; that while Sarah, a witness to the assault, had received counselling, she, the victim, had not. 'Mum and Dad need to start talking about it as well,' Mandy said. 'And Gran. It can't have been easy for them keeping a lid on it all this time.'

'No, indeed,' Evelyn said sadly. 'They've suffered badly.'

There was so much to think about, so much to consider now she knew, Mandy thought, it was overwhelming, and in some ways more frightening than not knowing. Slipping her hand from Evelyn's, she moved away. 'Will you explain to John before I come down?'

'Of course.'

'And if I get the chance, I'll tell Grandpa I know, and that everything's going to be all right.'

Evelyn smiled weakly. 'That will be a great relief to him. Thank God it's out in the open now and we can all stop pretending.'

Twenty-Eight

*D*awn was breaking as, an hour later, Mandy entered the study. The curtains had been opened and the lava lamp switched off for the day. Grandpa stirred but didn't wake. John looked up from his armchair with a mixture of alarm and apprehension. 'Don't worry,' she said almost lightly, sitting in the chair beside him. 'I'm not going to slap your face again.'

He looked at her, still uncertain despite her words, and then, reading her face, visibly relaxed. She felt his gaze on her as she looked across the room towards the bed. The only sound for some moments was Grandpa's laboured breathing. Then she heard John's voice, slight and imploring. 'The photos on my laptop were completely innocent, Mandy, I swear.'

She looked at him, and nodded. 'I know, Evelyn explained. But why did you behave so secretively? Guiltily – taking the laptop out to close the file?'

He rubbed his hand across his forehead. 'I thought you didn't want to see the photographs – that you would be upset by mementoes of your past. Because you never spoke of the time you spent here I assumed you didn't want reminders. Unlike Sarah. Her counsellor told us to compile the photo albums so she could see all the good times you'd shared. It was one of the things he suggested for helping her through that time. I never dreamt you could misinterpret them.'

'I never spoke of my past here because I couldn't remember it,' Mandy said lamely.

'I know that now. And you do believe it wasn't me who came into your room that night?' John asked, his anxiety returning. 'I always loved and treated you as a daughter. I would never ...' He stopped, unable to complete the sentence and voice the horrendous alternative.

'Yes, I know,' she said quietly. 'I believe you.'

He paused reflectively, collecting himself before he spoke. 'Mandy, I would have given evidence if it had gone to court. I would have given evidence against my own brother. But I understood why your father thought it would be too traumatic for you. I'd have probably done the same if it had been Sarah.' He stopped again, his face creasing at the thought of his daughter being attacked.

'I can appreciate why you and Dad would think like that, and want to protect us,' Mandy said. 'But how can you be certain Jimmy hasn't gone on and abused others?'

'I can't,' John said, 'and I'll live with that for ever.'

It was as if Grandpa knew that the demon of silence had been exorcized, Mandy thought, and the secret that had tainted the family's lives for so long had finally been exposed and was being dealt with, and he could relax. While she'd been upstairs the nurse had arrived and given Grandpa another injection, and although it was no stronger than the previous ones and was not expected to last any longer, the hour's release from pain stretched into two hours, then three, and Grandpa slept on, throughout the morning. It was a deep and peaceful sleep where he lay very still and comfortable with his head resting lightly in the small hollow of the pillow, his slow irregular breaths the only sign of life.

John had planned to attend a meeting at work at 1 p.m. but sent his apologies for absence instead. Evelyn phoned Sarah and said Grandpa was sleeping peacefully, and Mandy phoned her father at work and left a message on his voicemail saying the same. The atmosphere in the study, which had held so much darkness and pain, now seemed lighter, as though a veil had been lifted. Mandy knew that Grandpa had finally been released from his prison and the hourglass was slowly emptying its last few grains of sand.

When the nurse made his routine visit shortly after 2 p.m. they grouped around the bed and waited in silent expectation as he took Grandpa's pulse. 'He's very comfortable now,' he said gently, returning his arm to beneath the sheet. 'Two days at the most. I'm not going to disturb him further by examining him; he'll be dry.'

The nurse hovered with one hand on Grandpa's shoulder, reluctant to leave. Mandy thought how difficult it must be to keep having to say goodbye to the patients he'd grown close to – a continual cycle of bereavements. She knew she couldn't have done his job. 'Sleep tight, Mr Edwards,' he said at last, patting Grandpa's shoulder one final time. 'You deserved it; good man.'

The nurse said he would look in again that evening, but to phone if they needed him sooner. John and Evelyn saw him out, which left Mandy alone with Gran. 'I don't think I'll phone Dad and tell him to come,' she said.

'No,' Gran agreed. 'There's no point. Will won't wake again now.'

Mandy hesitated. 'Gran, I know what happened ten years ago to make my visits stop. I can remember now.'

Gran nodded stoically. 'Evelyn told me.'

'And you're not surprised?'

'No. I thought you coming here would take the lid off it, one way or another. Dying is a great leveller – for everyone.'

And as if in agreement, as if the words had filtered down through the layers of unconsciousness and found an audience, Grandpa took an extra breath and the briefest of smiles seemed to flicker across his lips.

'He knows,' Gran said.

The afternoon gave way to evening and Grandpa slept on without any obvious sign of change or any need for medication. Mrs Saunders served dinner and before she left for the night she made a point of saying 'Goodbye, Mr Edwards' rather than her usual 'Goodnight'. There were tears in her eyes as she left. The nurse looked in again at 7.30 and took Grandpa's temperature and pulse. 'You're certainly keeping us all in suspense, Mr Edwards,' he said. 'Another night?' And they smiled, able to share the nurse's small humour. Grandpa was peaceful and no longer in pain. He was ending his natural life, naturally, as it should be.

At 9 p.m., having had her Ovaltine, Gran said she would go to bed. John offered to make up a bed in the study so she could stay with Grandpa, but Gran said not to worry, she'd said goodbye before he'd gone. John nodded. They understood what she meant, for it seemed there was just the shell of Grandpa left now, and whatever had made him – his soul? – was no longer there. Gran said goodnight and kissed his lips just as she did every night, and then added: 'See you soon, love. I won't be long.' Mandy felt her eyes brim.

Evelyn saw Gran upstairs and said she was going to lie down too, but they must wake her if there was any change or if they needed help. By 9.30 Mandy and John had settled in their usual armchairs ready for another night. 'It's like *University Challenge*.' John quipped. 'I've started so I'll finish.' Mandy smiled, relaxed.

John opened his laptop and began to work. Mandy answered a couple of texts, and then returned her mobile to her bag and rested her head back. She gazed across the room. The lava lamp once more bathed the study in its red glow as the bubbles continued their relentless journey going nowhere. Mandy knew she would never possess a lava lamp, nor any light with a red glow, for as long as she lived; it would remind her of this study and make her very sad. After a while John paused from tapping the keys on his laptop and looked at her. 'Would you like to see the photos in that album, Mandy?'

She nodded.

Closing the file he was working on, he opened another. Angling the laptop slightly towards her so they could both see the screen, he clicked the mouse to start the slide show. 'Album one,' he said. 'Baby to five years.' A photo of her as a small baby being cradled by Sarah filled the screen. They were in the sitting room of this house although the sofa and wallpaper were different. This photograph was replaced by one of Evelyn holding her, again on the sofa.

Mandy turned slightly in her chair to make herself more comfortable as one picture followed another at five-second intervals. Her as a baby – being cuddled by Sarah, Evelyn, and then John, taken in this house on one of her parents' many visits. Then she was a few months old and sitting on their laps, all of them smiling – a happy family group. Mandy knew there were photograph albums at her parents' house containing pictures of Evelyn, John and Sarah, but the albums had disappeared from the bookshelf years ago when Mandy's visits had stopped. 'I've put them away,' her mother had said when Mandy had asked where they'd gone. 'They'll make you upset.' Mandy had accepted this, perhaps too readily, and had never thought – or dared – to ask why.

The picture changed again and Mandy was a toddler playing in the garden with Sarah who, a year older, was leading the game of what could have been 'tag'. Next the two of them were in the paddling pool on a hot sunny day, then running naked across the lawn. She laughed; her nakedness seemed quite cute now in the context of how she knew the photos had been taken – within a normal extended loving family. Autumn followed summer, and then winter came. Sarah and she were posing proudly beside a large snowman with a huge orange carrot for a nose. A few photos later and it was summer again and the photo that now filled the screen was the one she'd found previously: Sarah and she playing naked under the sprinkler, their little bodies pale and flawless, glistening in the sun.

'Did Jimmy ever see these?' Mandy suddenly asked, looking up.

John looked slightly taken aback and shook his head. 'We didn't ever really see that much of Jimmy, even before that weekend. Although he was my brother Evelyn was never taken with him, right from the start.'

'Perhaps she saw something in him she didn't like,' Mandy offered, remembering her own feelings of unease when he'd come near her.

'That's what Evelyn said. But he was my brother and until that night I had no reason to doubt him.'

'No,' she agreed hesitantly, and returned her attention to the laptop as the first album ended with Sarah's fourth birthday party.

John closed this album and opened the next. 'Five to eight years old,' he said. 'This is when you started sleeping over.'

It began with another birthday party. A clown with a big red nose and brightly coloured costume was entertaining about a dozen children. Mandy saw herself seated on the floor with

Sarah's other friends laughing at the magic. Then they were in the garden, seated either side of long refectory table and eating a party tea. As with the other photographs taken when Mandy was old enough to remember, they were starting to become familiar. The next picture was of Sarah and her wobbling on bicycles as they tried to navigate an obstacle course constructed on the lower lawn. 'I remember that!' Mandy said. 'You helped us build those little bridges to ride over. The ones we built collapsed.'

'That's right,' John said, pleased. 'I did. And what about this next one? Which one is the donkey?'

Mandy playfully tapped John's arm for the photograph now showing was of Sarah and her on donkeys at the village fête. Gaily coloured stalls could be seen in the background together with a large Victorian-style merry-go-round.

'I know I had some very good times here,' Mandy said reflectively. 'Thanks to you and Evelyn. You were like a second mum and dad to me.'

'I'm glad you feel that way,' John said. 'I'm glad we can enjoy the past again.'

The slide show continued. Mandy smiled at the memories as John supplied the date and occasion on which the photo had been taken if she couldn't immediately place it. Engrossed in the pictures, it was a few minutes before she realized that the air had grown unnaturally still, and was far too quiet. That the deep and laboured breathing which had dominated the study for so long had finally stopped.

Twenty-Nine

Nothing could be heard save for the small swish on the laptop as one photograph replaced another. And as the silence grew and realization slowly dawned, Mandy withdrew her gaze from the screen and looked at John. He turned towards her and their eyes met. Not daring to breathe, they remained very still, waiting for the next breath. So quiet and still, the silence was deafening – palpable almost.

Then John slowly lowered the lid on the laptop and stood. Mandy rose too. She walked close beside him as they crossed the study to the bed, all the time listening, expecting, almost willing that next intake of breath. None came. The silence continued, disturbed only by the faintest brush of their feet on the carpet. At the bedside Mandy hesitated before looking down, afraid of what she might see. But with his eyes closed, head relaxed to one side and mouth slightly open, Grandpa looked exactly as he had done when asleep.

Mandy stood beside John at the bed and listened and waited some more. 'Is that it?' she whispered, expecting something different – something more dramatic almost.

'I think so,' John said. Lowering his cheek to Grandpa's nose he felt for any hint of breath. 'Yes,' he said, straightening. And neither of them moved, for being aware that Grandpa had stopped breathing was very different from accepting he was dead.

After a moment John reached out and drew the sheet up and over Grandpa's face just as Mandy had seen in films. Then, crossing the room, he switched on the main light. Mandy continued looking at the bed, not really believing.

'I'll wake Evelyn and Gran,' John said at last, taking control. He looked at his watch. 'Will you phone your parents and tell them Grandpa died at eleven twenty. Use the phone in the sitting room if you prefer.'

Mandy nodded dumbly and, finally taking her gaze from the shrouded figure that was once Grandpa, left the room.

It wasn't until she heard her father's voice break and her mother crying in the background that she too began to cry, and once she'd begun it was difficult to stop. 'It was very peaceful, Dad, really it was,' she sobbed, trying to reassure him and control her own tears. 'He was asleep, and then he just stopped breathing.'

'And he didn't say anything?'

'No. Nothing. He died in his sleep.'

'And he wasn't in any pain?'

'No, not at all.' Thank goodness she could say that honestly.

'And Gran?'

'John has gone to wake her and Evelyn now.'

He paused and blew his nose. 'I'll come over first thing tomorrow. Could you ask Evelyn or John to give me a ring when they come down, please?'

'Of course, Dad.'

'Thanks, love.' He hung up quickly so she couldn't hear him break down completely.

Mandy stayed on the sofa in the sitting room, tears silently falling, too exhausted to move. Her parents never cried openly; hearing them do so intensified her own sorrow. She felt completely overwhelmed, and tired to the point of collapse. It was like coming to the end of a marathon; stamina had kept her

211

going for so long but now there was no reason to continue she'd collapsed at the finishing line, drained and depleted. Presently she heard Evelyn and Gran come downstairs and go into the study. A few minutes later Evelyn came into the sitting room. Wearing a dressing gown and slippers, she looked as exhausted and wretched as Mandy felt.

'Gran is staying with Grandpa until the undertakers arrive,' Evelyn said, sitting on the sofa. 'She's being very brave, poor love.'

Mandy dried her eyes and tucked the tissue into her sleeve. 'Dad asked if you would phone him. He said he'll come tomorrow. Is there anything I can do?'

'No, we'll take care of everything now. Why don't you go to bed?'

'If you're sure, I think I will. I'll see Gran first.'

Evelyn nodded and reached for the phone. Mandy heaved herself from the sofa and kissed her goodnight. 'See you tomorrow, Mandy,' Evelyn said quietly.

Going along the hall to the study, she found the door open and tentatively took a step in. Gran, in her dressing gown, was sitting beside the bed, just as she had been doing every day since Grandpa had come here from the hospital. She'd drawn back the sheet from Grandpa's face and was holding one of his hands. Bent slightly forward, she was looking at him with the same concern and tenderness she'd always shown, as though he could wake at any moment and find her sitting there. She looked up at Mandy and smiled sadly, then returned her attention to Grandpa. Mandy went over and kissed Grandpa's cheek; his skin felt cool and damp. Straightening, she kissed Gran and said goodnight. 'I'm going up. I love you.' Turning, she quickly left the room.

Upstairs she went into her bedroom and, switching on the light, stood for a moment in the centre of the room, unsure of what she should be doing or feeling. Dear Gran, now alone after nearly sixty years of marriage – a lifetime. How would she cope? Mandy felt lonely too and wished she had Adam with her – to feel his comforting arms around her and hear his words of support. It was too late to phone and tell him of Grandpa's death now, he would be asleep, and it wasn't something you could put in a text. She'd phone in the morning before he went to work. Closing the curtains but leaving on the light, she undressed, then dropping her clothes on the chair, climbed into bed.

The sheets felt strangely smooth after so long sleeping in her clothes in the chair, too smooth, in fact, and distant – not enfolding. She lay on her back and stared at the ceiling as thoughts came and went. Like the photos on John's laptop, images flashed across her mind – charting a chronology of events since she'd first arrived. How long ago it now seemed since she'd woken to find her father throwing gravel at her window and been told of Grandpa's illness. How long it seemed since she'd come into this house a stranger, recalling almost nothing of the hundreds of visits she'd made as a child, her mind having blocked them out in order to protect her. But tomorrow she would be leaving, remembering and aware. Aware, but not healed, she thought. And she had yet to tell Adam what had happened, and talk to her parents. Perhaps Evelyn was right and a therapist would help, for she doubted the past would simply settle into its rightful place, remembered but not tormenting.

Some time later, exhausted yet unable to sleep, she heard the front doorbell chime and then male voices in the hall. Footsteps made their way to the rear of the house, then it went quiet. Mandy got out of bed and taking her kimono from her suitcase tied it round her. She quietly opened the bedroom door. All the lights were on.

Padding round the landing, she went to the small bay window at the top of the stairs that looked over the front. From the window she could see a hearse on the driveway below, gloomy in the half-light of the lamp. The rear door was up and the back of the hearse was empty. Voices came from the study, fell silent, then footsteps sounded in the hall again. Taking a step back from the banister, like a child hiding on the landing, she looked down. A wooden coffin, supported by four pallbearers, came into view and moved silently through the reception hall beneath her and out of the front door. John was with them; Evelyn and Gran must have stayed in the study. Returning to the window she saw the pallbearers slide the coffin into the rear of the hearse and lower the rear door. Taking a step back they gave a small respectful bow and then climbed into the hearse. Mandy watched it as it pulled to the end of the drive and then, turning right, disappeared from view. 'Goodbye,' she said quietly under her breath. 'Goodbye, Grandpa, love you.'

Thirty

The April sun shone through the curtains, lighting up the room, and for a moment, as she woke, Mandy wondered where she was. Then she remembered she was in bed at her aunt's and, with a mixture of sorrow and relief, that Grandpa was at peace. She must have finally dropped off in the early hours and had slept like a log. She'd no idea of the time. Reaching for her bag she pulled it on to the bed and took out her phone: 9.50 a.m. It was too late to phone Adam now, he'd be at work, so she texted: *Plz fone when ur free. luv m.* There was a text from her father confirming he and her mother would be arriving at midday. Returning the phone to her bag she got out of bed and opened the curtains. The view was breathtaking. She hadn't noticed it before; it had always been very early in the morning and dark outside when she'd come into the room for clean clothes to take to the shower. Now she stood for a moment gazing at the magnificent gardens and lawns which ran into the green hills beyond. The sun blazed high in the clear blue sky with some real warmth, suggesting summer wasn't very far away.

Twenty minutes later, showered and dressed, Mandy once again stood gazing out of the window as she brushed her damp hair into style. Her mobile rang. 'Adam, thanks for calling,' she said, and then quickly told him what she had to say, needing to get the words out and spoken: 'Grandpa died peacefully in his sleep last night.'

'I'm so sorry, Mandy,' he said, and asked after everyone. 'Shall I come and collect you?'

'Thanks, but Mum and Dad are coming later. I should be home by five.'

He hesitated, not wanting to sound insensitive, but wanting to see her. 'Shall I come to your flat after work? Do you want some company?'

'Yes.' But the surge of pleasure she felt at the thought of being with Adam again was quickly tempered by guilt for allowing herself to feel joy now Grandpa was dead. 'Yes. I'd like that,' she said, subdued. She had yet to tell him what she'd discovered about her past, but now wasn't the right time.

'Do you need anything?' he asked. 'Milk? Bread?'

'I suppose so. The stuff there will be stale and out of date.'

'OK. I'll put the essentials in your fridge at lunchtime. I'm at our North London office for a meeting. Text me if you think of anything else.'

'Thanks, Adam,' she said, grateful that he was taking charge. 'Thanks for everything, and thanks for being you.'

He gave a small laugh. 'Can't be much else. See you later, Mandy. I've missed you.'

'I've missed you too.'

Bread, milk, her flat: how distant that life now seemed – a world away. Yet very soon she would be returning home, with bills to pay, pictures to try and paint, and another job to find when her year out ended. With these thoughts came another stab of guilt, and great sadness, for Mandy knew that while her life would shortly be resuming Gran's would never be the same. And again she wondered how Gran would cope without Grandpa – indeed if she would want to cope at all.

Going downstairs she arrived in the hall and hesitated, unsure what she should be doing now. The house was quiet and for a moment Mandy wondered if everyone was out, then Evelyn appeared from the morning room, looking less strained and tired. 'Hello, love,' she said, kissing her cheek. 'Did you sleep well?'

'I did, thank you. And you?'

'Not too bad. Gran's having some breakfast. We're all a bit late this morning. John is in the study. He'd said he'd like to see you. I don't know what about.'

Mandy frowned, puzzled. 'Now?'

'If you wouldn't mind, dear. I'll tell Mrs Saunders you're down.'

Mandy couldn't imagine why John would want to see her and felt slightly unsettled by his request. And it would be strange going into the study, which had been the hub of the house, knowing Grandpa was no longer there. The study door was closed and she gave a brief knock. 'Yes,' John called from the other side.

Entering, she was surprised to see that the bed and all the trappings of nursing Grandpa had already gone; the room was once again a study. John was seated at his desk, which was now under the window. He swivelled round in his chair to face her and Mandy thought that, whereas Evelyn had benefited from a night's sleep, John looked a good deal worse: even more tired and strained. 'You've been busy,' she said, referring to the room.

He nodded. 'The lamp's broken,' he said anxiously, and pointed to the desk.

Mandy looked at the desk behind him and saw the lava lamp, their constant companion of moving red light, was on its side with the plug open. A screwdriver, fuse and bulb lay beside it where John had been trying to fix it.

'It stopped working last night,' he said. 'Just after Grandpa died. I noticed it while I was waiting for the undertakers to arrive. I can't find what's wrong with it.'

Mandy recognized the coincidence in the timing but thought it was unlike John to view it as significant. 'Is that why you wanted to see me?' she asked, hovering just inside the door.

'Not exactly. Close the door, will you?' She did as asked. He paused, ran his fingers agitatedly through his hair and then met her gaze. 'You won't tell anyone, will you, Mandy? Now or in the future?'

'Tell? What?' she said, not knowing what he was talking about.

He lowered his voice in conspiracy. 'Trying to help Grandpa end it. I mean I thought I was doing the right thing. I thought that was what he wanted. Thank God I stopped when I did. But if anyone found out – your parents or Sarah, they wouldn't understand. They'd never forgive me.'

Mandy's thoughts flashed back to the night before last when John had ejected her from the study. When she'd returned and accused him of assaulting her he'd been standing over Grandpa with a pillow in his hand. 'No, of course I won't say anything,' she said quietly. She felt uncomfortable that he needed to ask. Mandy realized just how different their perception of events was now, in the cold light of day, compared to that night, when their desperate desire to stop Grandpa's suffering had overridden all other considerations including their ability to think rationally. 'We did what we thought was right at the time. And you couldn't do it in the end, could you?' she said.

'No, thank God,' he said again.

She turned to go. 'It will be our secret then, Mandy,' he said behind her. She froze. It was the same phrase Jimmy had used when he'd attacked her: *Don't scream or I'll have to kill you. This is our secret, Mandy. Cry out and I'll kill you.* Their voices were so similar.

'I won't tell,' she said quietly after a moment, and left the study, bitterly wishing he hadn't used those words.

* * *

Gran was just finishing her breakfast as Mandy entered the morning room. She was dressed smartly in a dark blue dress. 'How are you, Gran?' Mandy asked, going over and hugging her.

'Not too bad, love. Sad. I miss him already and I know it will get worse.' She looked at Mandy with a small wistful smile. 'Get yourself some breakfast now, dear.'

Mandy went to the sideboard and helped herself to fruit juice and scrambled egg on toast as Mrs Saunders came in and refilled Gran's cup of tea. They exchanged a good morning and Mrs Saunders left.

'The lamp's broken,' Gran said, glancing at Mandy as she sat at the table. 'John thinks Will had something to do with it. Superstitious bugger. Mind you, I wouldn't put it past him. Will hated that lamp, but didn't like to say. Perhaps it was his parting shot.'

Mandy returned Gran's small smile; her irreverence was a positive sign that life was continuing. Mandy took a sip of her juice and picked up her knife and fork. 'And if Evelyn and John think I'm coming to live with them,' Gran added, 'they've got another think coming. I'm not being ungrateful but I have a home of my own to go to, and that's where I shall be going later today.'

Mandy looked at her, concerned. 'But how will you cope alone, Gran?'

'I'll manage, love. Don't you worry. I'll arrange for one of those home carers to help me have a bath and take me shopping. Sue, my neighbour, always kept an eye on us and I know she's there if I need her. And doubtless Evelyn will be popping in. I know I won't have Will and I'm going to miss him dreadfully, but we agreed whoever was left behind wouldn't give up. We lived in that bungalow nearly all our married life. I know he'll be watching over me. I'm determined to see out my days in my own home, and that's an end to it.'

Mandy nodded, and chided herself for ever thinking differently.

Her parents were expected at 12 noon so after breakfast Mandy packed her case and hauled it downstairs, so it was ready in the hall by 11.30. There was something else she wanted to take with her, something that was rightfully hers but seemed insensitive to ask for now. Yet if she didn't ask soon, her parents would arrive and her keepsakes would be left behind, just as they had before.

A few minutes later Mandy seized the opportunity when she saw Evelyn going upstairs. 'Evelyn, have you got a minute?' she called. 'I need to ask you something.'

Evelyn paused on the stairs. 'Yes?' she said, turning. Mandy could tell from her expression she feared she was going to be asked a deep and soul-searching question about the past.

'It's nothing bad,' Mandy said quickly. 'It's just ... I was wondering ... You know those china ornaments – the little dogs on the shelf in the Pink Room? Well, I was wondering if I might have them? To complete my collection.'

Evelyn's expression changed to relief. 'Yes of course, they're yours. You bought them with your pocket money. They've been there waiting for you all these years.' She smiled and her eyes watered. 'Come on, let's get them now.'

Mandy followed Evelyn up the stairs, round the landing, and into the Pink Room. It was only now she noticed how 'shut up' the room felt. The air was slightly stale, heavy, as though the windows weren't often opened, and there was a faint smell of mothballs. The wallpaper, paint and furnishings, chosen by her and once so bright and vibrant, now seemed dowdy and tired. 'I used to love this room,' Mandy said as Evelyn crossed to the shelf beneath the window where the ornaments were. 'Does anyone use it now?'

'Not really. It was always your room, and when you stopped coming no one had the heart to change anything. Sarah used to creep in here sometimes when she felt sad, and sit on the bed. She missed you terribly. Now we no longer need all the bedrooms so I've just left it. Sentimental, I suppose.'

Evelyn picked up the little china dogs and, cradling them carefully in the palm of her hands, came over and set them on the bed. Opening the drawer in the bedside cabinet, she took out three little boxes.

'Their display boxes!' Mandy cried. 'You've kept them!'

'Of course. As I remember you always kept the boxes so they travelled home safely.'

'I did! That's wonderful. Thank you so much.'

Mandy watched, deeply touched, as Evelyn carefully took each ornament – the poodle, collie and King Charles spaniel – and, lowering each into its box, closed the lid. 'There,' she said, sealing the third and handing them to Mandy. 'I'm so pleased they're going home at last.'

'Thank you,' Mandy said again, and kissed her cheek.

'You're very welcome, love.'

Downstairs Mandy tucked the three precious boxes into her suitcase and then waited in the sitting room with Gran until the doorbell rang, signalling her parents had arrived. She went into the hall to greet them; John and Evelyn kissed and hugged them too, easily and comfortably, as they used to. Her father had brought Evelyn a bouquet of flowers and Evelyn's eyes misted as she thanked him. 'You shouldn't have,' she said, but Mandy could see just how pleased she was and how much the gesture meant.

Gran cried a little when she saw them all come into the sitting room with Evelyn proudly showing her the flowers. 'I wish Grandpa could have seen you all together as a family again,' she said. 'Although he probably knows,' she added.

Evelyn gave the flowers to Mrs Saunders to put into a vase and they sat in the sitting room; her parents, Evelyn and John discussing the funeral arrangements while Mandy sat quietly with Gran, listening. Presently Mrs Saunders wheeled in the silver hostess trolley containing platters of neat triangular sandwiches, small pastries and tea. Some things never changed, Mandy thought: lunch dead on twelve o'clock. Mandy sat close to Gran as they ate, reluctant to put any distance between them. Her mother sat on the sofa beside Evelyn while her father was in an armchair next to John. Mandy thought that while it was heart-warming to see the family together again (minus Sarah, who was at work) it also highlighted the gap in the family: the missing family member whose lively conversation and ready humour would never be heard again.

Gran cried again when it was time for them to leave. Mandy kissed and hugged her and said she would phone that evening when they were both home. She helped Gran on to her walking frame and went with her to the reception hall, where they all embraced. John opened the front door and her father carried her suitcase to the car and shut it in the boot. With a final goodbye they climbed into the car – her father into the driver's seat, her mother in the passenger, and she in the rear. The engine started and her mother opened her side window to wave goodbye. Mandy turned and looked through the rear window at Evelyn, John and Gran standing in the arched stone porch. The wistaria, which had been no more than dry twigs when she'd arrived, had burst into flower in the last few days. Voluptuous bunches of lilac blooms, like exotic decorations at a party, covered the front wall and framed the porch. Mandy looked through the rear window and waved goodbye, the receding view a sharp contrast to the last time she'd left in her father's car ten years before. Then it had been dark and cold and no one had waved them off, and she'd been badly hurt and felt so alone and scared.

As the car turned from the drive on to the lane and the house disappeared from view, Mandy faced the front. 'Can we make a quick stop at the shop in the village?' she asked. 'There's someone I need to say goodbye to.'

'It wouldn't be Mrs Pryce, would it?' her father asked, meeting her gaze in the interior mirror.

'Yes,' Mandy said, surprised. 'How did you know?'

'I stopped off at the village shop on the way here – to buy Evelyn those flowers – and much to my surprise I was served by Mrs Pryce. She recognized me immediately.' He paused and met her gaze again. 'So I finally got the chance to thank her and apologize for shouting at her the last time we left.'

'You know I've remembered what happened?' Mandy asked.

'Yes, Evelyn phoned. We need to talk, Mandy, but later, I think, when you're ready.'

Thirty-One

Leaving her parents in the car, parked where the double yellow lines ran out, Mandy entered the shop and heard the bell clang as the door closed behind her. Mrs Pryce was serving at the till. She glanced up and, seeing Mandy, smiled an acknowledgement, then continued serving. Mandy waited by the display of greeting cards until Mrs Pryce had finished with the customer, then approached the counter. 'I was so sorry to hear about Mr Edwards,' Mrs Pryce said, her sincere sadness mingling with apprehension at seeing Mandy again. 'How is Mrs Edwards coping?'

'Gran's trying to keep positive. She's insisting on returning home this evening. She's quite determined to go.'

'That sounds like Mrs Edwards.' Mrs Pryce smiled kindly. 'But I think she'll find it more difficult than she imagines to begin with. I know I did when I lost my hubby. I suddenly had all this time in the evening and at weekends to fill and with no one to talk to. Shall I look in on her?'

'I'm sure she'd be very grateful. And we'll all be keeping an eye on her and visiting regularly.' Mandy paused. 'I'm going home too now – Mum and Dad are waiting outside.'

Mrs Pryce nodded. 'Well, all the best, dear. It's been lovely seeing you again. Although I wish it could have been in happier circumstances.'

Mandy lowered her voice, aware there were other shoppers in the store. 'I wanted to thank you before I left for all you did for me – especially on that night. I remember how you looked after me and comforted me until my father arrived. I have remembered what happened now.' Mandy stopped and looked at Mrs Pryce. 'But you seem to know that already.'

She nodded. 'Your aunt came in here first thing this morning, ostensibly to tell me that Mr Edwards had passed away, but I guessed that wasn't the only reason she'd come. I mean you don't sack someone, cut them off for ten years, and then arrive at eight a.m. to tell them of a family bereavement. She told me you'd found out, and in pretty distressing circumstances. She apologized for the way she and Mr Osborne had treated me. Then an hour ago your father came in. When he realized who I was, he apologized too, and thanked me. I've never had so many apologies and thanks in one morning in my life!'

Mandy smiled. 'It's not before time. You were always so good to me when I stayed. And I don't know what I'd have done without you that night when Jimmy … Anyway, I just wanted to thank you. I'm very pleased my aunt has finally seen sense and apologized.' She made a move to go.

'One thing, dear?'

Mandy paused. 'Yes?'

'Can I ask what happened to Mr Osborne's brother? Your aunt didn't say.'

'Nothing,' Mandy said tightly. 'My aunt and uncle stopped seeing Jimmy, but he was never reported to the police.'

Mrs Pryce's eyes widened in dismay. 'So it was hushed up. I thought at the time that was the reason they'd sacked me. I was the only witness outside the family. But with no one keeping tabs on him who's to say he hasn't done similar to others? If I were your aunt or uncle I wouldn't be sleeping happily in my bed.' She stopped. 'Anyway, it wasn't my decision and I've probably said too much. It's been lovely seeing you again, dear, and I'm so pleased you were able to spend time with your dear grandpa before he died. Come here and let me give you a hug.'

Mrs Pryce came out from behind the counter and opened her arms to receive Mandy, just as she used to when Mandy was a child. Mandy fell into her arms and caught the faintest whiff of the lavender soap she'd always used, and remembered the warmth and security of Mrs Pryce's embrace when she'd comforted her for everything from a grazed knee to the assault that night.

'Take care, love,' Mrs Pryce said, finally drawing back as a customer approached. 'Come in and see me when you next visit your gran. It's not so far out of your way.'

'I will,' Mandy promised. 'Thanks again for everything. I won't ever forget your kindness.'

'You're very welcome, love.'

No, she wouldn't ever forget Mrs Pryce's kindness, Mandy thought as she gazed out of the side window and her father began the drive home. She wouldn't forget Mrs Pryce's care that dreadful night, and neither would she forget Jimmy's attack. For now she had remembered she was finding the memory wouldn't leave her alone; it was ever-present, like a movie set to rerun continuously. Even when she wasn't consciously thinking about it, the horror lurked in the corners of her mind, waiting to be acknowledged and confronted. The terror of waking in the dark to find Jimmy on top of her; the pressure on her chest; the scratch of his moustache as his lips sought hers; the smell of his sweat mingling with his aftershave; and the searing pain as he tried to force himself into her as she relived it over and over again. In some ways not remembering had been the safer, preferable option, for now she'd remembered she could never forget.

Turning her gaze from the side window, Mandy looked towards the front – at the backs of her parents' heads. Her mother was directly in front in the passenger seat, and her father to the right in the driver's seat, exactly as she remembered them from outings as a child. Only now her father's hair was streaked with grey, and her mother's was highlighted and in a shorter style. Her mother never drove when her father was in the car, saying she felt her driving was being scrutinized.

'Why wasn't Jimmy reported?' Mandy asked, aware of Evelyn's explanation but wanting to hear what her parents had to say.

There was a pause before her father answered while her mother looked straight ahead. 'We didn't want to put you through any more distress – the police interview, court, and having everyone know.'

'Did we do wrong?' her mother asked quickly, as though she'd always had doubts.

Mandy concentrated on the back of her mother's head. 'I honestly don't know. But I think we should have talked about it at the time, or soon after. I'm having to go back and confront it all now, instead of then. It's very raw.'

'Our decision *was* wrong then,' her mother said, and her voice caught in her throat.

'I'm not blaming you,' Mandy said quickly, touching her shoulder. 'I understand you did what you thought was right at the time. But how can you be sure Jimmy didn't go on and attack others after me? Has anyone heard from him? Does anyone know where he lives or what he's been doing?'

'No,' her father said. 'We hardly knew him, thank goodness. We'd only ever met him twice – at Evelyn's wedding and at Sarah's christening. John severed all communication and never saw him again, which I understand from Evelyn placed him in a dreadful position in respect of his mother.'

And what about my position? Mandy thought, but didn't say. Then something occurred to her. 'Evelyn told me John visits his mother in a nursing home. I wonder if Jimmy visits her too? If he does it's possible John has seen Jimmy at the nursing home, if they were both visiting at the same time.'

'It's possible,' her father agreed. 'I don't know. Their mother refused to believe Jimmy had done anything wrong, which I suppose is understandable – he was her son. Does it matter if he visits her?'

Mandy shrugged. 'Probably not.' She looked out of the side window at the passing scenery. There were so many issues to acknowledge and deal with, so many pieces to fit into the jigsaw before she could even begin to let go of the past and move on. And while she felt angry that Jimmy's mother had refused to believe what he'd done, as her father said it was understandable – what mother wouldn't believe her son over a distant relative?

'When did I see the doctor?' Mandy asked after a moment, returning her gaze to the front. 'Evelyn said I saw a doctor but I don't remember.'

'It was the following day,' her mother said quietly. 'It was very distressing – for us both. And the upset, together with the results of the examination, helped your father and me come to the decision not to report Jimmy.' She stopped, leaving the details unstated.

'Mum, I need to know what the doctor said, distasteful and upsetting though it might be. This has all been shut away for far too long. I need to know what – what exactly Jimmy did to me.'

There was silence as her father concentrated on the road ahead and her mother sat motionless, looking through the windscreen.

Mandy felt their reticence and discomposure. 'Mum? It is important. I need to know.'

'The doctor had to examine you thoroughly,' she began in a hurry, 'where you'd been hurt. I hated putting you through that – a girl of your age, after everything, but it was necessary. The doctor took swabs – you know, samples – and had them sent away. We didn't get the results for two weeks but when they came back they were negative. You didn't have a venereal disease. And the examination showed you'd been bruised but not fully penetrated. The hymen was still in place, so technically you were still a virgin. The doctor said that if we were going to report it to the police it would have to be done immediately otherwise valuable evidence would be lost. Your father and I had to make the decision whether to go ahead and subject you to another medical by a police doctor, and all that would follow – being interviewed and going to court – or just try and get on with our lives. We decided to try and put it all behind us and forget; only of course the only one who "forgot" was you.'

She stopped and fell silent, and for some time all that could be heard was the distant hum of the car engine and the occasional swish as the wipers cleared the spots of rain.

'But it wasn't genuine forgetting,' Mandy said. 'It was like amnesia where somehow I'd blotted it all out.'

'And I always thought that one day it would come back to you and we'd all have to deal with it,' her mother said, glancing sideways at her father. 'I was right.'

'We'll pay for whatever help you need,' her father said, meeting her eyes in the mirror. 'Evelyn thinks a counsellor or therapist could help. If you think it will, we'll find one and I'll pay for it as long as you need it. I did what I thought was right at the time, Mandy, and if I was wrong, then I'm very sorry, I'll try and put it right in any way I can.'

'Thanks,' she said, and realized her father was finally calling her Mandy rather than the Amanda of her childhood.

Thirty-Two

They pulled up outside her flat at nearly 4.30 p.m. and, as her father took her suitcase from the boot, Mandy kissed her mother goodbye. 'I'll phone this evening,' her mother said for the second time.

'All right, but please don't worry, I'll be fine,' Mandy reassured her.

Her father insisted on carrying her case up to her flat despite Mandy's assurance she could manage. She wanted to be alone, was looking forward to it, just her in her flat, before Adam arrived after work in an hour or so. Going down the short garden path, with her father following, her heart skipped a beat as she unlocked the front door and stepped into the hall. After ten days away she was greeting it afresh: the high Victorian ceiling with its permanent damp spot, the wallpaper below the dado rail in need of a coat of paint, and the original mosaic-tiled floor slightly grubby from the comings and goings of the tenants – all shabby compared to her aunt's house but oh so welcoming as home.

She picked up the letters on the small table just inside the hall and quickly sifted through them, but none were for her. Adam had probably put her mail in her flat when he'd stopped by with the milk and bread. Leading the way up the wide balustraded staircase, she turned on to the landing and was finally outside her very own front door. Inserting the key, she unlocked the door, then pushed it open and heard the familiar squeak. 'That hinge needs oiling,' her father said, following her in with the case. 'I'll see to it if you have a can of oil.'

'I don't. I'll do it another time. Thanks, anyway.'

'Where do you want the case?' he asked, unwilling to simply pass it to her and leave. 'It's heavy.'

'On the bed, please.'

She waited just inside the room as her father crossed to the recess – the bedroom part of the studio flat – and lifted the case on to the bed. 'You will be all right, alone?' he asked, glancing anxiously around.

'Yes, please don't worry. I'll be fine. Adam will be here soon.'

'Well, if you're sure.' He hesitated, then came over and kissed her goodbye. 'Thanks again for everything you did for Grandpa. I'll phone later. There's no need to see me out.'

She went with him on to the landing and then waited at the top of the stairs as he went down. 'Bye,' she called as he arrived at the bottom.

He glanced up. 'Bye for now, love. Take care.' Opening the front door, he let himself out as Tina from the downstairs flat came in. Mandy knew her well; they'd texted while she'd been away.

'Hi,' Tina called, looking up and seeing Mandy. 'Glad you're back. Fancy a drink later?'

'Adam's coming. Tomorrow?'

'Sure. I'll knock for you about eight?'

'Great.'

Re-entering her flat, Mandy closed the door and wandered slowly around the room, savouring everything anew. The faded green leather armchair beside the Turkish rug; the massive oak wardrobe with the warped door that stuck; the three-quarter-size bed that squeaked; and the Japanese-style dressing screen with the nightclothes she'd been wearing on the morning she'd left still flung over it. It was home and it was hers. The room smelt faintly musty from being closed up and she crossed to the bay window and hauled up one of the lower sashes. The late afternoon air rushed in, sharp and fresh, stirring the curtains and breathing life into the room. Going to the kitchenette, she opened the fridge door. Not only had Adam bought milk and bread but also eggs, bacon, cheese, juice, a fresh cream éclair – her favourite – and a bottle of white wine. She smiled at his thoughtfulness. Resisting the temptation to open the wine, she took out the milk to make a cup of tea, filled the kettle and, while it boiled, crossed to her suitcase to start unpacking.

She removed two items and stopped, suddenly and completely overwhelmed by a debilitating sadness. Coming from nowhere and with an intensity that was frightening, it engulfed her as though the biggest, blackest cloud had settled over the sun, obliterating any chance of light, now or in the future. Straightening, she left the unpacking and sat on the bed beside the open case. She stared unseeing at the floor, her mind a blank. Her body felt so heavy and weighted down, it was almost impossible to move; everything seemed too much effort. Of course she was sad, she thought, her dear grandpa had died, but this was more than sorrow, it was as if she were being buried alive. A darkness, a bleakness so dense that everything – her past, present and future – seemed completely pointless, her whole life not worth living.

She sat further back on the bed and curled her legs around her. The kettle boiled and clicked off; the old fridge hummed with the effort of keeping its contents cold; and the street noise filtered in through the open window. Gradually the late afternoon light began to fail and the room lost its sharpness. Mandy remained where she was on the bed, hardly moving and staring into space. She heard the doorbell ring; Adam was outside waiting for her to go down and let him in. She didn't move. A few minutes later it rang again and she knew he would assume she was in the shower or toilet and use his key to let himself in. A moment later he was knocking at her door and his key was in the lock.

Hauling herself to her feet, her legs stiff from sitting in one position, she crossed the room and switched on the light. The door opened. 'Hi, love!' he cried, pleased to see her. 'How's my Mandy?' She felt his arms around her, hugging for all he was worth, and then his lips seeking hers. She instinctively drew back. 'Sorry,' he said. 'Insensitive me. Let's sit and talk.'

With his arm around her shoulder they crossed to the bed. He lifted the case on to the floor to make room for them. She sat beside him, their legs outstretched, using the wall as a backrest as they often sat in the evenings. 'How are you?' he asked tenderly. 'You must be very sad. I can remember how I felt when I lost my granddad.'

She shrugged despondently. 'Yes, I am sad, but not only from losing Grandpa. There's something else, Adam.'

'What sort of something? You're not going to finish with me, are you?' he said lightly, as a joke, but with an underlying anxiety as though he feared it could be so.

'No.' She rested her head on his shoulder and, staring across the room, tried to formulate her thoughts. How she wished her sadness could just be put down to bereavement, how simple that would be. She knew she owed Adam some explanation; he was after all her partner; but how much she could tell him she wasn't sure. 'Something happened to me a long while ago,' she tried. 'While I was at Evelyn's I discovered something and I'm trying to sort through it and deal with it.'

'What sort of something?' he asked, looking at her anxiously. 'Why are you being so vague?'

'It was when I was just thirteen,' she began, and stopped. 'I don't know,' she said, shaking her head. 'I'm sorry, Adam; you're going to have to be patient with me.' For suddenly she'd found that she couldn't tell Adam. That despite, or possibly because of, the closeness of their relationship, the last person she wanted to tell – to know – she'd been sexually assaulted was Adam. 'I'm sorry,' she said again. 'You're going to have to be patient with me.'

He gave her shoulder a little squeeze of reassurance and kissed her cheek. They were silent for some time. She felt awkward and knew she should be saying or doing something after all his thoughtfulness, but what? 'Thanks for putting the things in the fridge,' she said at length.

'No problem. Shall we open the wine?'

'I don't mind,' she said unenthusiastically. And she really didn't mind; in fact, not only didn't she mind, she couldn't be bothered even to think about it. He could open the wine if he wished or leave it in the fridge – either way, it made no difference.

'Or would you like to go out for something to eat?' he offered.

'Not really. Thanks anyway.' He was trying so hard, and she felt wretched for not being able to respond, but she really didn't care right now – about wine, going out, or even him. And whereas, not so long ago – that morning and during the drive here – she'd been looking forward to being close to him again, lying in his arms and feeling his body caress hers, she now found that not only didn't she want him physically near her but she was feeling repulsed by the idea.

'You OK, Mandy?' he asked after a moment, sensing her disquiet and kissing her cheek again. 'Is there anything I can do or get you, love?'

She shrugged. 'Not really.' Then she realized there was some-thing he could do, cruel though it was to suggest it. 'Adam, I'm so sorry,' she said, shifting away from him. 'But I need to be alone.'

He looked at her, surprised. 'Do you want me to go?'

She nodded and hated herself. Good, kind Adam.

'Are you sure?'

'Yes, I'm sorry.' She could see his pain at her rebuff.

Sliding his arm from her shoulders he moved to the edge of the bed and stood up. 'I'm sorry,' she said again. 'I was looking forward to seeing you but it doesn't feel right – not tonight.'

He stared at her, hurt and confused; he didn't understand, but then why should he? She didn't either. Sliding off the bed, she walked with him to the door. 'Will you be all right alone?' he asked, as her father had done.

'Yes. I'll phone you.'

She saw his concern mingle with rejection as he leant forward to kiss her lips. Instinctively she moved her head to one side so his lips brushed her cheek instead. He opened the door and in silence let himself out. She watched him go and knew again she was a cold-hearted bitch. Loyal, caring Adam, who'd put up with so much from her and who, a few days before, had asked her to live with him and be his partner, now dismissed without explanation. It would serve her right if he never wanted to see her again, wanted nothing more to do with her. And whereas, before, she'd always been distraught at the prospect of losing him and had quickly tried to make up any argument, she now found herself thinking it didn't really matter, and in some ways it would be easier, a lot easier, if she didn't have a relationship to deal with.

Thirty-Three

Switching off the main light, Mandy crossed the room by the light of the streetlamp and took off her jeans and jumper. She dumped them on top of her suitcase on the floor and then slid under the duvet, where she curled foetally on her side. The curtains stirred in the evening breeze; the street noise slowly drifted in and then petered out.

When she opened her eyes again it was to the ringing of her phone. Dazed and disorientated from sleep, she sat bolt upright, expecting to be in the armchair in the study with Grandpa's bed opposite. With a jolt she realized she was in her own room and Grandpa had gone. Reaching out, she fumbled for her bag and took out her phone. 'I hope I didn't wake you,' her father said as she answered, 'but your mother was worried when you didn't ring last night.'

'Sorry,' she said. 'I must have fallen asleep.' She glanced at the time. It was 6.43 a.m.

'I told your mother that's what must have happened – that you were either asleep or out with Adam.'

'Yes. I'm sorry,' she apologized again.

'All right, love, I'll leave you to it. Just wanted to make sure you were OK. I'm on my way to a breakfast meeting. Give your mum a ring later, will you? You know how she worries.'

'I will.'

Saying goodbye, she dropped the phone on the bed and flopped back on to the pillows. Far from feeling refreshed after nearly ten hours sleep, she felt the same debilitating sadness that had engulfed her the evening before. More than sorrow, lethargy or exhaustion, it was a thick, dark mass which weighed so heavily, it took away the desire to do anything and made everything seem totally pointless. Even the basic essentials of washing, dressing or even getting out of bed seemed to require far more effort than she was capable of. And her wretchedness increased as she realized she hadn't even phoned Gran the previous evening as she'd promised. Mandy lay back on the pillows and stared at the ceiling, feeling absolutely worthless, and helpless to do anything about it.

Half an hour later she was dying for a wee and she knew she'd have to get up if she wasn't going to wet the bed. Hauling her feet to the floor, she stood, slightly giddy from spending so long lying down. In only her bra and pants she shivered in the early morning air coming from the open window, padded to the bay and lowered the sash. Crossing to her suitcase on the floor she pulled out her kimono and wrapped it around her, then opened the door to her room. She went along the landing to the communal bathroom, where she used the toilet. The house was quiet; it always was at this time. Most of the occupants were students and they never got up until much later. Returning to her room, she climbed into bed, where she propped herself on the pillows and lay back, very still. She stared into space, her mind empty of everything except the darkness, her body paralysed beneath the black mass.

How easy it was to do nothing and how quickly time passed, Mandy thought as the minutes blurred into hours. Time had no relevance when there were no goals or milestones in her day, it just went on and on. Her phone rang, and when she picked it up from beside her on the bed she saw it was already 11.40 a.m. She didn't answer; it was her mother's mobile and she really didn't feel like talking right now. Her mother knew she was safe; her father would have phoned her. She also noticed a text from Adam, sent half an hour before – *Hope u r ok. fone when u want 2 meet x*. She didn't want to phone or meet.

At 3.10 p.m., making a huge effort, Mandy drew herself higher up the pillows and phoned Gran. But the answerphone clicked in and Mandy was shocked to hear Grandpa's voice: *Sorry we can't take your call. Please leave a message and we'll call you back as soon as we return.* Gran must be out and hadn't thought to change the message yet. She hung up and redialled, just to hear his voice again, and then again. Dear Grandpa – his voice so immediate and alive, he might still be there. Tears stung the back of her eyes. She redialled and, savouring his voice one last time, made hers as light and even as possible. 'Hi, Gran. It's Mandy. Just phoning for a chat. I expect you're next door. Love you.' Closing the phone she put it beside her on the duvet, then lay back and wept.

At 7 p.m. the light began to fade again outside and Mandy realized with morbid satisfaction that she'd spent the entire day in bed doing nothing. She also realized she hadn't had anything to eat or drink, and while she wasn't hungry she was thirsty. She could hardly swallow, her throat was so dry. She pushed herself out of bed, wondering at the mammoth effort it took, and went to the fridge where she tore open the packet of fresh juice Adam had bought. She drank half of it straight from the carton, and then took the carton back into bed. Propping herself on the pillows again, she continued staring into space.

Some time later a knock sounded on the door together with Tina's voice: 'Mandy, are you still OK for a drink later?' Mandy had forgotten Tina's invitation from the day before, but no, she certainly wasn't OK for a drink later. She stayed where she was, very still and quiet. There was silence from the other side of the door. Tina knocked again, and finally went away. With no light on and no television or music playing she'd assumed Mandy had forgotten their arrangement and gone out. Later still Mandy's phone rang again and when she looked at the caller's number she saw it was Gran. Making a huge effort to sound normal, she answered, 'Hello Gran, sorry I didn't phone last night. I fell asleep. How are you?'

'Not too bad, love. I got your message. I've been with my neighbour most of the afternoon. It's a bit quiet here without Will. Evelyn came over earlier about the funeral arrangements. It's next Friday. Your dad has the details.' God, the funeral, Mandy thought, how was she going to cope with the funeral when she couldn't even get out of bed? 'So what have you been doing?' Gran asked. 'Keeping busy with your painting?'

'Yes,' Mandy lied, for it was easier than saying no. Then Gran talked about Grandpa and the little reminders of him that were all over the bungalow and which she was reluctant to put away.

'His message is still on the answerphone,' Mandy said.

'Is it? I'll have to ask John or Evelyn to change it; I don't know what you do. Evelyn said she'll help clear out his clothes and take them to the Oxfam, but there's no rush, is there?'

'No, none at all.'

Gran talked for another ten minutes, pleased to have someone to chat to. Mandy was pleased to listen. She found some comfort in the sound of Gran's voice — a familiar source of warmth in her present cold isolation. Gran finally wound up: 'Well, dear, come and see me as soon as you're free.'

'Yes, of course I will. Love you, Gran.'

'And you, dear.'

* * *

It wasn't that she wasn't free, Mandy thought as she once more dropped the phone on to the bed beside her and lay back; she had all the time in the world. But the organization and effort needed to get ready and then catch the train to Gran's were more than she could contemplate at present. Also, in her current state she was hardly the best person to be visiting and trying to cheer up someone who had just been bereaved. It seemed Gran was faring far better than she was at present; at least she'd been out.

An hour or so later she heard Tina and Nick from the attic flat leave the house, presumably going to the pub together. Mandy was still propped on the pillows; the only light in the room came from the streetlamp outside. The evening ticked past and she stayed where she was, vaguely listening to the comings and goings of the other tenants and their visitors. Some time later when it was completely dark she heard Tina and Nick return and call goodnight to each other before going into their separate flats. Her phone bleeped with a text. She drew it into her line of vision and saw it was 12.05 and the text was from Adam: *I luv and miss you x.*

His words, his forgiveness, opened a small crack in the black fog of her depression as she was reminded of what she stood to lose. Yes, she loved and missed him too, yet she couldn't bear the thought of him being close or touching her; neither could she tell him the reason why. Jimmy's attack, now remembered, had left her feeling dirty, violated and completely unclean. With a stab of panic she realized that if she didn't find a way of dealing with it, it would not only finish her relationship with Adam but very likely destroy the rest of her life.

I luv u 2, she texted, *but I need u 2 b patient. i hav to come to terms with sumthing. x*

He texted back immediately: *I understand. Hav all the time u need. hav you tried painting out yr feelings. it might help?*

Thirty-Four

Large splodges of black paint intermingled with swirls of grey, as though thunderclouds were gathering across an already dark sky. Mandy stood at the easel in her nightdress, clutching the paintbrush like a dagger, and daubed on more black paint. What the painting was supposed to be she'd no idea – it was certainly no prize-winning Turner. And while she was finding some release in expressing her anger, it wasn't providing the answers Adam had thought it might. It was more an outlet for her frustration, much like hitting a punch bag, rather than a gateway to her feelings. Or perhaps this *was* how she felt – a swirling mass of black and grey.

So it was hushed up, Mrs Pryce had exclaimed. Yes, but it wasn't my decision, Mandy thought. I had no control over the way it was dealt with – shrouded in secrecy and making me a slave to its legacy of silence. No wonder they thought I was odd at university; no wonder I didn't date. If it had been taken care of and dealt with at the time it would have been nothing more than a nasty memory for me now, instead of being fresh and raw. *Who's to say he hasn't done similar to others?* Mrs Pryce had rightly pointed out. 'Or still is,' Mandy added out loud, as another daub of black paint hit the canvas. But surely my parents, Evelyn and John must have considered this, she thought, when they made their decision not to report him. Unless there's something they're still not telling me? More paint landed on top of that already there, ran down and dripped off the edge of the canvas. Then she stopped, and her paintbrush hovered in mid-air. Slowly, very slowly, she lowered her hand and, dipping the brush into the water, began cleaning it on the rag. Painting out her feelings wasn't the answer. She needed answers and she realized she knew where to find them.

An hour later, showered and dressed, Mandy unpacked her suitcase and returned it to the top of the wardrobe. All that remained now were the three small boxes she'd put on the bed for safe-keeping, then she could begin her plan. Carefully opening the lid on each of the boxes she took out the three china dogs and set them on the bookshelf with the others. She stepped back and admired them. There was a sense of closure in seeing the collection complete, like putting the last full stop at the end of a very long essay. A full stop she was now hoping to put behind Jimmy's attack, if it was possible to find him.

Crossing to the small table that doubled as a desk, Mandy opened her laptop and, while it booted, took a writing pad and pen from the chest of drawers. She set the pad and pen on the table and drew her chair beneath her. She was now ready for some hard investigative work, which, thanks to the Internet, she thought, could largely be done at home. However did people manage before www? she wondered as the Windows page filled the screen. Presumably a lot of information was never discovered, and people and situations remained lost for ever? Clicking the mouse to connect to the Internet, the Google home page appeared. Now what? she thought, and her fingers hovered uncertainly over the keyboard.

What she needed was a website that held people's contact details, like the telephone directory or electoral register. She typed finding people into Google and a very promising-looking list of web addresses appeared. Starting with the top URL – *Trace-a-person* – she clicked on the link and read what information the website offered and its scale of charges; then she moved down to the next. The information on individuals these sites claimed to be able to obtain was staggering: medical records, criminal records, credit rating, in addition to the person's address, telephone number and marital status, which many of the sites seemed to offer for free. For £5 a month subscription, if you knew a person's mobile number, you could track that mobile and follow the person anywhere in the world! No wonder the public worried about the power of the Internet, she thought. Out of curiosity she entered her own name and date of birth for a free introductory search. A few seconds later she saw her full name and address appear, together with the full names of three of the other tenants living in the house. She learnt that Nick Granger in the top flat had a landline number; she'd assumed all the tenants relied on their mobiles as she did, and was even more surprised to read that Mrs Granger had lived with Nick, suggesting he was now divorced, which he'd never mentioned.

Returning to the Google list, Mandy clicked on the second website listed; it seemed the most comprehensive and also offered a free search. She looked at the two blank boxes where she now had to enter the name of the person she wanted to find and the area in which that person was last known to have resided. She felt slightly light-headed and queasy as her fingers typed in Jimmy Osborne, and then Cambridgeshire, the county where Evelyn and John lived. She'd have to assume Jimmy lived or had lived in the area, which seemed reasonable, otherwise she'd no idea where to start looking. Clicking *Search,* a holding message appeared: *Please wait, searching in progress.* She felt her pulse rise in a little rush of adrenalin as she stared at the screen. The word *Result* appeared and her mouth went dry. *Result* disappeared, immediately replaced by: *No person listed by that name in the area searched.*

'Drat!' she said out loud. If he's not in Cambridgeshire where the hell is he?

Moving the cursor to the button marked *More info* she clicked on it and two more buttons appeared: *Login* or *Join here*, with a list of charges for membership. The minimum was £5.99 and allowed twelve searches. Pushing back her chair, she stood up and fetched her bag from beside the bed, and then returned to the computer. Taking her debit card from her purse she entered her card details and clicked *Continue.* A message appeared stating a confirmatory email with her login details had been sent to her email address. She clicked on her email account, noted her password, and returned to the webpage where she logged in. She now had twelve searches to try and find Jimmy. She knew she had his name right and she now knew he wasn't living in Cambridgeshire so she decided to work through the other counties, starting with those closest to Cambridgeshire. It crossed her mind it would be a lot simpler to phone Evelyn or John and ask them if they knew Jimmy's address, but that would spark their curiosity, and they would want to know why. Also, as John had disowned his brother it was unlikely he'd have his current address, particularly as it appeared he'd moved out of the area. She doubted they were sending each other Christmas cards.

She began the wider search with Norfolk, which lay next to Cambridgeshire. Now she'd paid as a 'member' she automatically got more information in each search. There were six people in Norfolk listed as J. Osborne: Jack Osborne, Jeremy Osborne, Jessie Osborne, Jodie Osborne, John Osborne (not her uncle – John was a common name), Jonathan Osborne, but no Jimmy. She tried Suffolk; there were twenty J. Osbornes, but no Jimmy. Next she tried Essex. There were forty J. Osbornes. Surely this must produce a result. But as she moved the cursor down through Jackie, Jacob, James, Jean, Jeffrey, Jennifer, etc. to the bottom of the page, there was no Jimmy. Next she tried Bedfordshire and her heart skipped a beat as Jimmy Osborne appeared on the screen, but his date of birth made him only nineteen.

Encouraged by finding one Jimmy Osborne, she moved on to Hertfordshire. There were fifteen J. Osbornes listed, but no Jimmy. Next was Huntingdonshire where she found two Jimmy Osbornes, but one was eighty and the other thirteen. Spreading out from Cambridgeshire, she tried Northamptonshire: none; then Lincolnshire: three but none the right age. That Jimmy wasn't a popular name was helping as she could check their ages from the date of birth easily. John was far more popular, as was Jackie – there were dozens of John and Jackie Osbornes. One hour rolled into two; her neck was aching from leaning over her laptop, and although she had a glass of water at her side, she hadn't eaten and was hungry. Once she'd found Jimmy's address, she thought, she'd cook herself something nice to eat. Her spirits were quickly rising and she was feeling far more positive. It was only a matter of time before she found him. She was getting adept at scrolling down the names. If necessary she'd search through all eighty-six counties in Britain, although every twelve searches was another £5.99 on her card. Spreading out from Cambridgeshire she continued with Leicestershire, then Buckinghamshire, and then Greater London where there were four Jimmy Osbornes but none the right age.

Two hours later she entered Caithness, the last county at the very tip of Scotland, and clicked *Search*. The holding message appeared: *Please wait, searching in progress.* A couple of seconds, and *Result* appeared, followed by: *No person listed by that name in the area searched.*

'Shit!' she cried and slammed down the lid on the computer, tears of frustration stinging the back of her eyes. Eighty-six counties, nearly £50 on her debit card and all her efforts had come to nothing! She'd found sixty-two Jimmy Osbornes in all and not one was the right age or even near it. She'd even checked the details of the three who were deceased but they weren't the right age either. The Jimmy she was looking for was fourteen months older than John, which made him fifty-four.

Moving away from the table, she grabbed her jacket and bag and went out of her bedsit and down the stairs. She needed fresh air. Her legs were stiff, her arms and neck ached, and she felt lower now than when she'd started the search. She'd been so sure she'd be able to find him and confront him; it had given her something to aim for. She'd seen it as a cleansing exorcism that she was sure would set her on the path to recovery; now that hope seemed to have gone – for good. The only explanation she could think of for Jimmy not being listed on any electoral roll or directory, which was what the websites used for searching, was that he'd left the country or had changed his name. And for a moment it flashed through her mind that she could spend the rest of her life scouring the world in an obsessive but fruitless search to find him. For without doubt if someone wanted to disappear they could.

Head down, shoulders slumped, she walked towards the High Street. She needed something to eat but couldn't be bothered to make anything. She was feeling queasy from staring at the computer screen for nearly four hours and not having eaten. Bastard! she thought as she walked. He's got away with it again. It's too late! Why hadn't they done something at the time? And although she knew the answer and the reason why his crime had gone unreported – to protect her – it didn't help. Closure now was impossible. He'd escaped.

The supermarket at the end of the High Street was busy at nearly 5 p.m. Mandy picked up a wire basket and headed for the bakery section. She'd have a ready made sandwich; that was easy. There wouldn't be much choice so late in the day but she wasn't fussy, anything would do. She took one of the three remaining BLTs from the shelf and dropped it in her basket. Then she moved along the counter to where the cakes and pastries were. Picking up a bag of doughnuts, she dropped that in her basket and headed towards the chiller for some more milk; she'd nearly finished the pint Adam had bought her.

A young lad of about five who was playing up with his mother ran into her. 'I'm so sorry,' the woman said. 'Jamie, apologize now.' She took her son by the arm and pushed him in front of Mandy. 'Apologize now,' she said firmly. 'Or there'll be no treat later.'

'It's all right, don't worry,' Mandy said and edged away. She hated scenes in public.

'Sorry,' she heard the boy say from behind. She turned and smiled, and then continued to the milk cabinet.

She took a half-litre carton of semi-skimmed milk from the shelf and placed it in her basket. But instead of moving away from the chiller she remained where she was, staring into the cabinet. She felt her heart start to pound as her thoughts raced. Jamie. The boy had been called Jamie. Wasn't Jamie a shortened form of James? Hadn't there'd been a boy in her class at secondary school who'd been called James, but had preferred Jamie and then, when he was older – Jimmy? Yes, she was sure his name had been James but he'd always used Jamie, and then later Jimmy like the actor and singer/songwriter Jimmy Nail – who'd been born James but was known as Jimmy.

Why hadn't she thought of it earlier? Of course people used Jimmy as a name in its own right, but it was also a derivation of

James. Was it possible Jimmy Osborne had been born James Osborne but had always been known as Jimmy? In which case she'd been searching on the wrong name.

'Excuse me.' Mandy started and looked at the man on her left. 'Can I get to the milk, please?'

'Sorry.' Turning from the chiller, she ran down the aisle and to the checkout. *Please let it be so.*

Thirty-Five

Twenty minutes later, having run most of the way home, Mandy sat at the table in her bedsit with the carton of milk and the BLT beside her, and opened the laptop. The screen sprung into life and the last webpage appeared but with a message: Timed out. 'Blast!' she said. She'd have to enter her login details again. Clicking through to her Inbox she opened the email with her login details and copied and pasted the pass code into the *Login* box. The page for searching appeared and, hardly daring to breathe, she typed in James Osborne and Cambridgeshire. She clicked *Search* and waited. The familiar holding message appeared: *Please wait, searching in progress.* Please let him be there, please, this is my last hope. A few seconds passed and then *Result* appeared. There were two James Osbornes living in Cambridgeshire. Let one of them be him, she prayed, please, that's all I ask. She clicked on the first: James Mark Osborne, but his date of birth showed him to be forty-eight. Close but not close enough. With her fingers shaking she clicked on the second: James Simon Osborne. She looked at his date of birth. Her hand shot to her mouth and she stifled a cry. The right age. Yes, he was fifty-four! Was it really him? She hardly dared believe.

Clicking on the button for more information, she drew her pen and paper across the table. The information appeared and she made a note of his address and telephone number. There was a map symbol beside his address. She clicked on it and a map of the area where he lived filled the screen. Moving her cursor to extend the perimeters of the map, she calculated that this James lived about five miles from Evelyn and John. Closing the map she returned to James's details and *Other occupants over eighteen living at this address.* She clicked on the link and the name Natalie Jane Osborne appeared. Wasn't Natalie the name of Jimmy's wife? Isn't that what Evelyn had said? She tried to think back and remember. When she'd taken refuge in the Pink Room and Evelyn had come in and tried to explain, hadn't she said Jimmy's wife was called Natalie? Mandy was almost sure she had. She looked at Natalie's date of birth. She was three years younger than Jimmy. She made a note and then looked up and gazed at the screen.

Although his age and address fitted, and possibly Natalie was the name of his wife, Mandy had to be absolutely certain that this James Osborne was the Jimmy she was looking for. It wouldn't do to go bursting in and accuse an innocent man. A message appeared telling her she needed to pay another £5.99 before she could continue to search, which she did. It would have been cheaper to take out a year's membership, she thought, but she hadn't realized how much searching she was going to be doing. Returning to the page with James Simon Osborne's details, Mandy now clicked the button to search criminal records. The holding message appeared, and her stomach churned. *Result: no criminal record found.*

She wasn't sure if this made it better or worse.

She began clicking down the line of information buttons to the right of the page but the only other detail she was able to discover was that this James had a full driving licence and passport, both of which she could have reasonably guessed as most adults possessed them. Then she came to the search button for checking birth records. Of course! She had enough information to check his birth certificate. Leaning closer and hardly daring to breathe, she clicked on the link to the register of births and entered 'James Simon Osborne' and his date of birth. A moment later *Result* appeared. James Simon Osborne was born to a Mabel Elizabeth Osborne; it gave his mother's date of birth. Not daring to take her eyes from the screen, Mandy reached for the pen and wrote his mother's date of birth on the notepad. Close, so close; she was certain it was him, but there was one final check she needed to make before it was conclusive. Returning to the main menu, she carefully typed in his mother's full name, Mabel Elizabeth Osborne, together with her date of birth, and clicked *Search*. The holding message appeared ... *Please wait* ... then a few moments later: *Result*. Mabel Elizabeth Osborne lived in St Mary's Nursing Home, located almost exactly between John's and James's address. Evelyn had said John's mother was in a local nursing home. Too much for coincidence.

'Result!' Mandy said, satisfied, tearing off the sheet of paper with his details on. She folded it and put it in her purse for safe-keeping, shut down the computer, then finished the carton of milk and sandwich. 'Found you at last, you bastard!'

She wasn't sure exactly when she would be using the information, only that it wouldn't be very long. The anger, fear, hurt and resentment she should have felt in the months straight after the attack, but which had been denied to her all these years, were flaring with vengeance, and would very likely keep doing so. She knew if she didn't deal with them soon she would never be able to move on and leave the past behind. Being in possession of Jimmy's address had empowered her. She knew where he lived, and he had no idea she knew. Having the advantage made her feel more in control of events rather than at their mercy. Less of a victim.

Crossing the room, she went to the easel and the painting she'd begun in the early hours of the morning. She'd still no idea what the swirls of grey and black were and the 'picture' seemed even less appealing now than it had earlier. Taking down the paper, she screwed it up and put it in the bin, then clipped a fresh sheet to the easel. She took the cap off the tube of blue paint and squeezing a little on to her palette began to paint. An hour later she stood back and admired what she'd done so far. Not bad, not bad at all. The blue, cloudless sky stretched into the distance and the church spire that rose before it was a good likeness. Perhaps she hadn't lost her talent after all. Cleaning her brush, she picked up her mobile and texted Adam: *Im free if u want 2 meet l8r?* Almost immediately a text came back: *Dinner? red lion 7pm?* She felt a frisson of warmth as she replied: *Yes plz x.* The Red Lion was the pub they'd used once before to meet after an argument – neutral ground where they'd repaired their differences.

With an hour before she was due to meet Adam Mandy sat on the bed and returned the texts and calls from the day before. There were three texts from friends, which she dealt with first, then she phoned her mother. 'Are you sure you're all right alone?' her mother asked for the second time. 'You know you can always stay here.'

'I'm fine,' Mandy reassured. 'I'm keeping busy and I'm meeting Adam for dinner shortly,' which seemed to reassure her.

Mandy then spent the next twenty minutes, before she had to leave to meet Adam, getting ready. She made a special effort – straightening her hair, changing her T-shirt for a blouse and applying eye make-up and lipstick.

'Sorry,' she said, as soon as she saw him outside the pub. 'Sorry I was such a cow.'

He smiled and kissed her lightly on the lips, as usual willing to forgive even though he didn't know what was wrong.

'Thanks for being so understanding,' she said. 'I need to talk to you.'

He nodded and, taking her hand, led the way up the steps and into the carvery pub. The waitress showed them to a corner table where they ordered their drinks. Only once they were settled with their plates before them and Adam was concentrating on his food did she begin.

'Adam, you know when we first met at Uni you thought I didn't date because of a bad experience?' He nodded. 'You were right. I didn't know it at the time but I'd had a very traumatic experience as a child. I'd shut myself in emotionally and couldn't bear to let anyone near me. If you hadn't taken the time to get to know me I don't think I'd ever have had a relationship or fallen in love. I can't go into all the details now, I've only just found out.'

'While you were at your aunt's?' He'd stopped eating and was looking at her, his face deathly serious.

'Yes.'

'I thought as much.'

'I'm still trying to come to terms with what I now know happened. I'll tell you everything one day, I promise.' She paused. He was watching her intently. 'I need you, Adam, I love you. But if we are going to carry on seeing each other you'll have to be as patient now as you were at Uni. I want your company but I can't …' She stopped, suddenly very self-conscious and unable to say the words. 'Do you understand what I'm trying to say?' she finished lamely after a moment.

He nodded and, setting his cutlery on his plate, reached out and took her hand. 'I think we'll be watching a lot of television. Don't worry; take as much time as you need.'

Thirty-Six

Several days later Mandy stood in front of the easel, dry paintbrush in hand, and continued to study the blank canvas. Having finished the painting of the church with its spire rising high into the blue sky and been reasonably pleased with it she now found she was blocked again. Propped on the table beside the easel was her sketch pad; she kept flicking through it for inspiration but none came. It was mid-morning and Adam was at work; she was expecting him to phone or text later as he had been doing each day. Although they'd seen each other every evening, following her wishes he'd returned home to sleep.

With a sigh she moved away from the easel and wandered over to the window where she gazed out on to the front garden and street below. What was Jimmy doing now on this clear April morning? she wondered. Was he at work? Concentrating on a computer screen, with a client, or in a meeting? Or perhaps he was rich and didn't have to work and was playing golf, or was even at home, reading the newspaper, or out shopping with his wife. Or maybe he was on holiday, taking a week before the schools broke up for Easter. Since obtaining Jimmy's details Mandy found she kept trying to imagine where he was or what he might be doing. It was starting to become an obsession, overriding all her other thoughts. Knowing where Jimmy lived had brought him that much closer and made him more accessible and real, instead of the shadowy figure in the Pink Room or at the foot of the slide. But in bringing him closer, the horror of his attack had taken a step closer too. Mandy knew she couldn't put it off any longer – she needed to confront him, preferably before the funeral on Friday when she would see all her family again, which effectively meant she had to do it today, Thursday.

Two hours later she boarded the 12.05 at Paddington Station which would get her into Mowbury – the town closest to where Jimmy lived – at 13.40. From there she would catch a bus (No. 247) to the outskirts of the town, and then it was approximately a five-minute walk to his address. She'd worked out the route from maps she'd printed from the Internet, including a detailed street map of the exact location of his house. She sat in the carriage with a bench seat to herself and gazed out of the window as the train pulled away. She tried to silence her racing heart and not think about what she was doing, for she knew any more thought could weaken her resolve and she'd turn round and go home. Of course her family would be upset when she went to the police and the hurt of the past was reignited, but she was sure they'd understand. She was equally confident they would give evidence, and their evidence, together with that of Mrs Pryce and the doctor's report from the time, would surely secure Jimmy's conviction. She needed to make sure he wasn't free to do it again and also to see him punished.

Gazing through the carriage window, the offices and houses of Greater London were gradually replaced by countryside, peppered with the occasional town or village. It was only from a train or plane, she thought, that you realized just how much of England was still green – easily forgotten living in London. Her mobile bleeped with an incoming text and she took it from her bag. It was Adam: *Hav a gd time. take care x*, She'd told him she was going to see an old friend and wouldn't be back until late. She texted back: *I will thanks x*, and then felt guilty for lying to him.

An elderly couple sat across the aisle and the woman looked over. Mandy returned her smile, and then allowed her head to rest back on the seat. She hadn't been sleeping well with all she'd been thinking about, and the rhythm of the train on the track soon persuaded her eyes to close. But as happened at night her thoughts immediately began to race – now with the various scenarios of what could happen when she arrived at Jimmy's: no one was in; he was out at work but his wife or daughters were in; he was in with his wife or daughters; he was alone in the house. She'd considered all these possibilities over and over again since she'd made the decision to come that morning, and had worked out what she was going to say and do for each scenario. The last, finding him alone, was the least complicated and most direct: 'Jimmy Osborne?' 'Yes.' 'I'm Mandy, your brother's niece.' Then she'd watch the horror spread across his face as he realized his past had finally caught up with him. She could feel her pulse race again at the very thought of it: standing face to face with her attacker after all this time. If his wife or daughters answered the door, she'd ask for him, and if he wasn't in she'd ask what time he was expected, and return later. Yes, she was sure she'd covered every eventuality.

Opening her eyes Mandy looked again at the passing scenery, and then took the magazine she'd bought at the station from her bag and forced herself to read – of celebrity lifestyles and large glossy photographs of their luxurious homes. Every so often she took her phone from her bag and checked the time. The journey seemed to be taking for ever. Eventually it was 1.35 and she knew she had five minutes before the train arrived. She tucked the magazine into her bag, straightened her jacket and, taking a deep breath to calm her nerves, looked out of the carriage window for the first sighting of Mowbury.

Five minutes later the train began to slow as the station approached. Mandy stood, then waited by the doors until the train stopped. The doors opened and she got out, her pulse quickening and her breath coming fast and shallow. She looked the length of the platform and then followed the dozen or so passengers who were walking towards the exit barrier. She'd never used this station before; it was on a different network to the one she used when she visited her grandparents, twelve miles away. She fed her ticket into the turnstile and then followed the signs to the ladies' WC.

A few minutes later she was outside on the station forecourt, which was exactly as the Internet map showed. She went past the taxi rank and joined a woman waiting at the bus stop for the number 247. According to the timetable she'd downloaded the bus ran every fifteen minutes on a weekday, starting at two minutes past the hour. Keeping her gaze away from the woman so she wouldn't be drawn into conversation, Mandy concentrated on the ground. Her thoughts returned to Jimmy. She checked her mobile again. The time was 1.55. What was he doing now? If he was at work when she arrived it could be many hours before he returned and she wondered where she should wait. Her stomach contracted with anxiety as she pictured his wife asking her what she wanted and her offering the excuse she'd concocted that she was carrying out a survey.

'At last,' the woman next to her sighed.

Mandy looked up and saw the 247 coming towards them. It drew to a halt and the door swished open. The woman before her got on and Mandy followed her up the steps. 'Return to Cranberry Avenue,' she heard herself say and gave the driver £2. She knew from the map Cranberry Avenue was the nearest stop to where Jimmy lived. She took the 40p change and made her way down the aisle.

There were only half a dozen passengers downstairs and she went halfway down the aisle and slid into a window seat. Taking the street map from her bag she opened it on her lap. She'd marked the train station and Jimmy's address with a Biro. She knew the route the bus would take and the stopping points from the printed timetable, and that it would take twenty minutes. After that she had about a five-minute walk to Jimmy's house. Her pulse raced and her stomach churned. She took a deep breath and reminded herself she didn't have to go to his house and confront him – that if it all became too much she could go straight to the police, which is doubtless what Adam would have advised her to do had she told him. But confronting Jimmy was essential if she was ever going to move on, and she knew it had to be done before she reported him; after that he would be able to hide behind legal protocol and then his barrister in court. Confronting Jimmy wasn't something Adam would have understood, nor would anyone else who hadn't been in her position. It was about taking control of her life again and making the abuser responsible for his crime.

Mandy looked between the map and the streets passing outside, tracking the bus's stop-start journey. They had left the town and were now entering the outlying suburbs: rows of 1970s' semi- and detached houses with integral garages and neatly tended front gardens. It was nothing like the private road in which John and Evelyn lived, but it was pleasant and had an air of suburban respectability. Mandy felt another stab of anger that Jimmy had been allowed to continue his comfortable and respectable life uninterrupted for the last ten years, and she wondered again if he ever thought about what he'd done to her.

From her seat by the window she saw the boys' school and then the playing fields. She knew she was getting close. She began counting down the stops, checking the map, mentally ticking off the roads they passed: Rose Way, Tulip Close, Thorn End; she knew the next stop was hers. She stood and made her way to the platform at the centre of the bus and held the handrail as the bus shuddered to a halt. The doors swished open and she stepped on to the pavement followed by another passenger who headed in the opposite direction. With the map open before her Mandy walked along Cranberry Avenue and then took the second on the left. This was Berry Lane, although clearly it wasn't a lane but another road of similar 1970s houses. She followed it for about thirty yards as it curved to the left and then she stopped at the corner. The next turning on the right was Jimmy's. Jimmy. How she'd come to loathe that name since Evelyn had first spoken it and told her: *Mandy, it wasn't John who came into your room that night and attacked you; it was his brother, Jimmy,* and Mandy had been forced to remember.

She stood on the corner of the street, folded the map in half and tucked it into her bag. She checked her phone and then switched it off. She didn't want to be disturbed by the phone suddenly ringing and interrupting what she had to say; she needed everything to be calm with her firmly in control. Taking another deep breath and summoning all her courage, Mandy looped her bag over her shoulder and made the right turn into Hawthorn Drive. The first house was number 2, so she was on the correct side of the road for Jimmy's: number 22. With her stomach tight and her legs heavy she put one foot in front of the other and continued steadily along the pavement, bracing herself for what she might see. The road was quiet and appeared to be on the very edge of the estate; she could see fields in the distance. Doubtless it was deemed a desirable area, Mandy thought bitterly as she scanned the front door at the end of each drive for the house numbers. She passed number 12. Four more to go until Jimmy's. Fourteen, 16, 18 … Her heart thumped loudly. It wasn't the sort of street you could loiter in without attracting attention, not like a London street corner where you could wait almost indefinitely. Twenty, then 22. She saw the house. Panic gripped her. Quickening her pace she continued past, taking in what she saw. A small, respectable 1970s detached house, with a neatly mowed lawn and short drive leading to a garage, the same as all the other houses in the road. Could he really live in there? It seemed impossible. She didn't know what she'd expected to find but it wasn't this; not normality and conformity. Net curtains had hung at all the windows in his house, as they did in many others, so she hadn't been able to catch a glimpse of the inside.

Forcing herself to slow to a walking pace, Mandy continued up the road. Her breath was coming fast and shallow and her pulse beat wildly in her chest. She hadn't expected to be so affected by seeing his house. When she'd run through the possible outcomes in her head she'd always seen herself as anxious but composed. Now she was beside herself and wanted to get on the next bus home.

She finally came to a halt outside number 60. She stood in the centre of the pavement, took deep breaths and told herself to calm down.

'Can I help you?' a woman asked, suddenly bobbing up from tending her front garden. Mandy jumped. 'You look lost,' she said.

'No, I'm all right. Thank you,' Mandy stammered. 'I know where I'm going.' She turned and started back down the street, towards his house. The woman watched her go.

Mandy knew if she went past his house again and put it off any longer she would lose her nerve completely and go home, never to return. She couldn't go through this again. She began counting down the houses she passed: Fifty-two, 50, 48, 46 … She drove her legs forward, towards Jimmy's house, trying to keep her breathing even. Thirty, 28, 26, 24, 22, a small hesitation and she forced herself to make the left turn into Jimmy's drive. Keeping her gaze fixed straight ahead and her thoughts in check, Mandy went down the path beside the short drive and up to his front door.

She saw her hand in the air waver slightly, and then her forefinger went towards the bell and pressed it. One short sharp burst – she heard it ring inside – and then silence. She waited, trying to calm her pounding heart. Perhaps they were all out. Relief mingled with disappointment. Then she saw a faint movement behind the frosted-glass panel door. She stared at the door and steeled herself. The lock turned with a small click and the door opened.

A girl in her early teens, dressed in school uniform, looked at her questioningly. All of Mandy's well-practised opening lines vanished and her mind went blank. 'Yes?' the girl asked after a moment. 'Can I help you?'

Mandy forced herself to say the words she'd rehearsed so many times. 'I'd like to speak to Mr Osborne, please. Jimmy Osborne. Is he in?'

The girl's expression changed from polite enquiry to confusion, and then suspicion. 'Why? What do you want?' she asked brusquely – defensively, Mandy thought.

'I'd like to speak to him, please. It's personal.' She heard her voice quiver.

The girl hesitated and stared at her, quite clearly shocked. 'No, you can't speak to him,' she said. 'I'll get my mother.'

The door closed in Mandy's face.

Thirty-Seven

A cold chill settled down Mandy's spine and her heart beat loudly in her chest. This wasn't going to plan, not at all. There was something wrong. The expression on his daughter's face wasn't what Mandy had expected, and neither was her response. It wasn't appropriate. His daughter had appeared shocked and confused, but why? Mandy had only asked to see her father; what had made her so worried and defensive? Why had she said no? Why hadn't she just told Mandy he wasn't home? No, this wasn't going to plan at all, and she didn't understand why. Don't panic, she told herself; when his wife comes simply ask for him.

The door opened again and, unlike his daughter, whom Mandy hadn't recognized from ten years earlier, his wife did look vaguely familiar. 'I'm sorry you've been disturbed,' Mandy said straight away. 'It was Mr Osborne I wanted to speak to.'

Mrs Osborne was short and petite, with chin-length brown hair. Her skin was pale, she wore no make-up and her gaze was expressionless. 'What's it in connection with?' she asked, with the same edge of defensiveness her daughter had used.

'It's personal.' Mandy said too quickly, abruptly, and then added, 'I really need to speak to him, please.'

The woman held her gaze. Her daughter appeared behind her further down the hall. There was silence for what seemed like hours. Then she seemed to gather herself and, straightening her shoulders, almost looked through Mandy. With resignation – as though she was repeating something she'd had to say many times before – she said: 'I'm sorry to be the one to tell you this, but my husband is dead.'

Mandy heard the words but didn't believe them. It's a lie, she thought, a conspiracy to stop me from seeing him and confronting him with the truth. Someone has warned her I'm coming. He's hiding inside the house. She looked past his wife and down the hall to his daughter. Both women were looking at her, their expressions very serious. Mandy began to wonder if it could be true. Was Jimmy really dead? 'Dead?' she repeated. Mrs Osborne nodded. 'But he can't be. I need to see him. How am I going to deal with all this now?' She felt the colour drain from her face and her head began to spin. She grabbed the edge of the door to steady herself.

'Are you all right?' his wife asked, stepping forward and holding her arm. 'Do you want to sit down?'

Mandy nodded. The walls of the porch were tilting and felt as if they were closing in.

'Come in, through here.'

Mandy allowed herself to be led over the doorstep and into the lounge at the front of the house. 'Sit down,' she heard Mrs Osborne say, then to her daughter: 'Hannah, can you bring a glass of water, please?'

Mandy sat on the sofa with her head down and took deep breaths. She thought she was going to faint from the shock of what she had been told. Jimmy was dead and had therefore escaped, and for a moment she wished she was dead too.

Raising her head slightly, Mandy accepted the glass of water Hannah brought, and mother and daughter watched as she took a few sips. Gradually the room lost its tilt and she felt less sick.

She raised her head further and leant back on the sofa. 'Thank you,' she said, looking at his wife. 'I'm sorry.'

'Sorry for what?' Hannah asked, almost pouncing on her. Mandy saw her mother throw her a warning glance.

'For being such a nuisance.' She took another sip of water and looked up at the two of them standing in front of her. 'It was kind of you to ask me in.'

Neither of the women spoke. Mandy looked from one to the other. They were waiting for an explanation as to why she'd arrived asking for Jimmy. She wasn't sure she could, or should, give it now. It was obvious Mrs Osborne hadn't recognized her, and part of her said she should just leave, while another part said she should stay and confront her. Mrs Osborne had been there on the night of the attack and had presumably stayed married to Jimmy afterwards. Didn't she have a duty to tell her what she knew?

'How long ago did Mr Osborne die?' Mandy asked after a moment, looking at Mrs Osborne.

'Four months,' she said, as though it was a figure she held constantly in her head.

Mandy gave a small nod and looked at the glass in her hand. She knew she should really offer her condolences but couldn't bring herself to utter them. She wondered if John knew his brother was dead, and if he did, why he or Evelyn hadn't told her.

Mandy looked up from the glass to Mrs Osborne and before she had the chance to change her mind said: 'I'm Mandy, John's niece.'

Both women stared at her in disbelief. 'Mandy?' his wife repeated, clearly shocked. Hannah had visibly paled, which was odd, for while Mandy would have expected Mrs Osborne to have remembered her and what had happened, Hannah had been far too young. Had she heard her parents talk of her? Had they discussed what had happened?

'What do you want?' his widow asked, her voice slight and uneven.

Mandy paused. 'Does my uncle John know he is dead?'

Mrs Osborne glanced at her daughter before replying. 'No. Jimmy had been ostracized by John and his family. I saw no reason to tell them. Why?'

'And their mother?' Mandy asked, ignoring her question. 'She's in a nursing home. Did you tell her?'

Another glance between mother and daughter before Mrs Osborne answered: 'I phoned the nursing home and the matron said she would tell her. But his mother has advanced Alzheimer's so she wouldn't have remembered. What do you want, Mandy? Tell me, please, or leave.'

Mandy heard the edge of desperation in Mrs Osborne's voice. She and Hannah were still looking at her; they seemed almost fearful of her intentions.

'Do you know what happened to me?' Mandy asked quietly after a moment, looking at his widow.

She nodded solemnly.

Mandy looked at his daughter. 'Do you, Hannah?'

'Both my daughters know now,' Mrs Osborne said. 'I told them last year.'

There was another silence. Then Mrs Osborne moved from beside her daughter to sit with Mandy on the sofa. 'Mandy,' she said slowly, gently, partly turning towards her. 'Tell me why you've come here and perhaps I can help you. You're looking for Jimmy, but why now, after all these years?'

Mandy met her gaze. 'I came here to confront him. I know this sounds crazy but I didn't know what had happened on that night until last week, when I suddenly remembered. My mind had blotted it all out – a type of amnesia – and no one had told me. My parents never spoke of it and neither did my grandparents. My father stopped us seeing Evelyn, John and Sarah, and I never knew why. Then a month ago my dear grandpa became very ill and I went to stay at Evelyn's to help nurse him. It was the first time I'd returned to that house since the night Jimmy ...' She couldn't bring herself to say it even now. 'As soon as I walked in I started having strange thoughts – flashbacks to the last time I'd stayed, ten years before. Then I remembered what had happened. I'm still trying to come to terms with it.' She paused. 'Dear Grandpa died last week.'

'I'm sorry. He was a lovely man, a real gentleman.' Mrs Osborne sounded genuinely sorry.

Mandy nodded. 'Since then, since I remembered, I've been in turmoil. I'm confused, angry and upset. It's like an open wound. Because I never dealt with the pain and anger at the time I'm having to deal with it now. I am feeling now what I should have felt then. I came here wanting to confront Jimmy and force him to realize what he'd done to me, then I was going to report him to the police. I know ten years is a long time, but he's never been punished and he should have been. I needed him to be. That's what I thought, anyway.' She stopped and felt utterly defeated.

There was a long silence that seemed to stretch back ten years. Mandy concentrated on the glass of water in her hand and felt the weight of Mrs Osborne and her daughter's gaze on her. Then she heard Mrs Osborne take a breath. 'Mandy, would it help you if I told you what happened that night?'

Mandy looked up and saw Mrs Osborne's pain and regret. 'Yes, I think it would.'

She nodded and looked at her daughter. 'Hannah, if you don't want to hear this again, I suggest you leave the room.'

'I'll stay,' she said with a shrug, and sat in the armchair.

Mandy returned her gaze to Mrs Osborne and waited. For a few seconds nothing could be heard but the tick of the clock on the wall as Mrs Osborne stared at a spot on the floor a little way in front of her. Then with a sharp intake of breath she began, her voice flat and carefully controlled. Mandy knew that the image of what happened that night was as vivid now for Mrs Osborne as it had been ten years ago.

'We were staying at Evelyn and John's for the weekend. It was a hot day – scorching hot, and we'd all been in the garden until very late. The girls wouldn't settle in a room on their own in a strange house so I was sleeping with them. Hannah was three at the time and Vanessa was eighteen months. Vanessa is eleven now and is at her friend's for tea. Hannah is thirteen.' She nodded towards her daughter. 'I slept in a room with the girls and Jimmy slept in another room further along the landing. That house was so big we could have had a room each if we'd wanted.' She smiled reflectively. 'John did very well for himself, far better than Jimmy, in all respects.

'I was fast asleep in the middle of the double bed with Vanessa on one side and Hannah on the other. Suddenly I was woken by Jimmy roughly shaking my shoulder and telling me we all had to get dressed and go. I thought it was some sort of joke to begin with and told him to be quiet as he would wake the girls. He began pulling the duvet off and then dragging me out of bed. I realized it wasn't a joke. The girls were waking and were very upset. He was very agitated and kept tugging at me and repeating we had to get dressed quickly and go.'

'Didn't you ask him why?' Mandy said.

'Of course. All he would say was there'd been a dreadful mistake and he would explain in the car. He threw our clothes at me and told us to get dressed, and then began tossing all our things into the suitcase. I looked at my watch; it was two o'clock in the morning. I tried to pacify the girls and dress them at the same time. It was chaos. I remember thinking all the noise must have woken Evelyn and Mrs Pryce and I couldn't understand why they hadn't come to see what was the matter. Jimmy kept shouting at us to hurry. I finished dressing the girls and then scrambled into my own clothes. Jimmy took the suitcase and bags and I carried Vanessa and held Hannah's hand. All the lights were on in the house and we went downstairs and into the hall. The girls were still crying. John was alone in the hall; I looked at him for an explanation but he turned away. He didn't speak. He opened the front door and shut it as soon as we were out. He didn't say a word and he didn't see us into the car. I wondered where everyone was. It was later I found out you were upstairs with Mrs Pryce, and Evelyn was comforting Sarah in the lounge.

'I sat in the back of the car with the girls while Jimmy drove. It took me ages to settle the girls – they couldn't understand what was happening any more than I could. I remember I could see Jimmy's eyes in the rear-view mirror. He was concentrating on the road but there was something else, apart from anger – something cold and unforgiving. I remember thinking that whoever had upset him would have to work hard to earn his forgiveness. Once the girls were asleep I asked Jimmy again what had happened. He'd calmed down a bit by then. He said there'd been a terrible misunderstanding and he wasn't in any way to blame. He said he was furious with John for taking the word of an adolescent over his own brother. I asked him again what exactly had happened, and finally he told me. He said it was nearly one a.m. and he couldn't get to sleep. He was thirsty and decided to go down to get a drink of water. He didn't put on the landing light for fear of disturbing anyone. He crept along the landing but as he passed your bedroom door – you always slept in the Pink Room – he heard you cry out with a nightmare. He crept in to reassure you, but when he tried to comfort you you screamed out for help. Sarah woke and came in and saw Jimmy by your bed and completely misinterpreted what she saw. She started screaming too and her screams woke Evelyn. At that point Jimmy realized they weren't open to reason and went back to his own room. John went into his room a few minutes later and told him to fetch us and go.'

She stopped. The air was quiet again. 'And you believed him?' Mandy asked at length.

Mrs Osborne nodded. 'Yes, completely. At the time I had no reason to doubt him. He'd never been accused of anything like that before, obviously, and what wife wouldn't believe her husband over a teenage girl?'

Mandy said nothing. It sounded very reasonable.

'When I thought about it afterwards,' Mrs Osborne continued, 'the only concern I had with what Jimmy had told me was John's behaviour. It seemed an over-reaction to throw us out in the middle of the night for what had been simply a misunderstanding. Jimmy told me that John never wanted to see or speak to us again. It played on my mind, and a week later, when Jimmy was at work, I phoned Evelyn and asked her what exactly had happened. She was curt with me, and her version of events was very different from Jimmy's. She said Sarah had heard you cry for help and went into your room. She found Jimmy on top of you on the bed with his pyjama bottoms round his ankles. Evelyn heard Sarah scream and when she arrived Jimmy got off the bed and ran out past her. I was horrified. I didn't know what to believe. Evelyn told me never to phone again.

'When Jimmy came home from work that evening I admitted I'd phoned Evelyn, and told him what she'd said. He was furious – he had a terrible temper. He said it was ridiculous, and how could I begin to believe the nonsense of two hysterical teenage girls over him. He said if there'd been a shred of evidence the police would have been knocking on our door by now, which seemed logical to me. So I accepted what he said and we never spoke of it again.' She stopped and looked carefully at Mandy. 'Why didn't you report it to the police, Mandy?'

Mandy held her gaze. 'My parents thought I'd suffered enough and that they were protecting me. They didn't want me to go through another medical, police interview, and then have to relive it all again in court, and be cross-examined by a barrister. They thought it would be too distressing so, like you, we never talked of it again. I guess their decision was very lucky for you, Jimmy and your daughters.'

Mrs Osborne's eyes darted briefly to Hannah and then back again. When she spoke it was almost to condemn her. 'No, Mandy, you're wrong. It was the worst possible decision they could have made. And not only for you.'

Thirty-Eight

'   didn't doubt Jimmy,' Mrs Osborne continued with unsettling detachment. 'I believed him, and the fact that the police weren't involved confirmed what he'd said. If I'd had any doubts, if my suspicions had been roused, I'm sure I would have been more vigilant – more aware. But I didn't have doubts. We never mentioned that night, your family, nor John's family ever again – until last year.'

Mrs Osborne's voice had gone very cold and a dreadful sense of foreboding settled on Mandy. Mrs Osborne paused and in that moment Mandy knew that whatever she was about to hear could have been avoided if Jimmy had been reported, and therefore she and her family were at least partly to blame.

'Jimmy visited his mother regularly,' Mrs Osborne continued. 'She never doubted Jimmy, not for one moment, and was very angry with John for believing you. I understand she gave John a rough time for years and tried to make him apologize to Jimmy, but he never did. Eventually she stopped talking to Jimmy about his brother and the subject was dropped. Both her sons visited her at the nursing home, but never at the same time. John always went on a Saturday and Jimmy on Sunday. One Christmas Eve Jimmy stopped by unexpectedly and when he went into the sitting room, where all the residents were gathered, he found John already there. He left without being seen and waited in the car until John had left. As far as I know that's the only time Jimmy saw John in all those years. And for me, knowing that Jimmy's mother had so much faith in him confirmed his innocence in my mind. After the initial upset of being accused by John and banished from his house, life continued as normal for us, until last year when the police arrived and Jimmy was arrested.'

'*Arrested?*' Mandy asked, stunned. 'But I didn't ever report him.'

'No, not because of you.'

Mandy stared at Mrs Osborne and her stomach contracted with fear. 'So there was someone else?'

'Yes.' She nodded and rubbed her hand over her eyes. 'Unfortunately there was.' She paused before continuing. 'It was a Sunday evening and Jimmy and I were sitting here, watching the late-night film. Suddenly there was loud banging on the front door. Jimmy told me to stay put while he went to see who it was. He thought it might be yobs from the estate. The next minute the house was full of police. Three came in here with Jimmy and me, and stayed with us while the others searched the house. They wouldn't tell us what they wanted and Jimmy said he didn't know either. I thought it must be a mistake. Hannah and Vanessa were asleep upstairs and the police went into their rooms and woke them. I was only allowed to go up and comfort them after they'd searched their room. They were very frightened.' Mrs Osborne glanced at Hannah. 'Jimmy was so angry, he kept demanding the police tell him what the hell was going on, but all they would say was it was part of an investigation. Then they took him to the police station for questioning. They also took away our computer and Jimmy's laptop. I tried phoning the station to find out what was happening but they wouldn't tell me anything. I was at my wits' end but I had to stay calm for the sake of the girls. Jimmy finally came home at three a.m. and said he hadn't been charged, that there'd been a misunderstanding. Did this remind me of the other "misunderstanding"? No, why should it? I still didn't know why the police had taken him in for questioning. When I asked Jimmy he became very angry and told me to drop it.

'It wasn't until Hannah went to school the following day,' Mrs Osborne continued in the same flat and emotionless voice, 'that the girls and I found out. Hannah was in her first year of secondary school and she came home in tears. The whole school was talking about us. On the Saturday before Jimmy was arrested Hannah had had a friend, Katie, sleep over. I had put up a Z-bed in Hannah's room. When Katie went home on Sunday she told her mother that Jimmy had gone into her bedroom during the night and, while Hannah slept, had tried to rape her. Did he really think he'd get away with it? That Katie wouldn't report him!' She stopped, tears springing from her eyes.

'It's possible,' Mandy said quietly. 'He got away with it with me.' She looked from mother to daughter. Her stomach was churning and was so tight that for a moment she thought she was going to be sick. She knew what Katie had gone through – she could feel it. She also knew that she was responsible. If she'd reported Jimmy then Katie would never have had to suffer the same fate.

'Sorry,' Mrs Osborne said after a moment, wiping her eyes on the tissue Hannah passed her. 'I never dreamed I'd be telling you all this. Never, ever.'

'Did you believe he'd done it this time?' Mandy asked at length.

Mrs Osborne nodded. 'Yes, although of course he kept denying it. I also realized then that you'd been telling the truth. The thought that I'd been sharing my bed all those years with a … I had started divorce proceedings when Jimmy died.'

'Was he prosecuted for attacking Katie?' Mandy asked, aware her Internet search had shown Jimmy didn't have a criminal record.

Mrs Osborne shook her head. 'No. Like you, when Katie found out what was involved – the medical, and having to give evidence – she didn't feel she could go ahead. She was also told it would be difficult to prove as Jimmy was of sound character. Respectable, they said.'

Mandy looked away. 'That wouldn't have been true if I'd reported him. He'd have had a police record.'

'We'll never know for sure,' Mrs Osborne said. 'Don't blame yourself, love. If you want to blame someone now Jimmy is dead, blame me.' She sat back on the sofa, closed her eyes, and emotion overtook her.

Hannah came over and put her arm around her mother. 'Mum, it wasn't your fault. You weren't to know.'

Mandy looked at mother and daughter comforting each other on the sofa and her heart went out to them. She knew she should go now; staying any longer would be insensitive and intrusive. Jimmy was dead and hopefully she'd gain some closure from that, and also from what Mrs Osborne had told her. Although of course she now had to come to terms with knowing another girl had suffered as a result of her family's silence.

'Thank you for telling me all this,' Mandy said quietly. 'I really appreciate it. It has helped.' She placed her glass on the coffee table and stood.

Hannah took her arm from around her mother and they both stood too. Mrs Osborne turned to face Mandy. 'I'm so sorry for all you've been through, really I am,' she said. She gave Mandy a hug while Hannah hung back. She was obviously close to tears.

They went with her to the front door where Mrs Osborne apologized again. 'Look after yourself, love,' she said.

'And you.' With a small sad smile Mandy turned and walked down the path. She heard the front door close behind her.

She joined the pavement and glanced back at the neat, outwardly respectable house where Jimmy had lived with his wife and two daughters. As she would now have to come to terms with the past in order to move on, so too would his widow and daughters, and in some respects it would be worse for them. How did you ever come to terms with your husband or father being a rapist? She shuddered at the thought.

Thirty-Nine

Retracing her steps down Hawthorn Drive and along Berry Lane, Mandy came to the bus stop in Cranberry Avenue. She took her place in the queue with three others and switched on her phone. As it came to life it bleeped with two text messages, one from Adam: *Fone if u r back in time 2nite*, and the other advising her she had a voicemail message. She pressed call-back and heard her father's voice saying he'd pick her up at 9.30 a.m. It was Grandpa's funeral the following day and she was going with her parents in their car. She texted his mobile: *Thanx 4 mssge. c u 2mrrw. luv m*. Returning her phone to her bag she looked down the road in the direction the bus would be coming, and vaguely watched the passing traffic.

She hadn't thought to ask how Jimmy had died, and it didn't really matter. The end result was the same. She supposed it must have been a heart attack or cancer; that's what usually seemed to kill middle-aged men. She wondered again at the grieving process his wife and daughter were going through – losing someone they'd loved but at the same time hating him for what he'd done. And again Mandy's heart went out to them for what they were struggling to come to terms with.

The bus arrived; there were only aisle seats left and she sat next to a teenage girl who was listening to her iPod. It was about twenty minutes to the station and then, if the train and tubes were running a good service, two hours home. She should be home about 7 p.m. – early enough to see Adam. But before she phoned him to say she was home she knew she'd have to phone her aunt and uncle and tell them of Jimmy's death. She knew she had a duty to tell them and it was a duty she needed to discharge as soon as possible – certainly before she saw them at the funeral the following day. But it wasn't something you could say on a mobile in public, the bus was crowded, so she'd wait until she got home to call them in private.

Fifteen minutes later the bus pulled into the station terminus and Mandy got off. It was the start of rush hour and the station was busier that it had been when she'd arrived. She needed to use the Ladies before she boarded the train and she threaded her way through the commuters to the WC. Coming out, she crossed to the kiosk and bought a chocolate bar and bottle of water for the journey. Then she checked on the signboard for the time and platform of the next train into Paddington: 17.05 from Platform 3.

Suddenly she heard a small cry from behind and someone arrived at her side. 'Hannah! Whatever are you doing here?' Mandy gasped. The girl was still in her school uniform and was flushed from running.

'I need to talk to you,' she panted, looking at her anxiously.

For a second Mandy thought something dreadful must have happened as a result of her visit. 'What's the matter? Is your mother all right?'

'Yes, but I have to tell you something. Something Mum couldn't tell you and I think you should know.'

Mandy hesitated. What on earth could Hannah have to tell her that her mother hadn't felt able to? 'Does your mother know you're here?'

Hannah nodded. 'She tried to stop me from coming, but I insisted. I must talk to you. Please.'

Mandy could see her desperation. 'All right.' She looked around for somewhere they could go. There was a small coffee bar near the entrance to the station. 'We can go over there. Do you want a drink?' Hannah shook her head.

Going in, Mandy bought a coffee for herself and set it on the table between them. She looked at Hannah and waited. She was a plain but attractive girl with long fair hair. She had inherited her mother's features, which was just as well, Mandy thought, for she would have found it very difficult to sit opposite a face that reminded her of Jimmy.

Hannah fiddled with the cuff on her school shirt and then suddenly blurted: 'What my mum told you about my father not being prosecuted wasn't true.'

'No?' Mandy asked shocked.

Hannah shook her head. 'He was going to be prosecuted and would have gone to prison if he hadn't died.'

Mandy looked at her, completely taken aback but at a loss to understand what she was trying to tell her. 'I'm sorry, Hannah, I don't understand.'

She stopped fiddling with her cuff and looked up sharply. 'He would have gone to prison for a long time if he hadn't died. But not because of Katie, because of me.'

Mandy stared at her and turned cold. 'Why? Because of something you told the police?' she asked tentatively.

Hannah gave a small nod and looked down at her cuff again. 'I reported my father to the police because of what he did to me.'

Dear God, Mandy thought, not his own daughter! Surely not. She stared horrified at Hannah as she tugged at her cuff, and waited.

'There was enough evidence to convict him this time,' Hannah said after a moment. 'I made sure of it. I took the sheets from my bed and I let a police doctor examine me. I was prepared to go to court.'

Mandy reached out and touched her arm. 'I'm so sorry. I don't know what to say.' She felt her eyes mist and a lump rise in her throat. Hannah sat passively staring at the table between them. 'I'm sorry,' Mandy said again, helpless in the face of her suffering.

'I was ten when it began,' Hannah said in the same flat and emotionless voice and without meeting her eyes. 'He came into my room one evening when Mum was out, and raped me. It went on for two years – whenever he had the opportunity. It only stopped when I reported him to the police. I don't know why I didn't tell Mum. I think it was because he made me believe it was my fault.' She looked up sharply and met Mandy's eyes. 'He said I was sexy and since I'd started to get breasts I'd been leading him on and teasing him. He said if I told Mum, she and Vanessa would blame me and hate me for ever. He said I'd be put in a children's home and no one would ever visit me again. It sounds ridiculous now but I was so confused and frightened I believed what he said. He also said if I stopped him there was always Vanessa. She was eight at the time.' She shrugged. 'I guess I felt by letting him continue I was protecting my sister.'

Hannah was calm as she spoke, too calm, Mandy thought, as though all the emotion had been wrung from her and she had nothing left to feel. 'He wouldn't have got away with it this time,' Hannah added tightly. 'He would have been put in prison for a long time. But he died first.'

'I'm so sorry,' Mandy said again, completely overwhelmed. 'I can only guess at what you must be going through.'

Hannah looked at her. 'It was you who finally made me go to the police and report him.'

'Me?'

'Yes. Last Christmas Mum got out some old family photographs. We were looking at them, Dad as well, and there was a picture of you with Uncle John and Auntie Evelyn from when you were little. I asked Dad why we never saw Uncle John and he flew into a rage and tore up the photo. Then he had a right go at Mum. It was a rotten Christmas. Later I asked Mum why he'd been so angry and Mum said it was because you'd caused a lot of trouble by saying things about him that weren't true. I knew then that he'd done something to you. I just knew it. And to Katie as well. I knew I had to stop him. The day after Boxing Day I went to the police. Later that afternoon they arrested him and he died the following day.'

Hannah stopped and Mandy reached over and took her hand in hers. 'I'm so sorry,' she said again. Then with the need to now know everything she asked gently: 'How did he die?'

Hannah hesitated and Mandy saw her bottom lip tremble; it was the first emotion she'd shown since she'd started to tell her. 'After he'd been charged he was released on bail but he wasn't allowed to come home or anywhere near me. That evening the police came to our home and said he was dead. He'd committed suicide.' Mandy shuddered and held her hand tightly. 'He jumped under a train in London. So now I have to live with the guilt of being responsible for his suicide as well as everything else. I don't know whether to feel relieved or sorry he's dead. I'd like to believe none of it's my fault, but I can't.'

Mandy held her hand. It was some time before she spoke; words seemed totally ineffective beside the enormity of what Hannah had gone through – was still going through. 'If only I'd reported him,' Mandy said at last. 'You and Katie wouldn't have suffered.'

Hannah gave a small shrug. 'Mum says the only person to blame is him.'

They were silent again, then Hannah's phone rang from the pocket of her school blazer. She took it out and answered it. 'Yes, Mum, I'm with her now. No, at the station. Yes, I won't be long.' She closed the phone and returned it to her pocket. 'Mum worries about me all the time.'

'I can understand why.'

'Anyway,' Hannah said with a small shrug, 'I wanted you to know. And maybe we could keep in touch? I think it would help if I could talk to you sometimes – like an older sister. Is that OK?'

'Yes, of course. Give me your number and I'll put it in my phone, then I'll text you and you'll have my number.' Mandy took her phone from her bag and as Hannah recited the number of her phone she entered it in hers.

'Are you getting help? Counselling?' Mandy asked after a moment.

'Yes, I go once a fortnight.'

'Good.'

They were silent again. Mandy took a sip from the coffee which was now cold and, pulling a face, pushed the cup to one side.

Hannah smiled. 'I'd better be going. Mum will be worried. Thanks for listening.'

'Thanks for telling me. It was very brave of you. It helps me.'

Hannah shrugged. 'I don't feel brave. I often feel like shit. Sometimes I wish I hadn't said anything.'

Mandy leant across the table in earnest. 'Hannah, you did right. Believe me. I know how difficult it is now. You've suffered dreadfully but you did the right thing. If you hadn't reported him he wouldn't have stopped, and how long would it have been before he went on to abuse your sister? And others after her.'

'That's what Mum says. I guess I have to give myself time.' She shrugged, unconvinced, and stood.

Mandy also stood and walked with her out of the coffee shop and on to the station concourse. They turned to face each other and hugged. 'I'll text when I'm on the train,' Mandy said.

'Thanks.' Hannah turned, and Mandy watched her walk away. She'd been through so much, how was she coping? How could her life or her mother's ever be normal again? It made Mandy's own suffering seem manageable beside hers.

Checking the signboard Mandy saw the next train for Paddington was in five minutes, and she made her way to Platform 3. As she went she texted Hannah so she would have her number: *You did the right thing and it was never ever yr fault. luv mandy x.*

A minute later a text came back: *Thanks x.*

Forty

Flicking on the light switch, Mandy dropped her bag by the door and went to the fridge, where she finished the carton of orange juice. She should really have had something to eat but she couldn't face it yet – her stomach was churning with the thought of the phone call she had to make to John. How much of the detail surrounding the circumstances of Jimmy's death she should tell him she didn't know. She'd thought about it the entire train journey home and still hadn't decided.

She dumped the empty carton of juice in the swing-top bin and then crossed to the bay windows and pulled the curtains. It was nearly 9 p.m. and dark outside. She took her phone from her bag and sat in the armchair. She needed to get the call over and done with and then she would phone Adam. There was still time to see him, and she wanted to see him very much.

Flipping up the lid on her phone the screen illuminated. She pressed *Contacts*, and then *E* – John was listed under E for Evelyn and John. Their landline number highlighted and she pressed to connect. She felt hot and uncomfortable; she was after all about to tell John his brother was dead. If Evelyn answered she wasn't sure if she should tell her or whether she should ask for John. She hoped it wasn't the answerphone for it would mean phoning back later or very early the following morning – it wasn't a message you could leave on a machine.

'Hello?' a bright young female voice said, and for a moment Mandy thought she must have the wrong number.

'I'm sorry, who am I speaking to?' Mandy asked. 'I wanted John Osborne?'

There was a moment's pause and then a small laugh. 'Hi, Mandy, it's Sarah.'

'Sorry, I didn't recognize your voice.'

'Not surprising. It's over ten years since we last spoke on the phone. Dad is right beside me. I'll put him on. Simon and I were just leaving. See you tomorrow. Are you coming back here for the buffet after?' Mandy thought she made the funeral sound like a party.

'I expect so. I'm coming with Mum and Dad so it will depend on them. See you tomorrow.'

There was a small clunk as she handed the phone to John. Mandy heard John say goodbye to Sarah and Simon before his voice came on the line. 'Hello, Mandy. Everything all right?'

'No, not really.' She paused and took a breath. 'John, I'm sorry to be the one to have to tell you this, but I learnt today that Jimmy is dead.' There was silence the other end which Mandy took to be shock. 'I went to his house earlier today. I needed to confront him, and his wife and daughter told me.'

There was more silence, and then she heard John clear his throat. 'Thank you for telling me, Mandy, but I already know.'

'You do?'

'Yes. I knew the Saturday after it happened. When I visited my mother – our mother – at the nursing home, the matron offered me her condolences and said she was sorry to hear of my brother's death. I was shocked, obviously – Jimmy was only young, but I didn't let on to the matron I didn't know. Jimmy's wife, Natalie, had phoned the nursing home and asked if they would tell Mum of Jimmy's death. But of course with the Alzheimer's Mum hadn't remembered. She doesn't even know she has sons.' His voice fell away.

Mandy hesitated. 'Do you know how he died?' she asked tentatively.

'Yes. I went to the inquest. He committed suicide.'

She hesitated again. 'And the reason why he committed suicide? About his daughter, Hannah?'

'Yes,' he said sombrely.

She paused, and then her anger bubbled over. 'So why didn't you tell me?' she demanded. 'Why didn't you tell me he was dead or that he'd been accused of assaulting his daughter? Why didn't you or Evelyn say something when I remembered what had happened to me? I don't understand!'

There was a long pause before John's voice came on the line again, measured and very serious: 'We didn't think it would help you to know, Mandy. And there was the worry that if you knew about Hannah you might in some way feel responsible.'

'Too right I feel responsible. And who's "we"?' she demanded again. 'Who made the decision not to tell me?'

'Your father. And I agreed with him.'

'So he knows about Jimmy as well!'

'Yes.'

'And when did the two of you agree to keep this from me?' She was furious – having just been released from one set of lies she now found she was the victim of another.

'When you offered to stay to help nurse Grandpa your father was worried that Jimmy might still be visiting our house,' John said. 'So I told him Jimmy was dead. When he pressed me I told him the details surrounding his death.'

'And no one thought to tell me! What else don't I know?'

'Nothing. That's it.'

'Are you completely sure, John? Everyone in this family seems very good at sharing confidences without telling me.'

'Mandy,' he said, raising his voice slightly. 'It's the truth. When you decided to stay and help us with Grandpa your father told me that none of you had ever spoken of that night in all this time and he wanted it kept that way. I thought it was odd but that was his decision. Evelyn and I promised your father we wouldn't say anything to you, and we didn't. When you remembered what had happened I phoned your father the next morning and told him. Your father was adamant that you shouldn't be told about Jimmy's death and the reason he'd committed suicide. He couldn't see it would help you, and I agreed. He wanted to protect you, Mandy. If anyone should feel guilty for not reporting Jimmy at the time it's your father and me. And we do. It was a disastrous decision, given what happened since, and we're having to live with that.'

Mandy stared across the room, the phone pressed to her ear, angry, frustrated, yet reluctantly understanding that they'd only been trying to protect her. Her gaze moved across the room to her collection of china dogs, lovingly saved up for and bought with her pocket money. How long ago that simple pleasure now seemed; how far away the naivety of childhood.

'Mandy,' John was saying, 'when the funeral is over I might give Natalie a ring and see if there is anything I can do. It's time we tried to put the past behind and look to the future.'

'Yes, I'm sure she'd appreciate that.' She sighed, suddenly exhausted. 'I'll go now. Mum and Dad are collecting me early tomorrow.'

'All right. See you tomorrow. I'm sorry if we did the wrong thing.'

Mandy said goodbye, cleared the call and sat for some moments staring thoughtfully across the room. The future, yes:

John was right it was time to try and move on – to a future that wasn't complicated by the secrecy of the past. Returning her attention to the phone she pressed Adam's number and he answered immediately. 'Hi love, you're back early. Did you have a good time?'

'I didn't visit a friend,' she said carefully. 'I've been to Cambridgeshire to try and sort out my past. Adam, I know it's late but would you like to come round?'

She heard his hesitation, and for a moment thought he was going to say no – that he'd had enough of her blowing hot and cold, and thought it was best they parted. 'One problem,' he said. 'I've just bought fish and chips. How about I bring them with me and heat them up in your microwave?'

'Great,' she said, relieved. 'And I'll help you eat them. I've suddenly realized how hungry I am.'

'In that case I'll pick up another portion on the way over, together with a bottle of wine. See you soon.'

Forty-One

Half an hour later she sat opposite Adam at the small table in her bedsitting room; they were eating fish and chips with their fingers. The smell of fried fish drifted around the room and out on to the landing. She owned cutlery, of course, but there was something especially delicious about eating fish and chips straight from the paper, dripping in vinegar and coated with an unhealthy amount of salt. It was wonderfully reminiscent of holidays as a child. Adam had opened the wine and was soon refilling their glasses. Only when they'd finished eating, and Mandy had fetched the roll of kitchen towel to wipe the grease from their fingers, and had thrown the fish wrappings in the bin, did she begin to tell him.

She took another sip of wine and then, reaching across the table for his hand, began by telling him of the night, ten years ago, when Jimmy had come into her room. His horror was obvious as she described the terror of waking in the dark to find Jimmy on top of her, then the ten years when her mind had blocked it out and no one had spoken of it. She described the strange thoughts and flashbacks she'd experienced when she'd returned to Evelyn's house, culminating in the night when she'd remembered. Adam was quiet and very still as she spoke, his gaze not moving from hers. She finished by telling him of her visit to Jimmy's wife and daughter and the phone call she'd made earlier that evening to John.

'I don't know what to say,' Adam said at length, visibly shocked. 'But why didn't you tell me sooner, Mandy? I could have helped.'

'I couldn't. I had to sort it out in my own head first before I found the words or courage to tell you. And I guess I'm still sorting it out.' She looked away and felt his hand squeeze hers.

'And you're sure you don't want me to go with you to the funeral tomorrow? I can if you want.'

'I'll be OK with Mum and Dad, and I need to talk to them about all this. It will be a good opportunity.'

He paused. 'Mandy, there's something I need to talk to *you* about. It's been on my mind for a while. I won't be offended if it's not right. Just be honest and tell me what you think.'

She looked at him with a stab of unease. 'What have I done?'

'Nothing bad.' He smiled and turned to his jacket hanging on the back of his chair. Delving into the inside pocket, he took out a small paper bag and a folded sheet of A4 paper, which he tilted towards him so she couldn't see.

'I hope you haven't forgotten your promise,' he said. 'The one you made at your aunt's?' She frowned questioningly. 'You agreed we should move in together, so I've been looking at flats. What do you think?' He opened the sheet of paper and placed it in front of her. Mandy gazed down at the estate agent's details and a photograph of the outside of a flat. 'It's in a small new development,' Adam said. 'Ten minutes' walk from the station, which will be good for me getting into work. It's got a lounge, kitchen, one big bedroom and a smaller one.' He pointed to the photographs on the details as he spoke. 'The spare room is very light and would make an ideal studio.' He gave a small nervous laugh. 'The rent isn't too bad and there's my salary and also that bit of money my granddad left me. So there you go. What do you think, Mandy?'

She looked up and, smiling, felt her eyes mist. 'I think the flat looks wonderful, Adam, and I think you are too.'

'Good, because I've put down the deposit and we can have the keys next week.'

She gasped, but before she had time to say anything Adam was opening the paper bag and taking out a small jeweller's box. 'I know we agreed we would live together and not think about getting married, but I wanted to buy you something to mark the occasion. I haven't bought you anything in ages, apart from fish and chips. I hope you like it and it's entirely up to you which finger you wear it on.' He looked at her, embarrassed. Opening the box he set it on the table in front of her, beside the estate agent details.

She looked at the ring and her eyes filled. 'And I used to think you weren't romantic!' She laughed and blinked back the tears. 'It's beautiful, absolutely perfect, it must have cost a fortune.'

'You really like it?' he asked, concerned.

'Yes, it's exactly what I would have chosen. Thank you so much.'

He smiled, pleased. 'It should fit,' he said. 'I used my little finger as a gauge. I know your other ring goes down to my first knuckle.'

She felt him watching her intently as she carefully lifted the diamond solitaire from the box. It caught in the overhead light and its facets glinted all the colours of the rainbow. 'It's absolutely lovely,' she said again. Holding it in her right hand, she slowly slid it over the third finger on her left hand. It fitted perfectly.

Adam stood and came round the table. Taking her gently by the shoulders, he drew her to her feet and kissed her, first on the cheek and then fully on the lips.

'It's a bit late for going home,' she said as he drew back. 'Why don't you stay the night?'

'I will if you really want me to, Mandy.'

'Yes, I want you to.'

Forty-Two

Seated in the rear of the car behind her mother, Mandy gazed out of the side window with a warm feeling of inner peace. The familiar and repetitive scenery of fields running along the edge of the motorway encouraged her to daydream, and her thoughts had returned to the night before. Still gazing out of the side window, her fingers closed around the ring on her left hand and her heart skipped a beat. What a surprise. How romantic! She'd never have thought it of Adam. Finding the flat and then presenting her with the ring at the end of their fish-and-chip supper. She smiled. He'd left for work before her parents had arrived, but she'd shown them the ring and told them of their plans to move in together, and they were delighted. They liked Adam and had offered to help with the move. But now she needed to raise a subject with them that would be less welcome. If she didn't raise it now it would hang over her, growing in magnitude as grievances left unspoken so often do.

'Dad,' she said presently, bringing her gaze forward. 'Did John phone you last night after I'd spoken to him?' For it seemed the nature of their family's dynamics that he might.

'Early this morning,' her father confirmed.

'And he told to you I went to see Jimmy?'

He nodded, while her mother sat very still.

'Were Gran and Grandpa told of Jimmy's death?'

He nodded again. 'Shortly after he died, but not the details – not about his daughter, nor how he died. They didn't need to know, and your gran certainly doesn't now, she's had enough upset.' Mandy heeded the warning not to tell her. 'I asked your grandparents not to say anything to you. I didn't want Jimmy's name ever mentioned again. So if you are looking for someone to blame, it's me,' he finished uncharacteristically sharply, taking the criticism personally.

'I'm not blaming you, Dad,' she said quickly. 'I'm just trying to piece together the past. When I remembered what Jimmy had done didn't you think it was a good time to tell me he was dead?'

He glanced at her in the interior mirror. 'Clearly not. If I'd known it was so important to you, I would have told you. I thought the whole subject was best left alone. Perhaps I should have told you what John told your grandparents – that Jimmy had died of a heart attack. That way you would have been satisfied and not gone on a quest for more information. It's bad enough knowing that my decision allowed Jimmy to go on and attack others, without you feeling responsible too.' He paused. Mandy remained quiet, stung by his admission of guilt. 'As I said last week, Mandy, I'll do what I can to help you – pay for a therapist if you think it will help, or perhaps you'd like to go on holiday with Adam? I'll pay for it. But I can't turn back the clock. If I could, I would, believe me, love.'

Mandy looked at him in the interior mirror as he concentrated on the road ahead. She saw the familiar little creases in the corners of his eyes that had grown over the years; the lines across his forehead, deeper now from frowning; his grey hair and receding hairline; and the humility and sadness in his gaze.

'I know,' she said quietly. 'I know you did what you thought was best. I'll be fine, really I will. Moving in with Adam will be a fresh start. I'm just glad I found out now rather than later. There aren't any more family secrets I should know about?'

'Good heavens, no!' he said with a small tight laugh. 'I'd have thought that was enough!'

Easing out her seatbelt she leant forward between them and kissed their cheeks. 'Good.'

The atmosphere in the car grew sombre as they approached the crematorium. Although they were half an hour early there were already a dozen or so mourners standing in small groups in the car park. Mandy didn't recognize them, and neither did her parents. 'Friends and neighbours, I expect,' her father said. 'Looks like we're waiting for the service before to finish.'

He parked the car, cut the engine and opened the windows slightly for some fresh air. Through the open window Mandy could hear a lone song thrush trilling unseen in the branches overhead. The car park was surrounded by trees and shrubs, and the pathway leading to the chapel was lined with planters. The chapel itself was more like an ornate village church than a crematorium, and very different from the one she'd been to for Lucy's funeral while at university. Lucy's was the only other funeral Mandy had been to, and she remembered how she and her friends had cried continuously throughout the service, while Lucy's parents had remained so brave and dignified. It was the futility of someone dying so young that had torn through her; how parents coped with losing a child, she'd no idea. 'At least it's a fine day for it,' her mother said.

'Yes,' she agreed.

Three more cars pulled in and parked, but the occupants were also unfamiliar. A few minutes later the cortège appeared and Mandy was grateful they hadn't had to be part of it. Seeing the coffin was upsetting enough without having to journey behind it. The hearse drew slowly round and parked in front of the chapel, followed by the car with Gran, Evelyn and John. Mandy looked at the coffin, floating on a sea of flowers, and felt her eyes fill. Through the glass sides of the hearse the sun caught the brass handles of the coffin and they glinted in the light. On top of the coffin were three wreaths, one of which she knew was from her parents and her. The small groups of mourners who had been talking quietly were now silent and everyone was looking at the hearse. The pallbearers, in their tailed black suits, stepped from the front of the hearse and sedately put on their tall black hats. Her father raised the car windows, Mandy switched off her phone, and they got out.

John was helping Gran out of the car. Evelyn saw them and gave a little wave. Mandy felt the other mourners look at them as they made their way across the car park.

She kissed Gran first. 'Hello, love,' Gran said. She'd put on a little make-up – a touch of powder and lipstick – and Mandy's heart went out to her. Dear Gran, so frail and sad, but wanting to look nice for her husband's funeral. She hugged her and felt her thin shoulders beneath her coat.

'You look very smart, Gran,' she whispered.

'So do you.' She smiled. 'Sarah and Simon are over there.'

Mandy looked over at the silver Mercedes sports which had followed in the cortège. Sarah and Simon were climbing out. As Gran began talking to her father Mandy went over to say hello. She wanted Sarah and Simon to see she wasn't the hysterical wreck that had fled the house at their last meeting, and that there were no bad feelings. As usual they made a smart couple: Simon in a well-tailored grey suit and black tie and Sarah in a slim-fitting black dress and cardigan.

'Hi, Mandy,' Sarah said easily, air-kissing her. 'You look well.'

'Thank you. So do you.'

Simon shook her hand with more reserve. 'Hello, Mandy.'

'I'm not looking forward to this,' Sarah confided. 'I get so emotional at funerals. I can't stop crying.'

'I know what you mean,' Mandy agreed. 'Gran is being so brave.'

The three of them looked over to where Gran stood in the small circle talking with Evelyn, John, and Mandy's parents.

'Mandy,' Sarah said, suddenly looking at her. 'There's something I have to tell you.'

'Yes?' Mandy asked lightly, guessing she was about to hear another of Sarah's dramatized tales, like the one she'd told about the mouse that had got into her beauty salon and wreaked havoc.

'You weren't the only one Jimmy attacked,' Sarah said bluntly.

Mandy looked at her, astonished, and wondered what had brought this on. Simon was looking at Sarah too. 'I know,' Mandy said. 'Didn't your father tell you I went to see Natalie and Hannah?'

'Yes. But I'm not talking about Hannah or her friend Katie.'

Mandy continued to look at Sarah, as Simon took her arm. Clearly he knew what she was about to say.

'Mandy,' Sarah said, her face strained and serious, 'six months before Jimmy attacked you, he tried to do the same to me.' Mandy stared at her and felt her legs tremble. 'I didn't tell anyone at the time. I was too scared they wouldn't believe me. It seemed impossible – my own uncle! It was only after he attacked you I found the courage to tell Mum and Dad. I'm sorry, Mandy. If I'd spoken out it might have saved you.'

Mandy continued to stare at her. Simon was watching her carefully.

'So that's why you had all that therapy? Not because of Jimmy's attack on me, but because he attacked you?'

'Both, really. I was in a right state. I'm OK now. I felt so guilty. I knew if I'd spoken out there was a good chance you wouldn't have suffered. I am so sorry, Mandy,' she said again. 'Can you forgive me?'

Mandy gave a small smile. 'There's nothing to forgive. I understand why you didn't report him – for the same reasons Hannah didn't for all those years. Does your father know you're telling me?'

Sarah nodded. 'He said you should know. There have been enough secrets in our family to last a lifetime.'

'I couldn't agree more.'

As Sarah reached out and hugged her, Mandy caught a glimpse of the person she'd once known – the open Sarah who'd been her best friend and with whom she'd shared everything.

'Thanks for being so understanding, Mandy; I hope we can be friends again.'

'So do I. Perhaps you and Simon would like to visit when Adam and I are in our new flat?' She showed her the ring. Sarah gave a little squeal of delight and kissed her again.

The side door of the chapel opened and as they looked over, the mourners from the previous service begin to file out. 'Shall we go and join your parents?' Simon said.

Sarah linked his arm and Mandy walked beside them as they crossed the car park. Another car pulled in and Mandy saw Mrs Pryce sitting in the passenger seat.

'Good,' Evelyn said, 'I'm pleased she felt able to come.' Then to Gran: 'Mum, Mrs Pryce is here with her brother. I invited her. I know she always thought the world of you and Dad.'

'She still does,' Gran said dryly. 'You know, we didn't stop seeing each other just because you fired her.'

Mandy saw the look on Evelyn's face and had to stifle a smile. 'Behave, Gran,' she whispered.

'I'll try. But your grandpa and I never did like funerals. He swore he'd never go to mine. Looks like he kept his promise, the old devil.'

Mandy smiled sadly and kissed Gran's cheek again. Then an air of expectation descended as the pallbearers opened the rear of the hearse. Everyone stopped talking and the other mourners began slowly moving forward in their small groups towards the entrance of the chapel.

'The other mourners go into the chapel first,' her father explained to her. 'As chief mourners we walk in a procession behind the coffin.'

Mandy nodded. They were silent as the rest of the congregation filed into the chapel. Then the pallbearers began slowly sliding the coffin out of the back of the hearse. Raising it on to their shoulders they waited at the entrance to the chapel. Mandy's father linked Gran's arm over his and took up position immediately behind the coffin. Evelyn linked John's arm and stood behind them. Her mother and her were next, and then Sarah and Simon. Organ music drifted through the open door of the chapel; there was a brief pause, and the music rose a tone, signalling their entrance. Their procession began to move slowly forwards. Mandy looked at the coffin riding high in front, her eyes welled and her fingers closed around the tissue in her pocket.

Forty-Three

'Please be seated,' the Reverend said. He waited for absolute quiet before continuing. 'We are gathered here today to celebrate the life and mourn the passing of William Anthony Edwards. Born on 11 November 1922, he was the first child and only son of Emily and Wilfred Edwards. Despite a bout of scarlet fever which put the five-year-old William in hospital he grew into a fine and sturdy young man ...'

Mandy looked at the Reverend standing behind the lectern as he continued with the tribute – the words of appreciation for Grandpa's life. Then she looked over to the coffin and tried to rid her mind of the image of Grandpa as she had last seen him, emaciated and dependent on others. She tried to replace it with the image of the man the Reverend now spoke of; the man Grandpa had been before he'd fallen ill. The man who at the age of nineteen, the Reverend said, had been one of the first to sign up to fight for his country when war had broken out in 1939. The man who, not one to wait around, had quickly courted and married Lizzie, his childhood sweetheart, on returning home in 1946.

'He was a successful businessman and proud,' the Reverend was saying, coming up to date, 'but kind, loving and loyal; a family man. The last time I saw William was when I visited him in hospital and he asked me to make special mention of his granddaughters, Sarah and Mandy.' Mandy looked again at the Reverend and swallowed hard at the mention of her name. 'In a society which doesn't always value the family as much as it should,' he continued. 'it is heart-warming to learn of the special bond which developed between Grandpa, as he was affectionately known, and his granddaughters. His love for Sarah and Mandy was unreserved, as I know theirs was for him. Even when the girls were away at university they phoned and visited regularly just as they had always done. Sarah fondly remembers the afternoon not long ago when she taught her grandpa to use his new and highly sophisticated mobile phone, for he was quite determined modern technology wouldn't leave him behind.' A murmur of agreement ran through the congregation and Mandy smiled. 'It was fitting, therefore,' the Reverend continued, 'given that special bond between him and his granddaughters, that when William's life on earth was coming to its natural end one of his granddaughters, Mandy, should help nurse him. Indeed she was with him at the end.' Mandy met the Reverend's gaze and swallowed hard. 'How lovely for a man who placed so much value on his family to leave this world surrounded by those he loved and cherished. I'm sure he knew his family were there, and appreciated it. It would have meant a lot to him in his final days to hear the voices of those he loved; to feel the warmth of their hands as they comforted and nursed him.' The Reverend paused and looked first at Sarah and then at Mandy, addressing them personally: 'I know how painful it is to lose a loved one, but please find comfort in the knowledge that your dear grandpa lives on in you both. Let us all now spend a few minutes in quiet reflection as we think of the life and lament the passing of William, beloved husband, father and grandpa.'

Mandy lowered her head and closed her eyes as the rest of the mourners were doing. She felt her tears run freely down her cheeks and drip unchecked on to her hand as she thought of Grandpa and all she had lost. Dear, dear Grandpa, I hope you know how much I love and respect you. Life isn't the same without you; it never will be. I miss you dreadfully. I miss so many things about you. The sound of your voice on the phone when I called every Tuesday at 6 p.m. All those discussions we had that went on for ages, when Gran was so worried about my telephone bill she made you phone me back. If I was speaking to you this Tuesday I'd tell you about the ring Adam has given me and how we are moving in together. I know you'd be pleased.

I remember my visits to you, Grandpa – as a child with my parents, and then as I grew up, alone. You always greeted me in the hall with a big hug and the same words: 'So what's my little Mandy been up to? Come in and tell me all.' I can hear you saying it now; I can still hear your voice, it's very clear. And I remember how we'd sit together, either side of the hearth in winter, or beneath the apple tree in summer, and I'd tell you what I'd 'been up to'. And you'd listen carefully and then advise me. Strange, I never minded you giving me the benefit of your advice, indeed I welcomed it, but for years if my parents tried to give me advice I rejected it out of hand. I guess that was part of the special bond you and I had. How I wish I still had it.

And I remember your wooden pipe which you kept polished on the mantelpiece although you hadn't smoked for twenty years. I was intrigued by that pipe. As a child I used to put it in my mouth when you left the room and pretend I was smoking. I wonder if you ever knew? You never said if you did.

And the tie you always wore. Casual dress for you still meant a shirt and tie – even when you were pottering in the garden you wore a tie and your cap. It was always important for you to look smart, until the very end, when you were too ill and hadn't the energy to dress, let alone wear a tie. When you lay in bed, often in pain, wanting to be at peace. And now you are, my Grandpa, at peace. I haven't forgotten the promise I made when I knelt by your bed and stroked your hand, which was so thin and frail I thought it might break. I haven't forgotten my promise and I will start tomorrow, I promise I will. I'll make you proud of me, as I was of you.

'Let us pray,' the Reverend said, breaking gently into their thoughts. 'The Lord's Prayer. Our Father, who art in heaven ...' Mandy pulled a tissue from her pocket and quietly blew her nose and wiped her eyes. She could hear Sarah crying further along the pew. Others were sniffing and blowing their noses too as they began quietly saying the Lord's Prayer.

When they came to the end of the prayer everyone looked up and towards the front. The Reverend turned to the coffin and made the sign of the cross. There was silence as he began the Committal, the final words of the service: 'Almighty God, our heavenly Father, we praise you for the sure and certain hope of the resurrection to eternal life ...' Mandy braced herself for what was coming next. How could she bear saying her last goodbye? They stood as the organ began to play sombrely in the background. The large velvet curtains either side of the plinth on which the coffin rested moved slightly then slowly began to close; slowly, very slowly, as the Reverend spoke: 'The grace of our Lord Jesus Christ and the love of God ...' The curtains drew steadily towards each other, relentless and unstoppable. Goodbye, Grandpa, thanks for everything you did for me. I won't ever forget you. I love and miss you so very much.

The curtains closed, the coffin disappeared from view, and Mandy leant on the handrail and cried openly.

Forty-Four

She awoke with a start; her heart was racing and her senses were alert. Then she remembered where she was and that there was no need to be afraid. This panic on waking had begun soon after she'd remembered what had happened and continued since. It didn't happen every morning, but was troubling enough to be one of the issues she was going to work on with her therapist.

With a small sigh of relief Mandy turned on to her side to look at the alarm clock: 6.35 a.m. She could hear water running in the bathroom. Shortly Adam would return to the bedroom and apologize for waking her, just as he did most weekday mornings. After five weeks of living together they'd fallen into a routine and the predictability gave her a warm glow; it made her feel safe and secure.

A minute later Adam came into the bedroom with a towel wrapped around his waist. 'Sorry I woke you,' he said, coming over and planting a kiss on her lips.

'It's OK, I need to be up. I want to make the most of my last two weeks.'

Mandy climbed out of bed and slipped into her kimono. Adam met her in the centre of the room. Sliding his arms around her waist he drew her to him and kissed her again firmly on the lips. 'Are you sure you want to accept that job?' he asked. 'You know you don't have to. We can last longer on my income.'

She smiled. 'I know, thanks. But it's an opportunity too good to miss. Working in an art gallery and being able to show one of my own paintings! It's beyond my wildest dreams.'

'Well, if you're sure.' With a final lingering kiss, he let her go and began to dress.

She went through to the kitchen, which still appeared huge and luxurious after the kitchenette of her bedsit, and filled the kettle. At least she now knew where everything was. In the first couple of weeks she'd kept stowing things in cupboards and forgetting where she'd put them. Now, switching on the radio, she reached easily for the bread to make toast, and the butter and honey they both liked for breakfast.

The kettle boiled and she poured the water into the cafetière as Adam appeared in the kitchen dressed in his suit. She passed him his toast and he sat at the breakfast bar and began eating, while she waited for the coffee to brew. 'So what are you going to paint in your last two weeks of freedom?' he asked.

'You!' she returned with a grin.

'You'll be lucky,' he laughed. 'I wouldn't be able to sit still long enough.'

'Then I'll use a photograph, like I did for Grandpa's portrait. I've decided I've got a flair for portrait painting.'

'Absolutely!' he agreed, nodding as he ate. 'The likeness is incredible. I don't know how you did it. It's so realistic; you've made him come to life.'

She smiled, pleased, and pouring the coffee into two mugs joined him at the breakfast bar. 'I'm going to have it framed today, then we'll give it to Gran on our next visit.'

'She'll be in tears,' Adam warned. 'It's bound to stir up a lot of memories.'

'Good ones, I hope.'

He nodded and, draining the last of his coffee, stood, and kissed her a long and reluctant goodbye. 'See you tonight then,' he said. 'Have a good day. Friday, thank goodness. Lie-in tomorrow!'

She went with him to the front door and saw him off as she always did, waving until he'd turned the corner and was out of sight. Closing the door, she returned inside, but instead of showering and dressing as usual, she continued to the second bedroom: her studio. As she entered she felt a rush of excitement. The novelty of having her own studio was still fresh and exhilarating. A real artist's studio! She took it all in, savouring the moment again, as she did every morning. Her paints, brushes, palette, canvases, cleaning fluids, sketch pads and so on littered all the available work surfaces in bohemian disarray. It was fantastic; she loved the organized chaos. On the easel positioned for the best light in the centre of the room was the finished portrait of Grandpa, ready to be taken to the framers.

Mandy crossed the room and stood in front of the portrait: Grandpa as he'd asked her to paint him when she'd sat by his bed and held his hand. Aware he was dying, he'd smiled sadly and said: 'Paint a picture of me, will you, Mandy, and give it to your Gran. Something to remember me by when I'm gone. But not like this. Paint one of me young and handsome – when she fancied me.' Mandy had begun the painting, as promised, the day after the funeral, and had just finished it, six weeks later.

She looked from the portrait to the photograph clipped to the side of the easel. It was a wedding photograph, lent to her by Gran, which she'd used for the likeness. Grandpa, in his mid twenties, dashingly handsome in a dark suit, standing tall and proud beside his Lizzie on the steps of the church where they'd just married. Mandy was pleased with the result – as apparently was the subject, for despite Grandpa's serious expression in his wedding photo, she'd painted him smiling, and he seemed to be signalling his approval. Not only because she'd done a good job, she thought, but also because the portrait had started her painting again. Painting like a professional – focused and dedicated. She was sure he would be proud of her.

Turning from the portrait Mandy moved slowly across the studio and past the sketches – ideas for future paintings – which were pinned to the cork-board mounted on the wall. She'd had lots of ideas which she would paint up in the evenings and at weekends after she'd returned to work full time. Adam had been right about the light in the room – the natural light coming from the window fell at exactly the right angle and was ideal for painting. It had allowed her to work on Grandpa's portrait from first thing in the morning after Adam had left for work until 6 p.m. when he returned home and she made dinner.

Mandy came to a halt in front of another large canvas, propped on a wooden chair and hidden by a dust sheet. As soon as she'd taken Grandpa's portrait to the framers Mandy knew she must return and complete this painting before she began any more. It had remained unfinished for too long – utterly forgotten until she'd found it at her parents' in the move to this flat. A chill gripped her as her thoughts returned to the day she'd started the painting, as a second-year student at university. It had been a Sunday evening and she'd suddenly been overcome by the need to paint: an overwhelming desire, as though her very life depended on it. It was after 7 p.m. and she'd gone alone to the art studio where she'd set up a canvas and mixed paints. She'd painted furiously, frenziedly, for five hours, until midnight, interrupted only once by the caretaker. Only when she'd finally stopped, exhausted, her arm aching and her fingers cramped around the brush, did she actually see what she'd painted, and was horrified.

At the time she'd quickly wrapped the unfinished portrait in a dust sheet and put it away, not understanding what she'd painted and too afraid to confront it – until now. Now she understood.

Mandy stood in front of the covered portrait and tentatively reaching out, took hold of the edge of the dust sheet and slid it from the canvas. For an instant she felt the same revulsion she had done four years previously when she'd finally stopped painting and had seen what she'd created. She was shocked not only because the girl in the portrait looked grotesque with part of her face missing, but because of the message Mandy now realized her deformity contained: the message sent through the medium of her paintbrush that she hadn't understood until she'd remembered what had happened.

Mandy looked into the sad blue eyes of the girl she'd seen in the mirror at Evelyn's house. The portrait was of her, and was complete apart from the mouth, which was a gaping hole, the edges ragged and bleeding, where the mouth should be. The girl with no mouth, silenced for all these years, unable to speak until Mandy had remembered. Now she remembered, and as soon as she returned from the framers she would paint in the mouth and finally release the girl from silence.

With a small sigh of satisfaction, Mandy moved away from the painting and picked up the dust sheet. Carrying it to the table she cleared a space and then spread it open, the edges hanging loosely over the side. Going to the easel she carefully lifted down the portrait of Grandpa and, setting it in the middle of the dust sheet, wrapped it securely, ready to take to the framers. She thought she'd have the frame made of walnut, something ornate, with decorative inlaid wooden leaves. Grandpa would like that; he had other pictures with similar frames. But she'd have to ask for two frames to be made, identical, for Gran wanted her portrait painted too. 'Can't have Will sitting up there on the wall alone,' she'd said. 'Paint my picture, love, to put beside him, and I'll pay you for your trouble.'

Mandy said she would — her first commission, although of course she wouldn't be charging Gran. 'A labour of love,' she said to Gran, and somewhere close by Grandpa quietly agreed.

Cathy Glass

———

One remarkable woman, more
than **100** foster children cared for.

Learn more about the many
lives Cathy has touched.

Please Don't Take My Baby

Pregnant, homeless and alone

Just 17, Jade struggles
with the responsibilities
her daughter brings.

Another Forgotten Child

Eight-year-old Aimee was on the child-protection register at birth

Cathy is determined to give her the happy home she deserves.

A Baby's Cry

A newborn, only hours old, taken into care

Cathy protects tiny Harrison from the potentially fatal secrets that surround his existence.

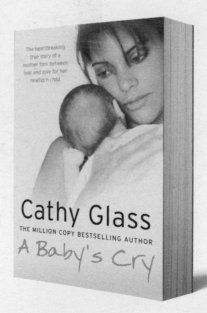

The Night the Angels Came

A little boy on the brink of bereavement

Cathy and her family make sure Michael is never alone.

Mummy Told Me Not to Tell

A troubled boy sworn to secrecy

After his dark past has been revealed, Cathy helps Reece to rebuild his life.

I Miss Mummy

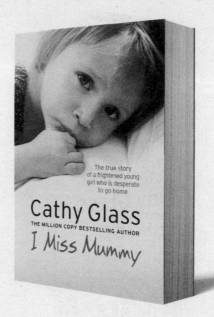

**Four-year-old Alice
doesn't understand
why she's in care**

Cathy fights for her to
have the happy home
she deserves.

The Saddest Girl
in the World

**A haunted child
who refuses to speak**

Do Donna's scars run
too deep for Cathy
to help?

Cut

Dawn is desperate to be loved

Abused and abandoned, this vulnerable child pushes Cathy and her family to their limits.

Hidden

The boy with no past

Can Cathy help Tayo to feel like he belongs again?

Damaged

A forgotten child

Cathy is Jodie's last hope. For the first time, this abused young girl has found someone she can trust.

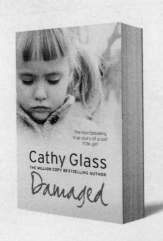

Inspired by true stories...

Run, Mummy, Run

The gripping story of a woman caught in a horrific cycle of abuse, and the desperate measures she must take to escape.

My Dad's a Policeman

The dramatic short story about a young boy's desperate bid to keep his family together.

The Girl in the Mirror

Trying to piece together her past, Mandy uncovers a dreadful family secret that has been blanked from her memory for years.

Sharing her expertise...

Happy Kids

A clear and concise guide to raising confident, well-behaved and happy children.

Happy Adults

A practical guide to achieving lasting happiness, contentment and success. The essential manual for getting the best out of life.

Happy Mealtimes for Kids

A guide to healthy eating with simple recipes that children love.

Be amazed
Be moved
Be inspired

———